ALTIRA

Jennifer Wherrett

Altira

First published in Australia by Jennifer Wherrett 2019
https://www.thelady.com.au

Copyright © Jennifer Wherrett 2019
All Rights Reserved

 A catalogue record for this
book is available from the
National Library of Australia

ISBN: 978-0-6482977-1-0 (pbk)
ISBN: 978-0-6482977-2-7 (ebk)

Cover design by Laura Wright LaRoche Publicious Book Publishing © 2019

Typesetting and design by Publicious Book Publishing
Published in collaboration with Publicious Book Publishing
www.publicious.com.au

Dance to the beat and rhythm of your <u>own</u> heart.
First, though, you must discover for yourself
How, exactly, your heart does beat,
For it will do so uniquely –
Your own unique beat,
Your own unique rhythm.
And then, of course,
You must give yourself permission
To dance to your unique beat,
To move through this reality
According to your <u>own</u> set of dictates,
No longer subject to or at the mercy of
The dictates of others.
Oh what absolute beauty will then be weaved
Into the fabric of human reality.
What absolute colour and vibrancy
Will be added to the human experience.
There will be no place for shadow and darkness
In this new fabric,
Because both of these will be overshadowed
By colour and vibrancy and beauty.
But only if you learn to dance
To the beat and rhythm of your <u>own</u> heart.

Table of Contents

Author's Note

These stories are deeply personal, as my stories always are. But these stories are not metaphors or analogies. They are real experiences, each in their own unique way, and, as such, their transcendent message is not hidden, disguised or embedded in a palatable but mythical story. Their transcendent meanings are 'out there' for all to see. These are genuine memories of lives I lived in other times and places ... or two of them are. The third embodies the knowledge of what I know is to come in the human experience. The fourth comprises experiences I had in two visions, which makes them no less real.

With these stories, I have moved completely away from identification with the human experience in its current state. We've got things horribly, horribly wrong in our current collective reality – a fact I hope these stories begin to challenge. In truth, we have no idea of the true nature of our own realities, and nor do we have any idea of the true nature of our own history, such is the bedrock of chronic ignorance in our collective experience now. We are so Separated, it is doing us very great harm, both individually and collectively.

For those of us who consider ourselves to be 'spiritual', do we spiritualise our physical reality, or do we physicalise our spirituality (don't you just love inventing new words)? In other words, for each of us, does the physical serve the spiritual, as it should, or does the spiritual serve the physical? For a long time, I waged this very battle within myself. This is my true Work. Because, whilst ever we physicalise our spirituality; that is, whilst ever the spiritual serves our ego, we will lower, reduce, contain and limit our spirituality, and we will never ascend this physical reality.

And do you not now know? Many of us are here to do just that.

Also, as usual, I capitalise the first letters of some words, like Purpose, Will, Way, Work, Voice, Separation and Process, to distinguish these as higher-dimensional concepts from the common lower-dimensional definitions and use of the words. For capitalised words, the meanings are metaphysical, not physical.

Jennifer

Non-Celestial Orbits

Author's Note

With this story, I find myself in the unusual position of wanting and needing to provide any potential readers with the background. This story is a past-life memory in its most pure form. That is, I have laid out the story as I remember it exactly, authentically, without tweaking it at all, adding to it, or changing any part of it (which I sometimes do for the sake of reader palatability, to polish the stories a little, make them slightly more glamorous, and to facilitate the particular story I'm working on, or to give them happy endings, which virtually none of them had).

Having finally shed the third- or lower-dimensional mindset regarding any successes I might have as a published writer, my writing has become, for me, a powerful tool for processing, seeing, resolving my inner shadows and healing my inner wounds. As such, my writing changes me as I write because it is a pure expression of my visions, and it facilitates the visions themselves. It opens doors in my conscious awareness, allows me to realise and to know things I might otherwise not know, and, as such, it transforms me. And never more so than with this story.

The memory of the life I write about in this story has been with me since just prior to writing one of the stories in The Messiah Perspective. Two of the people just appeared in "Cornerstones, Constructs, Yardsticks and the Mask of Conventionality" - one of the stories in The Messiah Perspective – and I instantly recognised them because the visions that contained the memories of the life in this story had already begun. Since then, the memory has been with me, lurking in the background of my conscious awareness, every now and then making itself known.

I always recognise the memories of other lives I've lived when they come because, unlike daydreams and other visions, past-life memories appear completely involuntarily, without any prompting from me whatsoever, and they are incredibly clear, like watching a movie in digital. Also, when they come, I am able to watch them unfold, again without any effort on my part, as if someone has turned on a movie in my conscious mind and all I have to do is sit back and watch. And so I do. Once a memory comes to me like this, it stays with me in the forefront of my awareness until I process it through my writing. Once I write a memory into a story, physically, the memory recedes from my conscious awareness, although it remains accessible, so all I have to do is recall it at will to watch it again, like choosing a movie to watch from your own movie collection. Once I write a memory into a story, though, I don't tend to access it through my visions. I just re-read the story.

Recalling past-life memories is not an unusual talent. I believe we're all capable of processing our past-life memories if we want to. After all, they exist in our own unconscious minds. We carry them within us. Of course, many people don't want to know what has occurred in other lives, and that's fine. That's their choice. But if you are one of those who would like to know what has happened to you in other lives you've lived, you just have to learn to recognise the memories for what they are, and to pay them heed when they come. And, everyone will have their own unique way of recalling them, of bringing them up from the unconscious into the conscious awareness. I'm a Storyteller (I hold this archetypal energy within me in this lifetime), so it's natural for me to use my storytelling gifts to process what is within my unconscious mind. Often, memories like this come to people in their sleeping dreams, but people fail to recognise them for what they are and dismiss them as mere dreams. If you want to start processing your own past-life memories, you just have to learn to recognise how you do it, or, rather, how your own unconscious mind works with them or makes you aware of them. Perhaps you get visions, too, but you just don't recognise them for what they are.

So, as I said, the memory of this story has been with me for many, many years, floating in and out of my conscious awareness, and it was only when I decided in the dead of night recently, after being unable to fall asleep courtesy of watching more of the story unfold, that I knew it was time to write it up. Why haven't I written it up before now? Because the memory was snagged. I always got only so far with it, and then it stopped, for reasons that may become obvious to you. I saw to the end of the memory only when I started to work with it through my writing.

Importantly, though, and additionally, two of the people in this story are with me in my current life once again. I would love to share the whole truth *with you and tell you who they are to me in this life, but I have to respect the privacy of others. So I will not tell you who they are. The dynamics between us in this memory, this story, are still very powerfully operating between the three of us in this lifetime. Not all the dynamics are identical in their expression this time around, although, also, some of them are, but they are definitely still between us. In processing this memory by writing about it, distance from them became absolutely essential, as you will, I hope, come to understand when you read the story. The emotions generated within me by these memories were not something I could handle whilst being with them, especially as I am currently unable to talk to them about these types of things. Hopefully, this will not always be so.*

I wanted to mention, too, from the outset, that I see the two cities in this story very clearly (and others not in this story), but I know they are not here on earth. They are on another planet entirely. And, yes, before you ask, I <u>am</u> human in this story ... very much so. One of the two cities in this story is 'futuristic', for want of a better word. It is very much like something out of that old children's cartoon 'The Jetsons'. Remember them? There are no roads and cars in these cities as such, and their 'trains' or their transports travel in transparent tubes both on land and under water, both within and between cities, at very great speeds. Consequently, these 'trains' are used extensively and can travel vast distances very quickly. They look like monorails. So the two cities are a long way from each other, because this planet was much, much larger than earth, and they both have very different atmospheres or personalities, but they are not in different countries, as we think of countries. I think they are on a world where that world thinks of itself as a whole ... oh wouldn't that be wonderful. As to the world itself, I will deal with it more specifically in the next story — the one that follows this one.

I have used words from our present to refer to certain things in the story so that you will be able to relate to whatever it is I'm referring to and to whatever it is the characters are doing at any moment in time, words like tequila to describe a drink and nachos to describe food, for example, and words like doctorate and honours to describe the degrees I complete. And, as a further example, I will use the word 'train' to refer to the transports I just told you about, and I will use the word 'car' as well, even though I know they don't exist in this world I can see.

Also, and very importantly, in the life I lived in this story, I worked with an ancient script written on scrolls and parchments from an ancient culture, and I have called the script 'hieroglyphics' and the culture 'Egyptian', but they are, in truth, not either of these. This is important for you to know. I am NOT referring to the Ancient Egyptians of our past, but I use the words so that you will understand. It will save a lot of unnecessary explanation. The ancient culture in this story was the ancient culture of Mallona (Mallona being the planet I write about in 'Altira', the story that follows this one). I know the scrolls I translate in this story are from the red sands of a vast and ancient desert, and that someone, at some point before the story begins, discovered the ruins and remnants of this ancient culture. My memory begins, both for me personally and for you as a reader, when I am already passionately interested in the culture and especially in its writing, hence my choice to study it at university and then turn it into a career. I know that the ancient culture and its writings significantly impacted and influenced the society in which I exist, hence my passionate interest in it. But I also recognise, both here and as the person I was in the memory, that something significant, something vital, was lost, and, as a result, that world suffers. Sound familiar? This is what we do, after all, recreate the patterns buried in our unconscious over and over and over again, both individually and collectively. One of the reasons I'm writing this story now — one of the reasons I actually lived the life — is because we find ourselves in the same place, yet again, of course. Also, the ancient Wisdom that I worked with in this story does form the core of the wisdom in the Ancient Egyptian religion-philosophy, even though the Egyptian religion held only an echo of it and was, unfortunately, therefore a distortion of it. The Egyptians got many things absolutely right, but they got quite a few things wrong, too.

There is another person in this story I need to explain, someone significant in the story for me personally, and I think it's possibly also because of him that I am writing and processing this memory now. I've said before in my writing that I weave a romantic, male counterpart into my stories for a number of reasons, the most important of which is that of him holding the energy of me, outside of the primary female character. He is me. And by weaving him into the story, he allows me to bring up and out whatever it is he facilitates me bringing up and out. Not so the man in this story. The man in this story is real, outside of me. He exists as another soul. He is another soul. Is he with me in this lifetime? That's an important and valid question given the fact that other souls in this memory are with me now. The answer is no. He is not with me in this life. I needed to, and I have, extricated the memory of him, rather like pulling a splinter out of my mind. I really recognise him, though, despite not knowing him in this life. The memory of him is very powerful for me, and I'm sure you'll understand why when you read the story.

I hope, too, that as you read the story, you will come to understand why I have chosen the title I've chosen. I guess, at this point, I would like to point out a vital purpose for the planets orbiting the sun the way they do. Most of them orbit the sun in circular or near-circular orbits that automatically preclude them ever coming closer to the sun and to each other. They do not touch, do they? Nor will they, ever, or not without dire consequences. Their orbits are set and cannot be changed except by interference from a large and powerful external body or entity ... or force. At the same time, opposing forces of gravity hold them together, in position, as they are. Pluto and its slightly-smaller satellite Charon, for example, both formally moons of (probably) Neptune, unless Pluto really is a trapped comet, now orbit each other in this way, constantly spinning around each other, trapped in and by each other's gravitational pull. They very much remind me of two of the people in this story. In other words, the title I've chosen for this story is an allusion to the way we humans trap ourselves and, therefore, each other in unyielding, inflexible and sometimes unforgiving orbits. And these orbits can and do transcend single lifetimes. Often, souls journey together in these inflexible orbits over many, many lifetimes because, of course, we humans no longer possess the knowledge necessary for applying or bringing to bear that external force essential for releasing the entities – us – from these orbits.

This story and the next, 'Altira', are connected in that they both occur on Mallona, the planet I write about in 'Altira'. And, in fact, this story precedes 'Altira' chronologically. There is a growing conviction within me that it is of vital importance that we humans know about Mallona and the events that led to its destruction because we are in grave danger of repeating our own history, and that, for me, is tragic because it means Altira (Mallona's beautiful little moon) died in vain. I'll be damned if I'll let that happen. And so, you need to know, Gaia (earth) is, at least for some of us, not our 'home' *planet. Mallona was our 'home' planet, for many of us. We are interlopers here on earth, aliens in a sense (except that I hate that word). We destroyed our home planet, and now, of course, we are destroying this one. We're like a plague of locusts.*

This story happened to me in another lifetime and to the other souls in the story. Maybe they will see themselves in the story and remember, too, as I have. I hope so because acknowledgement of the truths and the dynamics in this story will go a long way towards resolving the karmic bonds within and between them, and it will help them resolve their own inner shadows as well. That's not why I'm writing it, though. I write this story not for them but for me. In writing my own memories, though, and in opening myself up, sharing what I am seeing and learning, I am re-introducing humanity to its own multifaceted, multidimensional truth, and, in particular, its true history. This, I can see. This, I know. And it is of vital importance that I do so.

Jennifer

1

An Invitation to go Back to the Past

"Jade, honey, your sister's getting married, and since I'm paying for half the damn wedding, I'm issuing you an invitation. I want you there, the past be damned. You're my oldest daughter, my favourite, as you well know. And I want to show you off. I want you to come home."

"Dad, seriously …"

"I know what I'm asking, hon. I know it won't be easy, but I've thought long and hard about this. I think it's time you came home and faced some of the demons from your past. Besides, there are some old friends who want to see you. I brag about you often enough, so they know what you've been up to all these years. Don't discount this opportunity. I've failed you in the past. I know that. But I won't fail you this time. I promise. You don't have to stay at the house. You can stay at the apartment, although Anne wants you to stay with her."

"She knows about this?"

"She does indeed."

"And she thinks it's a good idea?"

"Ah, no. She doesn't. She thinks I'm not honouring your choices. But she wants to see you again, as does Amy, and they both know they'll have far less trouble enduring the whole shenanigans if you're there. I won't force you, hon. It's your decision, but I'm asking you to come, and if I have to I'll beg and plead. You need to be there. I feel it, me who never has any feelings about anything. I've got a hunch on this, and I can't ignore it."

Jade was silent. She didn't respond. In truth, he couldn't have shocked her more. She was stumped. She didn't know how to respond.

"Jade, honey?"

"I'm still here, dad. When is the wedding?"

"In two months, but they're having this ... what do you call it ... a pre-wedding party the week before. I'd like you to come over in time for that. So you'll have to take at least a week off work. Do you think you can manage that? Actually, come to think of it, do you think Pravesh can manage without you for one whole week?"

Jade ignored the jibe. This was not a laughing matter, nor even a smiling one. "Is she marrying Stuart?"

"Stuart? Who's Stuart?"

"Stuart, you know. The guy she stole from me."

"Oh, Stuart. Good god, no. Stuart lasted barely a handful of months after you left. Did you not know that? Did I not tell you that? No, she's not marrying Stuart. She's marrying her boss, would you believe? The gods alone know what he sees in her, but he must see something 'cause he's marrying her."

Again, Jade was silent. Her thoughts were already beginning to race. If Jocelyn was marrying some guy whom she, Jade, did not know and had never met, then maybe Jocelyn had finally found her own identity. So, then, maybe, just maybe, it was safe to come home at last ...

"Jade, honey ..."

"Yes, dad, I hear you. I do. I'm not sure I trust your instincts on this, but I hear you. You could just be trying to patch up your own mess, you know."

"Thanks for the brutal honesty, hon, and, yes, the thought has occurred to me, believe it or not. I could also be making things worse. That thought has occurred to me, too. It's a risk I'm prepared to take. Now, what about you? Are you prepared to take a risk, too?"

"I don't know. I need time to think about it."

"Of course. Of course. Look, hon, whatever you decide, you have my full support. You know that. I think this is your last opportunity, though. If you don't take it, you won't ever come back, and you will never see them again. Is that what you want?"

"Yes," she replied, somewhat sullenly.

Her father laughed. "Well, I'm challenging that. Thought I'd be a father at long last. Better late than never, or so they say."

That drew a smile from her. "Yes," she said, the smile ringing in her voice so that he heard it, "they do say that, don't they? All right, dad, I'll give this due consideration. I promise. I'll let you know either way, of course."

Jade sat at her desk when she put the phone down, staring out through the glass windows of her office to the room beyond it, only half seeing the hive of activity there but registering it not at all. She sighed as she leaned back in her chair. Work was impossible now which was unfortunate given the amount of work they were all inundated with at the moment. She was already planning a late night, as was Pravesh she knew. They'd already agreed they would get pizzas delivered for everyone who wanted to stay late.

Leaning forward again, she rested her elbows on the desk, and cupped her hands against her mouth. Why was he asking her to come home? Not that Maestronne was home anymore. Home was here, here in the life she'd made for herself. She didn't even like Maestronne, never had, but was that because of the city itself or was it because of all the bad, bad memories she had of her life there – the life of her youth?

Ten years. That's how long she'd been away. She'd left one night, suddenly, without saying goodbye, and had never returned. So she hadn't seen her mother or her sister for ten years, and in that ten years of being away, she had pushed them so far to the background of her awareness it was as if they no longer existed for her. That was exactly the way she liked it. And now her dad was asking her to change that. Part of her thought he had no right to ask, no right at all. He had failed her, just as he'd said. She felt resentment flare within, but she also recognised, at the same time, that he just might be right, and she could not allow resentment to dictate her choice. But did she really need to face the demons of her past? Her life here was perfect, so the past was not impacting the present in any way that was adversely affecting her. So, why stir up old dust then, upset old apple carts? Why not just let the past stay exactly where it was – behind her?

There were only two people in her life whom she trusted enough to allow input into these sorts of life issues, which she rarely encountered, her life being smoother than the average one. They were the two people who knew her best, and it just so happened that one of those people pushed open the door of her office, walked in without knocking, and took a seat in front of her desk.

"All right," he said matter of factly, "what has happened? You look like you've just been condemned to the hangman's noose."

She smiled, an extraordinary thing given the circumstances, but he could always make her smile. That was his particular gift. He could make anyone smile any time he chose. Like a magician conjuring a rabbit out of a black hat, so, too, could Pravesh conjure a smile.

"That's a rather apt analogy, Pravesh. I don't think you're far wrong."

He raised his eyebrows, his only response.

"Dad wants me to come home. Jocelyn, my sister, is getting married, and dad wants me to be there. He thinks this is a good opportunity for me to face my demons from the past."

"Ah." He said the word on a long sigh. "That is interesting."

"Mmmm. So, now I have a choice to make. I don't want to even make the choice. I just don't want to go back, but ..." She faltered. But what? Did she have a niggling sense that her dad just might be right? "I have a question for you, Pravesh. If my life is perfect as it is, and we both know it pretty much is, then why do I have to stir up settled dust from the past? Why not just leave everything as it is?"

Although she couldn't have predicted how he would respond, she thought he would agree with her. She thought he would be sympathetic. So his response surprised her.

"Because," he said as gently as he could, "you are walled off from the rest of us. You are shut off. We," and he waved his hands to indicate everyone in the room beyond the office, "love you deeply, as you well know, but we know we only get part of you. The other part is hidden away, protected, walled in, inaccessible. And this is all right for us because we love what we get. But I do not think it is all right for you, my friend. You are and can only be half alive when you are closed off like you are, not open."

She stared at him, shocked. "Does Nita think so, too?"

"Of course. Nita is Nita, after all. She sees many things, and she knows you very well, so it is natural for her to see this truth in you."

"You've never told me this before." For seven years or so, she had been having dinner with Pravesh and his wife, Nita, every Thursday night, sometimes other nights as well. It was a time-honoured ritual between the three of them that all three loved. And so, over those years, they had talked about many, many things. They had come to know each other very well. She had told them about her past, but that was many years ago. Still, they never missed a treat, the two of them, so she knew they would know how her past had shaped and affected her. She just didn't think they'd seen **that** deeply, although she had let them close in a way she had no other soul, not even her father.

Pravesh shrugged. "This is not the sort of thing you can say to someone easily. One must be given the right opportunity."

And this was the right opportunity. The knowledge hung in the air between them, unspoken, but recognised and acknowledged all the same. She nodded. "True. So do you think I am walled off because of my past?"

He nodded once, a definitive nod of unmistakable agreement.

"And going back, how is that going to fix me or help me become 'un-walled'?"

He rested his elbows on the arms of the chair he sat in and put his fingertips together. "I do not know. You make the choice and then you follow the path that is laid out before you. The Process will take care of the wall, if that is, indeed, what this is about. All of this you know. I am merely reminding you." He smiled to soften his words even more than he had already, and then he asked her, "So, you are aware that you are walled off then, my friend?"

Again, she smiled. "Yes, I am aware. I can feel it … here." She put her hand over her gut, just below her heart. "I don't let anyone in, although you and Nita have come pretty damn close, closer than anyone else. You both occupy a very special place in my heart."

He nodded and smiled again. "We know." Then he lost his smile, sobered, and he looked at her steadily, in that particular way he always looked at her when he was seeing more deeply into her than was normal. She was used to it now. She no longer felt the need to squirm with discomfort when he looked at her this particular way. "You want my opinion," he said and waited for her to nod her confirmation. "I shall give it to you. I think you should go. I think your father is right."

~

Lying in the dark, on her back in her bed, Jade looked up at the darkness, but thoughts of the past filled her mind so that she didn't see the darkness at all. Even now, ten years later, she still relished the freedom of the life she had built for herself over here, in Stenna, far, far away from Maestronne and all its bad memories. She had been born almost two years before Jocelyn, at a time when her parents still had some sort of meaningful relationship. Cecily, her mother, always said throughout their entire childhood that Jade had been jealous when Jocelyn was born and took her mother's attention. That was the excuse Cecily made for everything that was to come, always, without fail, for every incident and event that occurred. That was the excuse Cecily made to herself so that she could continue to protect Jocelyn from herself thereby perpetuating the illness that should have been addressed, for everyone's sake. Jade had never felt the jealousy she was accused of, so she had always known her mother was wrong. That was one mercy. At least she hadn't believed her mother and taken on the false belief in a jealously that didn't exist. If anything, the jealousy was the other way around, in Jocelyn, although the dynamic was far more complicated than just mere jealousy.

As they grew older, it was obvious the two of them, she and Jocelyn, were different. They were different in ways that made it impossible for them to ever get on well. Really, Jade thought, they were as different as chalk and cheese, but one could equally use the analogy of oil and water. They certainly didn't mix. So as young girls, they tolerated each other, and Jade was very well aware that Jocelyn was her mother's favourite, although she was also aware that she was her father's favourite. The two of them, her mother and Jocelyn, were on a similar wavelength somehow – a wavelength that excluded Jade, that she couldn't tap into, and it was powerful. Initially, when she and Jocelyn were both still young girls, she just felt excluded when she was in their presence, but as they grew older, and the troubles began, she would feel a kind of energetic attack when she was with them, and she felt the threat of it. She felt unsafe with them. It was, to her, a palpable, almost tangible thing. Still, aside from the hurt she felt as a child over her mother's favouritism and an exclusion that bordered on rejection, beyond this, there were no real problems in their childhood. The real problems started when they reached their teenage years.

By the time both Jade and Jocelyn became teenagers, James and Cecily, their parents, had become all but estranged. Jade was aware of it even back then but she never spoke of it. It was just something she knew, something that simply formed part of the fabric of their lives together as a family. James spent a lot of time at work, which was good because it meant as a family they had lots of money – money Cecily spent frivolously. He even purchased an apartment in the city so that he could stay closer to work when he worked late. And when he bought the apartment, they really only saw him on weekends. He opted out, and in doing so, he abdicated his responsibilities as a father. He and Jade had talked about this in recent years, and he had acknowledged the truth of it. He allowed his relationship with Cecily to deteriorate to the extent that he could barely stand being in the same room with her. Instead of being honest about it, though, and either divorcing her or at least making an attempt to work it out with her, he simply stayed away, effectively avoiding the whole issue. Cecily, of course, knew it. How could she not? And she reacted by becoming even more attached to and focussed on Jocelyn. And she developed a spending addiction. Shopping, buying and having new things made her feel better about herself, or, rather, just made her forget how bad she felt about being her. All of this, Jade observed at the time. She pitied her mother in a way, but she could never have spoken to her mother about it all because Cecily, by this time, barely acknowledged her existence.

So, with the absence of her father and the obvious focus of her mother on Jocelyn, Jade effectively got herself through her teenage years. She did have a friend and ally in the form of Anne, her father's much-younger sister – a sister closer in age to Jade than she was to him. Anne could see there were problems, and she certainly had no time for either Cecily or Jocelyn. Other than Anne, though, Jade was alone. She certainly had no support from her parents. She thought of her mother now as an obstinate woman – a woman blinded by prejudices she stubbornly refused to let go of, to the detriment of both her daughters. But back then, she saw and sensed her mother's hurt, and she was also only too well aware of her own hurt. When she most needed the comforting embrace of a loving and understanding mother, Cecily was unavailable. Jade was wholly unable to reach out to or connect with her mother at all. And, in fact, whenever she was in her mother's presence, she always felt a gut-clenching tension that permeated every muscle of her body. Pravesh had spoken, today, of being walled up. Well, this time of her life, she knew, was when it began. And it began courtesy of her mother. When the troubles with Jocelyn began, Jade and her mother became even more alienated. With every incident brought to Cecily's attention, she became more and more cut off from Jade, shutting Jade down, so that, fearing punishment, Jade learnt to keep silent, retreating into a place within, and finding her own way to deal with the troubles. The wall Pravesh referred to was the only way she could have survived her teenage years because it closed her off from the intimate world around her. That intimate world was hurting her. She had no choice but to defend herself.

There was no real point at which the troubles, as Jade referred to them and thought of them, began, or not that Jade could pinpoint anyway. The troubles were just suddenly there, and it was merely a matter of Jade becoming aware of them for what they really were as opposed to just a collection of unfortunate incidents. They began with Jocelyn raiding Jade's wardrobe, helping herself to Jade's clothes. Jade would go to put something on and find it missing only to have Jocelyn appear in the very same article of clothing she had been looking for. When she accused Jocelyn of stealing her clothes, Cecily would step in, put a stop to the conversation, and bring out the old excuse: you're just jealous because your sister looks better than you do. Jocelyn would do it with jewellery, too, and perfume and books. She would only ever steal Jade's favourite clothes or her favourite pieces of jewellery or her favourite perfume or her favourite books. Lying in the darkness, now, Jade frowned in concentration. How had Jocelyn always known which were Jade's favourites? Instinct perhaps? Or observation? Perhaps, Jade thought, she had worn those particular things more often than others and Jocelyn had simply observed that.

With hindsight, the stealing of the clothes, jewellery, perfume, and, occasionally, books had been relatively easy to deal with, physically if not emotionally. After realising she would get no help from her father, Jade took matters into her own hands. She bought herself a lock and padlock, installed them herself, and kept her room religiously locked despite endless complaints from Jocelyn and recriminations from her mother. She did not give in to either. She made very sure her room was off limits to both of them. In this, her father became her ally not so much because he stood up for her but because he refused to listen to Cecily's constant demands that he force Jade to remove the lock on her room.

But it was the other things stolen, or copied, that were not so easy to deal with, things that could not so easily be made inaccessible with lock and key. Socially, it was as if Jocelyn became Jade. She would express opinions Jade had expressed, even so far as using exactly the same words. She would profess the same interests and speak about them as if she was an expert, getting facts wrong and mixed up as she did so. She would laugh exactly as Jade did, she would tell a story as Jade would tell it, and she would use identical hand movements and facial expressions. And, she would take their shared memories of the past and place herself in them in Jade's place, putting herself in the central position of Jade's personal stories. There would be times when Jocelyn would even correct Jade publicly if Jade was telling a story from the past, effectively removing Jade from the story and putting herself in it instead.

"No," Jocelyn said one particular time when Jade was telling a story about their father cutting his hand, "that wasn't how it happened. It wasn't you who looked at the cut and told dad to go to the hospital, it was me. You disappeared because you couldn't stand all the blood."

Jade had never had an aversion to the sight of blood. Even so, although she knew fact from fiction, at first, when she was corrected in the retelling of stories from the past, she had felt confusion, beginning to doubt and question her own ability to remember events as they had truly occurred. But then, when it continued, and more and more memories were usurped, she began to realise Jocelyn was stealing the memories the same way she'd stolen the clothes.

It got so bad that Jade would become silent in any situation where she and her sister were together in a group – at family gatherings, family dinners with friends as guests, friends' parties, school sporting events, school dances. No one else seemed to notice. But to Jade, her own whole persona, which was impossible to miss when she watched Jocelyn in a social context, did not sit well with Jocelyn, as if, to Jade, Jocelyn always wore ill-fitting clothes, or clothes that did not suit her. And it felt, to Jade, like a competition, one she retreated from completely. To Jade, Jocelyn seemed false, but to everyone else, she was outgoing and interesting. Jade would clench her teeth in these situations, everything within her screaming her abhorrence, as she listened to and watched Jocelyn holding court while she sat there, quiet, silent, knowing the truth but wholly unable to speak of it, and wholly unwilling to compete.

Now, in the darkness of night, Jade took a deep breath, forced to remember it all. Because then, there were the friendships. This particular trouble had, perhaps, been the most difficult to deal with. How does someone steal another person's friend? Well, it's actually quite easy. You must do two things at exactly the same time. You must charm that friend, win them over, and you must turn them against the person you're stealing them from. Jocelyn was masterful at both. She was pretty, with long ash-blonde hair and blue eyes. She was small, too, like a fairy, small and charming. She looked like an angel, and Jade came to realise that people wanted to believe Jocelyn was as much an angel on the inside as she was on the outside. There was nothing to dissuade them, either, nothing overt. Jocelyn was clever in her manipulations, and she was as charming as she was pretty. So she used these attributes to perfection and with great success. Whilst still at school, Jade lost many of her friendships this way, so that she began to distrust the whole notion of friendship and still did, in a sense, even to this day. She now never entered into friendships lightly.

By the time Jade was in her last year of school, Jocelyn had become a clone – Jade's clone – so that Jade constantly watched what she did and said, particularly when Jocelyn was around her. The problem with Jocelyn being a clone was, of course, that Jade still very much existed in her own right and in Jocelyn's world, and, as such, was a constant reminder that Jocelyn was a fraud, a copy. So Jocelyn became downright spiteful in her resentment. Jade found it intolerable, but she didn't know what could be done about it because the spitefulness was always hidden from others. She tried to talk to a few people, including her father, but no one believed her. Her father rejected what she tried to tell him outright, explaining to himself probably more so than to her that, as sisters, they were just very much alike. Even Anne, the only other person who could see the truth, tried to talk to James, the girls' father, but with no success. The trouble with James was that if he acknowledged there was a problem it would mean having to deal with it, and he had decided he didn't want to have to deal with anything in relation to his family. As far as others were concerned, the two, Jade and Jocelyn, were sisters, so it was natural they would have the same mannerisms, the same interests, the same opinions, the same expressions, the same beliefs, the same attitudes, the same taste in clothes and music and books …

When Jade left school and started her degree at university, things became easier, and she was given some breathing space. At first, Jocelyn was still at school, but then, when she finished school, she could not follow Jade into university. She simply didn't have the same mind, the same intelligence, so she did a course for a year and got a job as a personal assistant. She was good at it too, apparently. With Jocelyn busy in her new job and Jade spending a lot of time at the university, eating there, studying there, and working there, they hardly ever saw each other. Jade even convinced herself that Jocelyn getting her own job and being good at it was a sign that the troubles were behind them. Hopefully now, Jocelyn could begin to forge and discover and develop her own identity.

And then Stuart came into Jade's life.

She noticed he was always in the café where she worked whenever she was on shift but she just saw him as a regular customer, thinking nothing more of it. Her relationship with and experience of boys had, at that stage, been rather problematic. She'd been on a few awkward dates, had a few awkward kisses, but only because she thought she should. Everyone else had boyfriends so she thought she should, too. None of them ever worked out. She couldn't actually stand any of them, and hated the idea of commitment, of being locked into a relationship and of having to maintain it. And, she hated dating. She hated the inane conversations that bored her to tears, and she hated the awkwardness. So she stopped bothering. Jocelyn, on the other hand, was showing herself to be rather good at it. She was never short of a date and had already had a string of boyfriends. In this, Jocelyn was anything but a copy of Jade. In fact, Jade could probably have taken lessons from her sister when it came to boys and the whole idea of dating.

Stuart was different from those other boys. He got under her skin and then into her social sphere without the necessity of those first few awkward dates. She was relaxed with him because she had no idea he was romantically interested in her. Had she known, she would have erected her wall between them and ejected him from her life. But she didn't know, so they got to know each other in the café over many months, talking, laughing, flirting. When he finally asked her out, it seemed natural and easy and right, and so they began their relationship. They were together for two years, and in those two years, she kept him a secret. She never mentioned him to her mother or to Jocelyn, so how Jocelyn knew about him was, to this day, a mystery to Jade.

At the very end of her honours year, she was working furiously on her dissertation, trying to get it finished and, at the same time, her supervisor was trying to convince her to take up one of the doctorate scholarships she was being offered. He had encouraged her to apply half way through the year, and so she had, not expecting to be offered anything at all, let alone so many she was able to pick and choose. Whilst still at school, she had developed a passionate interest in the ancient culture of the Egyptians and, specifically, in their hieroglyphic writing system and their religion-philosophy. So when considering what she would study at university, there was no question she would study ancient writings with a view to focussing on Egyptian hieroglyphics. Over the years of studying, she had discovered within herself a unique ability to read the hieroglyphics in an innovatively-new way, especially when the hieroglyphics were used to write the ancient prayers, spells and incantations of the culture's religion-philosophy. She had discovered there were layers in the writing system, not just width and height, but depth as well – a new dimension. And whichever layer a particular word was embedded in dictated the meaning of that word. As such, one word could take on a whole new and different meaning just by being in a different, deeper layer. Her supervisor had immediately recognised the value of her work and her ability, and was, as he told her, determined to convince her to take the study further. Her discovery, he knew, had the potential to change the translations and, therefore, the meanings of whole pieces of already-translated works, and, as such, to open up the whole religious philosophy, to enable a far deeper understanding than currently existed. He was excited, not just for her, but for the field of study itself. While it was difficult not to take on his enthusiasm, and his belief in her, she was looking the other way, entertaining ideas of marrying Stuart and having his children. The thought of a career, as opposed to a job, conflicted with her idea of her own future. Stuart was studying economics, so her thoughts, at this stage, were of his career, not hers.

Fortunately, the decision she had to make about her own future was taken out of her hands and made for her. Thank the gods, she thought, breathing deeply, distressed by the realisation she had nearly, very nearly, made the most horrific choice regarding the direction of her life. In that sense, Stuart and Jocelyn had unwittingly done her a huge favour, although it was impossible to be grateful to them for that. Left to her, she would have gone down a very different road, one that would have led her to frustration, dissatisfaction and lack of fulfilment. At the time, she wasn't to know that. She really thought she and Stuart were in love. She had genuinely believed they would be together for the rest of their lives, and that, at the time, had been her focus.

Why had she come home early that day? Frowning as she lay in the darkness, thinking back to that fateful day, she couldn't remember why she went home early. She so rarely went home at all in those days, let alone early. Thank the gods, they hadn't heard her open the lounge room door, so they hadn't known she was there, standing in the doorway, watching them on the lounge together. It was obvious from the way they were with each other that they knew each other quite well and had been doing this for longer than a single afternoon. Standing there, in the doorway, watching them, she realised she had never brought him home, never introduced him to Jocelyn, so how did they know each other? He was lying on top of Jocelyn, and they were both only half dressed, kissing passionately. Stuart, her boyfriend, the man she was going to be with for the rest of her life was making love to Jocelyn, her sister. She could see, from where she stood, stupefied, frozen in shock, that he was doing things to Jocelyn with his hands that he'd never really done to or with her. Supposedly in the throes of passion, Jocelyn was trying to talk to him, but he kept silencing her with his kisses.

"You have to tell her. Tonight. You have to tell her."

"Not tonight," he said between kisses. "I have to find the right time ..."

Jade didn't stay to watch or hear any more. Their words thrummed through her body, unfreezing her, and galvanising her into action. She hardened her heart and felt her facial features respond accordingly. She would be damned if she would give them the satisfaction of telling her at all. Barely thinking, her movements jerky with the shock of what she'd witnessed, she grabbed what she could while they were otherwise occupied in the lounge room, throwing things into her backpack. She left the house without a word and, for the next couple of weeks, she stayed at her dad's apartment in the city. Her father had asked no questions at the time, and she had offered no explanation. It was only later, after she moved to Stenna and effectively became disentangled from Cecily and Jocelyn, and she and her father began to communicate via texts and phone calls and emails, that Jade told him what had happened.

Of course, the one hugely positive thing to come out of the whole experience as far as Jade was concerned was her acceptance of an invitation to undertake her doctorate at Stenna University, almost as far from Maestronne as she could physically get. She certainly had no regrets about that. Since leaving Maestronne, she had completed her doctorate, revolutionised the way Egyptian hieroglyphics were translated, particularly where they concerned the ancient Egyptian religion, met Pravesh who had become her professional partner, established and built a whole department/business in the university, translating the texts and parchments that were constantly being unearthed in the desert and making money from it in the process, and written and published copious books with Pravesh thereby opening up and facilitating a new and profound understanding of an entire ancient religion philosophy. She and Pravesh were now considered leaders in their chosen field.

She had never said goodbye to her mother, or her sister or to Stuart. Stuart had tried to contact her, but she refused to speak to him. She felt she owed him nothing, not even an explanation, but she had deliberately told a couple of their mutual friends what had happened so they would tell him. He had a right to know. She just didn't need to be the one to tell him. She had, at least partially, let her wall down where he was concerned. Standing in the doorway, watching the two of them together, the wall had come up again, hard and fast and implacable. There was, though, she had to admit, even after all these years, a perverse satisfaction in knowing they never got to tell her themselves. At least she had deprived them of that. And now, she had finally found out how they ended up, courtesy of her phone call with her father. Stuart hadn't lasted. He deserved that. He'd been so easily manipulated. She felt no sympathy for him whatsoever.

Whilst at her father's flat, after discovering the two of them together, she had worked furiously, feverishly, to complete her dissertation and submit it, and then she just left, with one oversized suitcase and a backpack. All her books she packed into boxes and left at her dad's apartment so that he could send them when she got settled. When she arrived at the university in Stenna, she was given a room in the postgraduate student dormitories. Her room was long and thin with dark wood panelling covering three-quarters of its walls, and dark wooden floors. A single big window allowed in plenty of light, which was as well given the darkness of the room's interior. The room itself was sparsely furnished with a single bed, a bedside table, a tall wardrobe and a small desk. But it was her room and she loved it. Eventually, she bought herself a colourful rug and quilt, some pictures for the walls, and a couple of matching book shelves that were filled with her books, her most prised possessions, and the room took on the warmth of home and was given colour. But that very first day, only a little more than two weeks since discovering her lover in the arms of her sister, she had sat on her bed in her empty room, with her suitcase unpacked beside her, for a long, long time, knowing she was all alone in the world and relishing the knowledge. Here, she would be able to build a life for herself free of the shadowed dynamics that existed between her mother, her sister and her. She knew she was finally free. She would not have to look over her shoulder all the time to see who was watching her, copying her, cloning her. She could be herself as a unique and individual personality. And so she had been, for ten years.

And now her father was asking her to go back. She really, really did not want to go back, but she knew Pravesh was right. She trusted him as she trusted no other. She had to make the choice and follow it through, but she made the choice not for her father or for her sister, or even for Pravesh, but for herself. She was really all that mattered. Nothing else mattered, nothing at all.

~

2

Demons from the Past

"**B**y the gods! That whole thing is his house?"
"Apparently so."

"Oh." The sound Jade made was barely audible, and her next words equally so. "He can't be stupid then."

Anne laughed. "Is that what you thought, honey child?"

"She's hardly a child anymore, Annie," Amy said as she steered the car around the driveway's central garden, her eyes sweeping the area near the house for signs of an empty park. "Don't you think it's time for a new term of endearment?"

"Habit of a lifetime," Anne replied. "Can't change now."

In fact, the particular term of endearment she still used to address Jade had been deliberately decided upon many years ago in the hope of communicating the love and support Jade had lacked as a young girl. As best she could, Anne had tried to fill the void she could so obviously see in Jade's life all those years ago. But she could also still see that same void in Jade, so she was not going to relinquish her use of the childhood term of endearment just yet and without a fight. Amy surrendered, knowing from experience this was one of those battles she would not win. The two had been together for twelve years. They knew each other well, too well at times.

"The thought had crossed my mind," Jade said enigmatically, responding to Anne's earlier question and completely ignoring the interchange between Anne and Amy. "I kind of wondered if he was, you know, a bit lacking in intelligence, or maybe just very shallow."

Again, the comment was enigmatic but both Anne and Amy knew exactly who and what she was referring to. "Have you met him?" she asked them.

"No," they answered together, in perfect unison.

"But your father has, obviously," Anne expanded. "I can assure you, the fiancé is not lacking intelligence, honey child. He owns and runs his own company, and it's not a small company either."

"Obviously," Jade said, unable to take her eyes off the house. Its gate and the long, sweeping driveway had hinted at the grandeur of the house even before she'd laid eyes on the house itself. And it didn't disappoint. Red-bricked, double-storied, with rows of large picture windows that obviously gave plenty of light to the many, many rooms inside, and an elaborate, white-columned front entrance, the house was impressive, and massive. "It's a mansion."

"It is, isn't it?" Anne agreed, peering out the car window at the impressive house.

When Amy parked the car and the three got out, Anne stopped Jade from walking towards the house with a hand on her arm. "Are you okay with this?" she asked, nodding towards the house.

"Yeah, I am. She's obviously made a good life for herself. I'm glad about that. I'm happy for her. She's found herself a decent guy. That's a good thing."

Anne took that in, nodding her agreement, and then she said, "That wasn't exactly what I meant."

"Oh," Jade said, and then, remembering Pravesh's very apt comment about the hangman's noose, she added, "Not really. I feel like I'm walking to my own execution."

Anne didn't smile. "Understandably," she said. "We won't stay long. We'll make a decent appearance, and then we'll get the fuck out of here. Right, Aimes? And if you need to leave even sooner, so be it. Your father will have to endure by himself. We're in your hands, okay? I need to be clear about that."

"That's right, Jade," Amy said, adding her support. "Annie's absolutely right."

Jade smiled her gratitude at them both and squeezed Anne's hand in her own. "Thanks."

"You know," Anne added, giving Jade the once over, "if you wanted to hide today, you picked the wrong outfit, honey child. You do know that, don't you?"

Jade looked down at her tailored cream trousers and the high-healed emerald-green shoes that matched her sleeveless, green, silk top, and then back up at Anne. The cream jacket that matched the trousers was slung over her arm, and a green handbag that matched her shoes perfectly hung over her shoulder. The green of her outfit matched and heightened the colour of her eyes, she knew. The clothes she'd chosen were not done so to stand out. They were armour, protection. If she was going to make an appearance among people she hadn't seen for a decade, she was damn well going to look good doing it. "You think I should've worn something less conspicuous?"

"Ignore her," Amy said, jumping in before Anne had a chance to respond. "You look beautiful, Jade. Be confident in that."

Anne shrugged her surrender. "You do look good. Go in there and bedazzle them." And then she added sheepishly for good measure, "Just not the fiancé."

Jade laughed. "The gods forbid," she said. "That'll be all we need."

The three of them were met at the front door by a maid in black trousers and shirt, and a white apron, and taken through the house to the terrace out the back. Able only to get a glimpse of some of the rooms as they passed them by, Jade was given an impression of a half-empty house, as if the owner hadn't lived in it for long and so hadn't, as yet, furnished it fully, properly. The house was shaped in a U, and out the back, between the arms of the 'U', was a large, paved terrace complete with bar-b-que area and swimming pool. The three of them had arrived slightly late, quite deliberately, so the terrace was crowded with guests. They stood together for a moment on the steps outside the house, surveying the scene before them. Looking at the crowd of people, Jade suddenly felt as nervous as she'd ever felt in her life. And then James, who'd been watching for them like a hawk, broke away from the group he was with, and came to greet them himself. He kissed Anne and Amy and then turned his full attention to his daughter, wrapping her in a huge bear hug.

"Hey, hon," he said. "It's good to see you. Thank you for doing this."

"Against my better judgement ..." she muttered.

The next hour or so was a blur to Jade. Her father took her around, holding her arm possessively as if he wasn't about to let her go, and introduced her, or re-introduced her in some cases, to old friends. She found herself being kissed and hugged over and over, and answering the same questions over and over again. Someone, she didn't know who, at some point, put a glass of champagne in her hand, and she sipped it, grateful for the effect it had on her taut and tense nerves. The people around her swept her away from Anne and Amy, or maybe the fault lay with her father who seemed to have taken it upon himself to steer her into and then away from every conversation she found herself involved in.

Of her mother and sister, she saw no sign. They stayed away.

And then her father was introducing her to someone she'd never met before, and she was quick to realise he was the fiancé.

"Blake Watford," her father said, "this is Doctor Jade Howlett."

"Jade," she said, smiling at the man as she shook his hand. He was taller than she was, even with heels on, so she had to look up at him, and she found herself wondering what he and Jocelyn looked like together. Jocelyn was shorter than she was, a fair bit shorter, so she thought they would, possibly, look a little bit incongruous together, like a petite doll and a bean pole. He was dark haired, blue eyed, tall and slim – nice looking, she thought, not dazzling, just nice to look at.

"Howlett?" he asked. "So you're ... ?"

"My eldest daughter," James said definitely, almost defensively.

The man, Blake, looked surprised. "Jocelyn has a sister?" he asked, not releasing Jade's hand in his confusion.

"An older sister," James confirmed.

"I'm sorry," Blake said, and Jade wasn't sure if he was apologising for holding her hand for too long or for his obvious confused reaction at meeting her. "Jocelyn led me to believe she was an only child."

Jade and her father exchanged glances. "Well, she would, I guess," Jade said. "I've been away for ten years, so you could argue she has been an only child."

"Rubbish," James said aggressively, only partially under his breath.

"Dad," she said, pulling her hand out of Blake's, and giving her father the empty glass she was holding. "Could you get me another glass of champagne?"

Her father nodded, somewhat reluctantly, getting the message.

"I'm sorry," she said, turning back to Blake after her father took the hint and went to grant her request. "He and Jocelyn aren't close."

Blake nodded. "So I gathered. She never talks about him. But then, she never talks about you either."

"We're ..." she hesitated, looking for the right, diplomatic word, "estranged."

"I see."

"Dad said you own your own company," she said quickly, forestalling any potential questions and changing the subject, feeling very uncomfortable. "What does your company do?"

"Property development is the best description. I trained as an architect but discovered I'd much rather redevelop existing buildings than design new ones."

"Ah, and did you redevelop this house?"

"I did. This is my parent's house, mine now, obviously. I redeveloped it when I inherited it. It was one of the first houses I did, actually."

"It's very ... big," she observed. Too big, she thought. "Your parents are no longer alive then?"

"No, they were killed in an accident."

"I'm sorry," she said sincerely.

"Thank you. It's fine. It was a long time ago."

She nodded, wondering what to ask him next to keep the conversation rolling but not wanting to mention her sister again. He saved her the trouble by asking her a question of his own.

"And what do you do? Your father introduced you as a doctor. Are you a doctor of medicine?"

"No. I'm a doctor because I have a doctorate."

"In what?"

"Egyptology," she replied. "I'm an expert in their ancient system of writing, so I translate the copious amounts of scrolls and parchments they're currently pulling out of the desert."

He looked interested. "Passion for all things Egyptian must run in the family," he commented.

She looked blank. "What do you mean?"

"Your sister is passionately interested in Egyptology."

A chill ran down Jade's spine. Involuntarily, she shivered. "That must be a new development," she said slowly, cautiously, feeling uncomfortable again and wanting to put an end to the conversation.

He inclined his head. "No, she's been interested in Egyptology all her life."

Of all the interests Jocelyn had copied from Jade in their younger years, Egyptology had never been one of them. Jocelyn had shown as much interest in the ancient Egyptians as she had in running marathons. That is to say, none at all. In truth, Jade had deliberately kept her interest in Egyptology hidden. That particular interest had been highly sacred, so she had been careful to hide it from Jocelyn so that it could not be copied or cloned.

A thought, or a suspicion, began to germinate within her, and it was sending more of those chills down her spine, raising goosebumps on her skin and causing the hairs on her arms to stand on end.

"Oh," was all she could think to say in response to his comment, and she said it tightly, her lips pinched and her body tensing, looking away from him, avoiding eye contact as she said it. This conversation was taking her back to those days when she had watched Jocelyn silently, withdrawing into herself as Jocelyn stepped into a persona that did not belong to her. Withdrawal had always been Jade's defensive, self-protective response to watching someone else become her, and now she was doing it to him, the fiancé.

He seemed to miss the hint to desist. In fact, he seemed not to notice Jade's withdrawal at all. Or, if he did notice and if he was picking up on the tension in Jade, he chose to ignore it for reasons of his own.

"She's particularly interested in their religion," he said. "She's kind of taken it on as her own religion, so she quotes it often ... Are you all right?" he asked, reaching out to steady Jade with a hand on her arm. "You've gone awfully pale."

"Thank you, I'm fine," she said, removing her arm from his grasp. But she wasn't fine. She wasn't fine at all, and she looked, to him, like she was going to pass out.

"Maybe you should sit down," he said, concerned. "You look like you'll fall down if you don't sit."

"No, I just ..." As full realisation coursed through her, she was wholly unable to stop herself bringing a hand up to cover her mouth, and she felt decidedly queasy. In fact, she thought herself in danger of throwing up right there in front of everyone. "You'll have to excuse me," she said to him, intent only on finding one of the many bathrooms in the house, locking herself into it, and taking advantage of the necessary solitude to regain her equilibrium. But she'd taken only a couple of steps before she stopped, turned round again and looked back at him. "God I hope you know what you're doing."

She said the words with such conviction that he stood rooted to the spot, shocked himself, watching her walk away. Something was wrong here, something he hadn't been told. Actually, he thought, there were quite a few things he hadn't been told ... obviously. And where was Jocelyn? She'd disappeared. He looked for her among the crowd of people on the terrace but failed to locate her. Then he looked at Jade again as she walked into the house. Her reaction to his very simple comments had been instantaneous, involuntary, almost violent ... and genuine. She knew something.

Inside the house, Jade desperately tried to find a bathroom, but there were so many damned rooms. Every one she tried turned out to have a different function entirely. And then she heard voices – familiar voices – voices she would've recognised anywhere even though she hadn't heard them for ten years. Heart pounding, she followed the sound of their voices, and saw them standing together in the middle of a large room at the front of the house, a room that looked like a lounge room.

"What's she doing here?" her sister was asking angrily, viciously, her fists balled, her face bright red. "She'll ruin everything."

"Don't be ridiculous," her mother answered brusquely, dismissively. "He loves you. He's gong to marry you, darling, and nothing can change that now. How could she ruin everything?"

"She just could," Jocelyn answered angrily. "Who invited her anyway? I certainly didn't."

"Your father invited her. Apparently he had some foolish notion about bringing the family together again. Why he couldn't just let bygones be bygones ..."

Jade had heard enough. She turned away. Bathrooms forgotten she was now intent on finding Annie and Amy. She had to get out of here. They weren't hard to find because neither of them had moved far from where they'd been standing for over an hour.

Anne didn't need to be told or asked. She took one look at Jade, touched Amy's arm, and said, "Time to go."

Jade was silent in the car, the kind of silent one is when one is very distressed and so has retreated into oneself. Anne and Amy exchanged glances, and they, too, stayed silent, except that Anne asked at one stage, "Where are we going, honey child? I gather you're in need of an alcoholic beverage … ?"

"You gathered right. Mexican," Jade said. "I need a few dozen shots of tequila. Are you up for it?"

"Up for it? Are you kidding? Mexican it is."

In the Mexican restaurant they found, the three made themselves comfortable in a booth – two long, red-leather seats facing each other with a table between them. Anne and Amy sat on one side, Jade on the other. Once they'd ordered nachos and a round of tequilas, Anne was quick to steer the conversation where the three, each for reasons of her own, needed it to go.

She waved her hands at Jade like a traffic cop urging the traffic forward. "Spill."

Jade glanced at Amy, unconsciously seeking support, but Amy held up her hands. "Hey, I'm with Annie on this one, my sweet. Spill. What happened back there?"

"Can we … ? I need a shot first," Jade said.

And so she did. When the shots came, she downed hers in one gulp and ordered another one. "You?" she asked them both.

"Definitely," Anne said. "I'm in."

Amy rolled her eyes. "All right then, I'll be the responsible grown up. You guys go ahead, get as drunk as you want. I'll make sure we all get home."

Anne leaned over and kissed her on the cheek. "That's my girl," she said affectionately. Then, sitting back again on her side of the seat, she turned her attention to Jade. "All right, honey child, no more excuses. Spill. What happened back there? You looked like you were about to pass out, honestly."

"All right," Jade said, half sighing, surrendering to the inevitability of having to talk about something she desperately did not want to talk about. "I had a wee, small chat with the fiancé." She closed her eyes and took a deep breath, feeling the tequila warm her body and relax her muscles. The tension in her started to ease, somewhat, although there was still a way to go – nothing a couple more shots of tequila wouldn't take care of, she thought.

"And," Anne prompted, impatience ringing in the tone of that one single word.

Jade opened her eyes. "You know I had to leave, right? And so I did."

"Yeah, hon, of course," Anne agreed. "There's no doubting you did the right thing all those years ago. You had no choice really."

"Right," Jade concurred. "But I think, somewhere in the back of my mind, I've sort of held the thought, or the hope really, all these years, that by leaving, I kind of forced Jocelyn to find herself for herself. I figured if I wasn't there, she would have no one to copy or emulate. Right?"

In the natural pause, she looked at Anne and Amy. They were both looking at her intently, focussed on her, almost hanging off her every word. Neither of them answered her rhetorical question.

"But what if ... ?" she faltered, bringing a hand to her mouth. She was struggling to say it.

"What if what?" Amy asked intensely.

"What if, in leaving, I paved the way for her to just become me completely, no holds barred, and with no one around who knew the truth. So, no one to stop it, or call it to account. I mean, aside from me, you're the only one who really knew the truth, Annie. Even dad still doesn't really see or know the extent of it because he hardly pays her any attention, and he certainly doesn't spend time with her."

"No, he doesn't," Anne said. "So ..."

"So, I thought, if I'm not there, how will she copy me, right?"

"Right," Anne and Amy said together.

"Except that everything I've done over the last years, everything I believe, everything I've worked on, both personally and professionally, is in the public arena courtesy of my two websites – my own personal one and the one Pravesh and I religiously maintain for the business."

Anne and Amy just looked at her, the realisation starting to blossom but not yet coming to its full fruition.

"If she wanted to copy me," Jade said, helping them out, "everything is there. I am laid bare in those websites, especially my own personal one. I've made it so easy for her. God, I've handed me to her on a silver platter. All she has to do to be me is just read what I've written and then quote me … which is exactly what the fiancé told me she does … often."

The waiter brought their next round of drinks and Jade, again, downed her shot in one gulp and ordered two more, one for her and one for Anne.

"So I met him, the fiancé," she continued once the waiter had gone. She was starting to feel wonderfully, gloriously light headed, and was fast losing her ability and desire to choose her words with care. When she talked, she echoed or emphasised what she was saying with her hands. "And the first thing I find out is that he has no idea I even exist. No surprises there. If I was her I wouldn't tell him about me either. Too dangerous. He might find out certain truths relating to a certain stolen boyfriend that are best kept hidden. But then he tells me Jocelyn's interested in … no," she corrected herself, "passionate about Egyptology. What a load of crap. She showed not one ounce of interest in Egyptology before I left Maestronne, even with all the copying. I always kept that one a secret. She never knew I was interested in them, the Egyptians, 'cause I made damned sure of it. She could have all the others," she held up a finger, "but she wasn't having that one. Then," she brought her hand back to the table, the tone of her voice changing so that she sounded tired, even defeated, "he tells me she's into the religion of the ancients, and she quotes it, often. Honestly, does she even possess the intelligence to recognise what that religion is, let alone take it on for herself, personally, as her own personal philosophy? She wouldn't understand the first thing about it."

Amy sat back, grimacing. "Ouch," she said. "That's harsh, but, I have to admit, true." She was a counsellor, so she was quite good with human psychology. Well, she was an expert actually. She easily grasped the subtleties of the wounded human psyche and its various expressions.

"Oh, crap!" Anne said vehemently. "Where the fuck is that shot? I need it. I've seen your website, honey child, your own personal one. Gods, you're honest in it, brutally honest. I've always thought you were extremely brave, actually. But you're right. If anyone wanted to become you, you've made it easy. Heck, you've handed yourself to them, like you said …"

"It's like a constant fuel source," Jade said, nodding. "Constantly updated."

"Oh crap!" Amy said, thinking of something and surprising Anne and Jade with both the vehemence and the loudness of her outburst. "You two are overlooking something here, something important."

Both Anne and Jade looked at her expectantly. "What?" Anne said. "What could be more important than this?"

"The man," Amy said. "The fiancé." She rolled her eyes, exasperated when the other two still looked at her with puzzled expressions on their faces. "If Blake believes himself in love, enough to marry, then who is it he's really in love with?"

She asked the question slowly, carefully enunciating each word in the question, and then she watched the facial expressions of the other two change and clear as realisation dawned. Jade brought her hands to her mouth.

"Bollocks," Anne said, looking at Jade. "What a fucking mess. I could curse your god-damned father, Jade. He should've paid attention all those years ago. He should have been the fucking father he's supposed to be, and he should've forced that sick little girl into therapy."

Jade nodded and removed her hands from her mouth enough to say, "He should've, Annie. He absolutely should have. But you know what? She knows. Jocelyn knows. I heard them talking inside the house just before I came to find you. No wonder we didn't see them outside. Gods, she must've seen me come in and done a runner, she and mother dearest. She was telling mum I would ruin everything – her words exactly. Mum didn't get it, and she was trying to reassure Jocelyn, but Jocelyn wouldn't be reassured, and no bloody wonder."

"What do we do about this?" Anne asked the other two. "Do we tell him?"

"How? What are we supposed to say to make him understand?" Amy asked.

Jade lifted up her hands as if in surrender. "I can't get involved," she said. "I know that sounds horrible, but I can't become entangled in this. Hopefully, she'll just continue being me and he'll never know the truth. That's the best we can hope for, don't you think? If he thinks he's in love with her, then who are we to take that away from them both? Don't you see?" she asked them, sounding a little desperate at the dubious expressions on both their faces. "He need never know."

"I don't know, hon," Anne said. "I think this could all end badly. I just don't know."

"I don't know either," Amy said. "But I think Jade's right. Who are we to interfere? In a very real sense, this is not our problem."

"You're right, Aimes," Jade said, and then she looked at Anne. "This is not our problem. This is not our mess. We have to stay out of it."

~

A brief knock on the door was all the warning he was given before Jocelyn opened the door and put her head through it.

"I'm going to bed, honey. Are you coming?"

"Soon," Blake responded. "I'm nearly finished here. You go ahead. I'll come soon."

He smiled at her to reassure her, but she still pouted prettily.

"What's so important you have to deal with it tonight of all nights? Can't it wait? Couldn't you give yourself one whole day off, today?"

"I know. I'm sorry. But the company isn't going to run itself, and it doesn't take a break just because I'm getting married. I won't be long. I promise."

Knowing she wasn't going to convince him to come to bed, to his enormous relief, she nodded and then shut the door behind her.

He'd waited for as long as possible, seething with impatience, knowing he couldn't politely excuse himself and leave his own party, his own guests. When it became obvious there were only stragglers left – stragglers who would, no doubt, continue to help themselves to the food and alcohol he'd provided his guests well into the night – he quietly disappeared, not even telling Jocelyn where he was going, and shut himself in his study. Once there, he wasted no time. He turned on his computer and googled her: Jade Howlett.

Now, many hours later, he'd studied both her websites, but especially her personal one. He'd read it, and he'd absorbed it. And he loved it. He loved what she'd written. Here, at last, he'd found what he was looking for in Jocelyn, like a man parched with thirst who'd been given a small glass of water and, ever since, had been searching for the water's source, the well where the glass had come from. Now, at last, he'd found the well, the source.

He knew those people in his social circle, only some of whom were genuine friends, were puzzled, even bewildered by his choice of bride. Some of them had even told him, as Jade had today, they hoped he knew what he was doing. He'd resisted marriage for so long, or so they thought, but the truth was somewhat more complicated than mere resistance. He'd never met anyone he'd wanted to spend the rest of his life with before now. Women were all the same to him. He couldn't be with someone who was the same as everyone else. Instinctively, he'd always known he wanted something or someone unique. So when he started to get to know Jocelyn, to really get to know her, below the surface of her, he'd recognised the uniqueness within her. Over the years she'd worked for him, she had revealed, and he had seen, an aspect of her that was incredibly, profoundly wise and beautiful. She would come out with these gems of wisdom, as if she plucked them out of the air around her, and they had made him believe that she contemplated the deeper things in life. Always, though, when she came out with one of these gems, he would try to get more out of her, but she would clam up, withdraw, retreat, become unreachable, and he would have to work to get her out of herself again. He'd thought that if he provided her with the safety and security of marriage and a good home, then more of this aspect of her would emerge, naturally. And if it didn't, he was determined to cultivate it, to bring it out of her himself. What he saw was so beautiful, he thought it worth the effort and the angst of putting up with some of her less redeemable qualities, because there were quite a few of those.

Now that he'd discovered and read Jade's website, though, it was impossible for him to miss those same gems of wisdom. Because there they all were. Jocelyn even quoted them word for word, like a well-rehearsed speech. What did she do? Sit and memorise them all so she could use them at an appropriate time? And he had no doubt which sister was plagiarising which sister's words. When Jade had so obviously reacted the way she had and walked away from him today, looking shaken and unsettled, he'd wasted no time, seeking out James, and grilling him relentlessly, not allowing him off the hook. At first, James had been resistant. But Blake had persisted, ruthlessly, like a diver prising open a clam in the hope of finding a pearl inside, and James had realised he wasn't going to be allowed off the hook.

So he had relented, and, slowly but very surely, the whole sorry truth about the sisters' past came out. Unbeknownst to Jade, James actually knew far more about the whole situation than he let on, so he was perfectly equipped to properly and completely paint the true and whole picture for Blake.

When the door of his study was, once again, closed, Blake stared at it for a long time, and then he leaned back in his chair, looking at, but not seeing the computer screen in front of him. He sat for a long time. And then he breathed deeply and closed he eyes, letting his head rest on the chair behind him.

He knew now. He was certain, absolutely sure.

He was marrying the wrong sister.

~

3

Demons in the Present

The atmosphere in the room was stifling, and Jade was finding it hard to breathe. Seated next to her father at a table in the front of the room, near the bridal table, she was sitting directly opposite her mother, but her mother was pointedly ignoring her. She didn't mind. It was actually easier that way, not to mention honest. Her mother could be false with everyone else, but not her, so Cecily didn't bother trying. This night was a triumph for Cecily as much as it was for Jocelyn. There was an unmistakable vibe in and around them both, and Jade read it easily, effortlessly. They were gloating. Jocelyn now had something Jade didn't have – marriage and a husband. The room was full of conversation, laughter, music, smoke, the clinking of glasses. Everyone was happy, or so it seemed. This was, after all, one of those festive occasions. She swept her eyes around their table, catching Annie's eye. Annie gave her a wink and a reassuring smile, and she returned it. At least the two of them, Anne and Amy, were not pretending. Not that Anne could ever pretend. There was never any pretence in Annie, the gods bless her.

Needing some breathing space, not to mention a break from her mother's heavy energy, Jade quietly leant down to pick up her bag and, she hoped, surreptitiously rose from her chair, making her way to the opened glass doors she could see behind their table. Walking out onto the terrace, breathing the fresh, clear air and feeling the chill of the night on the bare skin of her arms and neck, she looked out over the city she'd grown up in, trying to assess her feelings about it now. From up here, atop one of Maestronne's tall buildings, with the darkness of night covering the city, and, in response, the city's lights punctuating the darkness, she could almost, almost think of it as beautiful. She still didn't like it, though. Maestronne was a centre of business, a commercial city, with a pace of life and an atmosphere to match. The people of this city were obsessed with success, intent only on amassing the wealth the city was famous for. Maestronne was a Mecca for anyone craving any sort of success. In many ways, Stenna and Maestronne were polar opposites. Stenna was a traditional university town. It owed its existence to the university, and so its atmosphere was one of culture and learning. Unlike Maestronne, Stenna's buildings were old, traditional, and definitely not tall. The tallest building in Stenna was the bell tower on top of the old town hall. She smiled affectionately as she pictured Stenna with its narrow, cobbled streets, and its old but beautiful stone buildings. She suited Stenna, or, rather, Stenna suited her. She'd never fitted in here in Maestronne, but in Stenna, she'd found a place she truly belonged ...

"You look beautiful tonight."

She half turned, frowning. Blake had followed her out onto the terrace and he'd come to stand behind her, so close he was almost touching her, and he had said the words softly, almost caressingly. He sounded like a lover, but she had not seen him since that disastrous conversation at his party the weekend before. She'd not exchanged so much as two more words with him. He, on the other hand, had been studying her work and her writing all week, so while she knew him not at all, he had come to know her well.

"Thank you," she responded, moving away from him slightly, putting some distance between them. "So do you."

She shivered with tension, couldn't suppress it, although she tried.

"Are you cold?" he asked her, sounding concerned and removing his jacket without awaiting her response, placing it over her shoulders. And when the jacket was sitting on her shoulders, shielding her from the chill of the night, he didn't take his hands from her. Instead, he let them rest on her shoulders.

She didn't say anything. She couldn't think of anything to say. She was too uncomfortable.

"I know the people around me, whether friends or colleagues, don't understand why I'm with Jocelyn," he said, unwittingly increasing the tension in Jade with the mention of her sister. "But they didn't see what I saw in her, or what I was given a glimpse of so often. Tell me," he asked, applying the pressure necessary to turn her around so that she was facing him, "how am I supposed to live with the copy now that I've seen the original?"

They were standing so close it was utterly impossible for her to hide her reaction from him. She closed her eyes as pain, hot and potent, shot through her. "Oh god," she whispered, feeling breathless. And then she looked up at him. He was still holding her upper arms, looking at her intensely, so he couldn't miss or misunderstand the pain in her eyes. "If you know that, why did you marry her?"

"I couldn't humiliate her that way, or embarrass everyone who's here for the wedding. I'm not that sort of person, Jade. She's my responsibility. I can't just wash my hands of her. Besides, she and I have been lovers for nearly a year. You don't just switch that off and pretend it was never the case. I care about her. I don't want to see her hurt and I certainly don't want to be the one to do so."

"So you've tied yourself to her."

"Not forever," he said. "I'll wait a year and then I'll divorce her. I just need to make sure she's okay."

"Well," she said, stepping back out of his reach, "I wish you luck. You'll need it, I think."

She began to walk past him but he stopped her with a hand on her arm, and he wasn't gentle. He held her arm in a vice-like grip.

"Please, Jade, just … please, just let me be in contact with you. That's all I ask. Please."

Why didn't she just pull away and leave him to his fate? Why? He didn't know what he was asking, or maybe he did. But he sounded so pained, so desperate, so pleading. She wasn't so frozen and so walled off, as Pravesh had put it, that she could remain unaffected by his pain. On the contrary, she was affected by it deeply. She felt it as her own. It reached into the depths of her and penetrated every part of her.

"All right," she said softly. Although everything within her screamed resistance, she opened her bag, took out one of her cards, carried by sheer force of habit, as if she wasn't quite intact without them, and wrote her private phone number and email on the back of it. Then she handed it to him.

He took it. "Thank you."

She nodded. And then she pulled off his jacket and handed it to him. When he took it, they looked at each other for a long moment, saying much without using any words at all, and then she turned and walked away from him. At the opened glass door, Anne was waiting for her. They, too, looked at each other for a moment, and then Jade whispered, because her throat was so tight she couldn't speak properly, "I need to go."

Anne put her hands on Jade's arms, leaned forward and kissed her forehead. "I know, sweetheart, I know. Let's go."

Wrapping her hand around Jade's arm, as if she felt the need to hold Jade up, and wholly unwilling to let go, Anne walked them both around the reception tables, towards the back of the room and the lifts that would take them down, down, away from this farce of a celebration. Amy was waiting for them there.

Out on the terrace, Blake put his jacket back on and then he stood, his head bowed, holding Jade's card in one hand, unable to take his eyes off it. Only once before had he felt this incredible grief, this intense pain, such a profound sense of loss. Watching Jade walk away from him tonight had aroused in him that same incredible grief he'd felt when his parents had been killed. And tonight was only the second time he'd laid eyes on her. He raised his eyes and looked out over the city. Maestronne looked beautiful from up here. He'd always thought so.

He didn't think it at all strange that Jade's departure had left him feeling so empty, so desolate. He knew he'd fallen in love with her months ago, so it all made perfect sense to him.

❧

The bar was dark, dark with a very light cloud of smoke hovering over the room and its patrons. But it was classy all the same. The dim lights were more like chandeliers, and the chairs were leather, the kind of chairs you sank into. In the corner, on a stage, a pianist was playing a beautiful, black grand piano. For a moment, all three women listened to him playing, all three awaiting the drinks they'd ordered, and all three postponing the inevitable.

When the waiter brought their drinks, handing them to each of the women, and then vanished into the dim interior of the bar, Jade looked at the bubbles in her glass. She'd ordered champagne not because she wanted to celebrate. The gods alone knew there was nothing celebratory about the events at hand and the situation she found herself in. She'd ordered champagne because she wanted to pretend, at least for this small moment, that there was joy to be had in life. And who better to pretend with than Anne and Amy. There weren't many people in her life whom she loved as she loved these two. They had proved themselves genuine friends, not just in the last week, but in the years since she'd left Maestronne.

When she looked up again, they were both looking at her silently. She smiled at them.

"I guess it was too much to hope for, wasn't it? That he would never know."

Amy smiled a sympathetic smile. "I strongly suspect he was always going to know once he met you. It was inevitable, wasn't it? It's as if there's something in him that recognises you, sweetheart. He recognised you in Jocelyn, but she was never going to compare when he met you for real, as you."

"Do you think," Anne asked them both slowly, "James knew what he was doing when he asked you to come back here for the wedding?"

Jade felt the shock of the question. "No. I hope not. Do you?"

"Actually, I do, unfortunately. I wasn't going to say anything, but it's a niggling, nagging feeling I can't seem to shake. He knows more than you think he does, hon."

Jade processed that. What could possibly be his motivation if that was true? "Surely," she said out loud, "if that's true, he must know he's stirred up trouble, for all of us."

Anne rolled her eyes and pursed her lips. "Wouldn't put it past him," she muttered.

"So," Amy asked, watching Jade closely, "where do you go from here?"

Jade took a large sip of her drink. "He asked me if we could stay in contact, and I agreed to, against my vastly better judgement. I couldn't say no, as much as I really, really wanted to. It was the weirdest thing. I felt his pain more easily than I feel my own. I felt it in my entire being. And I couldn't, I just couldn't be a source of pain for him. Gods," she sighed, "what a god-damn mess. Surely this can only end very badly, surely ..."

"You don't know that, honey child," Anne said. "I think that's your fear talking. You don't know how this will end. No one does. If you want some advice, just go with the flow. Don't be afraid of getting hurt, and don't be afraid of hurting him. Just let it go where it wants to go. I strongly suspect neither of you are powerful enough to stop it anyway, so you might as well just let it go where it will and go with it, willingly."

Jade nodded slowly, knowing Anne was perfectly right. She wasn't powerful or strong enough to stop it, whatever it was.

~

"Hi, it's Blake."

Jade was so immersed in the translation she was working on that it had taken her a while to even realise the phone was ringing. When she answered the call, though, she wasn't so immersed and preoccupied that she missed the tension in his voice.

For nearly ten months, they had been communicating, so much so that they spoke almost every day, sometimes in a brief text or email but sometimes in the form of lengthy phone calls. She had been resistant at first, in those initial weeks after returning to Stenna, but after a while, she'd succumbed and relaxed into the rhythm of their communications. He was, now, an intrinsic part of the fabric of her day to day reality such was his success at worming his way into her life. She hadn't as yet analysed her feelings for him. In fact, she had become quite masterful at avoiding that kind of self analysis where he was concerned. They spoke on the phone at least a few times a week, and he always phoned her, but he always called at the end of the day when they could both talk freely. She glanced at the time on her computer screen. Right now, it was still only late morning, not even midday.

"Hi," she said, her voice ringing with her uncertainty and wariness.

He wasted no time in getting to the point. "I'm sorry to call you during work hours. I know you're busy, but I wanted to tell you myself, or, rather, I wanted to make sure you found out from me, over the phone, in case you had ... ah, well, questions. Jocelyn's pregnant."

"You have sex with her?" Jade asked loudly, involuntarily, before she could stop herself, and then wanted to bite out her own tongue. By unspoken mutual consent, they never spoke about Jocelyn. They talked about many things, but never that particular topic. So Jade had no idea of the form Blake's marriage to Jocelyn had taken, nor did she want to know. She had, however, just assumed they were no longer lovers, not properly married. "I'm sorry," she said quickly. "That's none of my business."

In truth, she felt the impact of those two words like a punch in the gut – a punch that had knocked the breath out of her lungs and increased her heart rate. This was unexpected.

"It *is* your business," he said. "For gods sake, Jade, it very much is your business. You have every right to ask. And no, we don't, or we haven't ... except for a couple of times recently." He hesitated, and she could almost hear him taking the deep breaths necessary to calm himself. "We've never talked about her, you and I," he said, and he did, indeed, sound calmer. "I didn't want her coming between us, and I knew if I talked about her, you would withdraw." Again, he hesitated.

"And rightly so," she interjected quietly.

"Well, it's been difficult these last months. You don't know, you can't know, how difficult it's been. She has temper tantrums, Jade. I mean, she really loses it. A couple of times she's hurt herself. And she's becoming more and more unstable, ever since the wedding. I thought I was doing the right thing by her, but ... I don't know. I think, maybe, I've made things worse. It's my fault. It's all my fault. I haven't been the same with her since I met you, and she's not stupid. She must know that. So I thought if she had a child, it would give her something of her own to focus on, something that would help stabilise her ... settle her."

"This is **not** your fault, Blake," Jade said forcefully. "None of this is your doing. She's ill. My parents should have dealt with this a long time ago. She needs help, and having a child is **not** the kind of help she needs. And so," she, too, took a breath to calm herself, "now you've tied yourself to her even more. You won't divorce her now. She's having your child. I know you well enough to know that." Again, she took a deep breath and breathed out slowly, exhaling through her mouth. "I can't do this."

"Jade, don't ... please, don't do this ..."

"Don't do what?" she asked, sounding utterly exasperated. "Don't end something that cannot be? I can't keep this going, whatever it is. It's not fair on any of us. Please, don't contact me again, Blake. Please.

Leave me alone. Let me live my life in peace. Please. And, for gods sake, get Jocelyn the help she needs … the help she's always needed. If you really care about her …"

"Jade …"

She hung up, but she left her hand on the receiver, breathing deeply, feeling sick, sorry, and upset. She knew, she just knew, she shouldn't have allowed their … whatever kind of relationship they had, to continue this long. Tears pooled in her eyes, and she ruthlessly wiped them away and bit down on them, refusing to shed any more. Putting an end to it was for the best. For ten months, wondering the whole time if she had gone insane for continuing to allow him in her life, she had felt as if the axe would come down on their relationship one way or another, severing it, and hurting them both in the process. She had felt it coming. In fact, it had been like a dark cloud on the horizon of her existence. Now, at last, the axe had come down, and everyone knew where they stood. It was better this way. He would have to deal with his pain, and she would deal with hers.

And then she would move on.

⁓

Pravesh lounged in her doorway, watching her while he waited for her. She checked her computer was off and then turned off the light on her desk.

"What's wrong?" he asked her suspiciously. "You've been very quiet today, not your usual self at all."

"Nothing," she lied as she grabbed her coat from behind the door, smiling at him to give some sort of credence to that one word. "I'm fine, just busy as usual."

He eyed her suspiciously, not believing her at all. "How is the translation going?"

"Slowly," she replied. "Very slowly."

"Are you having trouble with this one?"

"Not with the translation, no, just with my levels of concentration. Don't worry," she said as she pulled the door shut behind her and made sure it was locked, "I'll get it finished. I'll put in a concerted effort tomorrow. I promise."

He turned to walk ahead of her, preceding her to the set of stairs that would take them both up to the ground floor and the foyer of the building they worked in. "I have no doubt you'll finish it, my friend, no doubt at all. That is not what concerns me."

"What concerns you then?" she asked his back.

"A few things," he answered enigmatically.

"I'm okay, Pravesh," she said as they reached the stairs.

He stood back to allow her to precede him, and then he followed her up the two flights of stairs. "You can lie to yourself all you like," he said as they walked up the stairs. "You just need to know, you cannot lie to me. I know you too well."

At the top of the stairs, in the foyer, she swung her coat over her shoulders and waited for Pravesh to join her. Then, still shrugging her coat on, trying to juggle her coat and her bag, she responded to Pravesh's comment. Amused, she said, "The gods forbid I should ever try to lie to you, Pravesh. All right, I admit, I'm not okay. But I will be after Nita sets me right with some of her home cooking. What is for dinner, by the way? Do you know?"

"Ah, so that's it then," he said as they started walking towards the building's main entrance. "Evasive action, is it to be? Don't think you can just change the subject thereby avoiding the issue at hand."

She laughed as they walked through the building's beautiful foyer, passing the foyer's staircase with its carved, wooden balustrade, and then past the double carved wooden doors of its impressive front entrance. Once through the door, though, she lost her smile and stopped walking so abruptly Pravesh, who was just behind her, nearly collided with her back. And then, she just stood where she was, frozen, staring. Pravesh stopped beside her, and followed her line of vision. A man was standing at the base of the building's front steps, leaning against the stone balustrade, his hands deep in the pockets of his tailored coat, as if he had been waiting there for a while. Although Pravesh had not ever met the man, he could still see and understand the determined set of the man's stance, his body language. He wasn't moving until he got what he was there for.

"Is that him?" Pravesh asked Jade without taking his eyes from the man. "The issue we're not talking about, is that him?"

His words seemed to break the spell cast over Jade. She took her eyes off the man to look at Pravesh with a self-deprecating smile that was half grimace. "That's him," she confirmed. "You see too much by half, Pravesh, too much for my own good."

He raised his eyebrows as he turned to look at her. "For your own good? I think not. So," he said as he took her arm to guide her down the steps, not entirely confident she wouldn't fall and hurt herself, "at last we get to meet him, do we?"

She glanced at him, "I didn't keep him ..."

He squeezed her arm. "I know," he said simply.

She hadn't told Pravesh and Nita about Blake. She, who never kept secrets from the two of them, had kept her relationship, if relationship was what it was, with Blake a secret for nearly ten months. She had told them everything else that happened in Maestronne, she just hadn't told them she was in constant contact with her sister's husband.

Blake straightened as they approached him. It was, he thought, smiling slightly as he watched her, hard to believe this was only the third time he'd laid eyes on her. He knew her so well in one sense. It was the little day to day things he didn't know about her – what her favourite food was or her favourite perfume, what she wore to work, what she liked to cook, what she did with her evenings when she wasn't on the phone to him, which book she was reading at the moment.

"What did you do?" she asked him unceremoniously when she and Pravesh reached him. "Get on a train straight away, after we spoke?"

It was only that morning they had spoken on the phone, and she had asked him not to contact her anymore. The train trip from Maestronne to Stenna took three hours, so by her calculations, he must have left the office almost straight after their phone call and got a train straight here.

"Yep," he said in response to her question. "Pretty much."

He pulled a hand out of the pocket of his coat and extended it towards Pravesh.

"Hi," he said. "I'm Blake ..."

"My sister's husband," Jade finished the introduction.

"Ah, is that so?" Pravesh asked as he took Blake's hand. "Well, it is very good to meet you finally, Blake. What?" he asked sheepishly when Jade threw him a look. "We know you so well, my friend. Did you really think we would not know? You cannot hide him from us? You changed in Maestronne. And we could not miss the change in you when you returned from your sister's wedding. He lights you up, this one. You are radiant. You glow like a beacon." Ignoring Jade's narrowed eyes and pursed lips – if she could have subtly stood on his toes to shut him up, she would have – he turned his attention to Blake once again. "Jade normally has dinner with us on Thursday nights. Would you like to join us, too?"

Jade began to protest. "Pravesh …"

"What? There is always plenty of food. You know that. And Nita will be pleased to meet him at last. In fact, I fear for my life if I allow this opportunity to slip between my fingers."

Reluctantly, and marvelling at his ability to make her smile even in **this** situation, she looked at Blake. "Nita is the kindest, gentlest soul you will ever meet," she explained. "She's the least likely person I know to actually commit murder."

True to his word, at dinner, Pravesh and Nita, pleased as they were to finally have access to him personally and exclusively, bombarded Blake with questions. Blake seemed not to mind at all. In fact, it took Pravesh and Nita no time at all to realise Blake was decidedly forthcoming, without boundaries, or without anything being off limits. He was honest, and he was prepared to share his most personal, most intimate thoughts and feelings. And so he did. It was, Jade thought as she sat at the table silently, listening to the conversation without participating in it, almost like a true confession. So some of the questions Pravesh and Nita threw at him were very personal. And because he was perfectly willing to answer them, over dinner, Pravesh and Nita came to understand the situation between Jade and Blake very well, probably even better than Jade herself.

She had not made a conscious choice not to tell Pravesh and Nita about Blake. Sitting silently at the table while they extracted the truth, easily and effortlessly, from him, Jade tried to assess her own reasoning for keeping him a secret. Was it because she didn't understand the nature of the relationship between them? Or was it because she had known the axe would fall sooner rather than later, so that the relationship had no future? Or was it because she felt guilty? No, she thought, not guilt. Whatever was between them was what it was. She had not made it happen and, really, neither had he. And besides, even if she had felt guilty, that would not have been enough to keep the truth of him from her two closest friends – these people she trusted as she trusted no others.

And then the truth hit her, not surprising since this was the first time she had really allowed herself to contemplate the situation. By keeping the truth of him from Pravesh and Nita, she could still convince herself he was not real, or what was happening between them was not really happening. By bringing it all out into the open, especially with Pravesh and Nita, she would've been admitting and acknowledging there was something real going on – something indefinable given definition and form. Now he, Blake, was doing that for her, without her choices being involved. And that, she had to admit, was one of the key issues with all of this, really. She was in this situation without really choosing it, apart from the choice she'd made to give him her contact details, thereby also giving him permission to be in contact with her. But even in that there hadn't really been a choice. She could not have ignored his pain that fateful night, and she certainly could not have deliberately and consciously exacerbated it. Ironic, really, she thought, given the fact that those were his own reasons for going through with the marriage to her sister.

Now that she was fully contemplating the whole situation, she could see that by not talking about him here, in Stenna, to those she interacted with every day, she could keep him out of her life here. She could keep him confined to one little compartment of her life and stop it seeping into the rest of her life. Not talking about him was her way of trying to stay in control.

"They are lovely," Blake said after dinner as they walked home, side by side, Jade's unit being only a few streets from Pravesh and Nita's house. They were both careful not to touch, even accidentally, keeping a small distance between them. Jade breathed deeply, partly savouring the fresh, clear night air and partly trying to still her racing pulse. Now that she was alone with him for only the second time, she was nervous.

"Yes," she agreed, responding to his statement, wrapping her coat further around her and hugging herself for warmth and comfort, "they are. They're very important to me. I don't know what I would do without them."

"I can see that. I'm glad you have them. They care about you deeply. So why have you not told them about me?"

"Not sure," Jade said, wanting to evade the question. And then she changed her mind. "I think because I don't know what you and I are, and in not talking about it I could pretend it wasn't really happening. And because I thought this," she waved her hand between them both, "would not last. Have you got somewhere to stay? Or are you just expecting to stay with me?"

They both stopped walking to face each other.

"I don't expect you to put me up," he replied, "so no, but I haven't got anywhere to stay either. I left so quickly, I …"

"You can sleep on my lounge," she told him. "I don't have a spare bed, but the lounge is comfortable. I sleep on it when dad comes to stay."

They both resumed walking again. "He comes often?"

She nodded. "Every few months or so."

Blake processed that. "I don't think your mother has any idea."

"Well, she wouldn't. They live separate lives really."

When they reached her unit, she said, "This is me."

Inside, they both took their coats off and she took them into her bedroom to hang them up. When she re-emerged, her arms were full with a spare sheet, a pillow and her spare quilt. "I'll help you make up the lounge," she said as she walked back into the lounge room.

He stopped her with a hand on her arm. Again, as he had at the wedding reception, his grip on her arm was firm, strong, and he guided her to the lounge.

"Please," he said. "We need to talk. That's why I'm here. We need to talk face to face. I want to see what's in your eyes."

She was very quiet but compliant as she allowed herself to be pulled down to the lounge so that she sat beside him, and then she leaned over and put the linen on the floor. When she straightened, she looked at him and, for a moment, they just looked at each other, silently, without words, as they had the night of the wedding reception.

"I don't want to hurt you …" he started.

"But you are hurting me," she said, interrupting him. "You're making me like you …"

Now it was his turn to interrupt. "Like?"

She made a noise in her throat – a noise of defeat and surrender and sheer, unadulterated reluctance. "All right, love," she conceded reluctantly. "You're making me love you. But you're not free. And I'll be damned if I'll have an affair with my sister's husband. You know our history so you must understand why."

"I understand," he said, feeling his heart soar with her confession. He hadn't been sure of how she felt until this moment. "Of course I understand. I just … I know it hasn't worked in our favour, any of this. The timing of it all, meeting you, was appalling. But I can't lose you. If you sever contact, it will feel as if you've ripped the heart out of my life, out of me. You've become …" he hesitated, looking for the right words, "everything to me."

She absorbed that for a moment, feeling a mixture of surprise and bewilderment. "You managed pretty well before you knew I existed," she pointed out.

"Because I had the company. I devoted a lot of time, effort and energy to the company. It was all I had, before Jocelyn gave me a glimpse of something beautiful. You and she are fundamentally not at all alike, now that I know you both, but still, she was a perfect conduit for your … inner beauty, your wisdom, your spiritual essence. She channelled you perfectly."

Jade broke eye contact, biting the inside of her lip, trying not to squirm with discomfort. "I beg to differ," she said. "It used to be a perverse kind of torture watching her be me."

"Only because you knew the truth. You knew who you were, and you knew who she was. For anyone who didn't know her, she was you, and she was good at it."

"Was?"

He reached out a hand to tuck a wayward strand of her hair behind her ear. He knew it was forbidden, given the well-demarcated boundaries between them, but he couldn't help himself. Nor could he help trailing his fingers over the smooth skin of her cheek. She didn't try and stop him.

"She's changed," he said. "As I said on the phone this morning, she's become very unstable. Your mother just makes excuses for her, but I'm worried. It's not normal."

Now she did pull away from his touch, annoyed.

"I told you what to do about that," she said, her annoyance ringing through the words she spoke. "She needs help. She's always needed help. And you won't get any support from my mother, so don't wait for it. If you're so god-damned set on taking on this misguided responsibility for Jocelyn, then get her into therapy, with someone good, someone who really knows what they're doing."

He let his hand drop, knowing the mood between them had changed, and the intimacy between them shattered. He wanted to touch her, wanted it badly, but, given their current circumstances, thought it would probably not be fair on her. So he let the moment pass.

"You really don't like talking about her, do you?" he asked.

"No, I really don't. Can't you see, I would have nothing to do with her if not for you? You are dragging me back to a place I don't want to be. Can't you see that?"

"Yes," he acknowledged reluctantly, "I can see that. I'm sorry, Jade. Perhaps I'm being totally selfish, and in trying to do the right thing by her, I've done the wrong thing by you …"

"And by you," she said vehemently. "Don't leave yourself out of this."

"And by me," he conceded. "I just … I can't lose you, even if we are not, and cannot be lovers physically, I can't lose what little I have with you."

That night, Jade didn't sleep. Lying in the dark, tossing and turning in her bed restlessly, she couldn't help but be aware of him sleeping on her lounge in the lounge room, if, indeed, he was sleeping. Perhaps he was tossing and turning as she was. How did she get herself into this mess? And why didn't she just put an end to it? Because every time he begged and pleaded, her resistance to the whole thing melted away. She couldn't end whatever this was because of him. She couldn't cause him pain because she felt his pain even more than she felt her own, as if she'd suddenly developed empathic abilities but only where he was concerned. Ending the relationship would cause her pain now, her own pain, but only briefly, she knew. She'd become like a derailed train, and she knew if she ended what was between them, she would simply put herself back on the tracks she'd been on before she met him. For him, it was not that simple, or easy, for that matter.

He was calm as he lay sleepless on her lounge. Being here was a new experience for him, knowing she was in the next room, and he relished the closeness of her. He also soaked up the pleasure of finally being in her place, her space. Before he'd turned the light out, he'd taken in as much detail as he could, memorising what her lounge room looked like so he could picture her in it when he spoke to her. He noticed many things – the lack of family photographs and pictures, her extensive, impressive collection of books, the colour of the paint on the walls, the paintings and pictures she'd hung on the walls, the configuration of her furniture, and the many things – ornaments, trinkets – she'd collected over the years.

At the station the next morning, they stood together on the platform, facing each other, and he took her hands in his.

"Can we continue?" he asked her quietly. "I have your word?"

She nodded. "Even though this is going to end badly."

He raised a hand and, again, touched her cheek with his fingertips. "But until then, it will be good. I promise."

Partly because he wanted to and partly because he wanted to silence her, stop her responding to his comment, he leaned towards her and touched his lips to hers, lightly but lingeringly, his lips caressing hers. He didn't want to make things harder for them both, but surely one kiss could not hurt them. He felt her respond so he deepened the kiss, and, again, she responded. She opened herself to him, was powerless not to. As they kissed, they both moved, wrapping their arms around each other. When he broke the kiss, he held her against him as if he would never let her go.

"By the gods," he said, "I will fight for you. You must know that."

~

"Hey, it's me."

"Hi. What's wrong?" He sounded utterly exhausted.

"Jocelyn went into labour early. They had to cut the babies out of her, and now she's in a coma. I know I shouldn't ask, but I need you. Can you come?"

"Babies?"

"There are two, a girl and a boy."

Jade digested that in silence. This was the first she knew about twins. And the babies were, indeed, early. They weren't due for another six weeks. Even though twins were notorious for coming early, six weeks was still pretty early.

"Are they all right?" she asked.

"The babies are fine. They're doing well."

"But?"

He took a moment to answer and the silence was palpable in that moment. "But I can't touch them. They don't feel like mine."

Jade closed her eyes and put her head on her hand, still holding the phone to her ear. Could this get any messier?

"Okay," she said. "I'm coming. I'll let you know which train I'm on. I need to organise some things here before I leave."

"But you'll come tonight?"

"Yes, Blake, I'll come tonight."

The relief that flooded his entire being choked his throat and prevented him from responding. He didn't need to. She knew. She felt it.

~

He was waiting for her when she got off the train. Neither of them spoke. They just moved into each other's arms. He held her so tightly she felt as if she was holding him up.

"When did you last sleep?" she asked him, pulling back from their embrace. He looked utterly exhausted and, perhaps, defeated, as if he'd used up his last reserves of energy.

"I'm not sure," he replied. "I can't remember."

"Have you eaten?"

"No."

"All right," she said, looking up at him and putting a hand on his chest to make him pay attention and focus on what she was saying. "First, we get something to eat, and you can fill me in. I want to know everything that's happened. Then, you get some sleep. We'll go to the hospital tomorrow."

"Will you stay with me? I have plenty of rooms."

"I know. I saw them. And, yes. It'll be easier with me at your place if we'll be going back and forth to the hospital every day."

~

At the entrance to the hospital, as he held the door open for her, he asked her if she wanted to see Jocelyn.

She threw him a look – half annoyed, half surprised he'd asked, as if she thought he'd suddenly lost all sense of sanity and rationality. "No," she said definitely. "I don't want to see Jocelyn. I want to see the babies."

He smiled, the first smile she'd seen from him since arriving the night before. She couldn't help but return it. They'd stopped at a restaurant on the way home from the station, and over dinner, he'd told her everything that had occurred. She could see, even as they'd talked, the weight coming off him, the burden he'd carried alone now shared, halved. And then, they'd gone back to his house – that same large house she'd seen at the party the weekend before the wedding. He'd shown her a couple of rooms on the second floor, and she'd chosen one for herself, a safe distance from his. It was large, airy, with its own en suite bathroom. After making up the bed in her room, they'd both gone to bed, he to his own bed, she to hers. Now, after a good night's sleep, he looked almost normal again, certainly much calmer.

The nursery was on the third floor of the hospital. Although she didn't say anything, she thought it a good sign that he knew where the nursery was. When they arrived, he didn't hesitate. He opened the nursery door and walked in. She followed him inside. The nursery was full of little cribs, all occupied by sleeping babies, wrapped up like little peas in little pods, but in the middle of the room, one of the nurses was walking around in large circles, holding and rocking an obviously-distressed, screaming baby. She was matronly looking, an older woman with a round face, rosy cheeks, a large bosom, and kind eyes – eyes that currently looked concerned. When she looked up and saw Blake, relief replaced concern.

"Oh thank the gods," she said. "This one's a mite distressed. We can't get her to settle, no matter what we do, and we've tried just about everything we can think of."

She moved towards Blake, preparing to hand over the distressed baby, but Blake took an involuntary couple of steps backwards, unconsciously holding up his hands, as if to ward off danger and obviously not at all prepared to take the child. Jade looked at him, surprised by the strength and depth of his reaction, but the nurse didn't look at all surprised.

"He won't touch them," she said. "'Tis a shame, really. I've seen it happen a few times. He's not bonding with them." As she spoke, she handed the baby to Jade, and, without any time to think about what she was doing, Jade took the child.

Almost instantly, the baby's distressed screams were reduced to little whimpers, and then even those ceased as she settled into the comfort of Jade's arms.

"Well, I never," the nurse said, looking at Jade in surprise. "Do you have children of your own then, dear?"

Jade took her eyes off the baby in her arms to glance at the nurse, smiling slightly. "No."

"Well, you've got the touch. No doubt about that. Either that or she knows you."

"This is the first time we've met," Jade told her.

"Ah, yes, that may be, but that's not to say she doesn't know you."

Again, Jade took her eyes off the child in her arms to look up at the nurse, smiling, this time openly. "True," she said simply. "Yes, that's very true." And then, with the baby in her arms, she turned towards Blake who, with those couple of steps back, was now behind her. "What's going on, Blake? Why aren't you bonding with them? Why won't you touch them?"

He looked at her for a moment without responding. Both Jade and the nurse, standing together in the middle of the room, facing him, looked at him expectantly. He raised a hand and, completely unconsciously, ran it through his hair.

"Because," he said, "they should be yours. I have no connection with them."

"Oh, crap." His answer shocked Jade so she'd breathed out as she said the words, and, as such, the words were barely audible. The pain resonating in that one simple statement of his caused her heart to skip a beat. "Even though you are their biological father, and it was your idea to have them?" she asked him unnecessarily.

"Even so."

"Blake," she said quietly, conscious of the nurse standing next to her — a witness to hers and Blake's personal and very tangled relationship — "these babies would never have been mine. I've made a very conscious choice never to have children."

It was the nurse who responded. "Really, dear? Why ever not? You're good with them, a natural. Look at her," she said, indicating the baby settled in Jade's arms. "She's perfectly settled with you."

Jade looked at the child in her arms as she responded. "I've chosen to focus on other things this time around." And then she looked up at the woman who was still standing very close. Given the woman's earlier statement, Jade thought she might as well explain. "Truth be told," she said, "I think I haven't had children very often, if at all. I certainly have no memories of ever having had them."

The woman considered that. "Are you so sure? Maybe you're just choosing not to recall those particular memories."

"That's possible, I guess. Why would I do that, though, if I so easily remember other things?"

"Well," the nurse said, "I don't know. Perhaps you've suppressed them so as to suppress the desire to have children this time."

"Perhaps," Jade said, noncommittally. "What's her name?" she asked the woman.

The nurse looked over at Blake pointedly. "Perhaps you should ask her father."

Again, Jade looked at Blake. "You haven't named them?"

He shook his head.

"Why not?"

He shrugged his shoulders but so slightly the movement was hardly perceptible such was his reluctance to talk about his own children.

"Because he hasn't bonded with them, dear," the nurse answered for him. "I think you don't quite realise how much he is keeping his distance from them, emotionally, I mean. To name them would be to acknowledge his responsibility for them."

Jade had watched the nurse while she talked, impressed with the level of her understanding of human psychology. "You're a bit of a psychologist I see," Jade said to the nurse, smiling.

The woman returned Jade's smile. "Oh, you see everything here, dear, and I mean everything. Your situation is not all that unusual, would you believe."

"Really? How is it people get themselves into such messes, then?"

"I suspect you already know what the answer to that question is."

In response, Jade smiled at her again, and then, she turned to Blake. "Did Jocelyn have names picked out for them?"

"I don't know," he replied.

"You didn't speak to her about it?"

"No."

When Jade and the nurse exchanged dismayed, frustrated glances, he felt compelled to add, "Perhaps Cecily will know if Jocelyn had any names picked out."

"Trust me," Jade said definitely, "you don't want to go down that road. Let's leave Cecily out of it." She thought for a moment, and then an idea occurred to her. "What were the names of your parents?"

"Um, Zachary and Ruth."

"Perfect," Jade said. "Those names are perfect. Why don't we name them for both sets of your parents? Zachary James and Ruth Cecily. No, that doesn't go. How about Ruth Cecile? Zachary James and Ruth Cecile."

"Lovely," the nurse said beside Jade. "Quite lovely."

And then both she and Jade looked at Blake, again, expectantly. When he remained silent, Jade prompted him. "Blake? What do you think?"

Slowly, he nodded. "Yeah," he said. "I like the idea of naming them for both sets of parents ... or grandparents."

The nurse put her hand on Jade's arm and all but whispered, "Do you know what you've just done, my dear?" Without awaiting a response, she added, "You've made it possible for him to bond with them now because you've named them, and in his eyes, they'll be forever associated with you. Well done. Now," she said, resuming the brusque manor of a nurse, "I'll go and get the paperwork prepared. Without names, we haven't been able to do up birth certificates for them. Do you think we could push our luck and see if the little one will take the bottle from you?"

"She's not feeding?" Jade asked her.

"Not without a whole lot of trouble."

"Okay, yes," Jade said. "Definitely. Is there somewhere I can sit?"

"Of course, dear, of course. This way."

She led Jade through the nursery to the next room which was decorated like a comfortable lounge room complete with lounges, coffee tables, and television. The room was empty so Jade took her pick of lounges, sitting down and settling into it so as to make the child in her arms as comfortable as she could. Blake had followed the women and now he sat beside Jade. The nurse left them both alone while she went to prepare a bottle.

"Say we'd met years ago," he said, "long before I had anything to do with Jocelyn, and we'd fallen in love and married like normal people do. Would you have had children with me then?"

"Probably," she replied. "It's hard to say because that didn't happen, obviously. I've always known I could never have children just for the sake of it. If ever I had them, it would be because I wanted children **with** someone. I mean, I would've wanted **his** child, not **a** child. So, yeah, I think I probably would've in that case."

Her response aroused such emotion in him, he couldn't speak. He just looked at her as she sat holding his child, and then, unable to help himself, he reached out and touched her, caressing her cheek with the backs of his fingers.

"But it wasn't to be," she said softly, taking her eyes from the babe in her arms to look at him.

"I know."

"Here, poppet," the nurse said as she walked into the lounge room. "Let's see how we go with this."

Jade reached up and took the bottle from her, feeling the warmth of the milk through the glass. When she gave the bottle to the child she was holding, the baby took it as if the two of them had performed the feeding ritual many times before. The nurse put her hands on her hips as she watched the baby take the bottle with no trouble or resistance at all.

"Well, I never," she said. "Who would've thought it. You've got the touch, my dear. You've definitely got the touch. But I rather think she knows you. She trusts you."

She stayed a moment longer, watching the three on the sofa in front of her, all three looking for all intents and purposes like a normal, loving family. Although she would never say so aloud, she was privately inclined to agree with the father. These children had been born to the wrong mother.

~

"So, you've got no plans to come home, then? You've been there six weeks, you know."

"Six weeks?" Jade did a quick calculation in her mind. "Oh crap, I have, too. God, how fast has that gone? I feel like I've been here six days."

"Nope," Pravesh said, "definitely six weeks. We miss you, you know."

"I know. I'm sorry, Pravesh. I'll be home soon. I promise."

She watched his facial expression change on her computer screen. He didn't believe her and his expression reflected that. "Beware empty promises. I think you are in danger of never coming home at all."

He said the words quietly as was his way, and, as was his intent, they shocked Jade. "Really? You really think that?"

"Yes," he said. "Really. And that's okay, my friend. That's okay. You need to know that, Jade. Whatever you decide to do, you have my full support. We just need to make plans as to how we run the business now if you're going to be living over there."

"No," she said quickly. "I can't live here, Pravesh. My life is over there, with you. This is not my life. There will be no plans. Plans will not be necessary."

A while later, she thought about her conversation with Pravesh as she stood under the shower, the jets of hot water massaging the tension from her muscles. She spoke to Pravesh most days, but this was the first time he'd spoken about plans, and raised the possibility of her living here. She didn't realise he'd been thinking that way. She certainly wasn't. It was always her intention to go back to Stenna. Six weeks, though. Had it really been that long? But then, she realised, a lot had happened in those six weeks. Blake had hired a live-in nanny, an older woman with impressive credentials and vast experience with children, a gentle soul with a gentle touch, who absolutely adored the babies. And together, Jade and Blake had brought the twins home from hospital.

Jocelyn was still in a coma, so between them, Maria, the nanny, and Jade were taking care of the babies. Blake still struggled to hold them, but he was making an effort. Jade was quietly determined to make him touch them, one way or another, every day, and, so far, she had succeeded. He had returned to work not long after they brought the babies home, so he wasn't there most days. She tried to work when she could, but working from a distance and with constant interruptions was not easy. She wasn't getting much of her own work done.

Although she and Pravesh spoke almost every day, usually at this time when the babies were asleep and the house was quiet, it wasn't the same as being there, in her office, with Pravesh dropping in throughout the day, sometimes for no reason at all. She missed him, and she missed the work. She missed being in touch with what they were still finding in the desert. Her life at the moment had become pure routine – daily feeds, changing nappies, morning baths – routine dictated by the demands and needs of newborn babies. The routine was rhythmical, a pattern that was all the same. No wonder it didn't feel like six weeks, she thought. The days were all the same. They'd rolled into each other.

She turned off the shower, stepped out and wrapped her towel around her, moving to stand in front of the bathroom mirror, looking at her reflection. Gods, she thought, leaning on the bathroom basin, this wasn't who she was. This wasn't what she'd chosen for herself this time around. And was Pravesh right or was he simply expressing his own fears and doubts? Was she in danger of not going back? She hadn't even thought about when she would return home. Her life in Stenna had been well and truly relegated not just to the back of her mind but to the back burner of her whole life.

She was already looking in the mirror, so when Blake stood in the doorway of the bathroom, she saw him immediately, reflected, as he was, in the mirror. Surprised, she turned quickly, so quickly she couldn't fail to miss the raw, unadulterated desire she saw in his eyes, and nor could she help but respond to it. He didn't say anything, and neither did she, so they looked at each other for a long, long moment. And then he moved, like lightning. He walked towards her, threaded his fingers through her hair and kissed her as if his life depended on it. She tried to resist initially, but her resistance was feeble and futile, easily swept away by the current of the passion that flowed within and between them. So she surrendered. Utterly powerless against the sheer force of the attraction between them, and completely unable to determine whose desire she felt more strongly, his or her own, she kissed him back as passionately as he kissed her. Their movements became urgent, frantic, frenetic, even slightly violent as long-suppressed desire boiled to the surface and erupted. Feverishly, he tugged the towel from her body, and then, with no barrier to stop them, his hands were all over her body. Burning with the need to feel him inside her, she pulled his clothes off him, ripping the buttons off his shirt in her haste to get it off, neither of them hearing the noise the buttons made as they hit and bounced off the walls and floor. When he, too, was naked, they collapsed onto the bathroom floor together, and he kissed her, again, hungrily as he pushed himself into her, not gentle as he moved himself inside her, deeper, ever deeper. She matched him, arching back as her desire peaked and exploded within her, burning through every limb in her body. He cried out as he convulsed, and then she held him tightly against her as he collapsed on top of her, exhausted, both of them breathing heavily.

And then, when his breathing steadied, he simply got up, collected his clothes, and walked out, leaving her still lying on the floor of her bathroom. She lay there stunned, not just because of the suddenness of his departure but also because she had never experienced sexual desire like that. She hadn't even known it was possible to experience sex like that. With Stuart, sex had been a way, for her, of being close to him, but she had liked the aftermath of sex rather than the sex itself. Never, with Stuart, had she experienced anything like what she'd just experienced with Blake. Since Stuart, there had been a few experiences of sex, but the relationships had not lasted, nor had she wanted them to, and the sex had been anything but satisfactory.

She groaned as she moved to sit up. Why now? Why had he touched her now? He hadn't come anywhere near her for the six weeks she'd lived in his house. The last time he'd really touched her, they'd been sitting on the lounge in the nursery and he had touched her cheek with the backs of his fingers. Since then, nothing.

Sitting on the floor of her bathroom, she put her face in her hands. Oh god, she couldn't do this. This was so wrong.

Forcing herself to her feet, she held the basin while she steadied herself. And then she moved. Picking the towel up off the floor, she wrapped it around herself and then walked into her bedroom. Reaching under the bed, she pulled her suitcase out, all but threw it on top of the bed, and started throwing her things into it.

She was fully dressed and calm as she briefly knocked on the door of Blake's study, and then, without awaiting a response, opened the door and walked in. He, too, was fully dressed, and he was standing in front of the window looking out of it, his back to her and to the room.

She took only a couple of steps into the room, making sure she kept a safe distance between them both.

"Am I to be lover to my sister's husband then?"

He didn't respond, nor did he move.

"Am I to be mother to her children?" she asked him.

Still, he neither responded verbally nor moved.

"What becomes of me, then, when my sister wakes up and takes her place again in this family, in her own god-damn life?" His lack of response was arousing her frustration and so the words were coming out more harshly than she intended. "Am I to be swept aside?"

"No," he said without turning to look at her. "It wouldn't be like that."

His words shocked her into temporary silence. So he was expecting her to stay.

"Doesn't the irony of this strike you?" she asked him. "Here I am in my sister's life, fully. I'm living in her house. I'm being a mother to her children, and now I am lover to her husband." She laughed bitterly, close to tears. "The irony ... Who says Fate doesn't have a sense of humour?" She stopped talking to take deep measured breaths, trying to calm herself. "I didn't choose this, Blake," she said, sounding calmer. "This is not the life I chose for myself. This is not the life I planned for myself, nor is it the life I have built for myself." She turned to go, but there was one more very important thing she needed to tell him. "Ruth is very sensitive," she said. "And she's struggling to adjust to being in the world, in her life. Please, Blake, hold her, often. Hold her close, every day ... for me, if not for her. Let her know you're there, and you will protect her. Please give her what my father never gave me."

She closed the door quietly when she walked out of his study. He had not turned towards her. He had not said goodbye. He hadn't even said thank you. And he had not tried to stop her leaving. She left the house straight away without saying goodbye to Maria, and without seeing the twins. She didn't trust herself to see the twins. She knew, if she looked at them, if she touched them, she would stay, and there really would be no going back.

When, finally, she settled herself on the train, she thought she would cry. She thought she might cry all the way home, but she didn't. Instead, she fell asleep. When she awoke, the train was just coming in to Stenna. Standing, she lifted her suitcase down, and then alighted the train. On the platform, she stood for a moment with her suitcase in her hand, breathing deeply of Stenna's fresh, cool air. Relief and heartache mingled within her, vying for precedence. But only one thought played through her mind over and over again.

Here she was, back in her own life.

~

4

Demons in the Future

"Thank you for the honour of being asked to speak here tonight, and for listening so attentively. Enjoy the rest of your evening."

Applause, loud and genuine and appreciative, erupted and filled the room. Jade smiled and took a moment to thank the room for its applause, raising a hand in acknowledgement, and then she collected her notes and walked off the stage.

This was a typical gala event, a charity dinner attended by Maestronne's finest. Tickets for the dinner were ridiculously expensive, ludicrously so, Jade thought. To her, the whole event was not authentic at all. She was perfectly well aware of the fact that the people who filled the room to overflowing, all currently still seated at the many large, round tables, were not at all interested in the particular charity the whole night was arranged for, nor were they interested in raising money. They were far more interested in being seen, in mingling and rubbing shoulders with Maestronne's elite. This was nothing more than a social event. But, for reasons she hadn't quite fathomed, she had been asked to speak ... well, to entertain them all, really, and she had accepted because the tickets to the very lavish dinner for her, Pravesh and Nita were free, and because she and Pravesh had taken advantage of the free trip to Maestronne by organising an impromptu conference – a series of meetings – with their sister department at Maestronne's university. Nita, who was heavily pregnant, had insisted on accompanying Jade and Pravesh, not because she didn't trust them together but because, as she told them bluntly, this was her last foray far from her own little house.

Very soon, once her baby was born, she knew, these trips would, at least temporarily, become a thing of her past.

"Still with us then?" Jade asked Nita as she took her seat at the table again.

"Of course," Nita replied, rolling her eyes. Even though Jade's comment had been facetious, it still held an element of genuine trepidation. For the three days they'd been in Maestronne so far, both Jade and Pravesh had been overly vigilant, constantly watching Nita for any signs the baby might be on her way. Putting her hands over her very extended belly, Nita added, "Stop fussing, the two of you. Really. You need to relax. You're as bad as each other. The baby is not even engaged yet. She will not be coming any time soon, I promise."

Pravesh leaned across his wife. "That really was very good, Jade, my friend. You managed to make a very complicated topic interesting and entertaining."

"Yes," Nita agreed, "you were very good, definitely worth the free trip and the free tickets, I think."

Jade smiled at them. "Why thank you. I even quite enjoyed it myself." Public speaking was not something she feared. She did it so often, giving lectures and tutorials, speaking at meetings, conferences and at events like this dinner, that it had become almost second nature to her. "However," she added, "I still have to go and do a nervous wee. And then I'm going to indulge in a couple of glasses of their very fine champagne." She hadn't been able to drink prior to her presentation. One needed to be completely sober for such things. Now that her talk was over, though, she intended to make up for lost time.

"Shall I order you a glass?" Pravesh offered.

"Yes, thank you, Pravesh. That's a good idea, but you better make it a bottle."

Smiling at him, and focussed on him as she got up from the table, she turned to walk towards the bathroom and nearly walked straight into Blake. Her smile disappeared in an instant. He was standing in front of her with his arm around the waist of an attractive blonde woman.

"Blake."

She said his name completely involuntarily, and she said it flatly, blandly, with no emotion attached to it whatsoever, not even the shock of seeing him so suddenly, with no warning and, therefore, no chance to protect and fortify herself. She had wondered if she would bump into him tonight, but when she'd arrived, she'd scanned the ballroom, surreptitiously but thoroughly, and she hadn't caught sight of him so she'd assumed he wasn't there. It had been five years since she'd walked out of his study, leaving him to take care of his own children alone. And she hadn't seen him since. When she'd returned to Stenna all those years ago, he had finally done what she'd been asking of him – he'd left her alone. He had not pursued her, not contacted her even once, not even when he divorced Jocelyn.

Jade still hated talking about her sister but she had allowed her father to tell her enough so that she knew Jocelyn's doctors were convinced the coma was psychological, not physical, in its cause. After many months in the coma, Jocelyn had finally awoken, but she was, even to this day, in a catatonic state and, as such, had been in a psychiatric institution from the day she awakened. So, she never had taken her place again in the family. James had told Jade that Jocelyn responded to no one, not even the children. She allowed herself to be moved, showered, fed, and dressed, so she was compliant, but the rest of the time, she sat, with a vacant look in her eyes, staring at nothing. When her father had told Jade that Blake had divorced Jocelyn, she thought he might make contact, but he never did. And, unsure as to how he felt about her now, she had never tried to make contact with him. And now, here he was, standing in front of her with his arm around another woman. Obviously, he'd moved on.

"Hello, Jade," he said calmly, obviously not nearly as shocked to see her as she was to see him which made sense given the fact that he'd just seen her talk to the entire room. "May I introduce my partner, Vanessa? Vanessa, this is the children's aunt, Jocelyn's sister, Jade."

The two women shook hands. "Your speech really was very good," the woman said. "You were informative but entertaining at the same time. You had us all riveted, not easily done with this crowd."

"Thank you," Jade replied, smiling at her briefly. "It's very nice of you to say so."

An awkward silence descended on the three of them. Jade felt extremely uncomfortable.

"How are Ruth and Zachary?" she asked unnecessarily, wanting to break the uncomfortable silence. She knew exactly how the children were because she'd followed their progress closely, courtesy of her father, for five years.

"They're doing well," Blake replied. "They're a handful, of course, but they're both very well."

"And Maria?" Jade asked. "Is she still with you?"

"Maria will be with us forever. She's become part of our family. We could not function without her."

Jade nodded. "That's good. I'm very pleased to hear it. She was a real find, a gem."

Another awkward silence descended, and then Jade remembered that Blake had met Pravesh and Nita. She half turned towards them. "You remember Pravesh and Nita?" she asked Blake.

"Of course," he said removing his arm from Vanessa's waist to step forward so he could shake Pravesh's hand. "It's very nice to see you again." And then, noticing Nita's very round belly, he asked them both, "When are you due?"

"Very soon," Nita replied. "Very soon indeed."

"And this is your first?"

"Indeed, yes," Pravesh answered.

"Well, congratulations," Blake said. "I can recommend parenthood. It changes your life, but for the better, I think."

Jade said nothing verbally, but she was unable to stop herself raising her eyebrows in surprise. That was news, good news, definitely, but still news. The last time she'd seen him he was still struggling to touch his own children.

The awkwardness descended once again, and this time Jade felt she'd had enough. She had just entertained the whole room for nearly an hour, so she'd played her part. She damn-well wasn't going to stand around making small talk with a guy she hadn't seen in a very long time.

"Excuse me," she said. "It's nice to see you again, Blake."

She took longer than was necessary to wash her hands, holding them under the warm water, postponing her return to the main ballroom. The bathroom really was very posh with marble basins and linen towels, so it wasn't unpleasant hanging out in it in the hope that Blake and the blonde were gone when she returned to her table.

"Are you in love with him?"

Jade turned off the tap as she straightened and turned to face Vanessa who was standing beside her, facing her, making no pretence to use the bathroom's facilities at all. Jade instantly detected the lack of aggression in the other woman's demeanour and body language. She hadn't followed Jade into the bathroom to pick a fight.

"I don't know what being in love is," she answered honestly. "But I love him, yes."

"Thank you for your honesty," the other woman said. "I've known, all the time I've been with him, that he was in love with someone else." She smiled slightly, but her smile was sad. "A girl knows these things. I didn't know who she was or what happened. I've never asked and he's never told. But I thought it would be okay. It has been okay. But then I saw the two of you together tonight, and I knew. I can't compete with you. Not now that I've met you. I could've competed with anyone else, I think, but not you."

"I'm so sorry," Jade said because she didn't know what else to say.

The other woman put her hand on Jade's arm, gently, as she said, "It's okay." And then she turned and walked out of the bathroom.

"Oh god," Jade breathed as she turned back to the oversized mirror hanging over the basin. For five years, her life had been smooth and tranquil, as it had been before she met Blake. And now he'd been back in her life for all of two minutes and already ripples of disturbance were upsetting the smooth, delicate balance and rhythm of it. She should've known she could not return to Maestronne without upsetting at least one apple cart – hers this time, and Vanessa's.

When she returned to the ballroom, she could see no sign of Blake. And so, determined to make the most of the expensive tickets, she rejoined Pravesh and Nita, and followed up on her earlier promise, partaking of more than a few glasses of champagne. Knowing it to be futile anyway, she didn't try and hide her upset from them. They knew. They understood. They knew she'd never stopped loving him. They'd even talked about it over the years.

When she got home to her father's apartment – Pravesh and Nita were staying in a hotel near the station so they could leave early in the morning – she kicked her shoes off and flopped onto her father's comfortable lounge. As she stared at the ceiling, feeling euphorically light headed, her mind was blessedly empty of thoughts. The silence of the apartment, too high up in the building complex to capture the noises of the city below, was wrapped around her, and it felt good to be solitary and still, in the silence. Her body became nicely heavy and she started to drowse, but a sharp knock on the door brought her awake and shattered the silence.

When she opened the door, Blake was standing on the other side of it.

"Is your father here?"

"No. He spends his weekends at the house … still."

"Good," and then, "My partner of nearly two years just ended our relationship."

"Mmm, I know," she said, and then she opened the door wider and stepped back to allow him in. It was inevitable, she thought silently, surrendering to that very same inevitability.

"You know?" he asked her as she shut the door.

She nodded slowly. "We had a wee chat in the bathroom," she said, holding up her fingers to indicate a small amount.

He frowned. "Are you drunk?"

"Drunk is too strong a word," she said. "No, I'm not drunk … just happy not to be thinking … about you especially. But here you are." She held out her hands, indicating him, and then let them drop to her side. Narrowing her eyes at him suspiciously, she asked, "Was it your idea to have me speak tonight?"

"Of course," he acknowledged easily. "My company's one of the sponsors, and I'm on the committee, so it was easy to convince them you'd be perfect."

"You didn't know that," she said as if she was scolding a child. "You've never seen me speak."

He ran a hand through his hair, a gesture she remembered all-too-well. "By the gods, Jade, I knew you'd be brilliant. You're brilliant at whatever you turn your mind to."

His words shocked her, and silenced her. She didn't know what to say in response, so she didn't say anything, and, as they had done so often in the past, they simply looked at each other. And then he moved. For Jade, it was like déjà vu, almost. He took the steps necessary to close the distance between them, threaded his fingers through her hair and kissed her as if his life depended on it. This time, she offered no resistance at all. She opened herself to him, kissing him back, matching him passion for passion. This time, they made love slowly, lips following fingers as he explored her body, both of them savouring every touch, every caress. Afterwards, they lay in each other's arms.

"Why?" she asked him languorously, knowing there was not the need to elaborate.

"I was thinking of asking Vanessa to move in with us, but before I did, I needed to know."

She lifted her head off his chest and propped it on a hand so she could look down at him. "Needed to know what?"

"How I felt about you now."

"And what did you discover?"

He ran his hand up her arm. "Need you ask. Nothing's changed for me. I still feel exactly the same about you as I did all those years ago."

"Why the silence then? Why haven't you contacted me all these years?"

"Because, you were right. What you said to me before you left was right. None of it was your choice, and I had no right to inflict it on you. I knew I had to let you go. I knew I had to let you live your own life in peace."

She lay against him again. "And so, you did," she said softly.

"And so, I did," he repeated as softly.

"Well," she said against him, feeling his arms around her, "what do you call this, then?"

He laughed softly as he moved, rolling her over onto her back so he could kiss her again. "This," he said, "is an aberration."

She smiled briefly before his kiss stole it away. They made love again, slowly, and, again, afterwards, they lay entwined. They were almost asleep, but she remembered something important, something she thought he should know.

"Jocelyn's doctors want to speak to me. That's why I'm not going home with Pravesh and Nita. They want my perspective on Jocelyn's childhood."

"And you're okay with that?"

"Yes. It's important, I think. I'm meeting with them tomorrow."

He sounded sleepy as he responded. "They should've spoken to you years ago. You're the key. You always have been."

Jade was shown into a large room.

"Can I get you anything while you wait? Tea, coffee?"

Jade smiled at the woman who had escorted her into the room. "No, thank you. I'm fine."

"All right then. The doctors will be here soon. They know you're here. They're on their way."

"Okay, thanks."

Left alone, Jade looked around the room. Large, light and airy, with windows comprising one whole wall, the room was obviously a conference room. A large, polished-wood table surrounded by more than a dozen chairs filled the room, dominating it. A white board dominated one wall, and pictures were hung on the other walls. Jade breathed a silent sigh of relief. She was inordinately glad they hadn't decided to speak to her in one of their cold and clinical therapy rooms.

The words of her escort proved prophetic. Jade waited only a handful of minutes before the door opened and two men walked in, both wearing the white coats of the resident doctors. One was clutching a bulging folder under his arm. Jade stood and walked around the table to greet them.

The one with the folder spoke first. "Doctor Howlett, thank you so much for coming in."

Jade took his hand. "Please call me Jade," she said as she shook his hand.

He smiled at her. "Jade it is, then. I'm Doctor Michael Cavendish, but you can call me Michael, and this is Doctor Brad Murphy ..."

"But you can call me Brad," the other said, extending his hand, smiling at Jade.

Jade visibly relaxed. They weren't like doctors at all. They were both personable, and it was obviously their intention to put her at ease.

"Please," Michael said, indicating the chair she had vacated. "Have you been offered coffee?"

"I have," Jade replied, holding up her hands. "I'm fine."

"I understand you're back here on business," Michael said as both he and the other doctor sat. Jade had chosen a chair at the end of the table on one side, avoiding the table's head. They both sat in chairs opposite her, and Michael opened the very large, bulging folder, and took a pen out of the pocket of his shirt, obviously prepared to take notes. It was, she thought, like being interviewed for a new job, without the pressure, and without the nerves.

"Yes," she said, responding to Michael's comment about being in Maestronne on business.

"And you don't come back often?" he asked when it became obvious Jade wasn't going to volunteer any more information.

"That's right," she said. "I don't like coming back. This city is full of bad memories for me."

She had chosen those words deliberately, and they both understood. The small talk was over.

"Your father has been very helpful," Michael said. "But there are gaps in our knowledge of Jocelyn's past – gaps we suspect you might be able to fill."

Jade nodded. "I think you might be right. Actually, to tell you the truth, it's good to finally be able to talk about my ... our past with people who, I hope, will understand. I've never had that luxury before."

For the next two hours, Jade told them of her past – Jocelyn's past. She went back to the very beginning, their early childhood, and she left nothing out, even telling them the whole truth about her relationship with Blake. Quite often, one or the other of them asked questions or sought clarification, which Jade readily provided, but other than these brief interruptions, Jade talked. She was honest about how she felt about both her parents, and she was honest about how she felt about their culpability in Jocelyn's whole situation. In her view, her mother had made the illness worse, not just because she had refused to acknowledge it, but because she had then latched on to Jocelyn in a way Jocelyn simply could not handle. Jade was honest about everything, all of it. The two doctors, sitting opposite her, listened attentively. Not once did their attention waver, and Michael, the doctor with the folder, took copious notes.

"Are you still in a relationship with the ex-husband?" Brad asked her at one stage.

She grimaced slightly. "Well, I wasn't," she said. "I haven't seen him for five years." She smiled at them both, slightly embarrassed. "I saw him again last night, though, and ... well, I'd say, yes, we are in a relationship."

They both nodded in response. They were not there to judge, they were there to gather information about Jocelyn's past.

"We think he was the key," Brad told her, "to bringing the illness out of the shadows, so to speak. Once he met you, he mirrored the truth back to her, and she knew it."

"That makes perfect sense," Jade replied. "Jocelyn became very unstable after the wedding, so much so, she no longer tried to be me."

"That's right," Michael said, "because she knew that he knew the truth ... all of it, and she could no longer pretend. But if it was no longer possible for her to be you, what does she replace the 'you' inside her with, especially when she's you in the first place because she has no sense of her own identity? So," he asked her after a small pause during which he watched the realisation crystallise within her, "when was the last time you actually saw your sister?"

Jade thought back. "At the wedding, I think. I don't think I've seen her since then. That was more than six years ago."

The two doctors exchanged looks, obviously, given the fact that they were sitting next to each other and had to turn their heads towards each other. "We know it's a lot to ask," Michael said. "And it's not something we ask of you lightly. But could we ask you to come and see her now?"

Jade hesitated, suddenly, inexplicably nervous. She hadn't expected to see Jocelyn so she hadn't prepared herself to do so.

"You understand, don't you," Michael continued when she didn't answer immediately, "that Jocelyn did not develop a personality of her own, or not properly anyway? She grew up with no sense of her own identity, so, in a sense, it was natural for her to focus on you, hence the cloning, as you call it. That's a good word for it. We believe your father had a lot to do with you as her choice, too. He favoured you, so in her mind, to get some sort of attention from him, she had to become you. Of course, as we all know, the opposite occurred as a result. It pushed him away. He couldn't handle it so he washed his hands of the whole situation."

"He said that?" Jade asked, surprised.

"Actually," Brad qualified, "those are his own exact words."

"Well," she said, "he's right. That's exactly what he did."

"Our reason for asking you to see your sister," Michael said, "is really quite simple. She responds to no one. She acknowledges no one at all, not even her own children. We'd like to see if she responds to you."

She frowned. "You think I can bring her out of the catatonic state?"

"Truthfully? No. But it's worth a try, don't you think?"

"Yes," she said, "it is. If it will help you, then, yes, I'll do it."

Michael immediately drew his phone out of the pocket of his coat, and used it to ask someone to move Jocelyn into one of the therapy rooms.

"So," Jade asked as the three of them stood, "she doesn't speak at all?"

"Not at all," Michael confirmed as he held the door open for her. "Not a single word, even in her sleep."

Jade walked with them through the corridors of the hospital, feeling as nervous as ever she'd felt, but unsure as to why. When they stopped outside one particular room, obviously the therapy room Jocelyn had been moved to, Michael asked her if she would like to see her sister through the room's glass window before going inside. Jade nodded, and when she saw Jocelyn through the glass, she at last understood why she was nervous. Never, never had she seen Jocelyn look the way she looked, and it shocked her. Jocelyn had always been pretty. And she'd always known how to use and apply make-up to enhance her prettiness. Now, Jade saw a woman sitting at a table, staring at it – a woman with no animation at all – a woman with no interest in her own physical appearance. Her face was devoid of make-up, and she wore an unattractive hospital gown, an oversized smock. Her blonde hair was obviously clean, but limp, almost straggly, cut short but not styled at all. Although she sat in the chair, she was slumped in it, and she held her hands loosely in her lap.

Unconsciously, Jade brought a hand to her mouth as she watched her sister through the glass.

"Are you all right?" Michael asked her.

She nodded mutely.

"Are you ready to do this? We can do it some other time if you prefer."

"No," Jade said. "Now is as good a time as any."

Michael preceded her into the room, and the other doctor, Brad, waited outside, watching through the glass.

"Hello, Jocelyn," Michael said. "You have a visitor today. Your sister's come to see you."

Silently, using his hands to communicate, he indicated to Jade she should sit at the table opposite Jocelyn. At first, she just sat, looking at Jocelyn, recognising the fact that Jocelyn's eyes were not focussed on anything. And then, she spoke. "Hello, Jocelyn."

She suspected she wasn't the only one who expected no response, so when Jocelyn did respond, she also suspected she wasn't the only one surprised.

Slowly, ever so slowly, Jocelyn's eyes first became focussed. Then, slowly, she raised her eyes to look at Jade, and she was focussed on Jade. She recognised Jade. And then, she moved, so quickly, the doctor and the other medical attendant in the room, a male nurse, had no time to stop her. She flew at Jade across the table, snarling, using her nails to scratch and her fists to punch. And she screamed, over and over again, "I hate you. I hate you. I hate you."

Jade had no time to defend herself. In pure reflex, she raised her arms against the onslaught in a futile attempt to protect herself. Michael and the male nurse pulled Jocelyn away from Jade, and forced her back into the chair. The door opened and Brad, the other doctor, came in with a needle, plunging it into Jocelyn's arm while the other two held her down. Jade was breathing heavily as she watched them subdue her sister. Even as the sedative took effect, Jocelyn was still saying over and over, "I hate you. I hate you. I hate you."

Michael let go of Jocelyn as she sagged in the chair, losing consciousness, knowing the nurse would hold her. He came and squatted beside Jade. "I am so sorry, Jade. I never would've asked you to do this if I'd had even an inkling she would respond to you like that. I'm so sorry."

"It's okay," Jade said to reassure him. But she didn't feel okay. Her neck and cheek were stinging where Jocelyn's nails had scoured her, and her left eye was aching.

"Come," he said gently, helping her stand. She was so shaken, she couldn't walk properly. He held her, guiding her out of the room. "I'll take care of those myself," he said, referring to her scratches.

He guided her to a treatment room and helped her sit on the table.

"It's incredible," he said as he put on latex gloves and removed bottles and cotton swabs from a cupboard. "This is going to sting," he warned her. "She's responded to no one for over four years, not your mother or your father, not to her own children or to her ex-husband." As he talked, he dabbed antiseptic onto the scratches on Jade's neck and cheek, and onto the small cut on her lip. She tensed and held her breath as he worked, her way of dealing with the pain, both inner and outer. "But you," he said, ignoring her hissing intake of breath, "incredible." He didn't elaborate as he gently scrutinised and checked her left cheek and eye, touching her gently with his gloved fingertips. "I don't think there's anything broken," he said. "But you'll have one heck of a black eye I suspect. I'm so sorry, Jade," he said again as he took his hands from her and stepped back. "Had I known ..."

"It's okay, really. How could you know? How could any of us know?"

"We couldn't know. We've had no communication from her at all. But she spoke today, clearly ..."

"Yeah, three words. I hate you."

"She doesn't hate you. You know that, don't you? She's not capable of normal human emotions. You are everything she thinks she should be. And your presence is a reminder of her own emptiness. Without you, she could pretend. But with you there, she was forced to face the truth. You were like a giant mirror held up to her, and that's what she associates you with now. You know she was always going to crack one way or another, don't you? It was inevitable, but the husband brought it all to the surface sooner rather than later. Maybe with help years ago, we could've avoided that. But she never got the help she needed, did she?"

Jade couldn't speak for the tears clogging her throat. Silently, she shook her head.

"And that's not your fault," he added, correctly guessing her thoughts. "You must know that. None of this is or was your fault. If anything, you were as much a victim of her illness as she was."

She nodded, mutely. And then she asked him, "Did it help ... ?"

"Very much so. She showed us she's still there. She hasn't disappeared into the void within her. That's very positive. We can work with that."

"Can you help her?"

"We'll certainly try, but I think she will spend the rest of her life in here. She can't function out there, and nor will she, ever. Hopefully, we can give her some sort of life here, though. At the moment, she has no life, does she? She sits. She's been vacant. Now we know she's capable of a little bit more than that."

When she left the hospital, she knew she couldn't go back to her father's apartment, so she walked until she found a park with a bench, and then she sat. She just sat. She didn't cry. She didn't move. She didn't look at anything. She had no idea of the passing of time, and it was only when her phone beeped at her that she roused herself.

Opening her bag, she reached in and took out her phone. There was a text from Blake.

"Are you still at the hospital?"

She texted back, "No."

He phoned her. "Where are you?"

"Um, not sure. In a park."

He didn't need to ask her if she was okay. He could hear in her voice that she was anything but okay. She sounded dead, barely responsive. He made her tell him where she was.

"I'm coming to get you," he said and rang off.

"Oh god," he said much later when he found her and saw her face. "What happened?"

"She attacked me. They took me to see her, and she attacked me. She just kept screaming, 'I hate you' over and over, even when they'd sedated her."

"Oh god, Jade, I'm sorry. I'm so, so sorry." He pulled her against him and, at last, she released her shock and upset. She sobbed against him, but she sobbed for far more than the horror of what she'd just experienced. She sobbed for the past, for everything that had gone wrong between her and her sister, and for everything that had gone wrong between her and him.

That night, they both stayed in her father's apartment, and they made love again, carefully given her injuries, and then they lay together, holding each other.

"Do you think it's ironic that we would never have met if it wasn't for Jocelyn," she asked him. "Seriously, Blake. We live in different worlds, not just different cities. We would never have crossed paths if not for her."

"Ironic? I guess that's one word for it. I've actually thought of little else since I met you, believe it or not, as much as I've tried not to."

"Well," she half sighed, half said, "I'm so sick of fighting this. I can't fight it anymore. I made a decision today when I was sitting in the park. I want this to work. Whatever I have to do to make it work, I will do."

He tensed, and she felt it. "What? I don't think I heard you correctly. You'll have to repeat what you just said."

She raised her head to look at him, smiling even though it tweaked the wound on her lip and hurt. "We both have to make compromises, not just me. Right?"

"Right. Fuck it," he said vehemently, "I'll sell the business and move to Stenna if I have to."

She leaned up and kissed him. "Let's not rush into anything. First things first. I want to see the children. Okay?"

"Let's not rush in, you say. It's only taken us nearly seven years to get here. Who's rushing?"

She laughed as she kissed him again.

~

There was an artificial lake in front of the beautiful, old building where Pravesh and Jade worked. And, surrounding the lake completely was parkland interspersed with bar-b-que areas, seats, and picnic tables. The lake was home to a whole colony of different species of birds – ducks, geese, swans, ibises, herons. Jade had spent the last handful of weekends in Maestronne with Blake and the twins, coming back to Stenna during the week to work. So Blake thought it only fair that he bring the children to Stenna for this current weekend.

It was a beautiful day. The sky was all but cloudless, and the sun sparkled on the water of the lake. They spent the day picnicking, walking around the lake, feeding the birds, laughing as they tried to give the birds individual names. It really was a perfect day – one to live on in memory.

At the station the next morning, Jade said goodbye to Zach and Ruth, and then to Blake. He slid his hands around her neck and leaned down to kiss her, lingeringly. When he raised his head again, he looked into her eyes and said, "I love you."

"And I love you," she said.

She didn't stay to see the train leave. Smiling, her mind full of thoughts of him, she walked back up the platform, and out through the station concourse. She stepped off the concourse, onto the road outside the station, but with her mind full, she wasn't concentrating on anything else, so she didn't see the truck until it was upon her, nor did she register the screeching of breaks and tires as the driver desperately tried to avoid hitting her. In the end, he hit her on an angle so that her neck snapped on impact. She was dead before she hit the ground.

In the train, Blake was settling the twins for the long train ride ahead when he felt a tremendously potent and powerful sense of loss. It rolled through him. Sitting heavily in his own seat, he breathed deeply, rapidly, holding a hand to his chest in an absolutely futile attempt to ease the pain there.

Ruth, ever the sensitive one, said, "Daddy?"

He smiled to reassure her and said, "Daddy's okay, sweetheart. Daddy's okay."

But daddy was not okay.

~

They wanted to bring her back to Maestronne, to bury her there, but he fought them. He fought so hard and with such determination that, eventually, they listened to him and knew he was right. She hadn't liked Maestronne when she was alive, so why lay her to rest there, forever. Instead, they scattered her ashes on the lake outside the building where she had worked to achieve so much. Blake didn't bring the children. He didn't want to mar their memory of that last perfect day with her. He didn't want them to picture the lake with people, dressed in black, standing around it in sombre silence. She had brought sparkle into their lives in the brief time she'd come back, and the children were having trouble understanding why they would not see her again. Blake, himself, was having trouble with that very same thing.

After the small, private ceremony beside the lake, the people moved away, slowly, talking in hushed tones. Some funerals were a celebration. This one was not. Hers was a life cut short before its time. She was cut down in her prime.

Pravesh put his hand on Blake's arm. "Will you come back to the house?"

"Yes, Pravesh, of course. I just need to say goodbye."

Pravesh nodded. "I know."

Left alone, Blake found a bench and, for a long, long time, he looked out over the lake. Then, he leaned forward, put his face in his hands, and sobbed and sobbed and sobbed ...

5

Many Aeons Afterwards

Are you all right, dear one?

No. Of course I'm not all right. I had to write the end of the story quickly and with distance – a fact I'm newly grateful for every time I re-read the story. It's the only way I can be with the memory – briefly and with some sort of psychological distance. Although, distance is difficult whenever I re-read it. It breaks my heart, every time.

Yes, we know. We understand, of course. Some memories are best left undisturbed, but this one, unfortunately, is not one of those. Why else do you think you see this memory so powerfully, so clearly? And why else were you not to tamper with it in any way? The memory had to be processed exactly as it occurred. And why else do you think this memory has stayed with you so powerfully even after writing it into a story? Normally, memories you've written up move into the background of your awareness, do they not, dear one. Not so this one. This one has stayed in the foreground of your awareness. Is this not <u>the</u> most powerful of your memories?

Yes, it is. And, yes, you are right. This memory keeps coming back, despite the fact of it being written into a story. There are certain scenes I see so incredibly clearly, some of which I didn't write into the story.

For years, this memory played in my conscious awareness, but for years, I couldn't see how it ended. I tried to end it on numerous occasions in my visions, tried to make it work out happily, but

always I was blocked. Nothing felt right, and always, I couldn't go any further, or I couldn't take the story any further. And, then, when I started writing the story, thereby processing the memory in entirety, and I finally knew how the story ended, I wanted to scream at the universe in rage and grief and frustration. Why? Why? Why live a life like that? Why meet and cross paths and love, only to have that love snuffed out, taken away, so suddenly and implacably? Why? It seems so futile. It seems so cruel. And I don't know what's worse – his pain or my own.

We know, dear one. We know. All right, then, so now it is time to go a little further with the memory. Your sight is changing, is it not, so now is definitely the right time. You need to see deeper, and you need to understand the dynamics operating in Jade's life, not just within her, or you, of course, but in the others as well. This is why the memory is so powerful for you, because it is vital for you in <u>this</u> life you live now. Actually, it is pivotal, crucial.

Okay, I'm ready. I understand what you mean about the memory being powerful. I mean, I know from the power of it that it is important for me in this life. I just don't understand the whys and wherefores. I need your help with that.

We know, dearest one. We know. And you've needed time to absorb the memory in entirety, and to come to terms with how Jade's story ended in that life, have you not? And not just because you were severed so abruptly from your lover but because you liked Jade. You liked being Jade. And you certainly loved what she did with and in her life. Is that not so?

Yes, I have needed time, and, yes, I did love that life. I really did. So knowing it was cut short was hard to Process and hard to write, especially since I haven't loved this life I'm living now. It shocked me, the abrupt end of Jade's life, and it doesn't get any easier with time. It still cuts me deep, even now, many years since I first wrote the story in entirety. I should have suspected she died when I could never see to the end of the story, or when the visions always stopped and were blocked. I should've known, but I didn't.

We know, dearest one. We know. But the visions were blocked because you were not ready to know the truth, the whole truth, and nothing but the truth. Because, of course, the truth is much larger than just Jade's story and yours. And is it not a further measure of how important the memory is to you that it can still cut you deeply, even now?

Yes, it is.

All right. Let's begin with the easier aspects. First, of course, as you have already identified, you need to see that life you lived there precisely because it was not lived on Gaia, or earth as humans call it now. You see the cities on Mallona very clearly, do you not, dear one?

Yes, not just the two in the story – Stenna and Maestronne – nor the one in the story following this one – Carcisse – but another one, too, that very much reminds me of Chicago. I'm very attracted to Chicago for that reason. I guess that story, and that life I lived in that city, I'll end up telling at some stage.

We certainly hope so. Something very important was begun in that life, and we think humans need to know about it. Remembering your lives on Mallona is very important, for very obvious reasons, is it not, dear one?

Yes. Scientists can search for the evidence of orthodox theories of human beginnings all they like, but they will never disprove or contradict cellular memory. Earth is not our original planet, or not entirely anyway, for some of us, and humans need to know the truth of that.

Indeed. Right, then, to the second aspect of the story, another of the easier ones to process. Your sister. Even though you intended to keep her identity in this life secret to protect her privacy, we have deemed it not to be so. Humans are moving into the age of honesty and transparency, nothing hidden – something they will have to come to terms with because they have no choice but to move into it. The natural state of existence for humanity does involve telepathy or telepathic connection. Transparency is a natural and normal by-product and aspect of such connection, so humans will have to make the adjustment accordingly. She is your sister again this time around, is she not?

Yes, she is.

And Jade's mother is your mother this time around. And the dynamics between the three of you are very similar, are they not?

Some are, yes. Or they have been. She, my sister, still steals my memories from our childhood, believe it or not, and places herself in them. And she and my mother have been addicted to each other in a very toxic way, although my mum is beginning to change that hopefully. My father favoured me. My mum favours her. But in this life, far from cloning me, my sister became my absolute opposite in almost every way, and she did so to try and get attention, especially from dad.

The same dynamic, just expressed differently. You are, therefore, still very much informing the person she is in this lifetime. Are you not one of the most significant people in the landscape of her life, at least in terms of her shadows?

Yes, I am. I have withdrawn from her now. I have had enough of all the shadowed dynamics between us, particularly as they are beginning to affect her son. Her energy is horrible when the dynamics are operating within and through her, not to mention her treatment of me. As I said, I'm over it.

Something she will very much come to regret in the later stages of her life. And what other powerful dynamic is still intact within her in relation to you?

The jealousy.

Jealousy of what?

Of who I am. Of how I am. She believes she is not seen when I am around. She believes she is overshadowed when I am near, and she punishes me, lashes out at me, especially when men are involved.

Yes, indeed. We will deal further with this jealousy, but for now, tell us why you two are incarnate as sisters again this time around?

We are bound by karmic debt and obligation, very powerful karmic debt, actually. We are very bonded by karma. So bonded are we that it's like a thick, unbreakable chain linking us both.

Just so. As you were in Jade's life, too. Do you understand those karmic bonds, dearest one? Do you know what she did to bind herself to you so powerfully, so implacably, and so personally?

Yes, I think so. In an entirely different life we both lived, she was an acolyte, like a priestess in training, at the temple I've written about subsequently*. I was a High Priestess in the temple, and she betrayed me, turned others against me, including my mother in Jade's life and my own – something she still easily does when she sets her mind to it – and she was instrumental in bringing about my death at the hands of those who wanted to cut me down for being what I am. She went to my enemies, I think. What she did, exactly, I cannot see, and she asked the shaman healer I saw many years ago not to tell me.

Just so, dear one. So she is aware that she did something terrible. That is why she does not want to know what the shaman healer actually said to you about what happened. And why did she do this terrible thing? Why did she betray you to your enemies?

The jealousy. She was jealous of me and of my relationship with my lover in that life. Jealousy always fears that which it believes it can never have, and so it was with her. And when jealousy fears, it destroys, utterly. It tears down or removes that which it fears it can never have. As such, jealousy is actually one of the most dangerous

emotions. And so she has carried that jealousy within her, down through the aeons of human time, through many lives to this one we are both living now.

Just so, and she has carried it because she has never resolved it, never faced it, never confronted it, despite being given numerous opportunities to do so. She continues to allow it free reign in her psyche, and, as such, she continues to allow it to control her and, thus, to create her realities. Because, you are aware, are you not, dearest one, of other lives where her jealously destroyed you … a certain nobleman, for example … ?

Yes. A story for another time. But the grief I felt in that life passed through me in this life, and I've never felt anything like it. If that's what Blake felt … Anyway, yes, you are right.

In fact, when anyone so much as touches the jealousy within her, or alludes to it, she implacably turns away or shuts those people down, as you've experienced for yourself this time around. Whilst ever any soul turns away from the truth of his or her wounded reflection, he or she will not and cannot heal. And so it is with your sister. So it has remained a part of her very soul – a very great wound carried across many lifetimes, along with the wound of what she did to herself when her betrayal led to your death – the laceration of her own soul. How does a soul live with the knowledge that one's own choices and actions led to someone else's horrible, violent death? He or she must live in denial, and, again, so it is with your sister. And so her wounds shape each life she has lived since that fateful one, including that of Jocelyn, Jade's sister. Is this not how the wounds of the soul affect and influence the events of each life?

Yes, indeed, 'tis so.

She tore you apart, you and your lover, violently, tragically, in one life, so she was always destined to bring you together in another life, and so she did, so she did.

But you came together in Jade's life, not for her, but for you.
You do know that, do you not, dear one? You and he came together
in Jade's life for you in this one.

Why create my own death, then, and tear us apart again, suddenly
and tragically – the same way it happened in that original life˙?

Right, to the difficult, painful dynamics of that life, then. First, before we
deal with that question, we've a need to know. What was the true Purpose
of Jade's life, dearest one?

To bring the ancient Wisdom back from oblivion. To properly
and correctly translate the texts and scrolls and parchments of
a beautiful, ancient culture, the beating heart of which was a
beautiful, powerful, ancient priesthood.

Does that not sound familiar?

Yes. So you're saying the Purpose of Jade's life was the same as mine
now? To bring the ancient Wisdom back from oblivion ... as a
Scribe. Even though the ancient Wisdom was unable to prevent the
events in '*Altira*', the story that follows this one? The Wisdom could
not prevent the disaster that very nearly destroyed humanity.

Do not make the mistake of thinking Jade's life was for nothing in relation
to the Wisdom. Do not. You must not think of the effect of the Wisdom on
the collective, as you must not now. 'Tis each individual soul that matters,
dear one. And in that life, as in this, the effect of the Wisdom was and will
be vastly different for each and every soul in the human reality. For some,
the Wisdom had and will have no effect at all, as you've seen for yourself
in this lifetime. Yes, 'tis sad, but 'tis so. But for others, the Wisdom had
and will have a profound *effect, a truly profound effect. It will change,*
it will heal, it will influence, it will transform. And so it was with the
translations Jade worked so hard on, and loved so much, for that matter.
Those translations had a profound effect on many of the souls in the human
reality at that time. Including him.

Now, we would have you answer this question, dear one. How was it, do you think, that she so easily and effortlessly knew how to work with the ancient language of the scrolls and parchments pulled out of the red sands of that ancient desert?

She knew the language because she had worked with it before. Indeed, she wrote many of the scrolls in other lives, particularly the life of the High Priestess* . . .

The very same High Priestess your sister was so jealous of, and sought, successfully, to destroy. Yes, 'tis so. And there we have two vital links in Jade's life to that <u>original</u> life – your sister and the ancient Wisdom as written on those scrolls and parchments.
Now, what of the third?

The third? Oh god. Him. Blake. He was the third link.

Yes, dear one, he was, and the most vital one as it happens. There is something that doesn't come through in the story, primarily because when you first wrote it, you failed to see it in your visions. But you see it now, do you not?

Yes. I see it clearly now. And the fact that I didn't see it when I originally wrote the story is the reason those scenes are not in the story. He recognised her twice over. First, he recognised her in Jocelyn – her words, her Wisdom, her essence, her Voice. And, second, he recognised her when he first laid eyes on her. When she, Anne and Amy stood on the terrace looking at all the guests at the party the week before the wedding, he saw her, and he experienced a powerful shock of recognition. And then he couldn't take his eyes off her. Whenever he was with her he couldn't take his eyes off her. That is exactly why he followed her out onto the terrace the night of the wedding. He was watching her.

Just so, dear one. Just so.

**Oh god. He <u>was</u> with me in that life I lived as the doomed
High Priestess˙. That really was him. But I thought he was a warrior
in that life.**

*He was both Warrior and Priest. Do humans not hold more than one
archetypal energy within them in each life they live?*

Yes, they do.

*Is that not why and how he was so easily a part of the temple whenever
he came home? He was a part of the temple because he was a part
of the temple. He belonged there every bit as much as did you.
He was a Ranger – a concept you will deal with in another story,
and the reason why you feel so connected to the city on Mallona that
reminds you of Chicago – and he was fully initiated. As to his first
loyalty, he was equally loyal to both king and temple, and because the king
himself was loyal to the temple, also an initiate, there was no conflict of
interest, or investment, for that matter. He could be loyal to both, and so
he was. And so, too, did his heart lie with both because he loved you and he
loved the king … in different ways, of course.*

**Of course. All right, that makes sense. I did wonder how
he was so at home in the temple. So, we crossed paths in Jade's life,
and he recognised me, and I recognised him. Or I certainly
recognised the way I felt about him. So that brings us back to
my original question. Why love so deeply and be torn apart so
tragically in Jade's life?**

*You know why you loved so deeply, dear one. You know why. You are perfect
reflections, each of the other, like looking into a full-length mirror. And you
know what, exactly, you are perfect reflections of. Humans are obsessed with
the idea and concept of the 'soul mate', are they not?*

Yes, they are.

Why?

Because they are obsessed with the idea of the perfect mate, even though most of them settle for far less than perfect _in_ a mate, a lover. And they are obsessed because there is a hole, a void, at the very centre of them, the heart of them, and they mistakenly believe their 'soul mate' will fill that hole.

Ironically, a lover can only ever be a reflection of the way you feel about yourself. Or, put another way, a lover can only ever reflect back to you the extent, or lack thereof, of your own love for yourself. Since most humans struggle with self love, their physical lovers reflect that struggle.

Just so. The concept of the 'soul mate' is much over used in that dimension and wholly and soully misunderstood. In fact, a soul mate, in truth, is any soul that helps another heal or experience or evolve. More often than not, soul mates help each other. Or, put another way, the help is mutual, in both directions. And, of course, there are always many different soul mates humans encounter across their lifetimes.

Humans confuse this concept with that of the twin flame. Twin flames, as the term suggests (although the 'twin' aspect of the term is not entirely accurate because twin flames are not necessarily limited to two) are souls who vibrate at identical frequencies, like the same note played on different instruments, as we've said many times before.

Jade and Blake loved deeply for two reasons. First, they were twin flames, and, second, they had crossed paths many times before, in many guises, in many contexts, and in many incarnations. They had, in fact, been lovers many times before. They knew, and know, for that matter, each other very well. It is all but impossible for the two of you to cross paths and not become lovers, dearest one. This you know. Being lovers is the natural state for the two of you to exist in and as when you are incarnate together because this most closely reflects in the physical what you are in the metaphysical.

As to the whys and wherefores of you being torn apart so suddenly and so cruelly, you know the answer to this, too. The patterns of fear buried deeply in your psyche, and in his, were played out yet again in this life you both lived – patterns embedded in your psyches courtesy of those events we have mentioned, the life of the High Priestess, and in other lives you both lived and have written about, dear one.

Describe for us, and for those who may listen in to this, our dialogue, the patterns of fear that exist within you both – patterns of fear and shadow that have never been resolved.

Okay. Umm, for him, it's simple. He fears loss – an implacable, irretrievable, deep sense of loss and its accompanying grief. He created, in Blake's life, through and out of his fear of loss. For me, it's far more complex.

In Jade's life, we were kept apart courtesy of the circumstances we found ourselves in, and, ironically, whilst apart, Jade was able to live, quite literally. So much so that if they hadn't come together again, she would have lived a long life.

Just so, although that was not her destiny. So why did she create her own death when they came together at last? What is the fear dynamic that existed so deeply within her she was completely unaware of it?

He holds within him, inherently, in the very essence, the fabric, of who he is, an ability to bring out of me my Light, my metaphysical Self, my Truth, which is exactly what he would have done had we stayed together. We are like magnets in that sense.

Yes, dear one, 'tis so. He is your most powerful, most potent, purest reflection – the very thing you were severed from courtesy of those same events that befell the High Priestess of that original life'. You were severed from your own reflection to facilitate identification with humans in the abyss, and it was, quite simply, not time for you to be healed – for your reflection to be restored – for <u>you</u> to be restored. It was necessary for you to remain identified with humans in the abyss. Had you continued to be together, you and he, you would have shifted and altered each other's consciousness. Why else do you think he recognised you so powerfully in that *life, even when your essence was merely being 'channelled' by your sister? He recognised you in Jocelyn, and he was powerfully attracted to and by what he saw in her precisely because you are each other's perfect and pure reflection. He knew you – the <u>essence</u> of you – and the very reason he was with Jocelyn was to bring forth more of what he saw. So would it have been with Jade. The more he saw, the more he wanted to see, putting undue pressure, albeit unwittingly and unbeknownst to Jade, on her psyche. It was not time for her to come forth in her life. That was always marked only for <u>your</u> life, dearest one.*

Now, there is also another very important reason why Jade created her own death in that life, and so, to that end, we've a question to ask you. Why have you not encountered him in this life you live now ... or not properly, anyway? This life is the culmination of all of your lives in this incarnation stream ... well, actually, this life is the culmination of <u>all</u> of your human incarnations, so the patterns of fear in your psyche must be resolved. This you know. So why have you not encountered him in this life?

Christ. Because in this life I've had to do the Work to Ascend ... I mean, I've had to do the Work of Ascendance . . .

Which he naturally helps you with. So, again, why have you not encountered him?

Because it's been vital that I walk it, the Way of Ascension, step by step, putting in the hard, arduous Work necessary, and focussing on it as I do so.

Why?

So I can experience it, identify its steps, write about it, articulate it, document it.

Yes, dearest one, 'tis so.

And so I can cast the most pure reflection . . .

Ah, yes. Yes, indeed. And is this not a most vital truth? Ironically,
courtesy of their ignorance, Jade and Blake would have pulled their
relationship down into the abyss of physicality. That is, they would have
physicalised something that was always meant to be purely metaphysical.
Their relationship was <u>never</u> going to be allowed to be physicalised,
made heavy and dense courtesy of lower-dimensional perspectives and
mindsets and behaviours and focusses. And so, too, has it been for you
in this life. You are both, in short, metaphysical reflections, or reflections
of metaphysicality, and that will never be allowed to be sullied with
physical non-reflection.

Dear me. All right. Told you it was complex. So Jade died to
protect the wound in my soul – being severed from my own
reflection and fearing it – because it was not time in her life to
be healed of it? She died to protect the very thing that facilitates
identification with humans as they are in the abyss of darkness
and Separation?

Just so, dearest one. Just so. How many times have we said it?
How does a being of pure Light exist in darkness? Taking on the very
great wound of fear is the only way. And following Jade's life, there
has been much Work still to be done under the influence of that very
great wound. Much Work. Indeed, your Work had barely begun in
her life, and, as you've experienced for yourself now, that Work has its
culmination in your writing in this life. Had Jade not died when she
did, the five books you wrote and published during the early years of
your Processes of Transformation and Transcendence in this life would
not have been written.

Yes, okay, I see that, and I understand it. So why cross paths at all,
then, if we were fated, or destined not to be together?

Ah, yes, why indeed? For a very, very important reason. But, to begin with,
partly because of your sister's karmic obligation to you and to herself. She
discharged some of the karmic debt in that life, and in so doing she released
some of the heavy burden she carried, although, of course, not all of it. But
that is not the primary reason you crossed paths with him in that life. As to

*the very important reason, you were together in that life not <u>for</u> that life,
but <u>for</u> this one you are living now.*

**Oh god. You said that before. Really? We put him through that
intense pain for me in this life?**

Yes. And what of your pain, Jade's pain?

She died. She didn't feel the pain.

*No, she did not. But you feel it. You feel it very powerfully … in more ways
than the very obvious one.*

**Yes, I do. You're right. Then this dialogue, and the others we
have had in the writing of those other stories, is, in fact, the very
outworking of that important reason.**

*Yes, indeed, dearest one, 'tis so. You are not just seeing the dynamics
involved in Jade's life by Processing the memory, you are also sharing the
experience. For you are the living example, are you not?*

*Humans have lost the knowledge of how their shadow dynamics are
formed in their incarnations and then taken through subsequent lives.
They have lost the knowledge of how those shadow dynamics form the
terrain of their lives by underpinning the circumstances, events and
incidents in their lives, and by informing the relationships of their lives.
Is this not so?*

Yes, this is very much so.

How much does the entire story of a book impact any of its single pages?

**Completely. Any one single page would not be as it is without
the entire story. The story underpins and informs every
word on any one single page. So much is this so that any one single
page does not and cannot make sense without knowledge
of the entire story.**

Yes, 'tis so. In fact, when you began to Process the memories of your other lives and the shadow dynamics underpinning them, you were surprised by the strength, depth, potency and power, and the extent to which, those shadow dynamics shaped those lives as well as your current life, were you not, dear one?

Yes, I was. But it makes so much sense now because these shape Thought, and what is our reality if not Thought made manifest?

Just so. Just so, indeed. Perfectly stated, as usual.

'Tis exactly why we take these patterns of fear through the many incarnations we live, or through the many lives we live, because these shape and inform our deepest thoughts and beliefs until we resolve them thereby clearing them out of our consciousness. But what is there in current human reality to help with this clearing out Process, apart from a small number of precious souls who know about this and come here as true Healers? 'Tis also why the tricks, traps and lures of entrapment – the mechanisms of manipulation – set up here now by the priests of darkness, are so successful. Because humans are so distracted by these, they care not about the patterns of fear that are shaping their realities, and so they do not resolve them.

Just so.

So these very same fear dynamics continue to shape human reality at individual and collective levels, which is exactly why we see these dynamics played out again and again in human reality, like a needle stuck on a scratched and damaged record.

Just so. Eternal and infernal cycles of death and destruction, as you say so eloquently in the next story of this collection.

Now, you wish to ask us two other questions about Blake and Jade, do you not, dearest one? So go ahead. Ask.

Okay. In writing their memory into a story originally, I had to release the thought of him – that last thought that was trapped in my consciousness like a splinter courtesy of Jade dying with the thought of being with him filling her mind. I had to extract the memory of him from my psyche. I had to pull him from my psyche, like extracting a splinter that's deeply embedded in flesh, and discard him.

Nay, dear one. You misunderstand. 'Tis not him *you were throwing away, 'tis the memory of him* as he was in that life *you had to extract. 'Tis his soul that matters to you, not the character-identity he was in that life. His soul laid bare, stripped of the identity he was in that life – the successful CEO.* That *is what you had to extract in the writing of this story. The memory, or the thought you've held of him has become, for you, a blockage, a barrier, a trap. Yes, until now it has protected you, but now that protection has become superfluous. You know now you cannot be with a separated, third-dimensional human man, so what need have you of the protection afforded you by that last thought of Jade's? The memory, the thought of being with him as he was, is no longer necessary, and it was necessary for you to extract it and discard it. But that does not mean you discarded* him. *On the contrary, you freed yourself to be able to call him to you as he truly is, without the disguise of the CEO. You will never, never discard him.*

Ah, I see. So, once again, as is always the case with truly transformative, transcendent Work, I've had to deal with this memory in layers. When I originally wrote the story, I had to deal with and discard the <u>physicality</u> of him as he appeared in that life, to free myself of it. And I also had to deal with the dynamics between my mum, my sister and me. And then, once I dealt with the physicality of him – which took a whole year to Process, really – it cleared the way to deal with the <u>metaphysicality</u> of him, or of us.

Just so.

Without throwing him away completely – throwing out the baby with the bath water, so to speak.

Just so. It was vitally important that you keep him, as a matter of fact.

But that is also one of the reasons we crossed paths in Jade's life? So that I could hold the thought of being with him deep within me – the thought that has, really, prevented me from being with anyone else in this life? 'Tis very much like still being in love so that you cannot be with anyone else.

Just so. The thought prevented you from forming any so-called normal lower-dimensional partnerships in this life. This life was never going to contain such mundane partnerships, or, rather, this life was never going to comprise the distraction of such physical relationships and all that comes with them. It has been necessary for you to be free of such messy, unhelpful entanglements.

What is the other question you hold within you regarding Jade and Blake, because the question is actually very important?

Given the intact fear in Jade's soul, why did she not run in fear and terror from the reflection Blake was for her, and, therefore, from Blake himself? Because she didn't. She never ran in fear from him. I see that very clearly. She was always very calm and steady when she was with him. In fact, he kind of had that effect on her.

As did she on him. Because he pulled her, naturally, into her inner centre which is, itself, pure peace and calm. 'Tis exactly why meditation works so well for some people, because it pulls them away from the storm of physicality and into their calm inner centre.

And do you see, dearest one, how important that question actually is? No, Jade did not run from him in fear. The answer as to why is simple, and this you will come to see when you contemplate it. Have you not observed for yourself that Jade was not completely conscious? She was not completely <u>un</u>*conscious, of course, and the more she worked with the ancient writing system, the more conscious she became. She knew, for example, that she had worked with the ancient writing before, in other lives, and that was why she was so good at understanding and translating it. She did mention, in the nursery, her own memories, did she not? But the memory of the High Priestess was dormant within her, not ever brought to the surface of her conscious awareness. Thus, she was never made consciously aware* <u>that</u> *she was severed from her reflection, nor was she made consciously aware that she feared it so. In other words, she was hidden, from herself, of course,* <u>in</u> *the character identity she was in that life. She saw herself as a physical being, and so she saw him as a physical being, too. Crossing paths with him did not, therefore, arouse the fear of her reflection within her, or, rather, bring it into her conscious awareness. It remained dormant, deeply-buried, unstirred.*

Not so you, dearest one. In fact, for you, 'tis exactly the opposite. Very early on — actually, at the very onset of your Metaphysical Transition — you were faced with the intact, very great fear of your reflection and the effect of the fear on you. How so? How, exactly, were you made aware of it so early on?

I came face to face with it. It was my trigger, actually. It cracked me open so severely I couldn't pull myself back together.

How were you faced with it? Say it, dearest one. You must say it. You must acknowledge it.

Him. I came face to face with him. Only, somehow, despite being so steeped and entrapped in physicality at the time, the encounter, as brief as it was, was purely metaphysical, and so, therefore, the reflection was too.

Yes. Thus were you <u>made aware of it, and thus was it stirred, brought to life within you.</u> *And, thus, for the last nearly-two decades, you have been made aware of the whys and wherefores, indeed, the very source of the fear. Because, of course, you must resolve it within yourself. Not so Jade. The fear was to remain intact within her, remember? That is, perhaps, the greatest difference between your life and Jade's. You are conscious where she was not. You are aware of the fear dynamic that has shaped every life you've lived since it was put there, in your soul. She was not aware of it. Furthermore, cocooned by her ignorance as she was, he reflected that to her – her own ignorance, that is. He, too, was ignorant of the events that tied them, bound them together, even though those same events greatly influenced them being together in Jade's life. Neither of them were aware of what happened.*

That's not to say, of course, that the fear was not affecting her. It just didn't cause her to run from him in the way you're referring to. Tragically, it <u>was</u> still affecting her life, and it <u>was</u> instrumental in creating her death in her reality thereby taking her from him irrevocably. After all, unresolved fears, buried deep in the psyche, shape and control the landscape of an individual's reality, as we've made very clear. This you know well.

Yes, they do. 'Tis why human reality is so hellish, as we said.

Just so, dear one. Just so.

Jade's life can be likened to a sign post for <u>you</u> – a stepping stone from your life to that life of the High Priestess. Her life urges you to look beyond, to go further back. To use your vision to go back, back, back … which you have done, very powerfully and very successfully. Your life is a direct reversal of the life of the High Priestess. She was a metaphysical being who descended into physicality deliberately, consciously. Whereas you have been a physical being who is now ascending into the truth of your metaphysicality consciously. She was your alpha, and you are your omega. She was the beginning of your human incarnations, Jade's life included, and you are the end.

So, it seems to us there is still one outstanding question, and it is the one question you are resisting, powerfully.

Mmmm.

For someone who hates loose ends, there is one awfully big loose end among the threads or themes that have run through your incarnations, dearest one.

Mmmm.

What is to be done about this awfully big loose end, then?

Well, obviously it needs to be resolved, or tied.

And how is this to be accomplished, and what form is the tying to take?

Jesus. You are relentless . . .

And you would not have us any other way.

Mmmm. There is, really, only one way. I have to come face to face with him, the one who is the most powerful and pure reflection of my metaphysicality. And this time, I have to confront and resolve the fear of that reflection once and for all. This time, I have to live, not die.

Yes, dearest one. This time, you have to remain wonderfully, powerfully, vibrantly alive. Yes, indeed. So, to Work, then ... to Work. It is time. And you are ready. You <u>are</u> ready.

～

*The events referred to in this dialogue – the events at the end of the life of the High Priestess – are written into three stories: "The Golden Dragon", "The Living Death" and "The Fallen" in the collection of stories entitled "Transcendence" (accessible only on my website: www.thelady.com.au) and "The Fallen" respectively.

Altira

The Lesson of Altira and Mallona

This world is cloaked and shrouded in darkness,
Like a heavy, dense fog of pollution wrapped around the planet.
Oh how it chokes the Light,
That heavy fog of utter corruption that is wrapped around this planet.
Gaia hates it.
She rails against it.
And despite the help She has from within Her,
From those beings who live in Light,
She is burdened, weighed down with the fears of humankind,
Her children for whom She mourns.
The real tragedy, though, is that you have all been here before,
Not once, but many, many times.
It is for this reason that your true history is kept from you.
Because, you see, every time you reach this place,
This place of utter corruption,
And the trauma and tragedy of Perpetual Separation,
You bring destruction upon yourselves, annihilation actually.
Do they who have led you here yet again
Really think they can avoid the cataclysm
That always accompanies such a place of fear?
Do they really have to live this truth over and over and over again
Without the lesson penetrating their obsessions and addictions –
Their obsessive need for power and control,
And with it, their need for blood?
For they feed on you,
Literally and metaphorically.
But they need you more even than this,
More than you can possibly know.
They need you to create this reality,
For they cannot do it without you.
They cannot be here without you.
This is why they have turned you into Slaves and Zombies.
So you will not buck their systems of control,

Or question what you see and what you are told;
So that you will not break free of the programming,
The many, many mechanisms of indoctrination and mind control
Used to lull you into an anaesthetised existence.
And this is why they bury and suppress the knowledge
That will set you free.
This time,
Now that you are here in this place of darkness and Separation yet again,
There is a Way through the death and destruction.
There is a Way into freedom and Light.
'Tis the Way of Ascension,
And it may be walked by any who have the courage to do so.
They who have led you here,
Here to this place of darkness and fear and trauma,
Know the Way of Ascension may be walked,
And they know that you are perfectly capable of walking it,
And they fear it greatly,
Because they cannot come with us,
And they will lose control of you.
And then they will lose their power.
They will become powerless.
In truth, 'tis humans who hold the real power,
Because they hold within them such Light in their souls.
They who have led you here to this place of darkness
Greatly fear the Light of the human soul.
That is why they work so hard to suppress and repress it.
So set it free, your Light.
Let it shine brightly.
Let it bathe Gaia in wondrous Light.
Let it banish the darkness forevermore.
And let us, together, take the lessons of our past
Apply them to our present,
And end, once and for all,
An existence in and of Perpetual Separation.

Jennifer

1

A Vision of Doom and Destruction

She stood, silent and still, as was her wont whenever she was deep in thought, with her hand wrapped lightly around the pillar beside which she stood. This was, in truth, one of her favourite places to contemplate. The scenery, stretched out below her, was stunningly beautiful – a forest of tall, green, conical-shaped trees broken only by a large rocky outcrop, or cliff, that was wrapped around the vista like a frame, and a river of rushing water that wound its way, in a great hurry, through the tall trees. In the silence of the temple, high above the forest, the water was easily heard. The temple itself, of which the pillar beside her was but a small part, was built high up on that same rocky cliff that framed the forest. And so, the temple overlooked the forest, and the forest, to those in the temple, was turned into a green carpet of tall trees, as if you could reach out and run your hand over them.

This was her world, this little moon that accompanied its much larger parent, and she adored it. The entire moon was covered in the forest of tall trees, with its network of rivers running through the forest like the vascular system in the human body, nourishing, vitalising. And the cliffs and mountains of red rock that framed the forest were like its bones. The little world was spectacularly beautiful, like a green, red and blue ball of coloured glass. And the air here, unlike that of her parent, Mallona, was clear, fresh and pure. Unlike her parent, Altira was as yet untouched by the stain of darkness, and uncorrupted by the stench of pollution and corruption that had settled over Mallona like a heavy, dense shroud … or cloud.

But that was, she knew, beginning to change.

She closed her eyes and bowed her head as the intense sadness washed through her, altering her breath, causing her breaths to come in gasps. They, those of the darkness, had all but bled Mallona dry, and so they were, now, turning their greedy, destructive eyes upon her little moon … with dire consequences.

She had seen those consequences for herself. Or rather, she was seeing those consequences almost constantly, whether awake or asleep, in her visions. She who possessed a sight that was bound not by time and place, had seen something so terrible she could not tell anyone else for fear of burdening them beyond their ability to keep living their lives, as they must. Altira was doomed. Altira, this beloved, beautiful little world, would soon be caught up in the destruction of her parent, and although she was destined to take her place in the Circle of Nine – a very great honour for one such as she – she would do so at the cost of her own very soul ….

The determined tread of boots against the stone floor behind her disrupted her contemplation, pulling her attention from the view below and, mercifully, slicing through her thoughts, distracting her so that her thoughts were silenced, at least temporarily. She sighed softly, recognising the tread without having to turn her head to look, and surrendering to the inevitable. She should have known Isaiah would not allow her to stay on Altira once she told him of what she could see. She should have known he would insist she come in person to tell the Council of what was to come, of what they had done, ultimately. Surrendering to the inevitable, inwardly, she forced herself to acknowledge she understood Isaiah's motives. Such knowledge could not be shared in any way other than in person really.

The owner of the boots stepped into the periphery of her vision, bowing low, his eyes lowered – a mark of genuine respect and homage – and his hands curled around the edges of his dark cloak, holding it back to keep it off the floor of the temple as he bowed, and unwittingly revealing the uniform and the silver wheel of a Ranger.

"My Lady," he said simply.

"Hello, Jerone," she responded, turning her head to look at him, and then, with a half smile lifting only one corner of her mouth, added, "So I am to have an escort then?"

Jerone straightened and looked at her, his own smile sparkling in his eyes but altering his mouth not at all.

"He thought you'd be more comfortable with your own personal escort. The transports are becoming more and more overcrowded, and, of course, they're never on time ..."

"Rubbish," she said softly. "He doesn't trust me to come." She turned away from the Ranger to cast her eyes over the forest once again. "Nor do I blame him, Jerone. I do so hate the necessity of having to set foot on Mallona again. It makes me ill, being there."

"Are you referring to the stench of corruption that shrouds the planet in a fog of heavy darkness or are you referring to the gravitational effects of being on a much larger planet than the one you're used to?"

She looked at him again. "Both, I would say." And then she frowned. "Does it not affect you at all, then?"

"What? The stench of corruption? I am used to it, unfortunately. I only notice the difference when I come here." Now it was his turn to cast his eyes over the vista stretched out below him. "There is such a lightness of being, here, and I always feel as if I can take the largest and purest of breaths." He turned back to her with a smile in his eyes, but his smile died when he saw the depth and the intensity of sadness in hers.

She had cast her eyes downward, avoiding his all-seeing, all-knowing eyes, but she had not been quick enough.

Concerned, he stepped towards her and placed his hands on her arms. "My Lady, what is it? What saddens you so?"

"I am sorry, Jerone," she replied, avoiding his eyes. "I would that I could hide the truth from you, as I will from others. There is not the need for you to carry the burden of what I see, of what I know. Why else would Isaiah ask me to go where I desperately do not want to go if not for the gravest of tidings? 'Tis not for a social visit that I make this trip to Mallona." Now she looked up at him. "You know, do you not, that it is only a matter of gravest concern that would induce me to set foot on Mallona?"

He frowned. "Of course I know. So tell me what you know."

She shook her head. "I told you," she said, "I would not burden you with this. 'Tis not fair to do so."

He pulled her against him, holding her close, his embrace firm, steady, strong. She allowed herself to melt into him, absorbing his warmth and his strength. She allowed herself the luxury of laying her head against his shoulder and closing her eyes to savour the feeling of being this close to him. She allowed herself this one precious moment ...

"Tell me," he said again, and his voice rumbled in his chest against her making her smile despite the gravity of her thoughts and of the knowledge she was all too well aware of. "Let me share this burden with you, Miri-Ani [*an official title, but used like a name, meaning 'First Lady' or High Priestess*]. It will be much lighter for you if we two carry it together, will it not?"

She was silent in response. And then she felt his lips against her forehead.

"Please," he whispered against her. "Please tell me. I've not ever seen you like this. I would know what it is that saddens you so."

She pulled back slightly, not so much that she was released from his embrace, just so that she could look at him. "They will destroy Mallona. Nay," she corrected herself, "they have already destroyed Mallona. It just hasn't happened yet. And Altira will be caught in the destruction. Both are doomed. I have foreseen it."

He frowned again. "How doomed?"

She laid her cheek against his shoulder again. "Mallona will be utterly destroyed. All that will remain as a testament to his existence will be a giant circle of rocks and debris orbiting the sun, and debris scattered throughout the solar system. And Altira ..." She faltered. Oh how she would mourn Altira, her beloved little moon, until the day she breathed her last breath ... and very possibly well beyond.

He touched her cheek gently. "And Altira?" he prompted.

"Altira will remain intact, barely, or only just. She will be flung out to take her own place in the Circle of Nine, but at a very great cost. She will lose her atmosphere almost completely, and with it the forests and rivers and streams that cover her, that make her beautiful. She will be naught but dry sands and red rock. Her face will change irrevocably, so much so she will lose her feminine energy. She will no longer even be a 'she'. The new planet will hold fragments of Mallona, enough to partly take on his soul, so that the two will be as if merged. But Altira will effectively die."

"Ah," he sighed, "no wonder you wear your sadness like an overly-heavy cloak. It weighs you down. When will this happen?"

Again, she pulled back so she could look at him. "Soon, I think. Very soon. In a year, maybe a little longer. I have tried to gauge the time in my visions, but it hasn't been possible, which means I'm not meant to know, or not yet anyway. Our people are doomed if we do not do something to save them ... or some of them, because we cannot save them all. Perhaps that is how it should be. Are we to find ourselves another planet only to destroy that one too? Perhaps we should just accept our fate. This was our time and we squandered it."

"Or perhaps we can learn the harshest of lessons and be given a chance to start again."

"Perhaps. I might be more inclined to agree with you if I thought we **could** learn from our mistakes. The greatest tragedy of all of this is that most of the people on Mallona have no idea what is being done to their planet. They have no idea that Mallona is being bled dry, and that those who control and dominate are in the process of going too far ..."

Again, he frowned. "You're saying it's not nature that will do this?"

She looked surprised by the question. "No. Nature will not do this. The darkness will do this ... **is** doing this. They have machines, Jerone. I have seen them in my visions. I'm not sure what the machines do, perhaps harness energy, but I know they are changing the atomic structure of Mallona's core, and, although we are yet to see and experience it, they have begun a chain reaction that will ultimately bring about Mallona's complete destruction. The planet will explode from the inside out sending debris through the entire solar system."

"There must be a way to stop them. Maybe this is why you've had these visions, as a warning so that they will stop what they are doing ...."

"Jerone," she said gently, silencing him, "it is too late. There is only one hope for our people now and that is to find a new home. Mallona is lost to us. It is too late."

"Gods," he said, sounding pained and pulling her against him again, holding her tight, whether for her sake or for his she could not tell. "How many will die in this destruction?"

She did not reply. There was not the need to say it out loud. He knew the answer anyway. The question had been rhetorical, and the purpose in asking it was to make a point. The entire population of Mallona and its moon – billions and billions of people – would die in the destruction if they did not find a way to save a tiny proportion of them – the seeds of a new beginning, a new community, a new culture, a new hope – the tiny remnant of a once-great, once-glorious culture.

He seemed to rouse himself. He pulled away from her slightly and, again, he placed his hands on her upper arms.

"Visions of the future notwithstanding, my Lady, there is another reason Isaiah bids you come to Mallona. There is something in the present he wishes you to see, something important. In truth," he added, "now that you've told me of what you've seen in your visions, I think Isaiah would have you see and know and understand it all. There are not many who are able to see and to understand what he has to show you, but you are such a one. There is a reason, or so it would seem, that you are to see and to know it all, not just the consequence but the cause and the source as well."

She nodded, understanding, and then she sighed softly. "Oh dear," she whispered on the sigh. "It really is that bad, then, as bad as I thought."

"Yes," he said sombrely, seriously, "it really is."

~

2

The Cauldron

"**A**re you ready?"

"No," she said, sounding slightly desperate.

Ignoring her, he leaned over to check her safety belt, tightening it just to be sure. Then he returned his attention to the controls of his craft, his transport. He gave her no warning. They moved forward so quickly and so powerfully she barely had time to blink and was pushed back into her seat with such force she could not have moved even if she'd wanted to. In an instant, Altira disappeared behind them, and in almost the same instant, Mallona appeared larger in front of them, looking from the distance like a giant, red-brown ball hanging silently in space. Mallona was one of the giants of the solar system, not as big as his nearest neighbour, the planet humans would come to know as Jupiter. No other planet came close to being as large as Jupiter because Jupiter performed a unique and important function for all the planets in the solar system. Still, Mallona was not dwarfed by his neighbour, so that should give you some indication of his size.

As they drew closer, Jerone concentrated on the controls of his craft, speaking into the transmitter sitting comfortably in his ear and around his mouth. While one of the ground controllers of Mallona's inbound and outbound air and space traffic spoke back, and Jerone listened to his instructions, she studied the planet she could see out of the transport's main, front window. Mallona was Altira's parent, Altira being one of four of Mallona's satellites. Altira was in the middle of the four satellites in terms of size – neither the smallest nor the largest –

and she was the only one of the four that was habitable. Unlike his moon which was covered in forest, there were only three great forests left on Mallona, and none of them were visible from the direction she and Jerone were currently coming in from. There were seas and lakes and rivers on Mallona, and there were, also, quite a few vast and rolling deserts. There were plantations and vast tracks of farmland that provided Mallonians with their food, and there were mountains and valleys and rocky outcrops similar to the rocky outcrops on Altira. In the past, Mallona had suffered upheavals, and evidence of one such was visible in the form of a large and long fault line, where the landmass had been raised, forming a single straight cliff for leagues in Mallona's ancient desert. Aeons ago, the remnants of Mallona's ancient culture had been discovered in this desert, obviously destroyed in the upheaval, and, with the discovery, the scrolls and parchments of a beautiful, ancient Wisdom. She knew of the Wisdom because she served it still. Many thought it dead. She knew otherwise. The Wisdom was not dead, it was just ignored.

So, while the planet was still possessed of natural formations of great beauty, by far the greater majority of the planet's surface was covered in sprawling cities, metropolises of civilisation and habitation. Some cities were so big they covered vast amounts of Mallona's landmass and could be seen as one approached the planet from outer space. Some cities were so big, they touched other cities so that the end of one city could not be determined from the beginning of another. Like most cities, whether on Mallona or elsewhere, Mallona's cities tended to have particular purposes. And the city she and Jerone were approaching was Mallona's capital – it's seat of government and power. Mallona was governed by a council, and it was here, in Carcisse, that the council sat.

As Jerone neared the helipad where he would land the transport, manoeuvring the controls of his craft so that it first hovered over the helipad, and was, then, lowered onto it, slowly, she could see Isaiah awaiting them. Despite his vast age, he was still a senator, and he was also, she thought, still handsome. Even from Jerone's transport, she could see Isaiah's trimmed white-grey hair and neatly-trimmed beard, and she could see that he wore his senatorial robes – a long tunic of white with wide, elaborately-embroidered, sapphire- and turquoise-blue trim around its collar and hem, and, over it, a sapphire-blue, full-length coat, with white and turquoise-blue trim around the edges of the cuffs of the coat's wide sleeves.

"Thank you for coming, my dear," he said when she and Jerone joined him. He put his hands on her shoulders and kissed both her cheeks. "I know you do not like coming back here, Miri-Ani. I asked you to come, not for the reason you think, but because there is something you must see for yourself. Well," he said, changing his mind slightly, "I would have you see it because I would have you know everything. And now," he continued quickly, still with his hands on her shoulders, looking into her eyes intensely, "I am going to ask you to do something else you do not like doing. We are going to attend the next session of the Council."

Knowing the gravity of the situation they now found themselves in, she knew he had not asked these things of her – first coming to Mallona and then attending one of the sessions of its council – lightly and for no good reason. Still, she was unable to contain a groan of protest, nor to keep her reluctance off her face. Coming to Mallona always made her feel sick, and she was, indeed, already starting to feel slightly queasy. Feeling sick always lowered her tolerance levels.

"All right, Isaiah," she half said, half sighed. "I know you do not ask this of me just for the sake of having my company."

He smiled into her eyes, such was the effect she had on him, always. No matter the state of his mind, and his emotions, for that matter, she always drew a smile out of him. "Your company will be most welcome, my dear, as it always is. But no, that is not why I asked you to come, and it is not why I ask this of you now." As they began to walk towards the Cauldron, Jerone falling in beside them so that she was flanked by the two of them, Isaiah spoke to her about the day's session. "When we're in the Cauldron," he said, "you must only speak to us if you have nothing important to say. This is terribly important, Miri-Ani. No matter what you see, or what you observe, do not speak of it until we three are in a place where we can speak freely."

"Everything is monitored?" she asked him.

"Everything," he confirmed. "And it is all kept on record and scrutinised. I would not have you put yourself in danger, my dear. So stay silent."

She nodded. "All right."

They walked through one of the transparent tunnels that formed the walkways of the city, criss-crossing it at different levels, like arteries carrying blood cells to a body's different organs. The tunnels, all of them, leagues and leagues and leagues of them, were all carpeted in maroon carpet, and they were strangely, eerily silent, even if they were crowded, which they invariably were. From the tunnel she, Isaiah and Jerone were in, she could see the Cauldron. Unconsciously, she stopped walking for a moment to look at it so that Isaiah and Jerone were forced to stop, too, and wait for her. From this distance, the Cauldron looked like a giant, circular pod. Certainly, its appearance from afar gave no indication of its true function, although there wasn't a soul in this city who didn't know its true function. It stood out from the buildings around it, probably because of the extensive landscaping around it – not many buildings in Carcisse could boast their own landscaping – but she thought it looked innocuous, insignificant somehow, certainly not impressive. The Cauldron had always reminded her of a child's toy. She laughed softly, thinking it a rather apt metaphor.

"Come, dear one," Isaiah urged her, holding out his hand to her. "We've not much time."

She nodded and allowed him to take her arm to propel her onward.

As they reached the end of the system of tubular walkways, Isaiah hesitated, holding her back with pressure from his hand.

"Remember, Miri-Ani," he said, "remain silent. There are eyes and ears everywhere inside and outside the chamber."

"Even in the gardens?"

"Even so. Everywhere."

"All right," she said softly. "I understand. No talking now unless I have something irrelevant to say."

Satisfied, he allowed her to leave the tubular walkway, and, together, the three walked through the landscaped grounds and gardens that surrounded the Cauldron. The gardens were impressive and beautiful but so out of place in Carcisse where gardens were as rare as hen's teeth. Every piece of this city was used for something specific, and gardens were considered a waste of its space. She tried to contain her resentment as she walked through the Cauldron's gardens. This kind of landscaping should have been provided for all the people of this city, not just its Council.

At the Cauldron's impressive entrance, the three were waved through the security checkpoint. There were certain citizens in Carcisse and, in fact, on Mallona as a whole, who were exempt from such invasive scrutiny, and the three of them were three of those, each for different reasons. Isaiah was a senator, Jerone a Ranger, and Miri-Ani was an Altiran priestess. All three wore the robes or uniforms and cloaks of their rank and station, so the guards on duty at the entrance to the Council's chamber recognised and honoured the rank and station of each, not just allowing them through, but nodding at each respectfully.

As instructed, she walked up the grand staircase in silence, noticing certain changes since last she'd come. The carpet was new – deep, rich red – as was the ornate and impressive chandelier above them, lighting the Cauldron's grand staircase. Already slightly queasy, she began to feel nervous, too, but was at a loss as to the possible whys and wherefores of her nervousness. Perhaps, she thought, it was the Cauldron itself that made her nervous. As they ascended the staircase, they were not alone. In fact, both the entrance and the staircase were crowded. Isaiah and Jerone stayed close to her, and both kept their hands on her arms, ever protective, not willing to let her go.

Like any arena, sporting or otherwise, the Cauldron had many points of entry, many doors, and it was always advisable to use the right door, that closest to your particular seat, otherwise the potential for getting horribly lost easily came to fruition. When they entered their door, she was able to look down at the arena itself – the Council's very great, very impressive chamber. She had forgotten how big it was. How was it possible to forget that? The chamber was perfectly round and shaped like a giant bowl, and it was this that gave it its nickname. No one ever referred to it as anything other than the Cauldron. In the Cauldron's centre, on a tall, elevated stage, rising up off the flat floor, was the lectern from which the Council's current president presided over Council sessions. On the sides of the Cauldron's bowl, surrounding the lectern in a full circle, were many hundreds of what looked like balconies in an opera theatre. Each balcony seated between five and eight people, and each balcony belonged to a particular senator. So, each senator was free to invite to the sessions of Council whomever he or she chose, and each senator had complete jurisdiction over his or her balcony, like a piece of owned real estate. Thus, at any one time, the Cauldron could seat over seven thousand people, not all of them senators obviously. And, for each session of Council, the Cauldron was usually full.

For this session, she and Jerone were Isaiah's only guests. He had brought with him no assistants, no clerks, no other visiting dignitaries as had others. They sat in the front row of Isaiah's balcony, leaving the back row empty, she between the two of them. From her seat, slightly less than half way up the bowl, she had a good view of the Cauldron as a whole.

"Are you comfortable?" Isaiah asked her.

"Yes. You?"

"Very, thank you."

"How long is this likely to go on for?"

"Many hours, I would think."

She threw him a look that made him chuckle in response.

"You are welcome to leave any time you would like to, my dear. People may come and go as they please while Council is in session. And so they do. So they do. It can be very distracting."

She nodded, feeling slightly better, slightly less ... trapped.

And then the president walked up the stairs that brought him to the lectern, and the current session of Council officially began.

For the next couple of hours or so, she watched and listened and observed many things. Although she was not one to ever take anything on face value, especially a session of the Council, it still took her all of that time to work out what was truly going on. And it was the cloud of chaotic emotion slowly gathering in the Cauldron's very centre, over the president, that finally caused full realisation to impact her. So she concentrated her focus on the president, watching him closely, observing.

The president was elected by the Council every three years. But this current president, she knew, had been in power for longer than that, much longer. He was, in fact, currently serving, and coming to the end of, his fourth term, unheard of in the history of Mallonian politics. And so, it was not surprising that he conducted the Council session like a maestro conducting an orchestra. With his words, he said all the right, politically-correct things – things like 'we need to find common ground', and 'we need to arrive at outcomes that are beneficial to all', and 'we need to find a workable solution', and 'we need to work towards a satisfactory compromise', and 'we need to have all parties operating from the same page', and 'we need to temper accusations to arrive at a satisfactory resolution' ... we need to do this, we need to do that ... But with his actions, he deliberately stirred up conflict. He actively and consciously generated it. He set senators and their officials each against the others, and then he fuelled the flames of their conflict, teasing it into life so that the consequent emotional tumult was palpable. She watched him manipulate them, and as she watched, tension gathered in the muscles of her limbs, and her stomach clenched in frustration. Why could they not see through his manipulations? Why was it so obvious to her and not to them, those who he was very successfully manipulating?

And, as a result of the emotional chaos generated in the Cauldron, a cloud of that same chaotic emotion was gathering around the president, over him. So thick did it become that she could see it, although not with her physical eyes. With her inner vision, though, it looked like a thick, dark, heavy fog that surrounded the president, and, as it grew, it became enormous, sitting in the bowl of the Cauldron, slowly filling it. Was this why the Cauldron had been designed the way it had? To capture and hold the emotional chaos generated by the conflicts arising in the Council's sessions? She began to wonder what would become of it, the dark cloud of emotion. Where would it go, and what would he do with it, because he was causing it to be for a reason? Of that, she was certain. Surely he wouldn't just let it dissipate. What would be the purpose in that? Or was the purpose simply control?

As if in answer to her silently-voiced questions, the cloud suddenly lifted and began spinning, at first slowly and then more rapidly. She lifted her eyes to watch it. A churning mass of dark, foggy cloud, it moved and spun like a large, upside down tornado, smaller at the top, not the bottom, gathering speed and working itself into the shape of a giant funnel as if a giant hand was moulding it the way a potter moulds his clay. Briefly, she took her eyes from the spinning cloud to look at the president, wondering if he was controlling it. He seemed to have become passive, no longer controlling and manipulating the Council. Was that because he was concentrating on the cloud? She couldn't tell if he was controlling it, but if not the president, then who? Who was controlling the cloud, and how? What strange kind of power could control such a thing?

And then, slowly but surely, the cloud began to split, forming itself into three distinct thinner tornado-like spirals. For a moment, the spirals snaked around the Cauldron's bowl like turned-on, out-of-control garden hoses. And then they touched and latched onto something, becoming grounded at three distinct and separate points in the bowl. Once grounded, they disappeared in an instant. They were swallowed, sucked in, absorbed, and the cloud and its spirals were suddenly gone.

The atmosphere in the Cauldron felt decidedly clearer, but was flat as a result, as if everyone in the bowl was suddenly exhausted. She leaned forward in her seat, slightly, trying to focus on the area just below Isaiah's balcony. One of the points in the Cauldron where one of the spirals of cloud had disappeared was very near where they were sitting. Straining to see, she could not make out what could possibly have swallowed one of the spiralling tentacles. All she could see was people, just like her.

And then Jerone laid his hand over hers. Her attention drawn, she sat back and looked at his hand. Silently, subtly, he motioned, indicating left with his thumb, then holding up three fingers indicating three balconies over, and then pointing down with his forefinger, and holding up first five fingers and then one, indicating six balconies down. She got the message. Three across and six down. She nodded, silently and slightly, to let him know she had understood, and then she leaned forward again, counting three across and then following, visually, with her eyes, down six. At first, she wasn't sure what she was seeing. Three people sat in the front of the particular balcony Jerone had indicated, just as did she, Isaiah and Jerone. But in the back row, there sat a dark shadow, by itself, and it was large, far larger than the size of a normal man. At first she thought the shadow a trick of the configuration of the dim lights in the Cauldron. But as she concentrated her focus, the shadow took form, although it was not her physical eyes that perceived it. It was cloaked, cowled, covered from head to toe in its black robes. And light was not penetrating it. If anything, it was there as a complete absence of light, a blob of insubstantial darkness in the dim interior of the Cauldron.

She watched it intently, honing and concentrating her focus. Silently, in the deepest recesses of her own mind, she asked it, "What are you?"

As if in response, it turned its head towards her so that she was given a glimpse of what was hidden beneath the hood of its dark cloak. Darker shadow looked out from that hood, although its eyes glittered like black agate. It changed position, shifting as if it needed to make itself more comfortable, putting its hands on its knees, and out of the long sleeves of its cloak, shadowy fingers appeared, like talons, with long, black nails sharpened to a point.

She sat back in her chair, suddenly feeling very ill. Dear Lady! She knew what it was. She had seen these creatures in her visions, her sleeping dreams and her waking ones, but she had thought them symbolic, somehow, of people's inner fears. They were not symbolic, though, these creatures. They were real, actual, and they were in control. And, if today's experience was anything to go by, there were three in this chamber, right here, right now ...

She stood up so fast she nearly knocked her chair over. She had to get out of there or she would disgrace herself by throwing up in front of everyone around them. Barely aware of what she was doing, she pushed past Jerone and left the balcony. Half running, half walking, she ascended the stairs that would take her out of the Cauldron, uncaring that others could see her desperation to escape. Half way up, she stopped, breathing deeply, holding a hand to her chest in a vain attempt to calm her heartbeat, fighting intense nausea and an insane desire to burst into tears.

And then, Jerone's strong hands were around her arms, and she could feel his strength beside her.

"Come," he said quietly into her ear. "I will help you. Stay calm."

She knew what he was telling her. Hold yourself together. Don't fall apart here.

Drawing on every ounce of strength she possessed, she did pull herself together, and she continued to walk up the stairs more calmly. He stayed close, holding her arm with one hand while he guided her out of the Cauldron, down the staircase of its entrance, and out into the landscaped gardens of the surrounding parkland.

"Keep going," he commanded. "We cannot stop here."

She nodded, remembering Isaiah's warning they would be monitored even in the gardens. But she breathed deeply, savouring the clearer air of the city. The air in the Cauldron had become stifling.

She held herself together until they stepped beyond the gardens, and then, in the foyer of some unknown building, away from prying eyes, she collapsed against him. He held her close, knowing she needed his strength. He knew how she felt. He had felt the same when Isaiah had first shown him the truth. Gradually, her breathing settled as did her nausea. When she could, when she'd conquered the need to throw up everything she'd just witnessed, she pulled back.

"Now I understand why he did not ask me here to speak to the Council. Speaking to the Council would have been naught but an absolute waste of my breath, would it not, an act of pure futility?"

He was still holding her, but he raised a hand to put a wayward strand of her hair back in its place, behind her ear. "I'm afraid so."

"How long have you known about this?"

He thought before he answered her. "Many years."

"Why did you never say anything? Why did you not tell me?"

"For the same reason you were not going to tell me about your visions."

"So," she said, frowning at him, "you have carried the burden of this alone."

"Not quite. Come," he said, "we cannot stay here. Isaiah will meet us at his place. We need to keep moving."

They rode the city's transport system away from the Cauldron and its dark secrets. A priestess and a Ranger were an unlikely couple, a fact reflected in the numerous interested and curious glances they received, some people openly staring. Uncaring, she pretended not to notice, as did he, because there's no way he would have missed them. He, like her, was too observant. It was part of his mandate as a Ranger to be observant, in fact.

Isaiah's 'place' looked like a giant bubble on a stick. It overlooked the city, high up, perched on one of Carcisse's thin, tall buildings, and the outside of it, at least around its very centre, was a continuous ring of large glass windows. When the city's low cloud of pollution was at its worst, a regular occurrence these days, Isaiah's 'place' disappeared from view if you were standing on the ground. And, in fact, so, too, did the view of the city disappear through the bubble's continuous glass window. Inside the bubble, the space was light, airy and spacious, with a modern kitchen, sunken lounge, a library, three large bedrooms, and numerous green, lush plants. As much as she hated coming to Mallona, so much so she rarely did come these days, she loved being in Isaiah's bubble, as she liked to refer to it. Walking into the interior of the bubble from the city outside was like walking into a different world entirely, or like stepping into another dimension.

While they waited for Isaiah to join them, she and Jerone made dinner.

Laying places at Isaiah's round table, beside the kitchen, she hesitated, looking out through the glass window at the city beyond it.

"It's a nice day today," she observed. "The pollution is quite clear. You can actually see the city for a change."

In the kitchen, Jerone glanced at her before returning his attention to the food he was preparing. "You're not becoming cynical, are you? Cynicism does not become you, Miri-Ani."

She pretended to consider the possibility, and then she shrugged. "Forgive me," she said sweetly, "I did not think it possible to **be** cynical where this city is concerned."

He laughed and didn't bother replying verbally, not after what they'd both seen that day. She was right, and they both knew it. Carcisse had degenerated into a den of utter corruption and iniquity, and the recognition by an individual that this was indeed so was not cynicism, it was realism. They didn't have to wait long for Isaiah to join them. He hadn't stayed long after she and Jerone left the chamber. His purpose in being at the Council's session that day had been fulfilled when Miri-Ani saw the truth with her own eyes.

"Are you all right?" he asked her seriously, again putting his hands on her shoulders and studying her intensely. "At least you've got some colour back. Ye gods but you turned white, as white as my robe, I would say."

She smiled at him. "I'm all right," she said. "I should've known. I think I've been hiding the truth from myself, or hiding myself from the truth. Same thing. You opened my eyes today, my friend. It had to be, sooner or later. My inner sight has not been letting me off the hook even though I have been resisting seeing the truth. At least now I understand what I've been seeing."

He nodded brusquely. "Good."

"So," she said once they were seated at the table and had begun to help themselves to the fare laid upon it, "the Council is a farce. What is the extent to which it is a farce, Isaiah?"

"Are you asking me whether or not it still genuinely governs? The answer is no, it does not, and has not for a long time."

"Do the people know?"

"No, they have no idea. They believe the Council is the source of genuine governance. The truth has been very effectively hidden from them. As for its true purpose, today, you saw for yourself what that is."

"So those creatures can feed? That's it?" she asked, struggling with the full extent of the truth. "That's truly the reason the Council sits?"

"That's it, the sole reason. You saw that for yourself, my dearest. Did they actually achieve anything in session today?"

She shook her head. "Nothing achieved, nothing gained. Except, of course, for a very heavy, very dark cloud of chaotic emotion that was devoured once it grew thick enough to satiate their dark appetites. Who does govern then?"

"Need you ask? Really? Whoever those creatures control."

She nodded her understanding. "They govern. They control. They manipulate and dominate. They have created this mess, and they have all but succeeded in destroying an entire planet ... with our help, or course."

Isaiah raised his eyebrows in response to that last comment. She had already known the answers to her questions, although she was, also, still working through her resistance, and so she'd needed to hear the truth from him. So, even though her questions could have been entirely rhetorical, as he well knew, he still indulged her by answering when the answers were, in fact, obvious.

"And the president?" she asked him quickly to forestall the comment heralded by his raised eyebrows. "He is their man, obviously, but is he one of them or ..."

"He is controlled by them, of course, like a puppet whose strings are pulled by an unseen master. It is a form of possession, Miri-Ani, but the vessel of possession must give his consent. Many do so without knowing what it is they are actually doing. In that sense, he is one of them and, at the same time, he is not. Most people can be bought, my dearest. Everyone has a price, and it is frighteningly easy for those creatures to discover an individual's price. As for the president, I suspect he knew exactly what he was doing. There are rituals of binding, and he would have actively and consciously participated in those rituals. 'Tis a dark bargain he has struck, is it not? He gives them his mind and body, and in return they make him rich and powerful, although they never hand him control. He becomes their plaything. He does their bidding, dances to their tune. The price he pays, though, is that he **must** dance to their tune, their way. He cannot dance alone, and he cannot dance his way, at all."

As he talked, she stopped eating, biting the inside of her lip instead as she looked at him. "I confess I do not understand the kind of mentality that would so risk the very essence and well-being of its own soul ...."

"Because you are of the Light, my dearest. 'Tis simply not in your nature to allow such things. You would never put your soul in harms way the way those people do." He waved his hand towards the glass window near them, indicating everyone in the city. "One of those creatures could not possess you anyway, and if any of them tried, they would burn up in your Light. And Jerone's. And mine, for that matter. That is why I keep Jerone close. The darkness has no hold over him, and no means of having a hold over him. He works exclusively for me now."

She looked at Jerone and smiled at him as she said, "You can trust him. I've always known that."

He smiled back, but, as was his way, his smile barely altered the contours of his mouth. She caught it, though, and absorbed it. Then, looking at Isaiah once again, she asked, "What is the ..." she searched for the right word, "prevalence of this possession? And how is it that one was there, in the chamber, as it was? Does it not need to possess a human to be in this realm, this dimension? And," she added as the thought occurred to her, "why do I call them the Si'il?"

Isaiah sat back in his chair, chuckling appreciatively. Her mind was moving, rapidly, as it always did once she successfully processed something not easily digested. "So," he observed once his laughter subsided, "your visions really have been urging you to see the truth. No wonder you had to see what you saw today. Right then, where to begin. Let me answer your questions in reverse order. You call them the Si'il because that is what they are. Creatures of utter, unadulterated, if you like, darkness."

"They call themselves that?"

"They do. It is a title based on an old language, and in that old language, the word meant 'shadow'. They worship it, the darkness. They worship it and they use it. Just as you honour the Light with all that you are, so do they honour the darkness with all that they are. They are your antithesis, Miri-Ani, your absolute opposite. You are **of** the Light, they are **of** the darkness. You serve the Light, they serve the darkness. You **are** Light, they **are** darkness. Your own character and nature radiates all the classic characteristics of the Light – Love, Care and Compassion, Wisdom, Knowledge and Truth, Movement and Flow, and Beauty. The nature of the Si'il expresses and exhibits all the classic characteristics of a complete absence of Light – hatred, fear, ugliness, ruthlessness, abuse, exploitation ..." Again, he waved his hand. "You know how it goes."

"As to the three in the chamber today ..." he continued, but she stopped him.

"Are they conceived that way? Are they born of the darkness such that they can never be Light?"

He considered the question. "No one is ever really born of the darkness, although, yes, there are angels and there are demons, in a sense. But, of course, it is not so black and white, not so simple as all that. Angels and demons are symbolic of the two polar opposites – Light and the absence of Light or darkness. So, would an angel ever choose to become a demon? Yes, it has been known to happen, believe it or not. Can a demon become an angel? Yes. But here's the real issue. To become an angel, a demon must fight, within itself, an arduous and extremely painful battle. 'Tis a long way back from the depths of hell to the heights of heaven. Most of the Si'il did not start out as creatures of abject darkness. But you will find most of them descended to the pits of hell willingly, one way or another."

He allowed silence to descend for a moment to give both her and Jerone time to absorb what he'd said. Both, he could see, were thinking through the information given to them, processing it, assimilating it. Isaiah smiled, making sure his smile was concealed from them. Their remarkable minds worked in such similar ways. After a moment of silence, he continued.

"As to the creatures in the Cauldron today, they can be there, as they are, in their true form, but only briefly, or temporarily. They lower themselves, in a sense, so they cannot hold that lowered vibration for long. And they come in their true form to feed, as you saw for yourself.

"Now," he continued, "in order to answer the question of the prevalence of possession and control, as you put it, my dearest, you have to think in terms of the layers or strata of human society. At the lowest echelons of society, there are virtually none, unless someone shows promise. But then that individual does not languish for long in the lower echelons of human society. Invariably, he rises quickly through the ranks."

He paused to see if she was following. She was, and she nodded at him to signal the fact, and to urge him to continue.

"And the highest echelons?" she asked.

"No one rises to the highest strata of society without them, and no one stays there without them."

The blood drained from her face as his meaning impacted her. Now, finally, she was grasping the full picture, the full and brutal truth. "And you, Isaiah?" she asked. "They must have at least made an attempt to control you."

"Oh yes," he confirmed. "They did indeed. And they have not tried again. But they watch me closely. I cannot make a move without them scrutinising every word I utter and every action I take."

"Ah," she sighed. "No wonder you urged me to stay silent today. They target you specifically."

"And from now on, they will be targeting you. But that matters not, does it? You and I know the truth. And no doubt you have told Jerone. Or rather," he corrected himself, "I've no doubt Jerone would have extracted the truth from you by now. Our priorities have shifted, have they not, my dearest?"

"They have," she concurred softly. "Surely they know the truth, too. Surely. They would see the truth from their dimension."

"I've no doubt they've seen the truth, and I've also no doubt they are already making their plans for the future. Very soon, they will lose the grip they have on this dimension courtesy of Mallonians. But the priority for us now is to secure ourselves a future, Miri-Ani. We must see to the survival of the human race."

"So those creatures can get a hold of us once again?" Ignoring the concerned looks Isaiah and Jerone exchanged, she continued, "So we can allow ourselves to be used again as a conduit of utter destruction?"

Jerone was perfectly silent, and Isaiah sat looking at her for a long time. Finally, he asked her, "Would you see us utterly destroyed as a race in the coming cataclysm, my dearest?"

She breathed deeply as she turned to look at the city spread out below, or the part of it that could be seen from where she sat. It reached the horizon in every direction. "Yes," she said quietly as she turned back to him. "We had our chance, and we have blown it … and our planet with it."

Isaiah raised his eyebrows. "Did you know about this?" he asked Jerone.

"Did I know she felt this way? Yes, but only since this morning."

"And do you agree with her?"

Jerone shrugged, but the movement was barely perceptible. "I see her point of view. It's very tempting to agree, I must say."

"Do you blame me? Really?" she asked Isaiah.

"No, I do not. So perhaps it is as well we did not consult you before proceeding with our program."

She eyed him suspiciously as she felt chills run down her back. "What program?"

"There are, of course," he replied, "those of us who have known the truth for a while, the Si'il notwithstanding. Scientists have been monitoring Mallona's core for years with a view to predicting more of the upheavals of the past, and possibly preventing them. Oh the irony. You can imagine their dismay when they detected something even more alarming. Definitive action was required, immediately. And there are those of us who have, indeed, acted."

Unconsciously, she sat forward in her chair. Jerone looked down, at the table, and she caught it out of the corner of her eye. Suddenly, inexplicably, her heart increased its pace, and she was nervous again. "What have you done?"

"We have built transports capable of penetrating deep space. They can carry five-six hundred people at a time in addition to equipment, works of art, books, anything we deem worthy of preserving. Many aeons ago, we sent a group of pioneers – scientists, engineers, farmers and their families – to Gaia, the second planet in our solar system, to assess her as a suitable and viable option for establishing and sustaining a sizeable colony. She is perfectly habitable, Miri-Ani. In fact, she is beautiful." He hesitated and then added very softly, "As beautiful as Altira."

Suddenly, she felt as if she couldn't breathe. "No," she said, shaking her head. "No," she said again as tears welled in her eyes.

Relentlessly, despite her obvious distress, he continued. "So we established a colony there, successfully. Today, it is large and it is thriving, and we intend to send as many of our people there as possible. Those who will make the most constructive, the most positive contribution to the new colony have already been pre-selected, although they do not yet know it – engineers, healers, scientists, astronomers, teachers, artists, farmers. We will continue to send as many transports to Gaia as we can, until it becomes impossible. The transports cannot return. They will be disassembled once they reach Gaia, and their technology and the material of their inner core and their outer shell will be used to build in the colony. Therefore, anyone travelling on the transports cannot come back, so for anyone who leaves Mallona, it is a one-way journey. There is no turning back, and there is no changing one's mind." He leaned forward. "The first transport leaves in six weeks, and I want you and Jerone to be on it."

Her tears overflowed, and she wiped them away. "And what of you?"

"I am tired, my dearest, so tired." He did, indeed, sound tired as he spoke the words. "I am tired of fighting for good and for truth. I am tired of fighting the corruption. They have sapped my strength. I do not now possess the energy to start again. I have given much to Mallona and to Mallonians. I have nothing left to give."

"Then if you are not prepared to go, how can you ask this of me?" she said, vehemently. "You know I would die with Altira. You know this. How can you ask me to keep living knowing she and you will be dead?"

He reached for her hand across the table and was heartened when she didn't pull back from him.

"The new colony will need law and order. Law and order will be essential, especially initially with the sudden influx of people. It will need the Rangers, and there is none better than Jerone. You know this. But equally as important, perhaps more so, it will need the Altiran priesthood, Miri-Ani. You are still the beating heart of our culture, whether or not that is recognised, and even though that heartbeat has grown quiet in recent years, it will grow strong again in this new colony because it will be needed.

"This," he continued passionately, "is a chance for us to start again. But not," he held up the forefinger of his free hand, "with a clean slate. There is a lesson in our situation, this tragic circumstance we currently find ourselves in, a most vital lesson, one that must not, under any circumstances, be lost. And who better to carry that lesson and hand it down to the generations that follow than you, my dearest? Who better? You who sees what others do not. You who knows what others do not. You who now knows the truth of what has happened to us here, on this most beloved planet. But," he said, releasing her hand and sitting back, "these are not my reasons for asking this of you. My motives are purely selfish, for I would die knowing that you and Jerone have survived. You are both precious to me, such rare souls as yours. I will die happy knowing your souls still shine brightly in the human experience."

Silence fell upon them, such a profound silence. Her throat was burning with the effort of containing her sobs, for she would not allow herself to fall apart in front of these two.

"Miri-Ani," Jerone said, his voice sounding overly loud in the profound silence, "you need to know, this is entirely your choice. If you choose to die on Altira, I will die with you there. But if you choose to leave on the transport, I will leave with you. You are **my** beating heart, and I will not and cannot live without you. So, whatever you choose, so, too, will I choose. 'Tis not my intention to apply pressure one way or the other, nor to burden you. You do not carry the burden of the responsibility for my life or my death. That is still mine, as yours is yours. You just need to know. That is all."

She nodded silently, wholly unable to speak. And, again, the tears spilled over, leaving trails of moisture on her cheeks. She made no attempt to wipe them away. There was no point because more would simply take their place. She rose from the table to move towards the window, putting her hand on Jerone's shoulder as she passed him, wanting to communicate her understanding of what he had told her. This was the first time either of them had acknowledged their love out loud. Always, the knowledge of the way they felt about each other had simmered under the surface of their relationship, never overtly acknowledged.

Again, and for a long time, she looked out over the city, standing with her back to the only two men she loved, the only two people, actually. "Six weeks …" she said out loud.

"I want to make sure you make it safely," Isaiah said. "Surely you know that any transport on its way to Gaia when the cataclysm hits Mallona will not make it."

Without turning, she nodded. She stood in silence, and neither of the men moved. They waited, silently, although they exchanged looks. Jerone was strangely calm. Either way, he would be with her, at last. If she chose to stay, he would surrender the cloak and the wheel of the Ranger, and he would return with her to Altira, there to stay until they both died. If she chose to leave, he would leave with her. Isaiah, on the other hand, was not calm. His heart was beating, hard and fast, as he wondered what kind of fight she would put up. He would fight her all the way if he had to. In fact, he had already decided he would do whatever was necessary to ensure she and Jerone were on that transport. The old expression played through his conscious mind … by fair means or foul ….

"What if the lesson is lost?" she asked suddenly, slicing through his thoughts and turning to face him. "What if we go and the lesson is not learnt? Then we will have left you for nothing."

He didn't respond straight away. He couldn't. He was weak with relief because he knew her question signified the beginnings of her intention, whether or not she yet knew it. Knowing her, she did know it and was putting up one last gallant fight. Such was her way. But she was in the process of making the choice to go.

After a long moment of silence during which she looked at him, demanding his answer with her demeanour and her eyes, he gave her one.

"There is no point in saving our people if we do not take this lesson with us, Miri-Ani. This you know. 'Tis an act of utter futility saving our people if they cannot learn the lesson of our misguided, tragic, corrupt present. Then, Mallona and Altira really will die in vain. We have to try. You have to carry this lesson to Gaia. You have to record it. You must hand it down to the generations that come after you. And you are the only one who can do this. There is no other as powerful as you, no other capable of carrying the lesson within. You must do this. Do not let Altira die in vain. Do not." He curled his hands into balls as he said those last words.

"That is not fair," she said slowly, but she sounded tired, defeated.

"No," he replied by way of agreeing with her, "none of this is fair."

She moved then, standing behind Jerone and putting her hands on his shoulders. "All right, Isaiah, you have your way. I will make sure Altira does not die in vain. Jerone and I will leave on one of the transports …"

Isaiah shook his head. "Not one," he said. "The first. You will leave in six weeks."

She nodded. "The first," she agreed. "But I need to return to Altira. I need time to say goodbye."

"Of course, my dearest. Of course."

~

"Can't sleep?"

She smiled in the darkness. "No. You?"

"No," Jerone said as he joined her.

She was sitting propped in one of the window seats, wearing only a long white nightgown, her feet bare, her hair unbound, her knees against her chest so she could wrap her arms around them. When he joined her, he sat on the opposite side of the bench seat from her and adopted a similar position. He wore a loose tunic over trousers, and his feet, too, were bare, as was his hair which he normally wore pulled back and bound with leather. Neither of them had bothered turning the lights on, so they sat in the darkness, bathed by the city's lights and by the light of the smallest of Mallona's moons, the only one visible at the moment in the night sky.

"Did you know?" she asked him.

"About the transports? I knew they were building them, yes, but I didn't know the reason why until today. And, no, I knew nothing of Isaiah's intention to send us. He didn't tell me. He probably knew there was no point telling me without telling you."

She smiled again, slightly, as she leaned her head against the frame of the seat behind her. "I heard what you said today, and I believe you, but surely you want to live."

"Of course I want to live," he said. "I'm not ready to die, not yet anyway. But there would be no point in living without you. Then, I would be only half alive, and what is the point in that?"

She absorbed that in silence and then said, "I'm not sure ..." She faltered and then decided to change tack. "I'm afraid I may not be the same person on this new planet. So much lost. So much will change. I don't know how I'll handle it. And, the context, for me, will be very different ..."

He narrowed his eyes. "Are you saying you're afraid you won't be the person I love?"

Again, she smiled. "Thank you, that is a much better way of putting it. Yes, I am afraid of that, both for you and for me."

"You are you, Miri-Ani. Everything around you may change, but that will not. You are who you are, and you always will be."

Again, she absorbed what he said in silence.

"In my visions," she said, breaking the companionable silence that had settled between them, "I see Gaia as the third, not the second planet in the solar system."

He inclined his head, interested. "You think they have the wrong planet?"

"No. Gaia is the second planet at the moment. I wonder ..."

"What?" he prompted when she petered out and then stayed silent. "You wonder what?"

"I wonder if the force of the blast will throw the third planet out of alignment so that the second and third will change places. And if so, if that happens, then why? What is the significance of Gaia becoming the third planet? And, if this happens, then Gaia will, herself, suffer upheavals. We may not survive even if we make it to her."

"We may not. If we do not survive, then what will come to pass is as you would have it be."

She smiled again, at him. "Fate. You are saying what will be will be. At least then Altira will not die in vain, and all the other planets in the solar system will be safe from us."

They fell silent again, both thinking of the changes that were to come, to them personally and the wider ramifications and further-reaching effects as far as the collective was concerned.

Then she broke the silence. "I could not do this without you."

"And I," he said quickly, "would not want to do it without you."

~

3

Transport

She stood, silent and still, as was her wont whenever she stood here, looking out over Altira's beautiful vista. Her hand was wrapped lightly around the pillar beside her, and she concentrated on being in this very moment, focussing on the view of the forest laid out below her, trying to sear it into her memory, although there was, really, not the need. The view was already seared into her memory, and she would always be able to access it at will. She was possessed of such a powerful sight that accessing the memory in her mind's eye was almost, for her, like being there for real. This was, though, the very last time she would see this scenery for real, and, no matter the brilliance of one's inner vision, there really was no substitute for seeing it for real.

Behind her, in the rooms of the temple, crates and boxes were stacked high, ready to be transferred to Mallona for the long trip to Gaia. Miri-Ani was not just of the Altiran priesthood, she was its High Priestess. So she was not just its head, she was also, and therefore, its heart. When Isaiah had asked her to take the long trip to Gaia, he knew, and so did she, that he was asking her to take the priesthood itself to the new colony, and to see it established there. And so, there were more than a dozen priests and priestesses who would be making the long journey, although only half those would travel on the first transport with Miri-Ani. Old he may be and waning in his strength, but Isaiah still possessed the kind of power necessary for ensuring the priesthood was well represented in the new colony. He believed, and she knew he was right, that the priesthood was essential for many more reasons than just the spiritual well-being of the colony's population. The Altiran priests and priestesses were the custodians of Mallona's true history, and they were, therefore, the preservers of the true culture of their people. And part of the preservation of that very culture was packed into the crates and boxes behind her now.

She knew, courtesy of her visions and memories, that she had been one of those who originally, and prolifically, wrote the ancient Wisdom down on the texts and books and scrolls that were now packed into the crates. And she also knew she was instrumental in translating those same texts many thousands of years later. When first they had pulled the texts and scrolls out of the desert, they had not properly understood how the ancient language was used to record the prayers and incantations of the ancient religion. She had changed that, she knew, aeons ago. Now, every one of the texts and books and scrolls, and every translation that formed such an intrinsic part of the Altiran library had been carefully packed away and would accompany Miri-Ani on the first transport.

It was, she thought, strange that she should glean some comfort from knowing the library was intact and would be coming with her. It was as if her own past was accompanying her so that she was somehow, strangely, intact even though she was leaving behind almost everything she truly and deeply loved. She would do everything in her power to protect and preserve the knowledge contained in the library, and so would Isaiah ... so *had* Isaiah. Once she had made her choice to leave Mallona on the first transport, as difficult as that was, she had worked tirelessly in her preparations. Because, in making the choice to leave Altira for this new world, she had chosen to preserve the priesthood and its valuable heritage.

The determined tread of boots on the stone of the temple's floor behind her heralded his approach. When he reached her, this time, he neither bowed nor greeted her. Instead, he put his hand on her shoulder.

"It's time, Miri-Ani," he said.

She nodded without looking at him. "I know."

"I need to know," he said without removing his hand, "why are you doing this? Why are you leaving?"

Still, she did not take her eyes off the vista below. "Because I would see the priesthood preserved and re-established in the new colony. I have journeyed with it so far, across so many aeons, I cannot abandon it now. And because I cannot bear the thought of Altira dying in vain, even though I suspect that is ultimately what will happen. I have to try, though. I have to try and make her death worth something. And because I cannot bear the thought of you dying just to be near me."

He removed his hand from her shoulder, and, not sure what it meant, she turned to look at him.

He nodded silently, but he touched her cheek with his fingertips. She saw in his eyes that her pain was shared. They had each other, but the experience of leaving the only home they knew – Mallona and its beautiful moon – was breaking their hearts. She covered his hand with her own, glad that he truly understood, as one only can when one knows the same pain.

Desperately trying to rein in her tears, determined not to have her last glimpse of Altira's beautiful vista blurred by them, she turned to drink in the scenery one last time. And then, as determined, she dragged her eyes away and turned her back on the forest spread out below her.

"I am ready," she said quietly.

In the craft that was to take them all, those who were accompanying her, and the crates containing the priesthood's library, to Mallona, she allowed herself only one last look at her beloved little moon. Then she resolutely turned her back on Altira, deliberately looking away. She could not, she just could not bear to see her little moon disappear from sight as Jerone used the controls to propel the craft forward, towards Mallona.

~

After personally supervising the transfer of the crates and boxes containing the Altiran library into the transport that would take them, the next day, to the ship that awaited them, docked, as it was, high up in Mallona's atmosphere, and knowing the library would be safe, she and Jerone spent one last night with Isaiah in his bubble. As she had so often, she stood looking out through the glass window to the city below. Dusk was upon them – that time when the light of day begins to give way to the darkness of night – and the city's lights were coming on slowly but surely, gradually changing the colour of the cloud of pollution that hovered over the city from grey-brown to pink. At least, she thought, the cloud was thin today, so it wasn't blocking her view.

"I will not miss this city," she half said, half sighed to the two men who sat at the table behind her, and then, turning to run her eyes over the interior of the bubble, she said to Isaiah, "but I will miss this place." Then, looking directly at him, she said, "And I will miss you, my old friend."

Isaiah got up from the table to wrap her in his embrace. "I know," he said as he held her against him. "And I will miss you. You know that. Although, I very strongly suspect our paths will cross again, my dearest. Remember that. Draw comfort from the knowledge, as I will."

They had such a shared history. They had crossed paths in these lives they now lived when she was still only young. In fact, he had saved her life – a story for another time. After that, he had been quick to recognise her unique gifts, and her connection to the ancient priesthood. To him, she had radiated it, even back then. So he had introduced her to the Altiran priesthood, and its home, Altira, and she had left Mallona for good. Over the many years that had passed since, they had kept in close contact, seeing each other regularly. In leaving Mallona and Altira behind, she would be leaving a gaping hole in his life, and in not coming with her, he was opening up a gaping hole in hers.

"I will not be able to contact you," she said against him unnecessarily given the fact that he already knew this to be the case. "But you can contact me. Send me letters with every new transport that leaves Mallona. Do not tell me about Mallona, just tell me about you. Will you promise to do that?"

"I promise. I will have nothing else to do anyway. Once I see you leave on that transport, I am hanging up my senatorial robes. My work here will truly be complete."

She pulled back from him, smiling at the thought of him having nothing to do, wishing she could be there to see it. "What will you do with your days? You will be so bored."

"No," he said seriously, frowning at her. "I will be too busy to be bored. I will write you a letter every day, and I intend to read my entire library."

She glanced at his library, which she could see over the other side of the room. It was extensive, but still ...

"Right," she said cynically. "That will take you all of two months. What will you do then?" Before giving him a chance to respond, though, she sobered. "So much pain," she said to him. "So much loss. It characterises human life, does it not, Isaiah? Why do we do it, then? Why do we have lives if they are only full of pain?"

Still holding her with one arm, he raised his other hand and ran the backs of his curled fingers over the soft skin of her cheek. "It does not have to be that way," he said. "You know this, my dearest. Souls choose to incarnate and then they become trapped in the human experience, coming back again and again out of necessity to resolve their karmic debt, but deepening it instead. They must learn how to free themselves, not entangle themselves further, and they must learn how to create heaven for themselves instead of hell. You can teach them, Miri-Ani. And you can free them."

Involuntarily, she shook her head. "You have more faith in them than I do. Are you sure I am the right person for this very great responsibility you've seen fit to place on my shoulders, and I, for reasons I cannot quite fathom, have accepted."

He smiled at her. "There is none better suited than you. I am not the only one who thinks so. Far, far from it. There are many who follow you willingly. Do you not know this? You have but to call them to you and they will come. They will transcend the barriers of time and place and space, my beautiful Lady, for you, when you call to them. They will follow you through time and through the aeons of the human experience. They will answer your call."

"They will come? They will come to help us set humanity free from its eternal and infernal cycle of death and destruction?"

"They will. They will come. Remember that. Hold the knowledge close."

⌐

A group of three dozen or so passengers had been invited by the ship's captain to his viewing platform to watch as the ship left its dock. Jerone and Miri-Ani were two of those, and they stood together at the front of the crowd with the captain, looking out through the viewing deck's large window. The group of people around them were talking in hushed tones so that the buzz of conversation surrounded them in a cloud of muted sound. The captain leaned on the railing that prevented them all from touching the window, watching proceedings intently, and neither Jerone nor Miri-Ani spoke. Through the window, behind the docking station, Mallona loomed, larger than life, filling the window.

The ship shuddered, and then, slowly, very slowly at first, it began to pull away from the dock. Even as it gained momentum, slowly but very surely, gathering speed in the process, Mallona did not alter in size. Still, it filled the window. But as the ship's speed increased further still, the docking station became smaller until it disappeared against the backdrop of the large planet behind it. The buzz of conversation on the viewing platform ceased, and every person stood still and silent, watching as everything they knew and everything they loved – their culture, their way of life, their people, friends, family, the planet that had sustained them – gradually receded with the distance the ship put between itself and Mallona.

Miri-Ani found Jerone's hand and entwined her fingers in his. He responded, his fingers tightening around hers. Her throat was burning with the effort of holding herself together, and holding her tears at bay. She knew others were feeling the same. She could feel their pain almost as much as she could feel her own. Involuntarily, she looked for Altira, her beloved little moon, but could not see it. Relieved and saddened at the same time, she knew Altira must have been on the other side of Mallona, thereby hidden from sight. She would, she knew, never again see her beloved little moon.

As they all stood together and watched, Mallona gradually became smaller and smaller, so that it no longer filled the window. Then it appeared, to the watching group, to be the size of a large beach ball, then a basket ball, then a baseball, a golf ball, a pea, and then a tiny dot in the far distance. The crowd began to disperse, quietly, leaving the viewing deck, but Jerone, Miri-Ani and the captain watched until Mallona was no longer visible at all.

It was the captain, still leaning on the railing, who spoke. "So be it then," he said very quietly. "There is no turning back now. Our fate, both individually and collectively, is in the hands of the gods ..."

"And so is theirs," Miri-Ani said, indicating those who had remained behind on Mallona with an inclination of her head.

"Yes," he agreed, "so it is."

With her attention drawn his way, there was something she was intensely curious about, a curiosity she needed satisfied. "If you do not mind me asking, Captain, what will you do in the new colony? Because you will not be commanding space ships there."

He straightened and turned towards her, smiling at her. "No, I will not be commanding space ships in the new colony. Well you should ask, my Lady, because I intend to join the priesthood."

She hesitated, waiting for him to laugh. But he didn't.

"You're serious?"

He nodded once, definitively. "Very."

She smiled at him, unwittingly bathing him in her sparkle. "Well, we will be honoured to have you as one of us."

Watching her, Jerone felt enormous relief at seeing her smile. He hoped he would see more of it in the days and weeks to come, but he suspected he would not. Earlier, he had personally witnessed the look of horror on her face when she'd seen their cabin for the first time. He had, with her consent, arranged for them to share. His reasons for wanting to share with her were three-fold. First, he wanted to keep a very close eye on her. Second, he wanted to make it as difficult for her as possible to withdraw from him. And, third, he wanted to make sure he was accessible to her. With only a dozen Rangers on the ship to keep order amongst five hundred and twenty people living in very close proximity, he would be busy, he knew.

Their cabin was long and narrow, with a single bed on one side, a wider bed on the other side, and an attached bedside table between the beds. There was no window, nor were there any adornments on the walls, just recessed lights. At the end of the wider bed there was a wardrobe and cupboard space, and at the end of the single bed there was what looked like a large cupboard, built diagonally into the corner of the room, except that it wasn't a cupboard. It was a tiny shower room with a toilet and basin. The shower head hung from the ceiling, and the whole room became wet when it was turned on, so it was important to lower the toilet lid whilst the shower was on.

He had followed her into the cabin, so he didn't at first see the expression on her face. He just saw it reflected in the sudden tautness of her body. But in the centre of the tiny cabin, between the beds, she'd turned to look at him, and then he'd seen the look of horror on her face. "Tell me again how long this trip will take."

"Ten months or so. You'll get used to it, Miri-Ani. I promise."

"That's easy for you to say. You don't suffer from claustrophobia. Won't you feel cramped in here?"

"Rangers, by necessity, can go without. We can sleep anywhere, comfortably. No, I won't be cramped. We won't be in here for much of the time. We'll only sleep here."

"Yeah, right," she said softly as she looked around the tiny room, sounding doubtful. "Well," she said, sitting heavily on the single bed, sounding utterly dejected, "you'd better have the bigger bed. You're taller than I am. I'll have this one." She patted the bed beside her.

He sat opposite her and took her hands in his own. "It won't be so bad, Miri-Ani. You will get used to it. You'll have to trust me on that."

She nodded.

He dropped her hands. In an attempt to distract her, he gave her some practical facts about the ship and the trip they had begun to make.

"We will be simulating day and night," he told her. "At the same time every 'night', the lights will be turned off. And over the course of the journey, we'll gradually adjust the simulation to help us transition from a Mallonian day to a Gaian day."

"To do that," she responded, "the lights on the ship will need to emit infra red and ultra violet as well as white light ..."

"And so they do," he said, smiling at her affectionately. She was, he thought, just like Isaiah in that way, knowing much about much. "They would like you to conduct meditation classes to help keep the people calm and focussed."

"That could be problematic," she said, "given the fact that I don't meditate ... at all. I'll let Kobi know. He's very good at that sort of thing. He'll take your classes for you. I'd prefer to work with Mischa and the other healers … if," she drew out the word, "you insist on having me do something practical."

He smiled, caught out, because he did, indeed, want her to do something practical. She would need it in the months ahead.

"Do you want me to explain how they'll recycle the water," he asked her, "or create oxygen and filter out the carbon dioxide, or harness the sun's energy to power the ship, or feed over five hundred people for ten months?"

She shook her head. "No, best I don't know about all that. That's just too many systems that can malfunction. So long as we don't suffocate, I'm happy to let everything else take care of itself."

"We won't suffocate. You have my word on that. All right then," he said as he stood, extending his hand towards her to help her to her feet. "The captain has asked us to join him on the viewing deck. Would you like to watch the ship leave its dock?"

She nodded slowly and, also slowly, reached up a hand to take his. He knew, then, she was already starting to retreat into that place within which she became inaccessible. He hoped she wouldn't become irretrievable because reaching in to pull her back out, he knew from very personal experience, was an inordinately difficult endeavour.

Only time would tell him if he would be required to bring her back or if she would find a way to stay with them all without help from him.

~

Jerone opened the door of their cabin, not at all surprised when he found it empty. Earlier, they had been eating dinner in the dining room, but he had been called away to deal with an emergency. A fight had broken out between two men on one of the lower decks, and it had taken all his strength and skill as a Ranger to pull them apart. With Rodhi's help, one of the other Rangers on board the ship, he had put both men into makeshift brigs, cellars in actuality. When one of the men had protested, claiming he hadn't started the fight, Jerone had lost his temper, something he never did.

"You do know what we're doing here, right?" he yelled at the man. "We are the hope and the future of our people. So what hope do we really have when the likes of you can't control yourself enough to stop throwing punches, and disturbing and upsetting everyone else around you? You may not have started the fight, my friend, but you certainly kept it going." And then he'd done something utterly uncharacteristic of him. He'd strode forward, grabbed the man by the front of his tunic, hauled him to his feet, and pulled him close so that their faces were inches from each other. "You're not worthy to be on this ship," he said. Then he'd thrown the man backwards so that the man staggered.

Half disgusted with himself and half disgusted with the behaviour of the two who had fought, he'd stormed out of the store room.

"Lock it," he told Rodhi. "They stay in these rooms for twelve hours. That should give them enough time to cool off."

Rodhi nodded his consent, in complete agreement.

As Jerone walked away from the situation, he knew why his tolerance was all but non-existent. He knew why he'd exploded. He was worried about her. Determined to give her the time and space he knew she needed, he'd left her alone, resisting the need to apply the pressure necessary to bring her back to him. But she was showing no signs of coming back to him. Instead, she was quiet, withdrawn, and she had about her that eerie stillness she got when she was in that inaccessible place within. And, she wore her sadness like a thick, heavy cloak. He had not, as he'd suspected, seen her smile again after she'd smiled at the captain the day the ship had left its docking station.

When he found the cabin empty, he knew where she'd be. At the top of the ship, there was a small viewing area, like a small lounge room. No one used it. No one went there because there was nothing to see except the dark vastness of space. She went there, he knew, not for the view, but for the solitude.

When he ascended the spiral staircase to the small lounge room, she was, indeed, there, sitting sideways on the lounge with one foot tucked under the other knee. Her elbow was resting on the back of the lounge, and her fingers were curled under her chin as she looked out at the vast blackness of space. He knew she wasn't seeing the darkness, though.

"Miri-Ani," he said softly so as not to startle her, "they're about to turn the lights out."

She shifted. "All right."

As she followed him through the ship to their cabin, she asked him, "Did you sort out your emergency?"

He didn't answer her.

"Jerone?"

At the cabin, he slid the door open and stood back so she could precede him into it. She glanced at him as she stepped through the door and knew he was upset. He was tight-lipped with tension. She'd rarely, if ever, seen him this tense. Breathing deeply when she was in the room, she turned to him. She knew exactly what it was he feared.

"I'm sorry," she said, as he slid the door shut behind them.

"I could've killed one of those men tonight, Miri-Ani. I lost control. He's damn lucky I didn't hurt him any more than I did."

"What did you say to him?"

He frowned at her. "Say? It's not what I said ..."

"I know. You hurt him. I know. But you said something, too. What did you say?"

He raked a hand through his hair which had partially come loose in the skirmish with the two fighters. "I told him he wasn't worthy to be on the ship ... well, really, to be the hope and the future of our people."

"You were right. Perhaps we should just eject the two of them here and now, send them out into space."

He folded his arms as he looked at her, trying to assess whether or not she was joking. She decided to help him out.

"Unfortunately, I'm only partly joking. I wish I was completely joking, but I'm not. It is as well I am not in charge ..."

He moved, then, to pull her against him because she had signalled her willingness to let him back in, and he could feel her receptiveness. "You blame them ... us for what is happening?" he asked her.

"No," she said against him, wrapping her arms around him, allowing herself the luxury of absorbing his warmth and his strength. "And yes. What would humans really be like if they were left alone? Really, Jerone. What would humans be like if the Si'il didn't manage to get their claws into them so easily? They would fight, yes. Those men proved that tonight. But would humans go to war if left alone? Would they so easily and effortlessly pump pollutants into the atmosphere of their planet, the very thing that gives them life? Would they just stand by apathetically while their planet is utterly destroyed?" She pulled back so she could look at him. "Are they worth saving?"

"I don't know."

"You don't? Aren't you supposed to reassure me that we've done the right thing in sending our people to Gaia thereby ensuring us a future?"

He lifted a strand of her hair in his fingers. "I wish I could. Is this what you've been thinking of late?"

"One of many things. But, yes, I have been thinking about it a lot of late."

They looked at each other in silence. He wished he could take some of those thoughts from her, but her incredible mind was one of the things he loved about her.

"Tonight, will you hold me?" she asked him. "Can I sleep in your bed, with you?"

He didn't hesitate. "Of course."

"You won't lose me, Jerone," she said against him much later when they were both lying together in his bed, she with her head against his chest, he with his arms around her. "I know that is what you fear. That is why you became angry tonight."

The Altiran priesthood, in living on Altira, had withdrawn from Mallonian and, therefore, human society. They were known to be pure in that sense – pure in terms of what they put into their bodies: air, water, and food; pure of thought and belief; pure in their interactions with others; pure of intent; and pure of deed and action. But they were not necessarily celibate. Or, rather, celibacy was not demanded of them, nor was it a requirement of being a part of the priesthood. Sex was not considered impure. On the contrary, if they found the right partner, sex was important to them. But sex, to them, was also highly sacred, and given the fact that they had withdrawn from normal human life, the opportunities to have sex were rare. If a priest or priestess was to have sex with someone who did not understand the sacredness of the connection involved, this was recognised to be a violation of the sacredness and sanctity of it. No priest or priestess would violate the sacredness of sex in this way. Despite their love for each other, Jerone and Miri-Ani had never made love, and, in fact, over the years they'd known each other, he had rarely touched her and never sexually. Tenderly, maybe, affectionately, too, but never sexually. He held her beliefs and her choice and her calling as a priestess as sacred as did she. He would never have violated or dishonoured her by instigating sex between them.

"Yes," he said, responding to her statements about his fear of losing her. "I am afraid of that. What are you afraid of?"

"I'm afraid of what and of how much I will have to invest in this new colony. I am afraid it will drain me, require more of me than I have to give. And I am afraid it will pull me away from myself. On Altira, we were withdrawn from human society, although they could join us when and if they wanted or needed to do so. But they did so on our terms. In the new colony, I will be immersed in the society, not aloof from it, and I am afraid of that. I am afraid of what it will cost me."

"The priesthood will protect you, Miri-Ani. They will shield you ..."

"I'm not sure they will be able to. I'm not even sure they should."

"They should. You are their heart. They must ensure you have the energy to keep the priesthood's heart beating as it should."

"Mmm, maybe."

They fell silent, both thinking, and then she broke it.

"I want us to marry."

A long moment of utter shock filled the cabin with a stunned silence, and then he moved, reaching up to turn the light on over his bed so he could look at her for this conversation. Initially, she was forced to shield her eyes from the light with a hand while she adjusted to the sudden change from darkness to light.

He propped his head on his hand so he could look down at her, and he laid a hand across her waist.

"I am a Ranger, and you are a priestess ..." he started to say.

"So what? You are also a man, and I am a woman. We are making this journey together, Jerone. I mean, look at us. We're even sharing a bed. Marriage would just make official what already is in actuality. Marriage is the truth of what we are. Can you deny it?"

"No. Of course I cannot deny it. Nor would I want to."

"As for sex," she said, correctly reading his mind, and his concerns, "we can either stay as we are or we can change our relationship. Marriage will make no difference to us in that sense. Either we can be as we've always been, or we can become lovers and be married properly. That is entirely your choice."

"Why is it my choice?"

"Because sex would bring me down off the pedestal you have me on. I am ethereal to you, like a goddess. If you don't want to change that, I will understand, and I will honour your choice."

"As an Altiran priestess, you are untouchable ..."

"I am no longer an Altiran priestess."

Of all the things she had done and said recently, none concerned him as much as that one simple statement. "Miri-Ani ..."

"I am not losing my mind, Jerone. The moment we left Altira, we were all no longer of the Altiran priesthood. I will always be a priestess. That will not change. 'Tis who and what I am. But the priesthood must change and adapt now, as we all must, every soul on board this ship. What we will become, the priesthood, I mean, I do not know. I just know we have to let go of what we were and move into our future, embrace it with open and flexible minds."

"Is this why you want to marry?"

"No. I want us to marry because it is the truth of what we are. We are in this," she waved her hand to indicate the ship, "whole new experience together. We chose that. But if the priesthood must change, then so, too, must you and I change. Everything is different now. Everything."

Silence fell between them again while he processed all that she had said.

"Well," he said eventually, "you really have been thinking. Why have you not talked to me about any of this before now?"

"Because I didn't want to burden you. You have a significant responsibility keeping order on the ship. I didn't want to distract you."

"You are my priority, Miri-Ani. I am here, first and foremost, for you. Never forget that. If we are to move into our new future, as you put it, then you must know that."

"All right, I will remember. So, will you marry me?"

"Absolutely."

"And are we to be lovers or ... ?"

He smiled at her as he leaned forward to do what he had wanted to do for more years than he cared to count. He kissed her – their first kiss. She reached up to curl her hand around his neck as she kissed him back.

~

They stood, again, hand in hand, on the captain's viewing platform, watching as a new and different planet gradually filled the window in front of them.

"Dear Lady," she breathed. "It is beautiful. Isaiah was right. It is not so different from Altira … perhaps a little more blue."

This new planet was, indeed, beautiful. And she was, indeed, blue. Gaia was blue when seen from space, and she shone in space like a blue gem.

"If only he was here to see this," she whispered to Jerone.

"He knows," he said back. "He saw it in his own visions. And I suspect he will see it for himself, up close and personal, one day."

She laughed softly. "I suspect you're right, my love. He wouldn't let an opportunity like that pass him by."

Jerone didn't respond verbally, but he smiled his agreement as he absorbed her soft laugh. In that moment, that fraction of an instant, he knew she would be all right, and he knew they would make it through whatever it was they were about to experience. They were together, and together they could and would survive anything. He knew, too, that her strength and Wisdom, fortified by his, and her sight and insight, would lead the Altiran priesthood into its new future, allowing it to take shape anew, and as it did so, it would become, again, the strong heartbeat of a new culture, a new community, the new colony … the new hope for humanity itself.

~

4

An Addendum

Adaptations and Adjustments

Do you think humans can just move to a whole different planet and continue to live as they always have? They cannot. There are many deep, powerful, profound physical and psychological adjustments to be made. The new planet will be of a vastly different size, in this case smaller, with different gravitational effects on the human body. It will be of a different energetic make-up, and different energies will surround, penetrate and affect it. The new planet will have a different atmosphere, with a different oxygen content. And the sun's light will affect it differently, particularly in this case where Gaia (earth) is so much closer to the sun than Mallona was. The new planet will have a different rotational spin on its axis and, thus, will have a different length of day and night, and it will also have different lunar months. In this case, Gaia has one moon whereas Mallona had at least three, possibly more, so the gravitational effects and the energies surrounding Gaia would have been vastly different from that of Mallona for this reason alone. The new planet will also have a different year because its orbit around the sun will be of a different length. Mallona's year, in fact, was much, much longer than that of Gaia, as was the segmented time periods that broke up the year – we call them months – so this was, in itself, a significant adjustment. And because the years of both planets will be so different, the seasons will be different, too. The water on the new planet will be different, as will its soil, and so will its native flora and fauna be different.

As is always the case when such adaptations and adjustments must be made, some souls in the new colony adjusted to the new planet quickly, some more slowly. Some souls adapted easily, and for some, the process was difficult. Some became ill, both physically and psychologically, and some avoided illness altogether. The important thing was that very few souls were lost in the adjustment process. The colony already established on Gaia helped the adaptation process enormously. The many pioneering souls who were a part of the already-established colony were living proof, after all, that Mallonians *could* adapt to this new planet. As such, the colony of Mallonians survived the initial transportation and colonisation process.

How many transports made it to Gaia, and how many were destroyed en route? I do not know. What I do know is that many transports did make it to Gaia, many more were destroyed in transit, and many more never left Mallona. So, the colony already established on Gaia many aeons earlier increased suddenly and significantly, and sizeably. As such, there were, obviously, many more adjustments to be made than that of coming to terms with being on an entirely new planet. The cesspool of emotions generated in the newcomers by the sweeping changes they were making and by the knowledge those left behind were doomed and would never be seen again meant that, for a little while at least, there was a certain degree of volatility simmering just below the surface of the colony – a volatility that erupted all-too-easily initially. As you can probably appreciate, then, the Rangers were an important and completely necessary part of the physical and psychological adjustment process in the colony itself. I know Jerone worked to maintain order for many decades, so much so that it tired him, drained him. He gave much, and he passed, or died, long before Miri-Ani did, even though she, too, gave much. He went, or left her, reluctantly and could not do so without her permission. He also made sure she would be looked after in his absence. It was the captain of their transport who replaced him as Miri-Ani's companion and confidante.

But so, too, was the priesthood important, or vital, actually, in helping the Mallonians adapt to their new environment. Well versed in human psychology and very knowledgeable in handling the psychological wounds that were bound to surface in such extreme circumstances, the priesthood was an integral, vital part of the process of adaptation and adjustment. Furthermore, the priesthood was properly equipped to help the Mallonians come to terms with what was about to happen to their home planet, *and* they were a vital link to Mallona's past and its culture, its soul. Isaiah was right in ensuring the priesthood was well represented in the new colony.

The Explosion

Effectively turned into a virtual, giant bomb by the interference with its core, possibly a nuclear one, Mallona's destruction lit up the sky like a sun. The light from the explosion would not have reached Gaia straight away, but, still, many of the ancients who lived on Gaia at the time witnessed a 'sun' appearing in the ancient sky, lighting it up, albeit briefly. Some of the myths from the ancient world speak of it.

The Romans had their own name for Mallona. They called it Phaethon, and they told of the legend of Phaethon who, on discovering he was the son of Helios, the sun, sought out his father and asked him a boon. Phaethon wished to guide the solar chariot for a day, and his father, unable to deny him, granted him his wish. But, too weak to handle the chariot and its immortal horses, they bolted and he lost control of the chariot, threatening to set the whole world on fire, until Zeus (Jupiter) killed him with a lightening bolt. Jupiter, the planet, did, indeed, play a vital role in protecting the solar system when Mallona exploded. Phaethon fell into the Eridanus, a mythical river, where his sisters gathered his body and mourned him. As already stated, the explosion of Mallona did, indeed, rival the sun, at least temporarily, hence the legend of Phaethon and his misguided attempt to drive the solar chariot. So, the ancients, even in our time, knew of Mallona. It is only us, in the modern era, who have lost the knowledge of the planet that once existed where now the asteroid belt exists. And, of course, with the knowledge of Mallona itself lost, so, too, is the knowledge of the lesson of Mallona's tragic destruction lost.

The colonists, of course, knew where Mallona was in the night sky. Knowing where their home planet was in the sky was an essential way of still being connected to it, even if that connection was tenuous at best. So, they watched it constantly, tracking its movements through the sky. You do not need much of an imagination to understand and recognise the unadulterated horror that rippled through the community when the explosion occurred. Watching an entire planet explode into non-existence would be enough to send chills into the depths of one's psyche anyway because we think of the planets as being timeless and indestructible. They are the enduring stalwarts of our solar system. But with the explosion, the lives of billions and billions of people were snuffed out at once. Remember our horror as we watched the unfolding events of September 11, watching the twin towers of the World Trade Centre collapse, knowing people were still inside them? So how much more so would we feel the horror of watching billions die at once – billions and billions of lives snuffed out in a heartbeat – and watching the planet we had once called home disintegrate into nothingness? Wouldn't that little part of the sky where once Mallona could be seen become deeply, darkly, tragically empty?

Cataclysmic Events in our Solar System

When Mallona exploded, the explosion sent shrapnel and debris out through the entire solar system, wreaking havoc as it did so. But it also sent an unimaginable shock wave of powerful energy through the entire solar system. We take our solar system completely for granted, thinking the way it is now is the way it's always been. But this is not so. There have been changes and upheavals over its long life, and the explosion of Mallona was one such upheaval.

As per its very valuable and unique function in the solar system, Jupiter absorbed much of the explosion, as well as significant pieces of the exploded planet, and it is very possible, even probable that, to this very day, it bears the scar in the form of a giant red spot. Very possibly, a sizeable fragment of the exploded planet collided with one of Saturn's moons, and the consequent debris from that smaller explosion is still in evidence today in the form of Saturn's giant rings. At some point, Neptune and Uranus have possibly swapped moons, and both planets have rings of their own, very possibly fragments of an exploded or disintegrated satellite or satellites.

Again, we take the planets in existence now and their satellites for granted. But the truth is, planets have become moons, and moons have become planets over the long life of our solar system. Astronomers will tell you that many of the moons that orbit Jupiter, Saturn and Uranus are large enough to be small planets. But there are other signs and symptoms of upheaval in the solar system, too. Uranus is so titled on its axis that it virtually spins on its side. And it is very possible that Jupiter, too, has caught moons that did not originally orbit it. Jupiter, Saturn and Uranus all have moons that have, at some point, been forced into retro orbit. There is also a large entity orbiting the sun between Saturn and Uranus, large enough to be a moon, possibly ripped from either of the two planets. Pluto and its satellite were most probably both moons of Neptune, both thrown out of orbit to take their place in the Circle of Nine, but it is also very possible that Pluto is a piece of Mallona, hurled into the orbit of a comet but trapped within our solar system as a planet … sort of. There is, of course, much debate about whether Pluto should be classified as a planet, and those who argue against this seem to be winning the debate. And these are just a few of the anomalies in our solar system. There are also anomalies in the orbits of various ones of the planets, in the tilt of their axes, in their rotational spins, and in the orbits and rotations of their satellites.

Whether or not the explosion of Mallona is responsible for all of this, we cannot know. There is another known but officially unrecognised explanation for some of the catastrophic changes and upheavals in our solar system, particularly among the outer planets, in the form of a visiting planet (an intruder) – one that exists in separation from a sun of its own but is caught between two solar systems, our solar system being one. Unlike the planets that belong in this solar system, the intruder's orbit is extremely elliptical. As to its orbital time frame, there are many theories abounding, the shortest of which is 3,800 years or so, and the longest of which is between 10,000 and 20,000 years. However long its orbital time frame actually is, its periodic intrusion into our solar system would be enough to bring about the dramatic, cataclysmic changes and perturbations I've barely touched on here, especially where the outer planets are concerned, as I said. I believe the intruder's course through our solar system is responsible for the explosion of an outer planet, beyond Pluto, and probably the disarray where the anomalous characteristics of the planets and the various and numerous satellites are concerned. Imagine the gravitational effects of a fairly large entity entering our solar system and orbiting close to our sun, between Jupiter and Mars, and then making its way out again. The gravitational effects of a sizeable entity entering and then leaving our solar system would definitely result in the disarray already described, especially if the outer planets are anywhere near it when it passes through, as they obviously have been at one point or more. Apparently, according to some, the last time it entered our solar system was, very probably, approximately two thousand years ago, when ancient Chinese astronomers recorded the presence of a new bright star in the sky – the same star that no doubt caught the attention of three mythical wise men .... except that the three wise men in the Jesus myth didn't exist physically, being an inherent aspect, as they were, of a myth that encodes the knowledge of the three stars of Orion's belt. Oh well. Such is the inherent gullibility of the human psyche.

So, although this intruder is probably responsible for much of the upheaval in our solar system, it is not responsible for all of it, and it was not responsible for the explosion of Mallona, although it was responsible for upheavals on Mallona – one of the reasons they were monitoring Mallona's core. I know that Mallona suffered upheavals of its own before its untimely demise because those upheavals left their mark on the planet, one in particular that I can see very clearly, a massive fault line in its ancient red desert, probably because whatever caused this fault line was responsible for the destruction of the earlier culture I referred to in the previous story, the one that was the source of the scrolls and parchments Jade was translating. I strongly suspect those upheavals were caused by this visiting planet which passes between Jupiter and, now, Mars on its way through our solar system, as I said, and so would have passed very close to Mallona on its way through the solar system, on many occasions, particularly if Mallona was on the same side of the sun when the intruder (Nebiru) passed through. The intruder disturbed Mallona and Mallonians many, many times ... in more ways than one, unfortunately.

Of one thing we can be certain. The shock wave from the explosion of Mallona would have applied enough force to cause at least some of the upheavals and changes referred to above. Furthermore, it is fast becoming a recognised and acknowledged truth among astronomers that the explosion of Mallona did not just result in the asteroid belt that orbits the sun between Mars and Jupiter, it was also the source of the short-period orbiting comets that periodically visit our solar system (long-period orbiting comets have at least two other sources, and I wonder if the gravitational disturbance from the intruder is one cause of them being dislodged from those sources and being sent into our solar system). Short-period orbiting comets and asteroids have a common point of origin in the place where Mallona used to be. I will return to this point because it is important and still has ramifications for humans to this very day.

Altira, Mars, and the Circle of Nine

And so, Altira was, indeed, flung out of her orbit around her parent, as Miri-Ani foresaw, thence to find a new orbit of her own around the sun, taking her place in the Circle of Nine. The Circle of Nine – nine entities orbiting our central sun in steady, constant, near-circular orbits – is sacrosanct for reasons I won't delve into here, those reasons being higher-dimensional and, thus, beyond the understanding and frame of reference of most modern humans. Suffice it to say, there must always be nine entities orbiting our sun, just as there must always be the same number of electrons circling the nucleus of an atom as there are protons in that nucleus for that atom to be stable, for it to be what it is, and for it to be in balance. And, contrary to popular opinion, gravity is not the only force that holds the planets in their orbits. Far from it.

But Miri-Ani's beautiful little moon did, indeed, pay a high price for her place in the Circle of Nine. Her face and her innate energy, or essence, were irrevocably changed. She all but lost her atmosphere and became the small red planet we now call Mars. She very nearly exploded herself, becoming fragmented, courtesy of three large pieces of Mallona that she holds within herself even to this day. She held together, though, by some miracle, although a large fracture on her surface shows us just how close she came to no longer existing at all.

I believe her two moons, Phobos and Deimos, are tiny fragments of the exploded planet that became caught in the orbit of the new planet, Mars, instead of taking their place in the asteroid belt.

Despite losing her atmosphere, and with it, her beautiful forests, streams and rivers, there are still remnants of Mallonian civilisation visible on her surface. NASA can deny the existence of that evidence all it likes, but I know the truth because I have lived it. Let me ask you this. Why send probes and robotic cameras out into the solar system and beyond if you have no intention of finding and reporting the truth? If it is not truth you seek, then you must be spending billions of dollars on perpetuating deception, must you not? Nature, contrary to NASA's assertions, does not make perfect five-sided pyramids. Nor does Nature make perfectly-straight geometrical structures that are the remnants of old buildings. And the face that stares out at us across space, reported to have a tear coming from one eye, is not a trick of light and shadow, but rather a means of communicating a powerful message and warning across time and space: be warned, do not ever allow yourselves to be in the same situation again. Do not ever bring upon yourselves such utter destruction again.

The Warning Ignored

And yet, here we are, in the same place, again. While we sit glued to our phones, ipads, computers and television sets, what is being done to us and what is being done to our planet? We will not help her because we are crippled with ignorance and apathy, just as we were on Mallona in the period right before its destruction. Billions of people perished in the destruction of Mallona, nearly all of whom had no idea the destruction was coming. They were so inert, courtesy of their apathy and ignorance, they had no idea of the brutal rape of the very planet that sustained them. And, yet, as I said, here we are again. So, we force Gaia to protect herself from us. And why wouldn't she? She knows what we did to an entire planet, and she knows there is real danger we will do the same to her. She's right because we **are** doing the same to her.

When I first wrote this, at the true beginning of 2016 (April), there were three earth quakes in less than two weeks at various points around the globe, and as the years since have progressed, I have watched more and more natural events take human lives, and that includes the erratic and extreme weather events we are experiencing right now. Three years later, I am watching with interest as volcanoes erupt all over the globe, particularly in the Ring of Fire. Wildfires, too, are raging out of control in five countries even as I write this, and there has just been a powerful earthquake, and consequent liquefaction, in Indonesia. I can tell you we humans are in for a rough time ahead. There is a Process of massive change occurring now that will force us to awaken to certain truths. And there is an event ahead – a regeneration of this earth and its magnetic field – that Gaia is already preparing for. I hope this event causes us, those of us who survive it, to re-prioritise. It will, certainly, give us a clean slate. The question is, what will we do with that clean slate? End up in the same place yet again?

Time and Dimensionality

We humans have no ability to perceive time as time actually is. In fact, I would go so far as to say, we do not understand it at all because we are locked into a mindset that simply does not, in any way, allow us to know the truth. We flatten time out like a piece of ironed fabric or a giant piece of string laid flat with an end and a beginning – linear time, we call it. And, in flattening out time, we do two things to it that dramatically distort our perspective of it. First, we distort it, and second, we separate it from space when, in fact, time and space cannot and should not be teased apart. Have you heard of the space-time continuum? Time is anything but flat. Time is also not constant, nor is it separate, and time does not just move forward in a single straight line. Our obsession with linear time is linked to our belief in aging, to our very great detriment. Rather than time being flat and uni-directional, space-time, as it should be called, cycles – cycles within cycles within cycles. The shortest cycles we're very familiar with: the cycle of day and night as the earth spins on its axis, the cycles of the lunar months as the moon waxes and wanes, the cycles of the seasons and the harvest as the earth orbits the sun. But there are, of course, much larger and longer cycles involving the constellations of the zodiac, the solar system, and the galaxy. These are thousands and millions of years in duration.

At any point in 'time', the earth is at a place relative to the sun and the galaxy where she may have been already, such that if we opened a small tear in the fabric of space-time and took a single step through it, we could find ourselves at a place we would consider to be thousands or millions of years in the past, or thousands or millions of years in the future. To conceptualise this, think of a flat piece of paper. Now, roll the paper over itself so that its opposite corners touch, one corner on top of the other, and then put a small tear through the paper in the place where it touches itself, and there you have an idea of what I'm talking about. Makes for interesting theories in relation to travel in space, and travel 'through time', does it not? If we could fold space, we could leap-frog vast epochs of time.

Furthermore, and perhaps more significantly, humans do not realise that the consequences of their choices and actions ripple out in all directions of time. Thus, we are being affected now by choices we will make in our future, not just those we've made in our past. We *are* affected now by choices we've made in all directions of time, and this, of course, transcends single lifetimes. And, yet, humans make their choices with such little thought and almost no consideration of the consequences. You might want to consider the truth of this when next you make a significant choice.

And, then, of course, there are multiple dimensions. Once you bring dimensionality into the equation, the concept of flattened, linear time becomes not just laughable but ludicrous, such is human ignorance. Actually, dimensionality has such an effect on 'linear' time that it tends to get all tangled up, like an entangled ball of yarn. Dimensions are like different facets of a perfectly-cut jewel. But humans are, now, locked into a single dimension, a severely limited dimension that informs human perspective (one of the reasons why it is laughable that we spend billions of dollars attempting to find life on other planets when we are, quite simply, not capable of seeing it at all). How do you think it's possible to see the whole jewel if you are trapped in only one of its facets? You will, and you do, mistakenly believe the facet you exist in is all there is.

To use another analogy, the human predicament in relation to dimensionality can be likened to looking up at the awesome magnificence of Michelangelo's painting on the ceiling of the Sistine Chapel but being able to see only one shade, or hue, of green. What, then, of your ability to take in the whole – to see its beauty and understand it, to absorb its meaning and its message, and to appreciate the awesome talent of Michelangelo? What, then, of your ability to see the use of and the intermingling of all the different colours and shades and hues, the subtleties of light and shadow depicted in those intermingling colours, and, of course, to perceive and appreciate the depth Michelangelo was able to achieve on a flat surface? All you would be able to perceive is a flat painting on a flat surface. It would be and is impossible for you to see any more of either the painting or the whole jewel of dimensionality, and to experience the whole, and to know that the whole is, in fact, so much more than you could ever have imagined.

But even the analogy of the jewel fails when you understand that dimensions are anything but flat, and nor are they straight. Nor do they sit beside each other, nicely and neatly, as facets of a jewel do, and nor do they sit on top of each other, layered like the twenty mattresses in the old fairy tale "*The Princess and the Pea*". They curve, they interweave and interact and intersect, they touch, they twist and turn, they are a part of each other, they are within each other. And guess what? Humans are not of one dimension. They are merely *trapped* in one dimension. Human consciousness is multi-dimensional, and the reason humans are trapped in one dimension is because they are trapped in the most shallow layer of consciousness – the conscious awareness – and have been deliberately severed from the other dimensions of their own consciousness. To reconnect with and access those other dimensions that comprise us we have but to reach within ... deep, deep within – the very place humans are absolutely terrified to go.

Humans think the way they are now is the way they've always been. So, what if, for example, I told you the sexes were not always separate? In the very beginning of the materialisation that is the human experience, individuals were both genders, male and female, in the one body, and to a certain extent, they still are. Over the aeons of its existence, the human experience has changed, beyond recognition, actually. And so, the human experience, as it existed on Mallona, was both similar to and very different from current human existence. Mallonians were different, dimensionally, and, of course, they were not in any way constrained by the misguided belief that life existed only on their own planet. They of the darkness were working hard to turn Mallonians into something that resembles current human experience, but it was *not* so at that time. Humans were in the process of falling, but they hadn't quite got to the point they are now, although there was, at the time of Mallona's destruction, a powerful and profound schism in the human experience, between those who still walked in and served the Light and those who walked in and cavorted with the Darkness.

So, courtesy of our ignorance of dimensionality and our very unfortunate penchant for flattening out time, we think the destruction of Mallona occurred 3.2 million years ago, (ironic, do you not think, that the number of estimated stone blocks in the Great Pyramid number 2.3 million? And why, do you think, did the architects of the Great Pyramid reverse the 3.2 into 2.3? Could it have something to do with the fact that we exist inside-out ... or outside-in? Or with the fact that physicality and metaphysicality are inversions of each other?), and we think the event that wiped out the dinosaurs occurred 65 million years ago. Obviously, these were separate events, occurring at different places in the space-time continuum so that the one occurred 'after' the other, seemingly, particularly from our vantage point here on earth. But given the cyclical nature of time, and the convolution of dimensionality, it is entirely possible the events were reversed in the order in which we believe they actually occurred. I'm not saying they <u>were</u> reversed, I'm saying it's possible given the true nature of space-time. Such **is** the nature of space-time, and such is our ignorance where space-time is concerned. We do know that we and the dinosaurs did not co-exist, and we do know we have found remnants of them, so it is obvious these events were not reversed. Instead of asking the question of when the destruction of Mallona occurred, perhaps it would be better to ask *where were we in the space-time continuum relative to where we are now*. Either way, if we accept the convoluted idea of linear time, then humans have walked upon this earth for over three million years. What does that do to the orthodox theories of human evolvement on this planet?

Time itself has actually been split into two in the modern era – nature's time and man-made time. The end of one year and the beginning of the next according to man's year (December 31st and January 1st) do not in any way coincide with the end and beginning of nature's year (currently April 18th and April 19th or thereabouts), nor do man's months in any way coincide with nature's months. In fact, man's months and years are fixed and inflexible whereas the times of nature's months and years move and alter and are fluid courtesy of the powerful cycle of precession (known as Precession of the Equinoxes). And, just as there are thirteen cycles of the moon, so, too, are there thirteen months in nature's calendar, not twelve, just as there are thirteen, not twelve, constellations in the zodiac. The removal of the significance to us of the thirteenth is exactly the same principle or concept of removing the capstone of the Great Pyramid – it facilitates Separation. And, of course, the official beginnings of our seasons do not in any way coincide with nature's markers of the changing seasons. But since our human bodies naturally follow nature's cycles – our bodies being part of the fabric of nature itself here on earth – we are discordantly and harmfully out of sync with nature, and, therefore, with ourselves, courtesy of mentally adhering to the unnatural, man-made concept of time … merely one of many ways we are out of sync with nature to our own very great detriment. We are, for example, courtesy of being able to walk into a supermarket and buy food all year round, completely out of sync with the profound, fundamental, significantly-rhythmical cycle of the harvest.

Put another way, we are discordant within ourselves, body at odds with mind, mind set against body, courtesy of the harmfully ridiculous fabrications of our concept of time and its various sub-portions.

The Shock Wave and Gaia

As for Gaia (earth), she suffered upheavals of her own courtesy of the shock wave and the debris blown out into the solar system by the explosion of Mallona. Did Venus and Gaia swap places in the explosion? It's certainly possible – a possibility I would never discount. I do think it's possible Gaia was the second planet in our solar system when Mallona existed, although she was not as close to the sun as Venus is now, and I think Venus was either the third planet or she was a satellite of Mallona's. Did the force of the explosion send Venus so far out of her orbit that she and Gaia danced around each other temporarily, like children holding hands, leaning back and swinging around and around, then letting go of each other's hands so that they spin off, finding and settling into new orbits? It is very possible this did happen. Astronomers are beginning to believe Venus is a relative newcomer to our solar system. I think not. I think she has always been here, just in a different position, either as the third planet in the Circle of Nine or, perhaps even more likely, as I said, as another of Mallona's moons thrown out of its orbit to take its place in the Nine. But, then, she could also have been one of Jupiter's moons. I think it's also possible that one of Jupiter's large moons, Ganymede maybe, or Callisto or Io, was the third planet in our solar system when Mallona existed, and Mallona was the fourth, or vice versa. Thus, I think the explosion of Mallona threw Ganymede out of its orbit around the sun and into orbit around Jupiter, and I think Venus was thrown out of orbit around Mallona thence to take her place in the Circle of Nine. Both Venus and Mercury show very distinct signs of being battered by asteroids and debris on one side of them; that is, in one event. This would indicate to me Venus was, indeed, in the solar system when Mallona exploded.

Earth's atmosphere would have destroyed a lot of the asteroids and debris that impacted it in the explosion, protecting those on the surface of the planet from the smaller pieces of debris, but many larger pieces of the exploded planet would still have made it through, impacting the surface and causing massive upheavals on Earth – earthquakes, volcanic activity, tsunamis and tidal waves. And if Gaia and Venus did, indeed, dance around each other temporarily, the gravitational effects, particularly on the seas and oceans of the earth, would have been devastating for those on the planet. The gravitational effects of the Gaia/Venus dance would have pulled all the waters of the earth into a giant wave, and the release of those same waters would have caused massive floods and upheavals. Many of our ancient legends speak of extensive floods, and they speak of a destroyed entity in the sky or planet – a god, in other words – but we won't go into that here. Suffice it to say, for now, that the ancients, of course, knew about the existence of Mallona, and they knew about its complete and total destruction. As for the myriad of flood myths, they have another potential source, and I will discuss that in a moment.

Obviously, the new colony of Mallonians survived the upheavals on Gaia as well. The shock wave from the explosion would have taken a while to reach Gaia, longer than the light generated by the explosion, but it would have come, and it would have hit hard. And it would have been traumatic and difficult. But survive the colony did, and, eventually, the colony of Mallonians thrived to become the foundation for the new human race, or at least a vital part of it. Humanity's future was secured, at least back there.

Human DNA and Genetic Diversity

I have another question for you. Was, or is, many tens of thousands of people or thereabouts, or even double, triple or quadruple this number, enough to ensure the genetic diversity necessary for populating the entire planet of earth? Was this relatively small number enough to seed the human race as we know it today? Well, here we must delve into the realm of genetic tampering, splicing, fusing, merging. Also, you have to remember, there was a semi-indigenous species of upright beings already in existence on Gaia. These beings were highly adapted to conditions on earth, so parts of their DNA would have come in very handy. Did we interbreed with them? Very possibly, although I think not. But there has been a human/Neanderthal hybrid skull found, and we now know that humans living outside of Africa have approximately 2% of Neanderthal DNA in the make-up of their own genetic code. Apparently, Neanderthal DNA holds the alleles for straight hair and a propensity to put on weight (god damn!). Neanderthal beings became extinct around 30,000 BCE, and they only existed in very small numbers by this time, and in a very specific location – central Europe. But we've obviously carried parts of their DNA in ours for a very long time. So, if we didn't interbreed with them, how do we have a part of their DNA in ours?

Do you really think we 'walked out of Africa' as ape-like beings over two-hundred-thousand years ago and evolved into modern humans? Really? Even Charles Darwin himself knew that his theory of evolution could not explain how we came to be, nor how we came to be here. Evolution is, in actual fact, an extremely slow process (millions not hundreds of thousands of years), and there are just too many gaps in the evolutionary chain from the early ape-like beings to us as we are now. We are not genetically related to those early beings. And where do you think the allele for blue eyes came from? Did it just spring up out of nowhere, and then become so prevalent, despite being recessive? A ridiculous notion. No, Mallonians brought it to this planet. Prior to our arrival, there were no blue-eyed beings on this planet. Dare I say it, but the intermingling of Mallonian DNA and the near-amimalistic DNA of the beings who were already here has lowered human consciousness, reduced human intelligence, physically and transcendently, thereby facilitating the Separation – a Separated third- or lower-dimensional existence – that so characterises the human experience – the very reason humans cannot conceptualise dimensionality.

There has been significant and extensive tampering with human DNA over the aeons of our existence here on earth, and by both sides, those of the Light and those of the Dark. Those of the Light have 'seeded' human DNA; that is, they have intervened to raise it so that it is able to retain the Light of Knowledge (higher Knowledge). I believe the Jewish people were one such 'seeding'. It's one of the reasons why Jews have been so persecuted down through the ages, because those of the Darkness, and those who serve the Darkness, know that Jewish DNA is better able to hold the Light of higher Knowledge. Oops! Does that mean Jewish DNA is superior? Yes, I'm afraid it does. And well do those of the Darkness know this. But as humans in general, we are, in truth, much, much more intelligent than we seem to be. Or, rather, we are much more capable of holding the Light of Knowledge. But layers of our DNA have been rendered dormant and inactive so that we mistakenly believe we have only two layers, the two we can see when we put strands of human DNA under a powerful microscope. In truth, we have twelve (with a very high frequency thirteenth) layers of DNA. Our DNA has also been deliberately altered to drastically reduce our life spans. We are, or we should be, capable of living ten times longer than we do now.

And what can we do, really, with such short lifespans? In other words, why reduce human lifespans? Because with such short lives, we easily increase the burden of our karmic debt but do not so easily balance and resolve it. It is a whole lot more difficult to build on our intelligence and experience, but particularly our higher intelligence, when we live such short lives. In other words, our short lives are crippling us. Who would dare make such alterations to lower and reduce human intelligence and lifespan? Who would dare play 'God' in this way? The answer can be found in the story I have just told you – an inconceivable Darkness that gets its claws into humans over and over again, time and time and time again. That same Darkness has its claws into us now. That same Darkness has turned humans, again, into slaves and zombies, and the tampering with and altering of human DNA is only one of the many ways they have achieved this.

It is at this point that I will mention the Anunnaki, because it was, really, the Anunnaki who destroyed Mallona, with our help. Their planet has no sun (their planet is the intruder I referred to earlier) and so they desperately try to harness the energy of the sun and planets in our solar system. It was their interference with Mallona's core that triggered the catastrophic chain reaction that was the cause of Mallona's destruction. And it is they who have deliberately interfered with and altered human DNA, although they are, apparently, obsessive with preserving the purity of their own 'elite' bloodlines. I am not going to explain the Anunnaki to you. Many before me have already done so. Suffice it to say, they exist. They are here, and have been for a long, long time. They are real, and they think they are in control of the human experience and human affairs. I am not interested in the Anunnaki, so I will leave it to you to investigate the truth of them for yourselves. I am interested only in the Darkness they serve, and, in particular, the dark priests of Si'il, as I call them. For, you see, the Anunnaki are slaves to a higher power, just as they believe we are their slaves. They mock us and ridicule us and believe us to be very gullible, which we are, but, in truth, **they are naught but puppets with a proverbial hand up their proverbial asses,** and they are manipulated accordingly. In the new paradigm of human existence, there will be no place for them. And the very thing they so fear will come upon them, as per the nature of fear. They know it, and they are panicking, as well they should.

The question of whether or not there is life on planets other than our own is so ludicrous it indicates either a distinct lack of intelligence in any individual asking it or an incredibly small-minded perspective, or, more likely, both, which, tragically, perfectly sums up the human state. Even if you hold within you the moronic belief that life on this planet, for all its beautiful complexity and diversity, and the intricacy with which it intermingles, like a symphony, is naught but a fluke and freak of nature, how can you think, with the sheer vastness of the universe, and the trillions and trillions of suns and planets out there, that the same fluke and freak of nature hasn't occurred elsewhere? Statistically speaking, it's not just possible. If it happened here, it has happened elsewhere. As Carl Sagan put it so succinctly, if there isn't life out there, then it's an awfully big waste of space. But I know there is because I have seen it and lived among it, more than once. The Universe is absolutely teaming with life. Just because we are not capable of seeing it, locked in this limited dimension, and being manipulated, as we are, into thinking we are alone in the Universe, does not mean life is not there. It just means we can't see it or connect with it. My little aged fox terrier lost his sight and hearing in his old age, and so he used to (try to) confidently cross roads thinking that just because he couldn't see or hear them, the cars were not there. Of course, they *were* there. He simply had no ability to perceive them so *they didn't exist for him.* So, too, is it with humans in relation to the true nature of the Universe, the galaxy, and the solar system.

We humans hold the power within us to change the status quo, of course. First of all, we can simply open our eyes, and, while we're at it, our minds, and see and recognise how we're being manipulated. And then, we can begin to reconnect with and rediscover our own memories, because many of us here now had many incarnations on Mallona. Furthermore, human DNA is a truly remarkable thing, adaptable, flexible, able to be changed in direct response to our thoughts and beliefs.

So, to keep human DNA as it is, our thoughts and beliefs must also be kept as they are, imprisoned, trapped, contained, and controlled. Utterly stagnant. Food for thought. We are perfectly capable of bringing the other layers of our DNA out of dormancy. Perfectly capable ... although not, of course, while we exist in this apathy. But, how magnificent would we be if those other layers of our DNA were to be activated fully and properly? We can change this existence easily. The question is, will we? To do so, we will have to shake off our apathy because that, alone, is crippling us. And then we really have to address our chronic ignorance because *that* is causing us to be oh-so-easily manipulated.

Atlantis and Atlantean Cultures

In the modern era, Atlantis has become synonymous with the high culture, or the antediluvian civilisation, that existed prior to 10,800 BCE or thereabouts. It is possible that the culture at that time called itself Atlantis, but I do not think so. In the higher dimensions, we refer to the human reality as the 'Atlantean Reality', for good reason. 'Atlantis' is a very ancient word, from a very ancient language, and it refers to something very particular. Ironically, humans are, currently, living in Atlantis.

When humans were first created, it was definitely not with the intention that they fall so low and so completely into materiality – spirit taking form in matter – that they forgot, completely, their spiritual truth and origins. And, yet, that is exactly what has happened. Self-aggrandisement – the satiation of egoic want – and the obsessive pursuit of material things like wealth, power, eternal youth, status, fame, pleasure, and even immortality have caused spirit to fall so far and so low into materiality that many, many souls are, now, trapped by it. These souls are heavily weighed down and burdened by karmic obligation and imbalance, and they are burdened by chronic ignorance and Separation, and so, they cannot rise above the material existence, transcend and ascend back into spirit. *That* is Atlantis, or, that is exactly what Atlantis means, and *that* is an Atlantean culture: one that is utterly trapped in materiality, stagnating, Separated, caught up in shallow, material pursuits and priorities.

That an Atlantean culture fell so low into materiality that it cared not what it did to an entire planet ... that an Atlantean culture fell so low into materiality that it *destroyed* an entire planet horrified those of us in the higher dimensions. We saw what the soul-state of Atlantis, or, rather, the soul-*less* state of Atlantis, is truly capable of doing. Or, rather, we saw how utterly destructive Atlantis is. And so, with the destruction of Mallona, those on high who watch over the human experience determined that never again would an Atlantean culture be allowed to destroy a planet. In *Lady of the Lake*, I warn humans they will never again be allowed to destroy that which is not of their creation. And so, down through the aeons and aeons of human existence, as humans have risen again and again to great heights of culture and civilisation, they have also sunk, at the same time, to unimaginable depths of Atlantean existence. When this happens, to prevent them destroying the very thing that sustains them, *they* are destroyed instead, and in being destroyed, they are recalibrated, given a clean slate so that they may start again. And lesser destructions have, by necessity, occurred in between.

The last global destruction here on earth occurred in approximately 10,800 BCE or thereabouts. The evidence is mounting and scientists are fast realising and acknowledging that the high culture of Atlantis that existed at this time was destroyed in a cataclysm that resulted from multiple impacts of fragments of a sizeable comet*, or a stream of debris that orbits our sun and regularly crosses Gaia's orbital path*. The impacts hit at different locations in the northern hemisphere which was, at the time, largely buried under massive sheets of ice at the end of the recent great Ice Age. The temperatures involved in the string of these events caused melting of the ice sheets on an unimaginable scale, the result of which was flooding so vast and powerful that it has left its scars on the landscape even to this day. *This* is the source of the myriad of flood myths that abound and have been handed down to us from far older cultures. The truth of this cataclysmic event has been preserved in these ancient flood myths, the most well-known of which, courtesy of the Bible, is that of Noah and his ark, which is, itself, a slightly-altered Babylonian myth. The impact of these comet fragments plunged the earth into a deep freeze, akin to a nuclear winter, that lasted approximately 1,200 years. But with the sudden melting of the massive ice sheets, these impacts also caused sea levels to rise to such an extent that vast and very ancient cities – the cities of the antediluvian high culture and civilisation – were forever submerged, effectively removing them from the archaeological record. Without proof, therefore, it has been all-too-easy for those of the Darkness to remove the knowledge of our own history and, in particular, the Cycle of Recalibration, from the human psyche.

Unfortunately, humans also suffer from locked-in paradigms of thought, and this, too, prevents them from looking at old and new evidence with clear, unprejudiced eyes. The rigid paradigms of thought form set-in-stone theories or impenetrable boundaries beyond which no one treads, and this, unfortunately, applies to just about every field of research and exploration and science. Usually, it takes people possessed of incredible intelligence and enormous courage – people capable of looking and thinking 'outside the square' who also possess within themselves the wherewithal to withstand the ridicule and criticism that is, invariably, the consequence of going beyond the paradigms of thought. It was, for example, only four hundred years ago that Galileo was imprisoned for daring to suggest the earth orbited the sun. So, archaeologists, historians, geologists, etc. fit the evidence they find into the locked-in paradigms, and they see only what they expect to see, or, rather, they see only what they're *told* to see.

The Great Cycle of Recalibration

So what if I was to tell you that the asteroids, comets and debris thrown out into the solar system by the explosion of Mallona have been used to destroy these Atlantean cultures when necessary? Because so they have. Does that not take karma to a whole new level – the same karmic lesson repeated over and over and over again like a needle stuck on a broken record? The destruction of Mallona is still impacting humanity even to this day. Well, humans are now living, once again, in an Atlantean culture, and have, therefore, once again, reached that extreme point in their civilisation that necessitates cataclysmic destruction in order to recalibrate the human experience.

And, of course, the ancients did not just know about the *recent* cataclysm that caused the recalibration of the human experience, they also knew that the *recent* cataclysm was merely the last of a long, long string of them – merely one of many. This was, in fact, one of the important functions of the ancient priesthoods – to preserve this most crucial, most vital knowledge and to ensure it was made available to future generations. It serves, of course, as a warning, that same warning that is constantly and consistently ignored. Many priests and priestesses of the ancient world – those custodians of this ancient knowledge – are incarnate today to bring this knowledge back from the oblivion it has been deliberately consigned to. Are you attracted to the knowledge of the Cycle of Recalibration, or does the knowledge strongly resonate within you? Then perhaps you are one of these custodians, here to bring this knowledge back to humanity.

The Cosmic Clock of Precession

There is something else you should know. The Cycle of Precession, known as 'Precession of the Equinoxes', powerfully governs human existence. And the great cosmic clock of the Cycle of Precession is about to tick over, with one great Age of Precession – the Age of Pisces – being replaced by another – the Age of Aquarius. That humanity will soon be governed by an entirely different great Age of Precession is anything but insignificant. On the contrary, the human experience will look very different under the Age of Aquarius, but the changes and adaptations as one great Age is replaced by another are always expressed physically. This alone will have significant impacts on humanity, energetically and, therefore, physically, and, in fact, is already *beginning* to have significant impacts, even though we are only on the cusp of this great change.

But there's more. The Cycle of Procession is divided into two periods, or epochs, of approximately 13,000 years (or just under: 12,960 to be as precise as possible), and this aspect of the precessional cycle is more like a cosmic year such that it can be likened to the descent of the sun culminating in the winter solstice and the ascent of the sun culminating in the summer solstice of the annual earth year. (Although, it is the 'ascent' and 'descent', or, more precisely, the position in the sky, of the great constellation of Orion and his companion Sirius that is the true marker for the passing of these great epochs of time. This, the ancients knew well which is why they built a perfect reflection of the *whole* constellation of Orion on the ground in Egypt, of which the pyramids of the Giza Plateau form its belt. I would love to know what lies at the marker on the ground for Sirius. In fact, I believe the three stars in Orion's belt point to the 'hour' of the great cosmic precessional clock in the same way the little hand on a watch points to the hour. The big hand of the great clock, pointing to the 'minutes', is the sunrise at the vernal equinox in the northern hemisphere.) And this cycle with its two great epochs of time is associated with the Cycle of Recalibration. The current 12,960-year period following the last destruction of the last Atlantean culture is fast coming to an end, and the clock will, very soon, reach its zenith, rather like the extreme point a pendulum reaches before turning to swing back the other way. Humanity exists, now, in a convergence of the end of a number of significant cycles and epochs.

In short, humans are due for another cataclysmic destruction. Or, put another way, we have reached a point where cataclysmic destruction has, once again, become necessary, and the cycles of nature are supporting this. Time is up. For a long time I thought we were approaching the stroke of midnight. But Graham Hancock's work* has made me realise we are not approaching the stroke of midnight, we are *at* the stroke of midnight. This is it. I was born in it. Humans can change the need for a recalibration, of course, but will they? Will they? Humans themselves are simply not capable of changing, but there are many, many souls here now who, although incarnate *as* humans, are *not* human. These souls are powerful, and they are capable of causing significant transcendent shifts in human consciousness. These souls *are* capable of raising the collective consciousness of the human experience ... and so they will. But there are, too, many energies at play, now, also affecting human consciousness, and they are powerful enough that it has become impossible for human consciousness to stay as it is.

It is only now that we are beginning to remember the truth that we have reached these heights and depths before, although so many are paying no attention to the truth of it at all. It is only now that we are beginning to awaken to the truth that our history is not at all as we've been led to believe, although, again, many are resistant to this truth, reluctant to acknowledge it. The truth has been deliberately kept from us because the Darkness takes us again and again to this same point of utter destruction, and they do not want us to know the truth of that, just in case we decide we will do something about it this time.

The Lesson of Mallona and the Last Atlantis Lost

For me personally, I chose to survive the cataclysm that destroyed an entire planet and all-but-destroyed my beloved little moon. It was a promise I made, both to myself and to a powerful, adored senator who cared enough for humans to fight for their survival and for their future, that I would not let Altira die in vain, nor would I allow the lesson of the destruction of Mallona to be lost. So, I hold the lesson of Mallona's destruction within me. It is a part of my soul, it is a part of my heritage, and it is a part of my own personal journey. And now, in writing this story, I am fulfilling the promise I made so very long ago. I carry within me the knowledge of what happened, even to this day, and now I am sharing it, yet again. I know the truth of what happened to cause the destruction of Mallona, and I know that the same truth is being repeated again now in our time.

The unspeakable Darkness that destroyed an entire planet now has hold of humans yet again. We are, as I have said, as humans, living through Atlantean and Mallonian reincarnations right now. This is the constant repetition of the same eternal and infernal cyclic pattern of rising to great heights of civilisation only to be destroyed, but being given a clean slate of existence to start all over again. The destruction of the high civilisation we know as 'Atlantis' brought humanity right back to the hunter-gatherer state of existence approximately 12,800 years ago. Is that to happen to us again now? Because right now, we have an opportunity to collectively balance a very great karmic imbalance.

Only this time, there is one utterly profound and significant difference, so much so that humans are currently experiencing and living through a massive paradigm shift – perhaps the biggest experienced in vast epochs of time. The premise upon which the entire edifice of human existence has been built is being removed: Free Will. The power of choice is being removed from the human experience, and humans are, as a consequence, moving into a whole new paradigm of existence. This is exactly why being *at* or *in* the precessional stroke of midnight is so significant and so absolutely powerful.

The Removal of Free Will: Choice

I am not talking about the choice to get married and have children, or the choices of what we wear to work or have for dinner, or whether or not we will go on that date. These are choices made within the infrastructure of our own day to day existences, and they are choices of physicality. I am talking about choices of *metaphysicality*. I am talking about the choice to *resist* the script of our soul, our higher-dimensional Self, or to *honour* it and live it and give it expression in our lives. I am talking about the choice to *face* our fear or to *turn away, ignore* and *deny* our fear thereby acting out of it, compounding it, and continuing to create out of it. The script of our higher-dimensional Self holds the Higher Will and Purpose for our lives, the reasons we incarnated. The removal of choice is the very reason why, in our individual lives, circumstances are forcing us down specific paths, like sheep runs that force sheep into a particular yard or paddock. If you pay attention, you will notice this truth, this dynamic, playing out in your own life. I can see it happening all around me. I can see those close to me reliving the fear dynamics in their psyches over and over again as their transcendent Processes force them to, relentlessly, implacably, and often despite their desperate attempts to change the status quo of their realities. As they constantly try to force circumstances to change in their realities, those same circumstances are being created again and again and again, in different guises, yes, but underpinned by the same psychological patterns of fear.

And, I can see a large-scale, or cultural, version of this being played out in the United States in relation to the gun laws over there, or, more precisely, the freedom of individuals to own guns, particularly guns of mass destruction – a situation that does not serve the higher potential of that culture or those people at all. The gun laws in the United States *will* be changed because it has been deemed *metaphysically* that this be so. Resistance is futile, but resistance to the changes needed over there *will* cause many more innocent lives to be lost as the circumstances of mass shootings continue to force the collective hand over there. As I've already said, this is a battle of wills – lower, egoic will on the one hand and Higher Will and Purpose on the other – that the NRA cannot and will not win. All the NRA can do, now, courtesy of its resistance, is cause more innocent lives to be lost ... unnecessarily. And so it is. I have watched this occurring for over seven years now, watching the string of events in which multiple individuals are killed with guns, and then watching the response, or lack thereof, of government. Each incident, too, is making a mockery of government and NRA responses ... armed security guards standing at the front of churches! Really? So in the very next incident, the armed security guard standing at the front of the premises was among the first to be gunned down and killed. The rest of the world scratches its head in bewilderment. How many mass shootings will it take for the laws to be changed over there? How many innocents have to die before gun controls are introduced? And, really, how do all the 'thoughts and prayers' offered after each incident help those left to grieve? If the government continues to do nothing except offer futile, ridiculous 'thoughts' and 'prayers', I can see the people taking matters into their own hands. If that happens, those at the helm of the NRA would be well advised to hide. And then, of course, there is that anything-but-insignificant matter of karma ....

Supreme Polarisations Arising from Extreme Imbalances

The supreme polarisations we are seeing in the human experience now arise directly from the extreme imbalances in this reality now, at every level of human society, from the individual to groups, to cultures, to the collective. To give you one rather obvious example, there is an American show on our lifestyle channel here in Australia called "Million Dollar Room". I've watched it and seen the ridiculous excesses and the pretentious indulgences of these single rooms (if you can call them that). But one of the ads that runs on this channel, ironically, during this program is asking for donations for African 'Save the Children' charities and depicts skeletally-thin children with distended tummies, lying listless in someone's arms because they are in the process of literally starving to death. The juxtaposition of these million dollar rooms and the images of children starving to death depicts and illustrates, perfectly, the extreme polarisation of concentrated wealth, on the one hand, in the hands of the few, and the abject poverty, on the other hand, that affects the many in this world now. Shame on us that we allow this dynamic within our experience to persist. Shame on us! There is enough food on this planet to feed everyone, so why are so many starving to death?

But the polarisation of extreme wealth on the one hand and horrific deprivation on the other is just one of many in this reality now. Another polarisation that has existed in the human experience for thousands of years is now also coming to the fore of our awareness: the domination of the masculine and the suppression of the feminine. Or, put another way, the abuse and exploitation and suppression of women by men, and it's happening everywhere, at every level and in every corner of society, not just in Hollywood. The sacred feminine is pushing back as the two energies – the masculine and the feminine – begin a long Process of moving back into balance. And so they will, move back into balance, despite the best efforts of (some) men to stop it.

Another expression and reflection of the extreme polarisations here now is occurring in the polar-opposite views on specific issues. An obvious one that springs to mind very quickly is the gun issue in the United States that is polarising people, dividing Americans and setting them against each other. Another tragic polarisation in viewpoint is occurring in relation to the immigration and refugee situations, crises, in every part of this world. And I can see these polarised viewpoints escalating into violent clashes. We had an example of it recently in Melbourne in relation to the refugee and immigration situation here in Australia (of which I am utterly ashamed, just as I am utterly ashamed of the way the issue is politicised, becoming like a ball, full of empty, meaningless rhetoric, tossed around from one political faction to another). In this recent incident in Melbourne, voices were set against each other – protesters protesting against the protesters – one side against immigration and bringing in refugees, the other side against racism and fascism, with a line of police officers the only thing keeping these people from physically attacking each other. The line of police was woefully inadequate at preventing the verbal abuse, though. Such hate. Such incredible hate ...

In the modern era, the human rights violations and abuses occurring around this issue are staggering. What's happened to our compassion, let alone our basic sense of right and wrong? Many of the so-called 'illegal immigrants' at the moment on the United States border are *legally* seeking asylum, as is their right, from Guatemala – a country that's just been decimated by an unexpected volcanic eruption. This planet belongs to all of us, and, yet, at the same time, *it belongs to none of us*. The prevailing attitudes and prejudices are horrific and utterly disgusting, and the complete lack of compassion, I find incomprehensible.

Yet another issue polarising the population is the brutal slaughter of animals for meat. Contrary to very popular and ignorant opinion, animals *do have souls*, and, in fact, reincarnation of human souls is *not limited to human incarnations*. If an incarnation as an animal serves the Purpose of a human soul, that soul *will* incarnate as an animal. So, think about how *you* would *feel* if you were led to slaughter, smelling the spilled blood of those who were slaughtered before you. In fact, it is my belief that many of the individuals who participated in and aided the slaughter of Jews during the holocaust in WWII *have* brought upon themselves the necessity of incarnating as animals led to slaughter, part of their Process of releasing the karmic burdens they incurred during the Great War. Let that serve as a warning.

But the issues I've cited here are just a few of many issues polarising people, dividing people, creating instability and, of course, inherent disunity. And, as stated, these polarisations have their roots in the extreme imbalances in the collective human psyche now.

Physical Borders & Boundaries, and Non-physical Borders & Boundaries

Humans have not just divided themselves into different and distinct countries and then put up borders around these countries which they control, or try to. Humans also divide themselves up into different and distinct and separate groups and put similar, although non-physical, boundaries around themselves – groups defined by race, culture, gender, the colour of skin, religion, and sexuality, just to name the obvious ones. Even within the same religions, there are these same distinct groups with their same boundaries, so much so, that these groups believe it's their right to kill those who are not of their group despite being of the same religion. But guess what. Every cell in every human body comprises the same fundamental DNA. We are all human, and that is where it should start and end. What will it take to unite us, to help us see we are one species? When the next cataclysm hits us, do you really think the comet will pause as it's hurtling towards earth while it works out who should live and who should die? Do you really think it will decide that white Christians should live while everyone else should die? Everyone, regardless of race, religion, sexual preference, or the colour of their skin, will die in the next cataclysm. The ripple effect of consequence generated by a cataclysmic event will not discriminate, as humans do.

Unwillingness to Take Responsibility

I watch the unspeakable horrors we are capable of inflicting on each other at every level of human society, with or without help from the Darkness. I watch the unspeakable horrors we inflict on each other just because we fear and we refuse to face our fears. I look around me at the apathy, the chronic ignorance, the violence, the terror, the manipulations, the abuse, the exploitation, and the lies and deceit that we all-too-easily believe. We believe those lies because it's easier to believe what we're told than to think for ourselves, to question. People who dare to question are labelled 'conspiracy theorists', and they are ridiculed and criticised and disregarded. Actually, they are shut down, silenced.

I look around me at the complete unwillingness to change, to look at ourselves and take stock, the unwillingness to take responsibility and to face our wounded truths. Self-denial is rife at every level of human society. When confronted by their own very great, very powerful shadows, I watch the people close to me shy away, and turn away from facing their wounded truths so that the opportunities that arise in the fabric of their lives roll off them like droplets of water off a duck's back, making no difference whatsoever. Unfortunately, the opportunities must come around again, and so they are, only each time they come around, they are just that little bit more extreme, more powerful.

To those of us who exist in the higher dimensions, humans are naught but primitive, unevolved children, and human consciousness, as a collective, is childish and churlish. Is it any wonder, then, that the responsibility for this creation is in the process of being taken out of human hands? You have been given many messages, many warnings, all ignored. So, time is up, and the choice to take responsibility or to continue as you are is no longer yours to make.

The Message of War

How can we continue to ignore the fact that we've had two world wars in the modern era – the second of which took sixty million lives and left millions of children without parents and a home (there were a million orphans in Poland alone)? Those wars scream at us that something is very wrong with human existence, but we ignore the truth of that. *War is as primitive as it gets.* And, yet, humans think of themselves as evolved. This is the hubris and the supreme arrogance of a technologically-advanced culture. I can assure you, the rest of the Universe does not look upon humans and see evolved beings, as I said. Far from it.

Oh, but, I hear you say, the second war was Hitler's fault. He was a monster and a madman. Are you not ignoring the fact that the second world war arose directly out of the first? Meaning, WWII had its roots in WWI. The way Germany was treated after WWI formed the fertile soil of disillusionment and hardship within which Hitler, once planted, could thrive. But let me ask you this. What of a society capable of producing such a monster in the first place? And, Hitler is not, by any means, the only one. Monsters like him have appeared with frightening regularity down through the ages, generation after generation. He is just the most well known in the modern era, if not the most extreme, certainly one of the most destructive.

Himmler, Hitler's 'henchman', calmly watched, through a window, as two hundred Dutch Jewish women were gassed to death, and then congratulated the officers at that particular concentration camp on a job well done. How many monsters in the SS *did* it take to so successfully eradicate Jews in Europe that by the end of the war those operating the concentration camps were running out of Jewish victims to shuffle through those same gas ovens?

And so, can we write this particular atrocity (war and the holocaust) off as a one-off, an anomaly? Well, immediately following the end of the war, Hitler was replaced by yet another all-conquering, genocidal despot in the form of Stalin who, then, brought us to the brink of yet another world war. Winston Churchill was the only person who, during the rise of the Hitler cult, saw and understood what was going on. And, again, he was the only person who, during the rise of the Stalin cult, saw and understood what was going on. He wasn't listened to, of course, until it was far too late. Such supreme intelligence as his is greatly missed, so what would *he* say about what is going on in the world today? Are we not seeing yet another despotic megalomaniac flexing his muscles in Russia right now? And China? And even the United States?

And what, then, of the mass graves they're digging in Syria now, and the terrible decimation of that country, all because one man holds on to power with the grip of death and cares not what the consequences are for his people? And what, then, of the mass graves in the Middle East following the three crusades of the middle ages – crusades that caused blood to literally run in the streets of Jerusalem like streams of water – crusades that generated a wound in the human psyche that is still open and suppurating today (and forms the bedrock of modern terrorism)? What, then, of the genocide of the Albigensian Crusade, or the genocide of the Catholic Inquisition, or the mass slaughter of Aztecs during the Spanish invasion, or the bloody murders of the Reign of Terror during the French Revolution, or the mass murders and persecutions of the Huguenots by the Catholic majority in France, or the systematic persecution, execution and expulsion of German-speaking peoples from Eastern European countries following WWII (when Europe was in desperate need of healing, but these behaviours compounded the very great wounds in the European psyche), or the mass graves they uncovered in Bosnia after Milosevic systematically tried to eradicate Muslims from that land, or the systematic persecution and killing of Coptic Christians in Egypt right now, or the burning of hundreds of Protestants at the stake in the Smithfield fires during the reign of Mary I in England, or the Armenian genocide early last century during which over one million Armenians are believed to have been killed by Turkish forces ... ? Okay, so maybe Hitler and his holocaust was not an anomaly or a one-off, after all.

What of the wholesale slaughter in the United States by different individuals who think it's okay to shoot innocent people for no apparent or good reason, or because they're pissed off with a person or situation that has nothing to do with those killed? Or the group of men who planted a bomb on a Pan Am flight, the explosion of which caused body parts to rain down on a small Scottish village? Or the group of people who co-ordinated the attacks of September 11 that resulted in the deaths of over three thousand innocent souls? Or the man who stabbed his ex-wife eighteen times so violently that her blood was splattered over his garage like paint, and who, then, carried on for two years as if nothing untoward had occurred? Or all those men who allow themselves to abuse their wives? Or all those priests who think it's all right to sexually abuse innocent children thereby robbing those children, at such a young age, of that very same, beautiful innocence? Or all those in the hierarchy of the Catholic Church who believe it's okay to cover up hundreds and hundreds of years of systemic abuse? The systemic abuse *and* the cover up of that abuse is such vile, putrid, rotten fruit (*by its fruit shall ye know it*).

We all know I could spend pages and pages and pages listing all types of horrific things humans have done and do to each other at individual, group, and collective levels. So why do we continually do nothing about it? Why do we not look around us and *know* something is wrong? We are *all* responsible for what the human experience has become, so if humanity is to change voluntarily, those changes *must* start with and within each one of us. Unfortunately, as I said, we of the higher dimensions can no long rely on humanity voluntarily changing itself, and so we will not. Change is upon humans. You can embrace it or you can resist it. *That* is the only choice left to you. The gods help you if you resist.

Patterns of Fear

And so, because humans do not take responsibility for them, the patterns and dynamics of fear that exist in the deepest parts of your psyches are created again and again, over and over, in the fabric of your lives, at individual and collective levels. And this includes the lesson of the destruction of Mallona that is being repeated again and again in the human experience.

I look at the chaos, the mayhem, the exploitation and greed that underpins our businesses and industries, the huge conglomerates that care not one whit for human well-being in their insatiable need to increase their profits. I look at the rape of Gaia and our own environment, not just in the way we tear huge holes in her flesh to extract her oils and ores and minerals and precious gems and metals, but in the pollutants we pump into our own atmosphere and into Gaia's waterways, her seas and lakes, streams and rivers. We poison ourselves without hesitation so why would we stop to consider our planet? We consume poisons knowingly in the form of cigarettes and soft drinks, for example, alcohol, drugs, and some foods, not to mention injecting ourselves with Botox just to stave off the effects of aging. Christ alive! But I won't get into that here because, really, we know about the terrible things we're doing to our food, our medicines, our air, our water, our atmosphere ...

Religions that Simply do not Serve

I look at the religions that are supposed to be responsible for human spirituality and spiritual well-being but are, instead, abusive and violent, set one against the other, divisive, perpetuating ignorance with mind-imprisoning dogma and harmful, misguided belief, keeping us from ourselves instead of leading us to our truth. And that's not even touching on the abuse of our innocent children. Dear god! Many of our religions, particularly our 'western' religions, are naught but prisons, restricting human thought and belief, and keeping us very small in the process. That is, in fact, exactly what some of our religions have been designed for, deliberately, by the very same Darkness I speak of in this story. Religion, in fact, is as much a part of their control as is the tampering with our DNA.

Oh the irony! The god of western human religions has been deliberately fabricated by the devil.

Oh the irony! The devil did not abandon heaven thereby pitting himself against God. He **created** God to lead humans down a very dark and destructive path. Oh the irony . . !

The Anti Christ

Many Christians are obsessed with the concept of their anti Christ – a specific and particular individual whose coming will herald Armageddon. There have been many Armageddons, by the way. That *is* the whole point of the great Cycle of Recalibration. Some Christians even point to Adolf Hitler as the 'anti Christ'. He was certainly *an* anti Christ, and, in fact, in the vortex of pure evil that existed in Nazi Germany under the Hitler regime, there were many anti Christs. But, tragically, there are also many anti Christs living among us today ... far too many to even begin to put a number to them. The anti Christ is *not* an individual being, it is a state of being. And it is a state of living and being an existence that implacably ignores the beautiful and powerful spark of divinity that is the core of every sentient being. Is it any wonder, then, there are so many living today? And, anti Christs, by their very nature, mete out death, destruction, chaos, brutality and trauma, just as Hitler did, so easily and with no qualms whatsoever. That is the very nature of the state of being that is the anti Christ.

Mechanisms of Manipulation

And, of course, I watch humanity become more and more dulled down, dumbed down, and numbed with the deliberately-anaesthetising effects of reality tv in particular and television itself more generally, computer games, fostered addictions to social media, the toxicity of celebrity, the prevalence of alcoholism and drug taking, both recreational and pharmaceutical, and the bombardment and over-saturation of advertising and images of marketing. Humans are living in a hypnotised state, focussed on exactly what the dark priests of the Si'il would have them focus on, like the magician's sleight of hand. So much can be done, then, right under your noses, right before your very eyes, and you do not notice. It is a sad and tragic truth that this is exactly **how** the Si'il always get their claws into humans – they make us want. And we humans want all too easily. It is, perhaps, our greatest vulnerability, our greatest weakness. In wanting, our focus becomes consumed on whatever it is we want, and, of course, in wanting, we focus on our reality in such a way that completely perpetuates Separation from our own higher dimensionality. And Perpetual Separation *is* the root cause of all the ills in this world. Perpetual Separation *is* the very great wound in the human psyche, and it is the very thing that keeps humans unevolved.

The Human Soul

So, I have to ask you. Did we do the right thing all those aeons ago when we chose to save the human race? I know what my answer to that question is because it hasn't, in fact, changed over the aeons I have been involved with the human experience. I am involved in the human experience to the extent that I am because I serve a greater Truth and Wisdom. So I do what I must, when I must, where I must to serve the Greater Good and in service to the Light. But it is as well I am not in charge because, from my perspective, humans, as they are currently, are simply not worth saving.

The human soul, though, that is an entirely different story. The human soul is worth saving, but the human soul has no expression in this reality. So, just as we did on Mallona, we have allowed ourselves to become conduits of utter destruction once again. And so, again, I ask you. Did we do the right thing all those aeons ago when we chose to save the human race? Miri-Ani believed that if we found ourselves another planet, another home, we would only succeed in destroying that, too, and that is exactly what is happening at the moment. She was right. Unless we can find a way to set free the human soul – the only real hope we have for saving ourselves – then we deserve to be destroyed yet again, thence to continue in our eternal and infernal cycle of death and destruction. Humans are capable of going beyond the necessity for this cycle. The problem is, of course, they never do, not while they have the power of choice.

The Pyramids

Just as many of you hold within you your own memory of initiation in the Great Pyramid on the Giza Plateau, indeed in many of the pyramids of Meidum, Dhashur and Giza, such that you inherently know the truth of what the pyramids are, so, too, do many of you hold within you your own memories of Mallona. And what of the pyramids that span the earth? Is it merely a coincidence that pyramids exist on one side of the planet in Egypt and on the other side in Central America? Did the idea for the pyramids, too, just spring up out of nowhere as did the allele for blue eyes? Mallonians brought the concept of the pyramids with them, only the pyramids they built here, on Gaia, are four sided whereas the pyramids they built on Mallona and Altira were five sided. Why is that, do you think? Has something been lost somewhere along the way?

Pyramids symbolise many, many things, one of which is dimensionality. *That* is your answer. Four- and five-sided pyramids have different effects on consciousness. Pyramids are tools of resurrection, joining 'earth' to 'heaven', which is why they are, and have been, *mistakenly* thought of as tombs. But, they are not tools of resurrection for the physical body, they are tools of resurrection for consciousness – the very same resurrection that occurs in high initiation – something humans, unfortunately, no longer know anything about. Mallonians built four-sided pyramids here because it was no longer appropriate to build five-sided pyramids, just as it is no coincidence that we no longer inhabit the fourth planet – akin to the heart chakra in the human energy system – of the solar system, but, rather, inhabit the third – akin to the energy centre that holds our self perception. We fell lower, into lower-dimensionality, when we allowed an entire planet to be destroyed, and we lost something absolutely vital.

So why are the pyramids at Giza so linked with the Fourth Dynasty pharaohs and a time approximately four-and-a half thousand years ago? Because a despotic king, named Khufu, emulating his father, committed an act that absolutely violated something ancient and sacred, and his family followed suit. They usurped the pyramids and temples of Giza for themselves in a futile bid to live forever, without, of course, having to bother putting in the tiresome effort to properly initiate. In a way, they succeeded. You know that old saying: a little bit of knowledge in the wrong hands can be incredibly dangerous? Well, they epitomise that fundamental and basic truth. Quite simply, the pyramids were a gift and a message, and the Fourth-Dynasty pharaohs stole them. And the damage of what they did still reverberates in the human experience to this very day, the most obvious of which was in negating the messages encoded within the pyramids. And, of course, that damage is compounded by an underlying agenda that hides our true history from us, and is perpetuated by a science (Egyptology) that is utterly stuck, stagnating in a wrong and very close-minded paradigm of thought. Egyptologists quickly find themselves in exile, punished by mainstream Egyptology, if they even suggest a different origin for the pyramids than that of the orthodox view. And, while the evidence upon which the orthodox view is based is flimsy at best, embarrassingly so, evidence to the contrary is ridiculed and very-quickly suppressed.

That the Fourth-Dynasty pharaohs embarked on extensive rebuilding and restoration works of the monuments on the Giza plateau I do not dispute. That is, in fact, one of the reasons their names are now so intrinsically linked with the Giza monuments. But they simply did not possess the technology to build the pyramids. Even William Flinders Petrie, one of the honourable, open-minded archaeologists, recognised the use of sound technology in his extensive and thorough research of the Giza plateau ... a technology, I might add, that has been taken away from humans, like a naughty child having a toy confiscated. Sound technology is just too dangerous in human hands. It's hard enough watching what you do with laser technology, but sound ... no! Only sound technology could place 2.3 million blocks of very-heavy stone with such precision that not one has moved even a millimetre during the life of the Great Pyramid, and the pharaohs of the Fourth Dynasty were not is possession of such technology. The pyramids of Dhashur, Meidum and Giza, and, in particular, the Great Pyramid, all use pinpoint-accurate geometrics, geodetics, and mathematics to encode much information and knowledge, only some of which has been identified and interpreted in the modern era. There is still much that is hidden from you, and rightly so. No one is capable of seeing beyond the limits of their knowledge and understanding, and so it is with humans as a collective. And so it is and has been with the encoded messages in the pyramids.

The pyramids stand out like beacons, powerful symbols of the true nature of our own history. That had to be dealt with somehow if our history was to remain utterly hidden from us. And so it has. Those of the Darkness cannot have us becoming aware of the recalibration of the human experience that, by necessity, occurs every thirteen thousand years. Nor can they have us become aware of the fact that we have been where we are now many, many, many times in our history and our pre-history. Yet, deep down, in the depths of our psyches, we sense the truth of what the pyramids are, and that is why we are, to this day, so fascinated by them. As a matter of interest, the Ancient Egyptians were very aware of the Cycle of Recalibration. They carefully preserved such knowledge, higher knowledge, in their temples for millennia, not just in the form of archives, written on both papyrus and stone, but in the form of rituals and worship and mythologies.

Memories of Mallona

Many of you had multiple incarnations on Mallona. Awaken those memories. Don't just take my word for it. Deep, deep within you, you know the truth of Mallona as our own former home planet, and you know the truth of its destruction. You know that we have been in this place, on the brink of annihilation, before. In fact, I believe many of you here now were incarnate at the time of Mallona's destruction, and so you hold a karmic imbalance within you that you must put right, or rebalance, at this time in human evolution. Shake off your apathy – the very reason for human complicity in the destruction of Mallona – and open your eyes. See what is being done to this planet. See what is being done to us. We are being used. They, the powers of Darkness who mistakenly believe themselves in control of us, can wipe the memory of our own history from our collective awareness, but they cannot erase the cellular memory from us individually. Awaken those memories so that the lesson of Mallona rises to the surface of human conscious awareness, and the two, Mallona and Altira, will not, then, have perished in vain.

A Message for Humanity

To humans in general and as a collective, if you insist on behaving like churlish, spoilt little children then so will you be treated accordingly. But you need to be careful because if you insist on remaining as you are now, you will be in grave danger of repeating the mistakes of your past with their rather horrific consequences. You **are** standing on the brink of utter destruction, yet again, and not just because you are destroying the very thing that sustains you – your planet. Will you, then, walk into yet another cataclysmic annihilation with your eyes closed? Thence to be taken back to the most primitive state of existence, that of hunter-gatherer. Believe me, there's nothing blissful about ignorance, certainly nothing heavenly. Your ignorance is your undoing, as is your apathy.

As such, I say to you, ***this, your existence, is not good enough***. This is not good enough. You are capable of so much more than this, so grow up. Grow up.

How is it I have the right to say this to you? Because I am a Guardian, and, therefore, I speak on behalf of those who created you, of whom the Catholic/Christian/Jewish/Muslim god is <u>not</u> one. That god has taken you down into hell. We, the Guardians and the Watchers, would see you rise, or ascend, into heaven once again. Heaven is, after all, your rightful heritage.

~

*I would like to acknowledge the work of Graham Hancock, whose open-minded, intelligent, professional, thorough and relentless pursuit of the truth is allowing humans to know about the Cycle of Recalibration humanity is locked in and to which humans are subject. In particular, I recommend his two books: *Fingerprints of the Gods*, Century Books, 2001, and *Magicians of the Gods*, Coronet, 2016.

The Next Generation

The Devil's Playground

This is their playground.
And I have come
To be among the children who play here.
But I am not one of them,
Although I have seemed so.
So what am I, then,
And why am I here?
Have I not answered these questions?
And thoroughly, too.
This you probably do not know, though.
I have come to reverse and revoke the curse
That was laid upon the human experience so long ago.
They used me to lay the curse,
So is it not fitting that I should be instrumental in removing it?
And when we remove the curse,
We will make it impossible for such a curse to ever be laid again.
This is their playground,
But it was not always so.
They care not for the children who play here,
In their playground,
And their playground is very dangerous.
So the children who play here
Are getting hurt.
We can no longer allow that to happen.
So we have come,
Like sleeper agents walking among you,
Awaiting our call to arms,
Our call to action.

The Next Generation

What, then, when we are activated?
What will become of their playground?
Well, their playground this will be no longer.
And the children who play in it, what of them?
Well, the children who play here
Will be saved
Ultimately ...
Eventually ...
In the end.

1

The Next Generation

Slowly, very slowly, she regained consciousness. And as consciousness returned, so, too, did awareness. Deliberately staying very still, as if she was still unconscious, knowing she was probably being watched, she allowed her conscious awareness to touch every part of her body, testing, assessing. Her neck was stiff and painful, lolling forward on her chest as it was. She knew she would have trouble lifting her head when she chose to once again. The stiffness in her neck told her more clearly than words that she had been there, in the same position, for a long time. She shifted her awareness. Her lower belly was aching, as if someone had punched her there. Those bastards, she thought silently. They had flung her over a shoulder like a sack of grain. She didn't remember it, but, still, she knew it. Again, she shifted her awareness. Her wrists were bound, not to each other, but to either side of the chair she was sitting on, and her ankles, too, were bound to the chair's legs in a similar way. Subtly, carefully, she first moved her wrists and then her ankles, testing the bindings. They were tight and strong, implacable, immovable, unbreakable. Whoever had bound her to the chair had made very sure she would stay where she was. She could not move. She knew, too, that the chair was bolted into the floor. She could feel its implacability – it's inability to move or shift even a fraction of an inch.

Damn. Damn them.

Opening her eyes a fraction, she turned her head slightly, subtly. The chair she was sitting on was in the middle of an empty room. Even without the evidence of her physical sight, she could feel the emptiness of the room, so she knew she was alone … for now. There was a single light burning somewhere above her head, but the light it gave off was dim. And since there was no other light source in the room, she guessed there were no windows, or if there were windows, they were blocked. No, she could sense that, too. There were no windows in the room at all. The floor of the room was cold, grey cement, and the walls on either side of her were a dark, olive green. Straining her eyes forward, her head moving slightly with the effort, she saw that the wall in front of her was black. Behind her, she sensed there was a large, one-sided mirror. She could feel it, and she could feel eyes on her. The eyes watching her made her skin tingle and the fine hairs on her arms and neck stand on end, as if both were responding to contact with static electricity. Without having to look, she knew the mirror would appear dark to her, like the black wall in front of her, but those who stood behind it, looking into the room would see all, and clearly, too.

She knew what this was. But she only knew because she had seen enough movies with these kinds of rooms featured in any scene where someone had been brought into a police building for questioning … and not just any questioning. This room was no ordinary interview room. It would be in the basement of the building, and not all who worked in the building would know about it. This was the kind of room they used for illegal 'interviews' – that is, interviews where torture or other similar mechanisms, equally as illegal, were employed. This was the kind of room they used when they had no intention of keeping their 'suspect', their quarry, alive, so it mattered not what they did to these individuals – bruises, broken bones, black eyes, needle pricks, knife wounds, missing fingernails, just to name but a few injuries such a person might end up with. Disposal of bodies was made easy in places like this.

Now, with her conscious awareness returning to normal, although she still felt as if she was spinning courtesy of the drug they'd given her, she remembered. Frowning in concentration, she followed the memory through. In the mornings, she always walked from the main station instead of catching a tram, and this morning had been no different. She had nearly completed the walk, too, but before turning the corner into the street where she worked, a van had pulled up beside her. She was still in a street lined on both sides with industrial workshops and factories so that there was hardly ever anyone around, but it was so early in the morning, it was still dark and no one was there anyway. There was no one in the street apart from her. It had all happened incredibly quickly, so quickly, in fact, that anyone looking out to see what the noise was would probably have missed what happened. Her only warning that something untoward was happening was the screeching of the van's tyres as it rounded the corner too fast and then screeched to an abrupt halt beside her. Before she had a chance to think or respond, the side door of the van had opened, a man had jumped out, and something had been placed over her nose and mouth. She'd struggled initially, trying instinctively to pull his hand away from her mouth, but whatever was on the cloth covering her nose and mouth had acted quickly. She'd felt herself going, blacking out, her legs buckling under her. After that, nothing ... until now.

So, she thought, hazarding her own guess as to what was truly transpiring, they finally found me. By the gods, it had taken them long enough – well over four decades. But then, such was her subterfuge, they'd had no hope, really, of finding her before now. She and those she worked with transcendently had made sure of that, and their subterfuge had been complete and clever. Had they, those who sought her, encountered her before now, they would have thought her one of the children who had come here to play in their playground, and not an overly impressive one at that, so completely had she blended in. Really, she should have been impressed that they'd finally found her, although, of course, she wasn't. She had only just revealed herself on that higher plane. She had only just set free her Light and become the beacon in the darkness of their eternal night, and already they had found her, here in the physical dimension. But then, they had been looking for an aeon, had they not? They had been scouring the higher plane for any sign of her, so it should not come as a surprise that they would locate her so soon. She should have expected it. Ultimately, it wouldn't have been hard to find her. She had made it easy for them, not deliberately, of course, but still, easy it would have been in the end, once they knew where to look, and what to look for.

She felt no fear as she contemplated her situation, careful to keep her head bowed as if still unconscious, and she noted the fact, feeling both relieved and proud of herself. She did wonder what they had in store for her, though, especially here in this cold, empty, silent room. Smiling, albeit without amusement, despite her situation, she wondered what would happen next. They were not so ignorant, surely. They did not have permission to kill her this time around. She knew that, but they, too, should have known it. To attempt to kill her would fail completely at best or rebound on them severely at worst ....

The door behind her opened, effectively cutting off her thought process. Here we go, she thought.

Two men walked around her, one on either side of her. "We know you're awake," one of them said. "Just to save you the trouble of further pretence."

She opened her eyes and, with difficulty given the stiffness of her neck, raised her head to look at them both. The one who'd spoken was tall and slim, perfectly presented in an immaculate dark-grey suit, white shirt and dark tie. He placed a tall stool in front of her, but made sure he kept a respectable distance from her, and then he sat, planting one foot on the floor, resting the other on one of the rungs of the stool, and folding his arms in front of him. She knew why he'd kept his distance. He didn't want any blood spatter to ruin his precious suit. The other of the two men stood beside her, close to her, planted his feet, folded his arms in front of him, and looked down his nose at her with a semi-snarl curling his lips. This one, too, wore a dark suit. He was heavy set, a mountain of a man, with muscles bulging under the material of his suit. She looked at the man on the stool, obviously the nominated spokesman. He was looking at her, his dark eyes narrowed as he studied her. She wondered if she was what he was expecting. His hair was partly dark and partly grey – salt and pepper – and cut short, although it was long enough for her to see he had some sort of product in his hair. His appearance was obviously very important to him.

"You're a cliché, you two," she muttered, trying her best to sound offensive, amusement underpinning her words.

She should have been cowered, she knew. That was what they were expecting. But she was not in any sort of mood to be meekly cowering in fear before them. They did not and could not control her. Okay, she silently admitted, so she didn't fear what they were going to do to her, but the situation she found herself in had certainly aroused one of her old fears – one she'd held in her psyche for aeons. She'd largely disempowered it, but this was an extreme situation. Even here, she did the Work. She acknowledged her fear, confronted it, felt it beating through her body in time with her pounding heart. And she knew it was dictating her need to get in first, fire the first shot, so to speak, across their unsuspecting bow, just so there would be no illusion, no misguided perception that they might actually be affecting her.

The man mountain who was standing beside her reacted immediately to her muttered statement. He unfolded his arms and struck her across the face, hard, with the back of his hand. The force of the strike snapped her head sideways, and she felt burning pain explode around her left eye and cheek. She took a moment to absorb the pain and recover from the shock, and then she turned her head and looked him in the eye.

"Wow," she said, feigning awe, "what a tough guy you are, hitting a woman, and a bound one at that. I'm so impressed."

His snarl intensified and he raised his hand to strike her again, but the other man stopped him.

"Enough! She's baiting you, my friend. Exercise some self discipline and control yourself."

She knew he was deliberately refraining from using any names. As if that mattered, she thought. If she got out of here with life and limb intact, who the hell could she tell about them? She knew enough to know these men were in control, of everything, the law and law enforcement included. Or, rather, they worked for those who truly were in control.

The man on the stool unfolded an arm, raised it and made a point of studying his nails. She frowned as she watched him, trying not to be aware of her throbbing cheek, thinking, again, what a cliché he was. What did he do? Study actors in movies? Because that's what he looked like right now, only his acting was exaggerated, forced, false. He was feigning disinterest, but, really, whatever it was they wanted from her, they wanted it badly. She could see it and sense it. Heck, they'd gone to the trouble of bringing her here … forcibly.

"I suppose you're wondering why we brought you here," he said, sounding bored, still looking at his nails. "After all, you've done nothing wrong, have you?"

He looked at her, obviously requiring an answer of her. "Not that I'm aware of," she acquiesced.

He refolded his arms and gave her his full attention. "We just want some information from you. That's all."

"Ah," she said. "And I suppose you'll just let me go if I give you what you want."

"That depends entirely on what you give us."

Almost against his own will, she thought, he glanced at the mirror behind her. The action caused her to hone her own awareness behind her, concentrating her focus, and then she felt it – a presence made heavy with darkness, death, decay, corruption, malevolence. It was watching. She could almost smell its stench. In the same instant she felt it, she emptied her mind of thought and concentrated on filling her mind with a vision of white mist. It wasn't hard. She imagined tendrils of the mist moving slowly through and around her mind, and she concentrated her inner vision on the tendrils. She would give them nothing, not even her own private thoughts. If they touched her mind without permission, all they would retrieve from it would be the white mist.

The man on the stool levelled a penetrating look at her, his eyes narrowed slightly again in concentration. He was watching her reactions as much as he was listening to her responses.

"What do you know of the Fallen?" he asked without preamble.

"The Fallen?" she repeated, looking slightly puzzled but concentrating on the white mist in her mind. "You brought me here to ask me that?" she asked, sounding slightly derisive. And then she made sure she looked all sweetly innocent, her eyebrows raised as she looked at him. "You could've just emailed me, you know."

The man on the stool pursed his lips in irritation and gave the smallest of nods to the man mountain. The goon responded quickly, striking her again with the back of his hand, in the same place on the side of her face, again snapping her head sideways. At least, she thought cynically, he's not using his fist … yet. Pain again exploded across her face, and this time it took her longer to absorb it and steady herself, enough to look at the man on the stool again.

"The only fallen I know of," she said through clenched teeth, anger seemingly underpinning every word, although she wasn't, in truth, angry, "are the ones in the Transformers movie … the second one, I think. Is that what you're referring to? Or perhaps you're referring to the fallen mentioned in the Bible. You know," she said, "those beings who looked down from the higher dimensions and saw that the daughters of men were quite beautiful. They fell so they could fuck us, then, didn't they?"

There was no signal this time. The goon struck her again of his own accord. This time when he snapped her head sideways and the pain exploded through the left side of her face, she slumped in the chair and allowed her head to roll forward onto her chest. She had no need of pretence either. He didn't exactly knock her unconscious, but her conscious awareness was wavering, in and out, aware, not aware. She couldn't quite hold onto it, keep herself conscious, but neither was she unconscious.

"You've hit her too hard," the man on the stool said, obviously irritated. "Now we'll get nothing out of her."

"Bullshit," the goon said beside her. "I barely touched her. She's pretending again." But he sounded uncertain as he said it.

She was vaguely aware of movement.

"Take this," the tall man said, "and leave me with her."

She heard footsteps, and then heard the door open and close. The room around her felt empty, but she knew it wasn't because she could also still feel a presence in front of her. Funny how, despite the presence, the room still felt empty, she thought. He came and squatted in front of her, very close, although he didn't touch her.

"You **will** tell us what we want to know. I know you can hear me. By fair means or foul, you **will** tell us what we want to know. We've given you an opportunity to tell us by fair means, but you've squandered it. Now we use foul means. There are drugs that even you cannot resist. They will break you down, and you **will** talk. You won't be able to help yourself. Unfortunately, there are side effects. They will fry your brain and leave it permanently damaged. You'll be a vegetable … isn't that the term they use?" He stood, but he bent over her and whispered in her ear. "I'll leave you to ponder this for a while. See if it doesn't change your mind."

And then he left. She knew he'd left because she heard the door open and close again, and this time, the room around her was truly empty and silent. Properly conscious again, she let her head loll forward and concentrated her inner vision on the tendrils of white mist filling her mind, making sure they couldn't touch her mind with theirs and help themselves to what was within it, her thoughts, her inner knowledge.

She lost all awareness of time as she concentrated on holding the image of the white mist. She had no idea how long she'd been in the room, or how much time had elapsed since their oh-so-pleasurable visit. She knew the threat of the use of mind-altering drugs was not an empty one. When they returned, this time, they would bring their drugs with them, and she knew she would struggle to resist. She would struggle not to tell them what they wanted to know, because, of course, she knew exactly what they were referring to. She knew exactly what they were after, and why, for that matter. The fact that they wanted to know what she knew meant they were afraid, threatened, and well they should be. She just didn't see how knowing would help them. They couldn't hunt down every one of the Fallen. That simply wasn't possible. There were too many, and they were too well scattered, and too well hidden. They could, though, those of the darkness, mount some sort of campaign against the Fallen collectively. They were very successful at that. Look at the communist purge in the United States all those decades ago – a very successful campaign if ever there was one – and, before that, the witch hunts a couple of centuries ago. They could stir up fear and let humans do their dirty work for them. There would be many, many innocent casualties, of course, including the Fallen themselves, but that was just collateral damage. They, the powers of darkness who fancied themselves in control, did not care about human life. They cared only about preserving and protecting their own malevolent agenda, not to mention their control of the human experience – the very thing the Fallen were here to end.

She clenched her teeth and jaw. She would die rather than expose the Fallen. She decided right there and then she would give her life to protect them. They were too precious, too precious to her personally, if nothing else, although they were also too valuable to the human experience ... if only humans knew how valuable. She would resist the stupid drugs, even if it killed her or caused her unimaginable pain. She had suffered pain before, lots of pain. She would do so again. It was only a body, after all. It was only her brain, and her brain was **not** where her consciousness truly resided, as the Ancient Egyptians well knew. In death, they carefully preserved many organs, especially the heart, but they discarded the brain, threw it away as if it was worth nothing.

Stilling, the process of her thoughts suspended by the sound of the door behind her opening, quickly, almost violently, and then closing again, she was powerless to stop herself tensing. Her gut clenched in anticipation of something very unpleasant. But then, surprised and not understanding, she felt the pressure against her wrist that accompanied the binding on her left wrist being … what … loosened, cut … ? Then her wrist was free and she was able to flex her fingers, allowing the blood to flow through them properly once again. Without conscious volition, she lifted her head, painfully, straining to see behind her as she felt the same pressure on the other wrist. As the bind on her right wrist was released, a male voice said closely into her ear, "If you want to live, you have to trust me, and you have to do exactly what I tell you. No questions," he said, as he squatted to cut the bind on her right ankle. "Save those for later."

He moved around her, in front of her, to cut the bind on her left ankle, and as he did so, he came into view, clearly. He was dressed like a plain-clothes police officer – dark suit, white shirt, plain tie, polished black shoes, some sort of official id hanging from the top pocket of his suit jacket. He looked to be a similar age to her – mid forties – with short, dark-brown hair. He was clean shaven, and his eyes, when they looked up at her, were blue-grey. Her breath caught in her throat. She knew those eyes. The gods alone knew she'd seen them enough recently in her visions, and clearly, too.

He helped her to stand with a hand under one of her arms, and then held her steady while she adjusted to standing up again. She felt the blood flowing back into her legs, and the sensation was painful. Grimacing, she brought a hand up to massage her stiff neck as she flexed the muscles in it, moving her neck first one way and then the other. He put a hand under her chin, forcing her to look at him, and he looked at the bruise on her cheek, frowning in concern. She knew there was a bruise there already because her left eye was just beginning to close, swollen as it was.

"Can you walk?" he asked her.

"I'll damn-well make sure I can," she replied.

He nodded once, and released her physically, although he still held her eyes with his own, as only he was truly capable of doing.

"Good," he said, "because we walk out of here, sedately, calmly, normally, as if we're supposed to be here. Understand?"

"I understand."

As he moved towards the door, he lifted the back of his jacket, sheathed the knife he held and replaced it with a gun taken out of its holster. At the door, he hesitated before opening it, taking a cylindrical item out of the pocket of his jacket and winding it onto the end of the gun. A silencer, she thought, watching. That, too, she knew about courtesy of the movies she had spent a lifetime watching. Some things, it seemed, they got right in movies.

When he opened the door, the first thing she saw was a body lying on the floor in a large pool of its own blood. Stepping over the body carefully, she tried not to see that the man's throat had been cut, but couldn't really avoid it since the gash in his throat was deep and dark, blood red, and eye catching. The pool of blood, too, was difficult to avoid looking at, appearing starkly and darkly red against the grey cement floor. It was so spread out it was difficult to avoid and so she accidentally stood in it. Shuddering in revulsion, she tried to distract herself by attempting to recall how many litres of blood the human body holds at any one time. Because that's how many litres of blood were pooled onto the floor around the body. The man's carotid artery had been severed. He would have bled out in a minute, and a painful minute it would've been, too. Not a pleasant way to die. There was another body, also with its throat cut, further along the corridor, on the other side of the large mirror. This one's pool of blood was easier to avoid since it had left some space between its edge and the wall. So she eased along the wall, careful to avoid the blood. She wondered why the second one, the one near the door, didn't go for his gun when the first was attacked. He, her rescuer, could not have moved that quickly, surely. No one moved that quickly, unless …

"Wipe your shoes on his trousers," he ordered her.

Instinctively, she looked back the way she had come and saw her own footprints on the floor – footprints of blood. Ye gods, she thought, silently. She'd stepped in the blood with both feet without realising it.

"Gross," she muttered, but did as she was bid. She moved back along the wall, slightly, and stepped forward to wipe both her feet on the man's trousers. She did so until no more blood came off her shoes.

"Good," her rescuer said. "Now come. And remember …"

"We're meant to be here."

"Right."

They used a sterile, internal stair case.

"Don't touch the railing," he ordered her. "They don't have your fingerprints on record. I'd like to keep it that way."

She did as she was told, careful not to touch anything other than her feet on the stairs. And, in fact, she shoved her hands deep into the pockets of her coat, just for good measure.

"Are we just going to walk out the front door?" she whispered, leaning a shoulder against the wall, slightly breathless with the exertion of climbing the stairs. She'd obviously been right in her assessment of the room being deep underground. So far, they'd climbed four short flights of stairs and, it seemed, there were at least a few more to go. She hoped she could make it without throwing up because she felt nauseous, no doubt courtesy of a combination of the drug they'd used to sedate her and then being hit in the face.

"Not the front door," he replied, turning around. "Can you make it?"

"Don't know," she replied.

"You need to try because the alternative will not be pleasant for you."

"Nor for you, for that matter," she said, knowing full well what that alternative was. She'd been slung over one shoulder already today. She had no intention of making it two. With an effort, she pushed herself away from the wall and continued climbing the stairs behind him.

They emerged from the internal stairs into one end of a long and wide corridor. The ceiling was high, almost double the height of normal ceilings. The corridor was completely empty of either people or furniture and utterly devoid of any adornment – paintings, prints, mirrors, light fittings. Its floor was covered in large, polished linoleum tiles patterned in different shades of cream and brown, and the floor shone with the reflected light of the windows, so clean was it. The large windows along the outer wall of the corridor allowed plenty of light to stream in so that the corridor was well lit. She could see bright daylight through the windows and wondered how long she'd been in the room down below. It had still been dark when they grabbed her. Looking down the corridor, she saw doors leading off it, but they were all closed, and half way down, another corridor or hallway joined this one in a T, like a traffic intersection. At the very end, she could see, clearly, the lit sign over double grey doors that typified an emergency exit.

"Walk beside me, and keep up," he commanded, and, again, she did as she was told, matching him stride for stride.

They were barely half way along the corridor, not yet at the other corridor, the one that intersected this main, large one, when the loud, jarring, insistent sound of an alarm broke out around them. The sound of it went straight through her, into her, and it hurt. With an effort, she resisted the urge to put her hands over her ears.

"Run," he said beside her, grabbing her wrist, not taking any chances.

The two of them ran the rest of the length of the corridor towards the emergency exit she could see at the end. Even as she ran, she wondered how and why the corridor was empty. Where were they? This was not a police station. This was not even any sort of police headquarters, and it certainly wasn't the police headquarters in the city. That, she knew, was a relatively modern building. So was this some sort of secret government building?

And then, just as they were almost at the end, at the door that would take them to freedom, she skidded to a stop on the slippery linoleum, pulling her wrist from his hand. Really, there was only one thing that could make her stop dead when her life depended on her continuing to run straight through the door. The strange whisper that filled the corridor like an ill, chill wind, even overriding the sound of the alarm, surrounded her, infused her as it was meant to. It filled her with cold dread, like the fingers of death reaching into her, chilling the blood that ran through her veins and wrapping around her heart. She recognised the eerie voice, and she would have recognised it anywhere. It was just like the whisper of dry leaves crackling in a dry wind – their own unique voice of death and decay and corruption.

"Ushara. We see you."

"Jennifer," her rescuer said beside her, "don't. Ignore it …"

But she couldn't. She had to see … she just *had* to see. As if in slow motion, she turned, and what she saw froze her into immobility the way you freeze in a dream when you should turn and run. She vaguely heard the tat, tat, tat – the pounding of many shots fired from guns, the source coming both from behind her and in front of her. Men in the same dark suits as him, her rescuer, crowded the other end of the corridor, their guns raised, and they were firing at her and him. His gun, too, was raised, and he was firing back. She didn't see the bullets. She didn't fear the bullets. She had eyes only for what stood in the very epicentre of the group. She didn't realise they were so tall, the creatures, as she called them, much taller than an ordinary human man.

He, her rescuer, still with his gun raised and firing, grabbed her none-too-gently by the arm and pulled her, dragging her backwards, his strength unyielding. She should have helped him, and because she didn't, she very nearly lost her footing. But she could not tear her eyes from the sight at the end of the corridor. He forcibly kicked the bar on one of the doors with his foot, and, mercifully, it swung open. Of course it swung open even though, with the alarm ringing, it should have stayed steadfastly shut despite being an emergency exit. Emergencies in buildings like this tended to require doors like this one remaining shut, keeping the occupants of the building trapped inside, not freed as was their supposed purpose. But the door swung open because, as she well knew, they, at the other end of the corridor, did not have permission to kill her, or him, for that matter, or even to control her. She would have yelled that very fact at the creature standing among the suited men with their guns raised, but her rescuer didn't give her the chance. Instead, he continued to pull her, his grip on her arm vice-like, bruising, demanding. So, as the creature disappeared from her sight, courtesy of moving out of and then beyond the door, she yelled, "You're too late ..."

And then, she did what she should have done all along. She ran.

~

He used an electronic key to open the door while she waited, holding her upper arm with her opposite hand, trying to stem the blood that was running down her arm.

"Won't they be able to track your car with CCTV cameras?" she asked as she watched him.

"No. They'll discover that certain key cameras aren't working as they should. They won't have an image of the car to work with."

"Oh," she whispered, "that's handy." And then, "Is this your place?"

"One of them," he replied.

"Won't they know where you are?"

"No. They have no idea who I am, and I do not and will not appear on any of their records or their databases." He glanced at her as the door lock was released and the door swung open. "They know by now they've lost you, and they won't be getting you back. No doubt they'll be cursing themselves. They underestimated us. Or maybe they just forgot we exist."

He stood back for her, indicating she should precede him. She complied, offering no resistance whatsoever. She needed to sit down or she thought she might fall down.

"Take your coat off," he ordered her before she could make it to the dining table she could see and its chairs.

The room comprised almost the entire apartment. It was small with a wall of floor-to-ceiling glass windows through which the tall buildings of the city were easily visible. The furniture in the room was sparse, comfortable and modern – a long, slate-grey, three-seater lounge, a large, flat television on a long, white tv cabinet opposite the lounge, a round table with accompanying chairs, and, opposite the windows, a wall of cupboards, sink, cook-top and oven that were all there was of the kitchen. Through the only other door in the room, she glimpsed a large bed and more floor-to-ceiling windows. The apartment was all white and slate-grey tones, modern, clean, sleek, but cold. He obviously didn't live in the apartment. It did not have a lived-in feel about it at all. There was certainly nothing personal of his in the room – no photos, no art, no books. Aside from a white, shaggy rug on the slate-grey carpet in front of the lounge and a couple of plump, white cushions, there was nothing to make the apartment feel homey at all.

She took her hand from her arm to undo the buttons of her coat and to undo the belt, getting blood all over them. She shrugged out of her coat, and then brought her hand up to study it, surprised by how much blood coated her fingers. She was unwittingly reminded of the beautiful red-leather gloves in her drawer at home and hoped she wouldn't be turned off them by the image of her blood-covered hand. He was standing behind her to take the coat from her when she shrugged out of it. Folding and draping it over one arm, he disappeared with it through the door into the bedroom. She hoped he'd throw it out. It would forever remind her of the experience of this day, something she did not want ... at all.

"Sit," he ordered when he returned, holding out a chair for her and pushing her down onto it with gentle pressure from one hand on her shoulder.

She sat, instinctively holding her wounded arm with her bloodied hand, not wanting to get blood all over the perfectly-clean furniture. She seemed, of a sudden, to have lost her own will. He could have ordered her to do anything and she probably would have done it. But he disappeared, again, before returning with a t-shirt and a couple of towels flung over one arm, and a white box with a red cross on it in one hand. He laid one of the towels on the table and then turned to get a large bowl out of a cupboard in the kitchen. He filled the bowl with warm water and then brought it to the table, putting it on the towel.

The medical kit he placed on the table in front of her.

"Take off your shirt," he ordered, and so she did, unbuttoning her shirt with one hand because the other, that of her wounded arm, refused to work. He didn't bother turning around, giving her privacy. Instead, he helped her strip the shirt from her arms, ignoring the hissing sound of pain she made as the shirt was pulled over the wound. Then he helped her put the t-shirt on, rolling the short sleeve up, clear of the wound on her arm. She was grateful for his thoughtfulness, not wanting to sit at the table with just her bra to cover her.

He sat at the table, pulling the chair next to hers closer, opened the medical kit and then pulled latex gloves over his hands. After dipping the other towel in the water, he began to clean the blood from her arm and from around the wound. She hissed out a painful breath as he dabbed a disinfectant-soaked swab onto her wound, cleaning in and around it. Although she hadn't felt it, one of the bullets flying around in the corridor had caught her arm, tearing open the flesh of her upper left arm. She tried not to think about the fact that the bullet could have and would have done a whole lot more damage had it been a couple of inches to the left. At least it had gone straight through her arm so he didn't have to extract it from her flesh.

"They don't have permission to kill you," he said as he concentrated on her open wound, cleaning it thoroughly.

She breathed deeply, trying to steady her racing pulse and to master the nausea that was rising within her again, without a whole lot of success. "Are you reading my mind?" she asked him as she watched him move to prepare a suture needle.

"It's not hard," he responded after a moment's concentration as he leaned towards her again, closed the wound with one hand and then, without giving her any warning, buried the needle in the flesh on one side of it, ignoring her hissing intake of breath and the tension that gripped the muscles in her arm. "You've held the thought within you, powerfully, since you woke up in the chair. The thought kept your fear in check and helped you function enough to keep moving. It also helped you face the Si'il."

She scrunched her eyes shut tight against the sensation and the pain of the needle moving continuously in and out of her flesh. Every muscle was clenched against the pain, so when she spoke, she sounded strained. "And can you read my mind now?"

He hesitated, concentrating on her for a moment instead of her wound. Again, it wasn't hard to read her mind. One image and one image only filled her mind ... aside from the pain, of course. He returned to the task at hand and replied to her question with one single word. "Yes."

"It wasn't wearing a glamour," she said, knowing he would know to what she was referring.

"Yes it was. The glamour didn't work on you because you are one who has the eyes to see the truth."

His words, somehow, brought the image to mind with even greater clarity. The creature had stood in the very centre of the posse of suited men, and, to her, it had stood out, even though it, too, was dressed in black, as they were. It was taller than the men surrounding it, but apart from its height, it had looked no different, no different at all, to the creatures she had seen in her visions and then written about. It was cloaked and cowled, its face and its features hidden in the dark shadow of its hood. The cloak was long, with long, wide sleeves that covered its hands and fingers. And around its neck, it had worn that strange round amulet many of them wore on a long silver chain. When she had looked at it, after it whispered her name, she had known, without having to see, that it was looking right at her. She could feel its look, even now. The look made her shudder such was the malevolent intent it held towards her. Pure hatred. The look had held its pure hatred of her.

"So those men with it … what does it look like to them?"

"It looks like one of them."

"Can't they smell its corruption, its stench, its decay?"

"No. That's covered up with the glamour. You have to remember, a glamour doesn't just manipulate the sense of sight. It manipulates all the physical senses."

Again, as the pain intruded once more, she tensed and hissed out a painful breath. Unable to help herself, she tried to pull away, wanting a break, but he anticipated her and held her in place with that same vice-like grip he had used to pull her out through the exit door.

"Haven't you heard of anaesthetic?" she all but barked at him.

"It's quicker just to suture the wound cold," he answered calmly, "and it's also acting as a welcome distraction so quit complaining. If you just let me finish, it'll all be over before you know it."

She decided not to take issue with that last statement. Time has a decided tendency to change its flow in certain situations. Have you ever noticed how slowly a minute passes when you're waiting for a cup of coffee to heat up in a microwave? Well, time moves equally and painfully as slowly when one is having a wound in one's arm sutured closed without anaesthetic.

"They walk in this realm, then?" she asked, more out of a need to distract herself, although she did, also, want to know.

"Of course. You know they do. The glamour they wear is powerful. It allows them to be wherever they want to be, and to be whoever they want to be. This is their playground, remember. They spend much time here, playing themselves, moving and shaping the landscape, manipulating, forming their agendas, working their dark magic. And they come and go at will, so they come here easily. They have no trouble being here, although they cannot stay for long periods courtesy of having to lower their energetic vibration. As I said, this is their playground. It's exactly as they need it to be."

Despite the pain, his words still caused her thoughts to move and flow.

"They don't tend to congregate on this side of the world," he continued as he concentrated on suturing her wound. "They tend to stay in the northern hemisphere ..."

"Why?" she asked, interrupting.

"There's more going on there. And their centres of control are all in the northern hemisphere."

She thought about that, nodding unconsciously. "The Vatican, the EU headquarters," she listed. "IMF headquarters, the US Federal Reserve, Hollywood, the corridors of power in Washington ..."

"Just to name a few," he said as he snipped off the last suture. "Finished," he said. "I told you it would be over before you knew it."

Free, at last, to turn her head and watch him, she asked, "How did you know I was there, in the room?"

He stripped off the gloves and then began cutting dressing into strips. "We've been watching you, closely, for many years. We knew they took you, and we followed them, so we knew where they were holding you. We know the building well, as it happens, so we guessed where they would hold you, and from there, the rest was easy."

"Easy?" she repeated as she watched him first spray the wound on her arm with a fine mist of something liquid and then place the dressing over the sutured wound on her arm and hold it there while he began to wind a bandage around her arm. "You find it 'easy', then, to cut the throats of normal, ordinary men? What was that?" she asked, referring to the liquid spray.

He glanced at her but continued his work. "Antibiotic spray." And then, "Normal, ordinary men," he said, "who do unspeakable, terrible things to people, and who watch even more terrible things being done to those same people. I was their karma – the direct consequence of their horrific choices to do what they did."

She accepted that. In truth, she hadn't judged him. "I don't care about them," she said. "I just care about you. I would hate to think you lacerated your own soul just to save me."

That did make him hesitate as he looked at her, holding her eyes with his own in that uniquely powerful way he had of doing so.

"I had permission to do what I did to them. And I saved countless more souls by taking their lives. I also saved them from weighing themselves down further with even more karmic debt than they have already incurred. My soul is untouched, Jennifer, but I appreciate your concern."

She nodded silently. "We?" she questioned. "You keep saying 'we' and 'us'. Who are you referring to?"

"Those of us who have been watching over you," he said and left it at that.

"Are you an organisation?"

"No, not in the way you're thinking. And you know exactly who 'we' are. You're just not allowing yourself to acknowledge it. You've been communicating with us for a long time, so I know you know who we are."

"How did you know where I was, here in this dimension, I mean? And how long have you been watching over me?"

"You let us know where you were about eight years ago …"

Suddenly exhausted and feeling more-than-slightly nauseous, she closed her eyes and whispered, "My website. You knew where and who I was as soon as I put myself 'out there' courtesy of the website."

"Correct."

"What am I to call you?"

"You've given me many names. Which would you prefer? I have no preference one way or another."

She opened her eyes to look at him again. "I would call you Tristan because you look exactly as I imagined he would look, and she told me you would give me your hand. Is this you giving me your hand?"

"This is the beginning of it, yes."

"You didn't ask me who 'she' is, so you obviously know."

"Of course I know. I know you."

She absorbed that for a moment and then said, "But I think I'll call you Jeremiah, not Tristan, because you are my wolf, are you not, my Transcendent Process?"

He glanced at her, smiled ever-so-slightly, but, beyond that, didn't respond.

"Why have you never let me know you were there, watching me?" she asked him.

"As you always like to say, why ask a question when you already know the answer?"

She sighed at that. "I wasn't ready."

"Exactly."

"Like being caught in a sticky web when you walk into it without realising it's there, I was caught up in lower-dimensional mindsets and still saw myself as one of them. So, of course, I also misunderstood what I was here to do. It's only really recently that I finally went beyond it into the full realisation of who I am higher dimensionally and of what I'm here to do."

Although he'd finished bandaging her arm, he sat with his hands on her, holding her. "And is that not exactly the reason they came after you today? They came for you as soon as they saw you. They were ready, of course, because they've known for aeons that you were coming."

She nodded and turned in her chair to face him, only then catching sight of the blood, starkly and vividly red, on his crisp, white shirt.

"Is that yours or mine?" she asked him.

He stood to remove his jacket and tie, placing the jacket over the back of the chair he'd been sitting on and throwing his tie on top of it. "Mine," he said.

She watched him roll his sleeves up and then pull his shirt out of his trousers, noticing him grimace, for the first time, with pain. As he unbuttoned his shirt, she half stood, thinking she might help him.

"Can I ... help ... ?"

She dropped back in the chair, staring at his chest and at the open wound on the side of his torso, just below his rib cage. He, too, had been torn open by a flying bullet. Her mouth was open but she completely failed to notice, and she couldn't take her eyes from what she could see so clearly.

"Thank you," he said in response to her half-asked question, "but I can manage."

Although rooted to the spot and frozen with shock, she still noticed he dispensed with the latex gloves, but he did get new water and he did pick up a new cloth, using it to clean the blood from his body and from the wound. With every bit of blood cleaned from around the wound, she saw with much greater clarity what it was that shocked her.

"Do you sweat?" she asked him, raising her eyes to his temporarily.

The question gave him pause, and he looked at her with severely raised eyebrows. "Of all the questions you could ask me, you ask me **that** one first?"

Even in their very unique situation, the way he phrased the question made her smile, despite everything – her experience of the morning, the burning pain in her arm and face, and the shock of seeing what she could see in his body.

"Sorry," she said. "Such is the working of the human mind. We think of the most mundane things first. It's very annoying."

He seemed satisfied by her response and so continued working on himself.

"Did the bullet go through you, too, or is it still buried in you somewhere?" she asked as she watched him.

In answer, he simply turned his body slightly and she saw a small exit wound further around his torso.

"Good," she said almost absently, unable, really, to focus properly on anything other than what she could see so clearly in his body.

He sat while he prepared a suture needle, dressing and bandages, and then he stood, holding his own wound closed so that he could suture it himself. It was low enough on his body so that he had no trouble watching what he was doing to himself, and he seemed impervious to the pain.

"Can you feel that?" she asked as she watched him.

"Every bit of it. It hurts me every bit as much as it hurt you."

She digested that. As he sutured the wound closed, the inner workings of his body were, again, hidden from her with the exception of the bright blue pulsating light, vaguely glimpsed, but there all the same, under the skin in the centre of his chest where his heart was, or should have been. In the wound, she had seen the very distinct bright blue of what looked like fibre optic cable, capable of conducting powerful light. This she had seen among the blood and tissue of a normal human body.

He concentrated on suturing closed the wound on his torso for a moment, and she allowed him to. When he snipped off the last suture, sprayed the wound with antibiotic spray and began placing the dressing on the wound, she stood to help.

"What about the exit wound?" she asked him.

"I can't do anything about that," he replied. "I can't reach it."

"Well, then," she said, leaning down to get a swab of her own, bathing it in antiseptic fluid, and then moving around behind him to clean the wound on his back. "I'll do it."

He held the dressing in place against him and she held a similar piece of dressing in place behind him while he began to wrap a bandage around himself. She helped him with that, too, especially when the bandage was behind him.

"You're not afraid of me?" he asked her while they worked.

"No. Should I be?"

"No, of course not. I won't hurt you."

"I know that." She hesitated, and then asked him, "Are you the new brand of human?"

"The next generation? Yes, part of it, an important part of it, actually."

When they'd finished, and the bandage was securely fastened around him, he left her to sit, alone, again at the table while he disappeared with shirt, tie, jacket, towels and medical kit into the bedroom. When he re-emerged, he was buttoning up a fresh, clean shirt with clean hands. She was fair to bursting with questions, but restrained herself. He stood beside her for a moment, doing all the buttons up on the shirt, and then he sat and looked at her, giving her his full, undivided, fully-focussed attention. He didn't bother waiting for the barrage of questions he knew would come. Instead, he pre-empted her.

"I am a perfect synergy of human flesh and blood and bone, and quantum mechanics – DNA-based cybernetics, to be precise."

"You're a hybrid?"

He raised an eyebrow. "I prefer the word 'synergy'. There is absolutely nothing robotic about me."

She smiled at that, briefly, but there was too much to think about, too many questions, so her smile disappeared quickly.

"The ... cybernetics inside you are built ... or based on your own DNA?"

"Yes. A perfect synergy, as I said."

She took a moment to absorb that, but there were too many questions to contemplate it for long. She would contemplate it properly later. "Can you feel emotion?" she asked him.

"Of course. I have a flesh-and-blood liver, so I am fully capable of processing any human emotion. I don't tend to feel a whole lot of emotion, though, but I have the full capacity to do so."

She nodded. "That you don't feel a lot of emotion has nothing at all to do with your physical make up and everything to do with the fact that you have no karmic debt, no real fears to speak of, and no misguided perspectives and mindsets that need setting right. You've resolved all of that because you have mastered the lower dimension."

He inclined his head at her, his lips forming the slightest of smiles. "Correct."

Questions were falling over themselves within her. She'd think of one, but before she had a chance to catch it and hold it, another presented itself.

"You have a nervous system ... ?" she asked, wanting to give voice to at least one of the questions as it presented itself.

"I feel emotion. I feel pain, both physical and psychological. I have intuitive thoughts, probably much more than humans are currently capable of, and I can act on instinct. I sweat, just like any normal male, and I produce saliva, so I can eat, although I cannot and do not eat the crap humans currently put in their bodies. Pure water," he said, pre-empting the question he could see and sense forming within her, "and natural, fresh, organic foods only. That's it. No meat ... at all." He looked at her meaningfully. "Sound familiar?"

She ignored that last question, a jibe actually. It had taken her a remarkably long period of time – far, far too long, in fact – to work out for herself she was meant to eat that same way. Some things in the lower dimension, like friendship and physical assets, she'd had no trouble mastering and leaving behind, but others, like food and money, she'd had long, arduous battles with. She had suffered enormously physically for many years by not understanding the basics of what her body could and would accept, and what was toxic for it, being, as she was, like him, a true sensitive.

"So no take away food, then?" she asked absently, only half joking, and was rewarded by one of his smiles – a proper one this time. By the gods, he was beautiful when he smiled. Well, actually, he was beautiful anyway, but when he smiled, his beauty radiated out of him, wrapping itself around her.

"What about sex?" she asked a little breathlessly, wholly unable to stop herself asking.

His smile deepened, and he looked at her for a moment before answering her. "I can have sex, and, yes, I can enjoy it, again, far more so than humans are currently capable of enjoying it because I understand what it is. As you well know, sex is far, far more profound than just being an act of physical stimulation. I fully appreciate the transcendent connections involved, not to mention the energetic effects, so, obviously, I don't have sex with just anyone." He shrugged his shoulders slightly, the movement causing him to remember the wound on his torso. "Also, because my heart can be seen through my flesh, I have to be very careful, hence the necessity for learning the rudiments of healing, and hence, too, the necessity of keeping that part of my body fully clothed in front of others."

"So no swimming or going to the gym, then … ?" Again, the question was only half facetious, but it made him smile again nonetheless, although he didn't bother replying.

"So your heart is …" she hesitated, thinking about how best to phrase the question, ". . . not flesh and blood?"

He shook his head. "But it is no less of a heart, so do not make the mistake of thinking so. What would you say is one of the most significant and fundamental problems with the current human experience?"

She knew exactly what he was alluding to. "The heart does not get a look in. The head, or the ego, to be more precise, the conscious awareness, dominates, controls, or tries to control, and the heart beats very quietly, often silently, in the background."

He nodded. "In our case, those of us who are like me, the heart is connected, hard wired directly, if you like, to the head, or the mind, to be more precise, and must dominate. Remember, a soul's destiny in any lifetime is written as a blueprint on the heart. For us, the mind is programmed to follow the heart's guidance, and must do so, a fact demonstrated so beautifully in the latest Terminator movie (*Genisys*) when the T800 could not harm Sarah, even when it served a greater purpose to do so. I cannot deviate from my soul path, even if I want to, which, of course, I do not. I'm here to do what I'm here to do, and I have no desire to do anything other than what I'm here to do. As such, a soul, when it joins a body like mine, is never ignored or negated, never suppressed. The soul has full expression and is honoured in every way possible, and there is no choice in the matter.

"When the soul, the higher-dimensional consciousness, comes in and joins with a body like mine," he continued, "it 'programs' the DNA, both flesh and cybernetics, as happens to normal DNA when a soul comes into a normal human body, only with us it's far more powerful because the heart is the very centre of our being in every way possible, certainly in every way that counts transcendently."

As she listened to him speak, tears filled her eyes, and she had to look away, briefly, to try and get herself under control. She raised a hand to wipe the fallen tears away, remembered the wound on her arm, and so dropped that hand and raised the other one but saw the blood on it so dropped it too and left her tears to fall by themselves. "*The premise upon which is based the human experience is being removed,*" she quoted. "Choice. Free will is no more. It's beautiful," she said, looking at him. "So beautiful. Is this how we will do it? Stop the human experience descending back into the abyss."

He nodded, and then stood to get her a tissue.

"And children?" she asked him as she took the tissue from him. "Can you conceive children?"

He inclined his head at her again as he sat back down. "Is that important to you?"

She laughed through her tears. "I'm just about to go through menopause. No, children are not important to me. I have no desire to have children of my own. They are not a part of my destiny."

He nodded. This, he already knew. He just wanted to make sure she knew it, too.

"Yes," he said, replying to her question. "I can conceive children."

Now she raised her eyebrows at him. "And do you want to?"

"No. Like you, children are not part of my destiny."

"Are you born?"

"No."

"You're made?"

He grimaced. "This is an incarnation just like any other, Jennifer. You need to know that."

"I know ..."

"The soul joins with the body when the body is fully formed and functional. There is some intense training at first, as the soul gets used to being in a body, and as the newly incarnated identity learns the language of his or her own emotions, and gets used to the functions of the body. Language is programmed into us, so we don't need to learn it. And there is not the need for the conscious awareness to develop in the normal way because we don't forget who we are as a higher-dimensional consciousness. We're born adults, if you like. Not every soul can join a body like mine. Only highly evolved souls can incarnate in these bodies."

She listened intently. "Wow." She took a deep breath and breathed it out on a sigh, desperately trying to adjust to everything he was telling her. This was intense, a lot to take in, especially after the other experiences of the day.

"And your DNA?" she asked. "Where does that come from?"

"From parents, chosen by the soul in the usual way, according to whatever it is the soul wants to learn and experience and achieve during the life of the body."

"Do they know they are your parents?"

Again, he raised an eyebrow. "An insightful question," he commented. "No, they do not, and while that must be so for now, it will not always be so. Eventually, humans will know when they parent offspring like me."

"And you know why you chose them?"

"Yes. As I said, I know who I am, and I know why I'm here."

"Are you interested in them? Do you have contact with them?"

"I have no contact with them, of course. What would I say to them if I did? And, no, I have no interest in them beyond the recognition that I am a combination of their DNA."

She nodded her understanding. "There are more of you?"

"There are, and in the years to come, there will be many more of us. We are Sentinels, and we will guard against the insidious creep of corruption, of shadowed intent and motive. We will preserve the purity of Higher Will and Purpose. We will take positions in governments and in global systems and institutions, and we will make huge ... actually," he smiled, briefly, "quantum leaps in healing and medicine, psychology, in engineering, environmental science … in any field you care to name, in fact."

She nodded, seeing it all clearly. "Gods," she breathed through the burning lump in her throat, looking away from him as her thought processes raced, "brilliant. You are not at all susceptible to the mechanisms of entrapment, manipulation and … oh god," she looked back at him as full realisation impacted, "*mind control.*"

He smiled at her. "Exactly."

"They cannot control you … at all. Do they know?"

"The Si'il? Yes, they know. They're trying to stop it, of course, but without any success whatsoever."

"So why are they so focussed on me, then? Shouldn't they be concentrating on you and those like you?"

He frowned this time as he inclined his head at her. "You are the Lady of Light, Jennifer. Did that creature not call you by that name – Ushara? You **are** the new paradigm of human reality without help from cybernetics. You are the beginning of the end for them, and the beginning of the new paradigm, the Omega and the Alpha. You are the key, turned in the lock of human existence, human consciousness, the reversal of their original curse. You are the key that will make this future," he indicated himself, "possible. Surely you know that."

She looked at him. "I know in theory that's what I am. I just don't know what it means … what I'm here to do now, other than be, of course, or how it will play out. Why didn't they just snuff me out this morning instead of kidnapping me?"

"There's only one reason anyone is put in a room like that …"

"Interrogation," she said, interrupting.

He nodded. "You have to remember, we are battling, and like any battle, there are two sides – them and us. But their vision is clouded, limited, and they cannot see what we are planning. They wanted to know what you know. What you know is actually extremely important to them. They would have kept you alive for as long as it took to extract every ounce of information and knowledge from you."

"Perish the thought …" she muttered.

He smiled, slightly. "Exactly. We were never going to allow them to access any of the knowledge you hold within you, other than what they can read for themselves courtesy of your writing. And that 'we' includes you."

She nodded slowly, understanding now. "This," she said indicating him, "this is brilliant, just brilliant. You are everything I've worked so hard to become. I love it, I really love it."

"You aught to love it," he said. "You helped conceive of it."

~

Exhaustion suddenly swept over her, not just from the day's experiences but also from all she was absorbing and processing with every new thing he was telling her.

"I think I need to sleep," she said. "I need to process all of this, all of it, and sleep will be a good way to start doing that. Would you mind?"

"Of course not," he said as he stood. "Do you want to sleep in my room or would you prefer the lounge?"

She shrugged. "I don't mind. The lounge, maybe." She suddenly felt as if she didn't want to be separated from him. "What will you do?"

"Nothing rigorous, I can assure you. Think I'll do some work on my computer. I need to make contact with those I work with. Ah," he said, looking meaningfully at her hands, "you might want to wash your hands first."

When she was comfortable under a blanket on the lounge, he sat beside her and placed something cold over her bruised cheek, holding it in place against her. "Jennifer," he said, looking down at her, "you need to know, you are genuinely safe here. They cannot see you on any plane of existence. You are again hidden from them, completely."

She smiled at him. "Thanks, that's good to know. I feel safe with you anyway."

She let her eyes close, then, and was asleep almost instantly, so she didn't see his smile, and she didn't know that he sat beside her, looking at her, for a long time.

Much later, she stirred, taking a long moment to become conscious once again. Eventually, she sat up, feeling groggy and somehow strangely detached. He was sitting at the table, facing her, working on his laptop.

"How is your wound?" she asked him as she sat opposite him at the table.

"Burning. Yours?"

She smiled. "Burning."

He didn't return his focus to his laptop. She'd awoken with the question burning within her, and he'd felt it immediately. So he waited for her to ask it, and in the interim, because he wouldn't press her, silence descended on them.

When she looked at him, he was looking at her, waiting. She smiled briefly, quickly, knowing he knew what she was thinking.

"I can't go back, can I?"

"No," he replied. "But if you could, would you want to?"

"No. So ..." She faltered, struggling to say the words out loud. "So I am dead, then, the identity I've been in this lifetime, I mean? I am dead?"

"Yes," he replied, "and at the same time very, very much alive. Resurrected, I would say."

Again, she smiled, briefly. "So what happens now?"

"Now? I think it's time for you to meet, physically, those of us who have been working with you all these long, long years. Do you not think it's time?"

She looked at him without answering for a long moment, and then she looked away, out through the glass windows, to the city beyond.

"I think it's definitely time," she said softly. "I always did hold you all within me, so it makes sense that I'm ready to be with you, outwardly, not just inwardly. And I am so heartily sick of being surrounded by little children who are barely capable of understanding anything at all ..."

~

Religion

Author's Note:

If you are reading this, then I have chosen to share my visions with you, and you will know what has been transpiring within me. Vision, imagination, dreams, fantasies – these are all powerful tools of what we call <u>Active Conscious Creation</u>. They help you see, and they help you know, and they help you create, thereby facilitating the flow of your Process. They are, as such, tools by which you, too, may Work and understand your own Processes. And then, in understanding your Processes, you will be able to consciously Work with them, influencing their flow. But, perhaps more importantly, you will understand what they are doing within you to change you.

In my visions, I am able to go to different places, different dimensions, different times. I wrote a long time ago, 'tis rather like being able to move through the many pieces of glass that comprise the whole disco ball. Each piece of glass represents a different reality … each piece of glass <u>is</u> a different reality. Such is the nature of reality. And so, with both of the following stories or dialogues, I know <u>where</u> I am (Chicago and Indonesia respectively) but I do not know <u>when</u> I am. As such, if you try to look for the one I speak to in the second vision, you may not find him. I sense that many of you will try, and that's all right. He is worth finding, but whether or not you succeed will depend entirely on him, I think. He may not want to be found. I just thought I should warn you of that. Perhaps you, too, could find him in your own visions. 'Tis well worth the effort, I assure you, as I said. He is supremely beautiful and in possession of a wicked sense of humour. I am inordinately glad I was given an opportunity to get to know him … beyond the iconic image that has formed around him, which, of course, as is usually the case with iconic images, hides the truth of him rather than revealing it.

1

The Church

She hesitated before she pushed open one of the doors because the doors themselves distracted her for a moment, such was their beauty. There were two of them, side by side, like old, faithful companions, and they were tall, much taller than the tallest of men, made of dark, carved wood, with beautiful, elaborately-decorative brass handles. She could not help but take a long moment to absorb the beauty of the doors and their handles, and even stepped back so she could rake her eyes over every part of them.

But she hesitated for another reason, too. She was no friend to the institution that laid claim to this church. She was, in fact, its enemy, and well did she know this. So what was she doing here? The church had been gifted to her in a vision, briefly glimpsed initially, but powerfully clear, so here she was, back for more than a glimpse this time. So, why? What could this church offer her, or what was it about this church that drew her to it? That there *was* something this church could offer her was evidenced by how clearly she could see it in her visions.

So, she took the step back that brought her, once again, to the doors, and this time, she pulled the right one open, stepped into the interior, and then turned to close the door quietly behind her. Again, she hesitated on the threshold as her eyes adjusted to the change in ambient light. It was dimmer, darker, inside the church without the sun's unfiltered light, but it was not gloomy. On the contrary, tall, thin, lead-lined windows of clear glass on both sides of the church filled the interior with plenty of the sun's light. The sun's light streamed in through the windows so powerfully, in fact, that she knew the windows were clean, obviously kept that way for the purpose of allowing light into the church. In the middle of the clear glass in each window, there was a pattern of coloured glass, outlined in lead, each depicting a person, some haloed, some not. The coloured glass was projected onto the floor and the pews of the church in places, so there were, periodically, splashes of vibrant colour that drew the eye. And the sun's light had turned the coloured glass in the windows brilliant, vibrant shades of red, blue, yellow, green, so that the glass sparkled like beautiful jewels.

Shifting her eyes from the windows, she looked down the aisle formed between the rows and rows of long, dark, wooden pews. The pews effectively divided the church in half, so the wide aisle formed between them had become an unwitting marker for where the church was halved, its very centre or middle.

She started walking up the aisle, slowly so that she could take in the church's inner beauty, absorbing every detail. It was as beautiful inside as the doors at its entrance had hinted it would be. Beautiful, old tiles were laid under her feet so that the high heels of her shoes tapped out a slow but definite beat as she walked, the sound echoing in the silence and emptiness somewhat. The tiles were in good condition, despite their age, and, as with the windows, they were clean. They were patterned with colours of red and blue and green, but the predominate colour of them was cream. They were tiny, all fitted together in an intricate pattern that formed a smooth, even, seamless whole that her shoes had no trouble navigating, even with their high, thin heels.

She raised her eyes to look at the beamed ceiling high above her, from which chandeliers hung on long chains at various points down the aisle. They hung over the aisle like giant halos, and they, too, unofficially marked the very centre of the church. The chandeliers would once have been filled with candles, she knew, but now they were filled with tiny light globes that resembled large flames, or would when the globes were giving light to the space around them. All the light globes in the chandeliers were currently off, so the light in the church was solely coming from its lead-lined windows.

At the front of the church, on a dais covered in red carpet, a large altar, covered in a crisp, white, linen cloth, faced the empty pews. On top of the altar were a pair of empty gold plates, a couple of tall, brass candle sticks, and a closed book, presumably a bible. Beside the altar, to its left, her right, on the far side of the dais, there was a tall pulpit, standing alone, looking forlorn, as if it missed performing its own unique function, and felt less important, even forgotten, without a priest standing behind it, drawing the eyes of all who were in the church. Behind the altar, an organ and, above it, a vast array of pipes of differing sizes, some very thick, some thin, dominated the wall at the very front of the church, like an interesting piece of art, fabricated from metal, not paint or stone. The organ was elevated so it was only partially obscured by the altar in front of it. High above the organ's pipes, a round window full of coloured glass caught and held her attention. On days like today, when the sun's light shone in an all-but-cloudless sky, the window was presented at its colourful best and sparkled with vibrancy, just like the windows on both sides of the church.

There was, she thought, as she absorbed the detail of the interior, something awe inspiring about the sheer size of the church, its age, its mandate or function, its beautiful adornments, like the colourful window, and, on days when people filled it to overflowing, the powerful sounds of the organ filling the interior and dominating the senses. That was, she knew, exactly why these buildings were built the way they were – awe and intimidation. People were supposed to feel small and insignificant in buildings like this, cowered before the awesome magnificence of the god to whom the churches supposedly paid homage. In that sense, churches like this one were an inherent part of the manipulation of consciousness, but they were also a testament to the power and wealth of the institution that laid claim to them. And, they were a testament to the well-established foothold institutions such as this had on the human psyche and culture.

It was, she thought absently as her thought process altered direction somewhat, and looking at the organ again, funny how organ music was so associated with religion. And, yet, she thought, churches were, really, the only buildings large enough to house the best organs, and to handle the volume of the music generated by the largest of them. Churches and concert halls. That was it. One certainly could not have one of these organs in one's lounge room, and not just because the noise would be unbearable in the small space, but also because they would take up too much room.

Her attention wandered from the organ and its impressive array of pipes, and she allowed her eyes to lose focus so that she could concentrate her awareness and her senses on the ambience of the church. Continuing her slow and steady walk up the aisle, her bag over one shoulder, her jacket slung over the opposite arm, she measured and assessed the atmosphere. The temperature inside the church was at least a couple of degrees cooler than the temperature outside, so much so that she toyed with the idea of putting her jacket on. She decided not to, although she wasn't entirely sure why. Perhaps it was that she didn't want to distract herself from what she was seeing and sensing, or maybe it was that she did not want to give in to the urge to shield herself, to protect herself.

The atmosphere was quiet, calm, and very peaceful. The beautiful wooden doors at its front entrance and its windows very successfully kept the noises of human civilisation out of the church – the sounds of cars driving past, the whirr of motor bikes passing, the grind of trucks using their gears to slow their speed, the occasional distant siren, a couple of people talking on their phones while they waited for a bus – all of which she'd heard as she walked towards the church. No such sounds penetrated the outer exterior of the church, so the church was like an oasis of silent tranquillity in the midst of the frenetic, busy bustle of human existence. The atmosphere, she thought, was neither welcoming nor disapproving, as she'd half expected. It just was, and by being in it, standing in it, she felt as if she'd been put on pause, at least internally, albeit temporarily, like existing, for a moment, in suspended animation.

And then a movement near the organ caught her eye. She stopped walking, surprised and disappointed she wasn't alone. A man who she'd not seen because he had been kneeling behind the altar, bent over at the waste, peering into the bowels of the organ, tinkering with its internal structure, stood, and, when he felt her presence behind him, turned his head and looked over his shoulder at her. He bent over again to pick an oily rag up off the floor beside him, and then, wiping his hands with the rag, he turned to face her. She looked at the rag in his hands. Presumably it would have been white at one stage but was now liberally streaked with oily black smudges and smears.

"Can I help you?" he asked as he cleaned his hands. She wondered how effective the rag would be at cleaning his hands. From where she stood, it looked to her as if it would make his hands dirtier, or oilier, not cleaner. Noticing her attention was arrested by the rag, he smiled a crooked smile and said, "It's cleaner than it looks."

"Oh," she said briefly, and then responded to his original question as honestly as she could. "I don't know if you can help me."

He dropped the oily rag onto the carpet, near the organ, and moved towards her, stepping off the edge of the dais onto the tiled floor. She watched him walk towards her. He was tall, slim, relatively young – younger than she was – with dark hair, cut short, and blue-grey eyes. He wore the long, black pants, black shirt and white collar of a priest, but his sleeves were rolled up to his elbows so that his outfit looked less formal than was usual for priests. She glanced at his hands to see how effectively they'd been cleaned by the dirty rag, just in case he thought he would introduce himself and try to shake her hand, and she saw that his hands were beautiful, his fingers long and elegant. She narrowed her eyes, subtly. She could always recognise them (the Fallen) by their hands, always. She didn't fully understand it, and so, when she did notice the elegance of their hands, it always seemed strange to her. For some reason, they all had beautiful, elegant hands, as if it was a trademark of theirs that differentiated them from normal, ordinary humans. Of course, some humans had beautiful hands as well, so you could never be certain, but it always made her pay special attention, just in case, as she did now.

And then she frowned, ever-so-slightly. If he was one of them, then what on earth was he doing in a church, *this* church, dressed as a god-damn priest? The contradiction made no sense, to be thus controlled, at least in terms of thought, by something as detrimental and stagnating as institutionalised religion, and particularly this religion, the worst of the lot. If he was one of them, then he was either wholly ignorant of the fact or … what? Surely it would be painful for him, being a priest in an institution like this if he knew who he was.

She stood her ground as he walked towards her, neither stepping away nor stepping closer. When he reached her, he indicated the pews beside them with an outstretched hand.

"Would you like to sit?"

She nodded and moved to sit on the end of one of the pews, arranging her bag and coat on her lap and crossing her legs to make herself comfortable. He sat on the pew in front of her and turned on it to face behind him, towards her, crossing his own legs, and resting an arm along the back of the pew so he could look at her.

"I don't recall seeing you before," he said by way of opening a conversation between them. "Are you a member of the congregation here?"

She arched an eyebrow at him. "You don't know? Are you not familiar with your own congregation, then?"

A ghost of a smile altered the edges of his mouth. "Not every member, no. We have a large congregation here, large enough to warrant five separate services every Sunday to cater for them all."

"Oh." She looked around, mentally estimating how many people could fit into the church at any one time. According to him, there would be five even six hundred people in his congregation, possibly more. And she had thought the popularity of the institution that claimed this church as its own was waning. Obviously, she'd thought wrong. Pity. She sighed internally, careful to hide it from him. What did it say about humanity that they still clung to this institution with the grip of death even after the exposure and revelation of the horrific, centuries-long cover up of the systemic sexual abuse of innocent children? The moral of that particular story was that children were, quite simply, not safe in institutions like this. As to the very obvious rotten fruit of the systemic sexual abuse, she thought, didn't the institution itself say 'give us a child to the age of seven and we have them for life'? Indoctrination is a powerful thing in terms of the collective, as is its hold on the individual psyche, no matter how rotten its fruit.

She brought her eyes back to focus on his. "No, I am not a member of your congregation."

He inclined his head, interested. "Are you a believer?"

"In God?" she asked.

He looked amused. "Who else?"

"I believe," she said. "I believe your god was fabricated, long ago, by clever men who sought nothing more than total control of human consciousness. Thus did your external god become a mind trap, stagnating and imprisoning human thought and belief, as was the intent, so that humans would remain trapped as they are, not evolving as they are supposed to … except that they haven't stayed where they are. They have *de*volved, not necessarily entirely because of your god, but he has certainly made a significant contribution."

She watched him carefully for a reaction and was only mildly surprised when there wasn't one. He simply looked at her for a long moment, and then nodded slightly, subtly, and said, "I see."

Now it was her turn to incline her head at him.

"Do you know *when* was the inception of monotheistic religions with their one, single, masculine god? Almost three and a half thousand years ago," she continued without giving him a chance to reply, "in Ancient Egypt, the birthplace of modern humanity, at least in terms of thought and belief. That was Egypt's energy, and that was her role in the human experience, something the gods themselves were, and still are, very well aware of. Unfortunately, the one thing she birthed that has survived and matured and taken hold in the human experience is masculine monotheism. A shame, a very great shame.

The Natural Progression of the Energetic Birth-Inception Influence as it Shifts Around Gaia

"Tragically," she said softly, looking away from him, "Egypt is dead now, naught but a land of dry bones and dust, and so her contribution to and influence over the human experience is equally as dead." She looked at him again, and there was pain in her eyes. "It was not always so. Egypt was spectacularly beautiful once upon a time, and her energy was powerful and vibrant and hugely significant in terms of its influence on the development of human consciousness, thought and belief. We have but to look at the monuments of her past to know the truth of this – one of the reasons why we are, in the modern era, so fascinated by those very same monuments.

"Did we, as humans, cause the demise of Egypt's powerful energy? Yes, I'm afraid so, at least partially. The priests and pharaohs of the ancient world knew of the energy, its power, its influence, and they knew how to keep it in balance and to honour it, to harness it for the good of all. Although, also, with this knowledge came the knowledge of how to use the energy for personal gain, as some of them did." She smiled affectionately. "Egypt always fought back, though, when this happened. She didn't let them get away with it for long."

Her smile faded.

"But there is, too, a natural progression of a powerful energetic influence on consciousness that shifts and moves around Gaia, the earth, over time. Egypt's time has passed, the way individual incarnations pass, or die, or the way one pharaoh dies and gives way to another. But this natural progression of energetic influence has also been manipulated, used and hijacked by the malevolent agendas of those who believe themselves in control of the human experience. Egypt has been deliberately silenced, her energetic influence suppressed, one of the reasons why masculine monotheism survived. It survived because it served the dark agenda. Egypt was, back in her day, the custodian of a beautiful, ancient Wisdom, but that Wisdom has been deliberately suppressed and twisted into the modern monotheistic religions we have today. Those religions contain just enough of the ancient Wisdom to be palatable to human consciousness but not enough to evolve it, or to feed and nourish it.

"As for the natural progression of energetic influence, the energies at play in the human experience now are anything but natural. They are forced."

"You are speaking about the United States."

She looked at him, surprised, almost as if she had forgotten he was there. But the real source of her surprise was his ability to connect with what she was saying. His simple statement told her, very effectively, that he understood.

"Yes. 'Tis a fabricated, deliberately-shaped and moulded, much-manipulated society, but its influence is perniciously ubiquitous, infiltrating, affecting, every aspect of human existence. It is entirely possible, even probable, that the natural progression of energetic influence did genuinely move to the United States, but it was anticipated, hijacked, harnessed, and controlled. It was genuinely in Europe, particularly Italy and Spain early on, then in France and Britain up until the Great War, World War II. But then it moved, whether authentically or not, after the war, to the United States where it was utterly abused. Now, the energy has passed on, the influence of the United States is waning, rapidly, and that whole culture is in the process of imploding, just as the Roman Empire did at the end of its reign, so to speak."

"And so," he said slowly, "that begs the rather obvious question as to where the natural influence really lies now. If Egypt's and Europe's energy is no longer at the heart of the human experience in terms of its influence, then what is?"

Again, surprise flickered across her face as she looked at him. He wasn't just listening to her, he was *connecting* with what she was saying – connecting, acknowledging, understanding. That was unusual, to say the least, for a priest, especially a priest of his religion. Perhaps he really was one of them. No one understood energy as they did.

He easily read her surprise, even knew its cause, and was unable to prevent the very-slight, barely-perceptible smile of satisfaction from sparkling in his eyes. He knew exactly what her first impression of him was, and he also knew it was absolutely incorrect, understandably so given the context of their encounter and his priest's collar. So it was inordinately satisfying to begin to dissolve if not shatter her false first impression with just a few simple questions.

"Yes," she agreed, responding to his question. "That is the obvious question. I think the energy is shifting to the southern hemisphere, particularly Australia and New Zealand. It's not obvious at the moment because it's still embryonic, but soon it will become obvious as the energy there grows and matures. And it is doing so rapidly. Soon Australians, with New Zealanders, will find themselves leading the way in the human experience in terms of thought, belief, mindset, action, choice, behaviour. The energy is clean there, tainted only by their treatment of indigenous Australians when Australia was first colonised. But the fault of that lay not so much with Australians as it did with prevailing attitudes in Britain, the coloniser. Then later came the horrible episode they call the 'stolen generation'. Australians are now, however, reversing the damage done in their past as they recognise and acknowledge the importance and the beauty of the indigenous culture there, and as they honour the contribution of the aboriginal people. The aboriginal people are custodians of humanity's true history, and the rest of humanity could learn a lot from their interaction with and respect for the natural world. Australians are recognising this *and* the need to allow the aboriginal culture to express itself and to be what it is rather than being suppressed, distorted and damaged by western influences, alcohol being the very obvious one."

He absorbed that. "An interesting observation," he said simply. She was right, of course, and he knew it. He knew where the energy was located now … he knew very well where it was, and he knew very well where it *wasn't*.

Polytheism: The Gods and Goddesses of the Ancient World

"Anyway," she said, returning to her original point, "before monotheism was forced upon humanity, humans worshipped many gods, and rightly so because the gods and goddesses of the ancient world are archetypal, symbolising the myriad of different aspects of human nature, human thought and belief, and the human experience itself. Monotheistic religions were all but unheard of. People had their favourite gods they tended to pray to, but they still had many to choose from. And, of course, the gods and goddesses of the ancient world are linked with the natural world, as are their myths and rituals. Thus did they keep humans connected to the natural world and the cycles of the moon, the sun, the planets, the stars and constellations, the seasons, and the harvest. Your god does not keep humans connected to the natural world. On the contrary, he is disparaging of it and so keeps people *dis*connected from the natural world, and the consequences speak for themselves. Humans pay no heed to their environment and so do not live in harmony with their planet, and they are destroying it. They are destroying the very thing that sustains life here. How ignorantly foolish is that?

"But perhaps the most harmful dynamic introduced as a result of monotheism and the masculine, one-god cults that arose from it, is the lack of recognition accorded the sacred feminine. Thus do the sacred masculine and the sacred feminine become imbalanced, and so they have. Again, the consequence of this speaks for itself. The gods and goddesses of the ancient world kept the masculine and feminine in balance. Your god and his various religions, all with their different names and creeds, perpetuate the domination of masculine energy and the suppression of feminine energy." A shiver ran down her spine. So powerful was it that he actually saw it. "The damage done to human consciousness when these energies are out of balance is powerfully significant and inordinately difficult to repair, as we are seeing now."

He didn't respond verbally, and neither did his expression change. He listened. He absorbed. He observed, particularly the fact of her referring to humans as 'they', 'them' and 'their'. But he made no comment. She could see and sense he was very focussed on her, but she wasn't entirely sure why.

The Aten: Source of the God of Judaism, Islam, Catholicism and Christianity

Her own words, though, were taking her back to her own past, opening up memories within her, and the memories were robbing her physical sense of sight of its power. As she focussed on the memories and the visions and images they were evoking in her mind's eye, she looked away from him again as she asked him her next question.

"And do you know *what* was the source of your monotheistic god? Do you know how he came to be, how he came to exist in the psyche of humankind?"

She asked the question gently, softly, and then she paused, not to give him a chance to respond, but because of what she was seeing internally. Accordingly, her eyes became unfocussed. He could see for himself she was seeing something other than the surrounds of the church, and so he watched her but stayed silent. In truth, he sensed this was something she needed to do, and so he was loath to interrupt or disturb her vision. Plus, he was very curious as to what she could see of those circumstances she was speaking of.

"A psychologically-ill pharaoh, Amenhotep IV, ascended the throne of Egypt and declared his new god, the Aten, his sun god, to be the only true, living god. Archaeologists call it the 'Amarna

Period', and they see it as just a period in Egyptian history, albeit a fascinating one. But the truth is, this period of Egyptian history had lasting and significant consequences for the whole of humanity, and its impacts are still very much felt to this day. It was pivotal, and it altered the course and direction of the human experience in entirety. As I said, this was the time of the birth of the one-god cults that still predominate to this very day.

"Of course, when this pharaoh declared his Aten to be the one, true, living god (do Christians still not use this clichéd term to this very day?) he also declared himself to be his god's only earthly intermediary thus putting himself at the very centre of his cult and making sure no one else would ever replace him or even equal him – the fundamental and classic cult dynamic – only one of the reasons why monotheism is so harmful." She focussed, briefly, on him, her companion. "His god formed the basis of yours because it was his people who took his god out of Egypt and established what became the precursor for modern religion today. From his god, yours emerged, victorious apparently, over all other gods. That certainly has been the case in the long term."

Again, she refocussed on her memories so that her eyes shifted from his.

"The pharaoh changed his name to Akhenaten in honour of his one god, and he wiped aside the pantheon of gods that had existed in the Egyptian culture for thousands of years – a pantheon of gods that was deeply entrenched in the Egyptian psyche because those old gods had served our people well for hundreds of generations. He began simply by taking over our temple, the religious centre, or heart, of Egypt at the time, and installing his one-god as the primary god, having precedence over all others in the pantheon. But, then, still in the early years of his reign, he banned the worship of the old gods and ordered all their temples in our land closed. The people now had no choice but to worship his one god. This behaviour was, and still is, very telling for those who cannot decide if this man was villain or hero, tyrant or visionary. An authentically-spiritual person would never, *never* take people's gods from them and impose his own religious beliefs on them. Thus was this behaviour not about spirituality at all but, rather, power, and, in particular, the lust for it and for homage of his own very-wounded ego, as cults always are.

"'Tis natural, perhaps," she continued, still looking back at the past, "to wonder how anyone could hold the sort of power necessary to command an entire culture of people to simply stop worshipping their old, traditional gods and start worshipping a new and strange god. But he could because he had inherited genuine power from his father. His family, the 18th Dynasty, had established a real power base not just in Egypt but also in the regions we now know as the Middle East and north Africa. Egypt's might and power were supreme in these regions, not just physically, but economically, too. In fact, Egypt's supremacy was such that it maintained peace in the region. No one, in Akhenaten's time went to war with Egypt. No one would dare. And there were other things weaved into the power base established by the preceding members of the 18th Dynasty, things that should never be underestimated, like myth and reputation born of battles fought and won, peoples conquered, events experienced, territories gained, and hardships overcome. So the family, the 18th Dynasty, ruled authentically and completely.

The Seeds of Monotheism Sown

"But the seeds of Akhenaten's cult were sown not with the son, the IV of his name, but with the father, the III. The old adage we've all heard is never more aptly demonstrated than with these two: power corrupts, and absolute power corrupts absolutely. We saw the same dynamic much later with Phillip of Macedon, who established a real power base that was, then, handed on to his son, Alexander the Great. Amenhotep III, Akhenaten's father, inherited wealth and power beyond comparison at that time, but he was twelve when he ascended the throne of Egypt, still a boy, still a developing consciousness. How is a child to handle such wealth and power when most adults cannot? What sort of a distorted perspective would he have held of his world, his environment, and the people who surrounded him? And who was there to take him in hand and guide him, or to hold him in check, for that matter? Most of his advisers sought only to ingratiate themselves, to fuel and further their own selfish ambitions.

"So Amenhotep III, Akhenaten's father, was taught from a young age to feed his monstrous ego, a fact born out by the number of statues and temples he built to glorify himself. The statues created of him are among the largest *ever* built. They're even called 'colossi'. One in particular is known to be the largest ever built by any monarch in any culture in any time period. And no pharaoh ever built more temples than he did – temples that were ostensibly erected to honour the gods but, really, honoured only his ego.

"And so, is it not a sad fact that the more power an ego like his holds, the more power it *wants* to hold? The ego is always a black hole of want and need that can never be filled, especially when it casts such a shadow over the soul, as his did. The evidence of his megalomania still exists and is, even now, being unearthed in Egypt to this very day. The vast wealth he controlled coupled with the power he commanded was so supreme it was almost complete … almost." She held up her fingers to indicate a very small amount as she focussed on him again, this priest who was paying her the courtesy of listening. "Almost. Only one thing stood in his way, one very big thorn in his side, one challenge to the supremacy of his power, to its completeness, and it came not from outside Egypt but from within: the priesthood, especially the priesthood of Amun-Ra, the primary god at that time. The priesthood held real power, and its power was multifaceted. The temples were storehouses of great wealth, not just gold but grain, and, of course, as intermediaries of the gods and conduits for their power, the priesthood wielded real, genuine power over the psyches of the people and, thus, over the people themselves.

"Amenhotep III railed against this. He hated the power of the priesthood, and so conflict was generated between the two – a conflict that grew in intensity and gained momentum the longer he reigned. Regardless of culture or country, there is always trouble when church and state are at odds, out of alignment. But when they openly oppose each other, a very great wound is opened up in the psyche of that culture. And so it was during the reign of Amenhotep III. He became obsessed with breaking the power of the Amun-Ra priesthood, and he found a way. He sought and found, in the archives and records of the past, ironically, in the archives held in the temples, rituals practiced by the despotic Fourth-Dynasty kings – rituals that would make him a god in his own lifetime. So he stage-managed this ritual for himself with those of the priesthood who saw not the danger of what they were doing because they saw only an opportunity to further their own selfish ambitions. The ritual was accompanied by much pomp and ceremony to ensure they got the attention of the people, and the ritual itself was designed to transform the pharaoh into the living incarnation of the powerful and ancient sun god, Ra. Thus did he become a god in his own lifetime, as I said.

"But that's not all. This pharaoh did something else that was unprecedented at the time, something very foolish. He courted the power of Sekhmet, the goddess of chaos, and chaos has many forms: war and conflict, pestilence and disease, famine, turbulent weather events. Only an arrogant fool or an ignorantly foolish ego believes the power of Sekhmet can be commanded and controlled. Priests and priestesses underwent intense and specific training to be able even to interact with this power, let alone keep it under control, so dangerous was it known to be. And in focussing so much on Sekhmet, Amenhotep III would have been neglecting one of the primary roles of the pharaoh – that of honouring the Law of Ma'at – the very thing that kept chaos at bay in Egypt. Archaeologists believe the hundreds and hundreds of life size statues of Sekhmet discovered in the third courtyard of Amenhotep's massive funerary temple were about protection. But I know they were about harnessing Sekhmet's power to generate conflict. He wanted conflict with the priesthood. He wanted the priesthood defeated. But in courting Sekhmet's power, he was courting real danger and very serious trouble because her power cannot *ever* be controlled.

"It was, however, the son, the IV of their name, in whom the seeds of megalomania grew to their fullest fruition. The son inherited the father's conflict with the priesthood, but the son went a step further than the father, heedless of any dangers involved. He, too, declared himself the only intermediary of the only god that truly existed, and he threw out the old gods. In a single stroke, a single command, he broke the power of the priesthood, or so he thought. His odes to his god reveal it all very clearly: '*How manifold are thy works! They are hidden from the sight of men, O Sole God, like unto whom there is no other ... but there is none other who knows thee save thy son Akhenaten*'. The secular power of the throne was now combined with the spiritual power of a god. Thus was Akhenaten's power complete, or so he thought."

"Did you meet him?"

The question surprised her, and it pulled her back to the present. She focussed on him again, this priest who had chosen to sit with her and talk.

"Yes. I met him, only once, although I saw him many times." She smiled slightly, a smile of deep and genuine amusement that found greater expression in her eyes than in the curve of her mouth. "In the same instant he met me, he dismissed me as irrelevant and paid me no more heed. But I paid attention to him. His energy was chaotic and very unstable. He was dangerously one-eyed in his focus, and, as such, there were equally-as-dangerous imbalances in his psyche, and vice versa, too. The two fed off each other within him. There was madness and darkness in his black eyes, and wherever he went and whatever he did, he expected to be the centre of attention so that he sucked everything into himself, like a black hole. Such is the vampiric dynamic at the heart of every cult. Cult leaders truly are vampires, feeding off the homage of the members of the cult, draining them dry, and even discarding them like the scraps of a meal when they no longer serve a purpose. And, he held such animosity towards those of us of the old priesthood who openly opposed him, very possibly the reason he dismissed me so readily. He knew I would never become a part of the infrastructure of his new cult."

"Were you priest or priestess?"

"I was female in that life, and I was, initially, just a priestess, very young, not part of the hierarchy of our priesthood. But oh how easily did so many of our priesthood abandon their beliefs in favour of his one-god to ingratiate themselves with him. Many saw only the means by which they might further their own cause and fulfil their own ambitions. It was a thing to behold. It exposed their inauthenticity, but the shock of it, for me, was in how many of them abandoned us. How easily they abandoned themselves in the process. But at what cost? Many of them died."

"Why did you oppose him? Why did you not just worship his god?"

"Because," she said, her eyes losing focus again as the memory opened up within her, "I sensed the danger in what he was doing. Real danger. I could feel it. The truth is, no matter how powerful you think you are, you *cannot* simply wipe aside thousands of years of beliefs as if with the sweep of your hand or the click of your fingers. No one ever holds that kind of power, and if you try to exercise it, it will blow up in your face. And so it did. The old gods were entrenched in the psyche of our culture, our people, and he actually did not have the power to change that, command or no command. Thus was he playing around with the psyche of our people, and I knew there were going to be consequences, very serious consequences." Her eyes were filled with a great sadness, and she couldn't help but glance around the church. "If only I had foreseen just how far-reaching those consequences would be." She looked back to him, her companion. "But also, I saw then what is typical with a religious cult, or any cult, for that matter. His god was, really, naught but a means of having the people worship *him*. And he did, indeed, demand that of the people. Plus, I would never abandon the old gods. They had served us too well for too long."

"So what happened to the old priesthood?"

"We were harboured, sheltered by those who still believed. We still met, and we still served our people, and conducted our rituals, but we had to be very careful, and, of course, we had to do so in absolute secrecy."

"So what happened, from your perspective?"

"Deep down, in their collective unconscious, the people believed they would be punished for abandoning the old gods, and so the collective Egyptian psyche created that as a truth in their collective reality. I remember the day I knew chaos would reign down on our land. I see it clearly. I was looking across the river as the sun was setting. I was looking north, towards his new capital, although it was too far away for me to see it physically. The energy radiating from that place felt discordant and dangerous and destructive. Actually, it sent ripples of discordance and disturbance out across the entire land. I felt the chill dread of premonition. It filled my body and sent ripples from my head to my toes. And even though it was many long years before chaos did, indeed, reign and rain down on Egypt, it did come, and I lived all those long years with the knowledge sitting heavily within me. It was as if we were all walking into a dark storm cloud of chaos – Sekhmet unleashed, thanks to Amenhotep III, running rampant and out of control. And so she did. So she did. Thus were the sins of both father and son visited upon our people.

"Disease and plague ravaged our land. And the crops failed. Archaeologists have identified, in the mass graves at Amarna,

Akhenaten's fabricated religious capital, mosquito-born malaria and bubonic and pneumonic plague as well. Plague is a real killer. In Europe, plague ravaged the population in both the thirteen- and sixteen-hundreds, and even though the contagion of the sixteen-hundreds is the better known of the two, in the thirteen-hundreds, the plague wiped out fully one-third of the population in Europe at the time before it ran its course. There is no official record of anyone ever surviving pneumonic plague, and only a small number have survived bubonic plague. Plague ravages, as does malaria – the biggest killer of humans outside of war – and many died in the chaos that ravaged our land. It was frightening to behold, disease moving from person to person, striking them down quickly. Even Akhenaten himself was a victim of the chaos. He lost many of his loved ones to the disease that ravaged the land, including his own Great Royal Wife, Nefertiti.

"Ironically and tragically, the chaos ultimately worked in our favour. It served to restore the power of the old gods and, with them, the priesthood, and we were able to bring him down. And so we did. We restored the old gods, and we expelled the heretic pharaoh and his one-god cult from Egypt. He was banished, sent into exile. We tore down the edifices he had built to his god, including his false, fabricated city, and we expunged him from the annals of Egyptian history, albeit only back then, thereby expunging him from the Egyptian psyche – a fate worse than death in those days. How ironic it is, then, that the shared tomb of the much-younger brothers, Smenkhare and Tutankhamun, both of whom were pharaohs following Akhenaten, was, really, the only tomb to survive intact into the modern era thereby allowing the world to know about the family, including Akhenaten. But then, the tomb survived because it was meant to, and this despite the lies and deception, and the dishonest actions of those involved in its discovery. We should have thought, right back then, to expunge Akhenaten from the human psyche, not just the Egyptian one, because the damage rippling out from that time has been so utterly profound.

"The Bible calls it the 'exodus', his banishment, but it was, of course, the expulsion, or the exile. The pharaoh called himself the son of his god, *mos*, or *mosis*, in Egyptian, and the Greeks then flattened this out into Moses. He used to write psalms to his god, or odes that he made public, and when you read the psalms supposedly written by King David in the Bible, they bare a striking and startling resemblance, almost word for word in some cases, each to the others. *Thy rod and thy staff, they comfort me* (Psalm 23): to see what the rod and the staff are we have only to look at the depictions of the gods and pharaohs of Ancient Egypt, because these *are* Egyptian. Such is the distortion and the convolution of the biblical representation of our true history. And yet, no one wonders why there are no archaeological or official records of these men – Moses and David – ever having existed. Their only record is in a Bible that in no way represents or documents our true history. And do you know what the analogy of David slaying the giant Goliath represented to those who were responsible for writing it at the time? The young king, Akhenaten, accomplishing what his mighty father couldn't quite manage: the slaying of the mighty Amun-Ra priesthood.

"As for the ten plagues of Egypt described in the Bible, they were real enough, a domino effect of catastrophe caused by a massive volcanic eruption on the ancient island of Thera. But the eruption and, therefore, the domino-effect of disasters, did not occur during our lifetime. It occurred just before the beginning of Akhenaten's Dynasty, the 18th, and, in fact, I believe it was instrumental in Ahmose, the first pharaoh of the 18th Dynasty, arresting control of lower Egypt from the Asiatic invaders, the Hyksos, thereby unifying Egypt once again under a single rule. Thus was the series of cataclysmic events a vital part of the lore of Akhenaten's family, handed down from one generation to the next.

"What happens when the victorious speak of events after the fact? They get to tell the story exactly as they want to. What happens when cult members record events in history from their distorted perspectives, weaving their own agendas into the threads of those same events? Well, you get the narrative we have today in the Bible, a twisted, distorted, convoluted version of truths and half truths that humans today believe represent their true history. Myth becomes reality, and different events occurring at different times are folded up or rolled up into a single cohesive whole, like pieces of fabric gathered up and bunched together into a single handful."

Modern One-god Cults Born of the Quagmire of Megalomania

She shook her head sadly.

"We were so intent on restoring our land that we did not give a thought to anyone or anything outside of it. We allowed the next pharaoh, Smenkhare, to exile the heretic when we should have executed him for high, high treason. He betrayed our people. The Bible tells us pharaoh changed his mind, allowing Moses to leave at first but then going after him. Pharaoh did not change his mind. Pharaoh himself changed. Smenkhare ruled only for a few years before an untimely death, and he was replaced by Tutankhamun, whose name was, initially, Tutankhaten. We, the priesthood, could not fully control the former, but we got control of the latter." She looked at him, this priest who was allowing her to speak. "Our mistake," she said intensely, "was in allowing the heretic his freedom." She sighed as she looked away. "One-god cults do not sit well with the human psyche, not well at all. They are, in fact, harmful, even dangerous."

She looked at him again and inclined her head at him.

"*And so, out of the quagmire of megalomania – the supreme lust for and addiction to power and the need to be superior – the bedrock of all one-god cults – was born the god of Catholicism, the god of Christianity, the god of Judaism, and the god of Islam, for these were all born of each other. Thus are these all masculine, one-god cults. And within these, there are cults within the cults, which is why sects supposedly of the same religion fight and kill each other.*

"This is the inherent danger of monotheism: power and control."

Silence reigned for a moment between the two of them when she finished speaking. She could not determine what the silence held – shock, disapproval, surprise, anger. It seemed to contain nothing at all. He merely listened, and it seemed to her he was forming absolutely no judgements whatsoever.

"And when the old priesthood was restored, were you a part of its hierarchy?" he asked her.

She nodded. "I was. I was a high priestess."

"So you were actively instrumental in bringing down a king and expelling both him and his cult from the land?"

"No, I was not so much a part of that, although they had my full support. I was more focussed on restoring the old gods and restoring the natural order after the chaos. He violated one of our most basic laws – the Law of Ma'at. I was instrumental in re-establishing the law and seeing that it was upheld. It was as important to do that for the people as it was to banish the heretic pharaoh and his one-god cult."

"So Ma'at was the goddess you served?"

"One of them. I honoured Her, yes. My ..." she looked for the right words, "skill set was more conducive to serving the Lady Is't, or *Jst*, Isis in Greek, and so I did. I would never abandon Her because abandoning Her would have been abandoning myself, and so I did not back then."

"I see," he said again, very quietly. "And do you serve Her still?"

She didn't exactly smile, but a semblance of a smile sparkled in her eyes as she looked at him. "Her energy is a part of me. Always has it been thus. And always will it be. She is the great navigator, and sailors used to pay Her homage accordingly. But 'tis not the waters of this earth, nor the lands, that she navigates, but, rather, the labyrinth of the psyche. She is masterful at that, and She could always aid the people with the navigation of their own psyches. And so She did, and so, too, did I. And so, too, do I still. I suspect that is one of the reasons why I knew Akhenaten was taking us straight into supreme danger. Plus, Her words are magic. Her words hold Her power, and great, indeed, is that power – the power to affect consciousness. Yes, I serve Her still because I am Her."

He didn't respond to her smile, but nor did he take his eyes from hers. He responded to what she said with the merest, slightest nod of his head.

Modern Religious Rituals Formed out of Rites of Black Magic

"Do you conduct mass here?" she asked him, changing the subject, wanting to establish whether or not he was one of them, even if he did not know it.

"I do. I take the evening mass."

"Why?" she asked. "Why the evening one?"

"Because it's smaller, more intimate. Less people. No children running amok. And because there are priests of greater seniority here than I am, all three of whom conduct the largest services during the day." Again, he inclined his head. "If you are not a believer or a member of this church, then may I ask why you are here?"

His question did not hold judgement or criticism. He merely asked it, out of curiosity, although not curiosity as to why she was there, but, rather, curiosity as to whether or not she *knew* why she was there.

Again, she looked around her, as if the church itself would yield up the answer. "There's something ..." she said softly, absently, as if she was not so much answering his question as she was thinking out loud. And then she looked at him again. "This church was gifted to me as and in a vision. I say gifted," she said, anticipating the question she could see in his eyes and in his slightly-opened mouth, "because it came to me courtesy of someone else's description – someone I trust. The description caused the vision to open up within me, and it has stayed with me ever since. So I came back."

"I see," he said. "And you do not know why?"

"No, I don't. Is there a crypt here?"

He nodded, once. "There is."

"And do they conduct black magic rituals in it?"

This time he reacted to the question, but only with slightly narrowed eyes. "No."

"Is that no, they don't, or, no, not that you're aware of, or, no, you don't participate in them?"

"No, there are no such rituals practised anywhere in this church. I know that for certain." Again, his tone was not defensive, just informative.

She raised her eyebrows at him slightly. "But you conduct mass here," she said. "So you *are* conducting rituals of magic – rituals that hold more than an element of black magic, too. Take a step back from the tradition of mass, and communion, from taking the rituals completely for granted, and you will see the truth of my words: repetitive prayers that are incantations, wine that symbolises the drinking of blood, wafers or bread that symbolise the eating of human flesh. Those are powerful elements of black magic, as is their effect on those who partake of them. The strong link to masculine energy, too, means that the ritual magic in the mass you preside over stirs up negative masculine energy. You conduct mass in the name of a masculine god, and 'tis his blood and his flesh that you supposedly consume. Is it any wonder, then, the masculine has dominated and suppressed the feminine for the last two thousand years?" She narrowed her eyes at him. "'Tis an extremely successful manipulation, implementing mass in the religions of the west. It has effectively meant humans have, themselves, been complicit in the ongoing perpetuation of the manipulation.

"And couching the mass in religious overtones to make it palatable to the ignorant, gullible congregation of people does not change the truth of that." She sighed softly. "And humans wonder why there is so much aggression and anger in this world. Well, some of them do. Most of them don't even think about it, to their own very great detriment. Worse, most of them don't *want* to think about it. But things like your mass they take totally for granted so that they don't think about the ritual at all or its potential effects on them. They're told where it came from and how it came to be a part of the church service, and they simply believe what they're told, even though what they've been told is a lie. They just think they are earning their own ticket to a heaven that doesn't exist because they have been programmed to believe it, often since they were little children.

"I've said it many times before, but I'll say it again. Heaven and hell are not places humans go to after death depending on how they've behaved in their lifetime, and heaven is definitely not a place one can buy one's way into. Heaven or hell are states of being humans create in *this* moment, and whichever they exist in is entirely up to them. They *will* create one or the other, though, and, ironically and tragically, rituals of black magic will cause them to create out of fear, separation, aggression and conflict ... hell, in other words. Thus will they exist. Thus *do* they exist."

Silence again fell between the two, him and her. They both held and maintained eye contact, and the energy of both of them was neither aggressive, attacking, nor defensive. She wasn't attacking him personally by pointing out the truth of the rituals he presided over, and nor was he defensive, at least in terms of his energy. She would have felt it if so. That, she thought, was interesting, because, by rights, he should be very offended, given the context of their conversation.

Eventually, after a long moment, he asked her, "Do you not think it a little offensive to come into a church and speak to the priest here of the harm to his congregation of the religious rituals he presides over?"

She inclined her head at him. "Only if you find the truth offensive. And," she added, "if you were going to be offended, you would have been so long before now."

"Again, I have to ask, if you are no friend of this church, then why are you here?"

She uncrossed her legs and stood, arranging her bag on her shoulder, and tucking her jacket against her. Again, she looked around, and this time she looked troubled. "I told you. I don't know. 'Tis a question I've been asking myself since I stood at the front doors."

He didn't say anything. He just sat watching her.

"And so," she said, looking down at him, "it would seem you cannot help me, after all. I am sorry to have disturbed you."

"I'm not disturbed," he said, not moving from his place on the pew.

She smiled. "Good. I'm glad." And then she turned to go.

"Wait," he said, and the word was spoken with some force. It stopped her in her tracks, especially after the mild, gentle way he'd spoken to her up until that point. She turned and looked back down at him.

"Why do you refer to humans as 'they' and 'them'? Are you not one of them?"

"I am incarnate, so I am human in this lifetime, but, no, I am not one of them. Not at all."

He uncrossed his legs and stood so that he faced her.

"What are you, then?"

"I am a Guardian."

To her surprise, he nodded as if he fully understood and, in fact, had already worked out for himself what she was.

"So, as a Guardian, why were you in Egypt at the time of Akhenaten's cult? Were you there to stop him? Or were you there to put Egypt right after his expulsion?"

She shook her head. "Neither," she replied. "I was there as an observer. I was just there to observe, although I did help to put things right again in Egypt, as I said. Almost everything I've done up until this life has been *for* this life, and *for* this time in the evolution of human consciousness."

Again, he nodded. "Why did you ask me about the crypt?"

"Why? Because churches like this are, traditionally and where possible, built on strategically and energetically important sites, usually the convergence, or the meeting points, of the ley lines that run through the earth like veins. When they conduct their rituals of black magic, the darkest power is sent through those ley lines in such a way as to affect all and any beings who exist near them. Usually, they build crypts into their churches for just such a purpose."

"You are right about this church being built on an energetically significant site," he said, "because so it is. Very significant. There is real power here. This site is a convergent point of not two but three ley lines."

Now she was fully, intensely focussed on him. "How do you know that?"

He shrugged. "I know because I know."

"You can feel it?"

"Sometimes. Can you feel it?"

She honed her senses, sending her awareness out. And then she shook her head. "There is no dark energy in this place. I can feel that. I *could* feel that from the moment I walked in, so I believe you when you say black magic is not practised here … other than the mildly-powerful rituals of your masses, that is. But I cannot feel the power of the site beyond that. The church contains it, I think, and changes it, a bit like a coffin."

When she focussed on him again, he was amused, although neither his mouth nor his eyes had altered. She could feel it in his energy. "Do I amuse you?" she asked him.

He put his hands in the pockets of his trousers. "You interest me," he replied. "Which is a lot more than I usually say about most people."

For a moment, they looked at each other.

"I think I might know why you are here," he said.

"Why?"

"If you will trust me, I would like to show you something."

An expression flickered across her face, briefly, that he found impossible to interpret. "I will trust you," she said.

He nodded and moved. "Then follow me."

He brushed past her and she followed him to the front of the aisle, and then along the side of the red-carpeted dais to the very back corner of the church. Dark, wood panelling covered the wall, from behind the organ to the very corners of the room. She thought, for a moment, they were going to walk right into it, but he reached up and released some sort of latch. It made a deep and distinct clicking sound that echoed around them both for a brief moment. When the internal latch was released, the panelling popped open, and he pulled it, opening it like a door.

"Watch your step," he advised, preceding her through the door. "The steps are solid but steep."

When she followed him, stepping through and then past the wood panelling, she found herself on a small stone ledge that then descended into darkness courtesy of the steep steps he had warned her about. He turned and reached up behind her. For a brief moment, she thought he was going to touch her, but he reached past her and flicked a light on before stepping down onto the first step. The light was old and gave off inadequate light, although it was augmented somewhat by the natural light coming through the panelled opening. She followed him carefully, her right hand against the cold stone wall beside them to steady herself. Courtesy of the inadequate light, the steps were as much in shadow as they were in light, and they spiralled around and around. The temperature dropped significantly as she stepped down, and tiny goosebumps raised the hairs on her neck and arms, although she knew the goosebumps were not a reaction to the dropping temperature. The atmosphere in the stone stairwell was vastly different from the main hall, colder, and not just because of the much-cooler temperature and the cold stone. But nor was the atmosphere the cause of her physical reaction. With every step down, she became more certain that he was taking her where she needed to be. And, she knew instinctively that he did not take everybody down here – an understatement if ever there was one. He did not take *anybody* down here.

Even as she stepped off the last step, onto the cold stone floor of the crypt, she could see and sense light, and the light was different from that emitted by the old globe at the top of the stairs. Large, thick stone pillars prevented her from determining the light's source, but it radiated, gently, and it was pure white, somehow, soft but powerful at the same time.

She followed him further into the bowels of the crypt. Although the ceiling of the crypt was high, also made of stone, the heaviness of the stone in general made the crypt feel oppressive, as if its pillars and ceiling and walls were closing in on her, or as if she really had walked into a tomb. Aside from the gentle, white light that emanated from somewhere in the very centre of the crypt, the rest of it, especially around its edges was dark, and the darkness, to her, felt malevolent, so much so, she began to question whether or not she really did believe him about the black magic rituals. But then, as she followed him around one of the pillars, she saw the source of the light and knew it would not have been possible for any entity of darkness to be in this place, let alone conduct rituals of darkness.

She froze where she was, and she stared. He stood aside so that her vision would be clear, and then he came to stand right beside her, watching her closely.

Slowly, she put her bag and jacket down on the floor at the base of the pillar. And when she straightened again, she put her hands in the pockets of her jeans. Involuntarily, unconsciously, she took a couple of steps closer to what she could see. No wonder it was gentle but powerful, she thought. The source of the light was a shimmer hanging in the air, almost like very fine, gossamer material, or thin silk weaved from threads of light, suspended from nothing, although it almost touched both the floor of the crypt and its ceiling. The source of the light in the crypt wasn't light at all. It was Light. And in the absolute darkness and dinginess and coldness of the crypt, she could see clearly.

"Has this always been here?" she asked him.

He was standing slightly behind her. She'd taken a couple of steps towards the shimmering Light, but he had continued to stand where he was. "No, not always. The church was built over the convergence of the ley lines, as I said, not because of this. This came after, once the church was here."

"How long after?"

"Many, many decades, I would say. More than a century of them."

"Then it hasn't been here for that long?"

"No, it has not."

"Do the other priests know it's here?"

"Of course. We all protect it … religiously, if you'll pardon the choice of word."

She looked at him, then, a smile in her eyes in response to what he'd said. Because he was behind her, she had to turn her body slightly when she turned her head. "Do they know what it is?"

He nodded. "They do."

She inclined her head, a gesture that signalled her lack of comprehension. "How is that possible? Surely this would conflict with their religious beliefs. How do they reconcile the two?"

He noticed she referred to the other priests as 'they', such that, whether consciously or unconsciously, she did not include him with them. He wasn't entirely sure she was aware of it but she was shifting her mindsets, letting go of old ones, taking on new ones, especially where he was concerned, a little like being caught between two worlds, or, more aptly, two dimensions.

"*They*," he said, emphasising the word, "think of it as a gateway to heaven." He shrugged his shoulders and held out his hands. "And who am I to disabuse them of the notion?"

"Perhaps," she said, "they are not far wrong."

"That depends entirely on the individual. For most people here, now, this," and he lifted a hand to indicate the shimmer, "would be incredibly dangerous. Even standing this close to it could potentially be incredibly dangerous."

She narrowed her eyes. "In terms of their sanity, you mean?"

He nodded.

"So the other priests have not stepped through it, then?"

"No," he replied, "and nor would it be advisable. They would not handle the experience … at all. But they understand that, so they would not attempt to step through it. I suspect they believe they will not return if they step through it."

"Like death?"

He nodded. "Like death," he repeated.

"So how did you know I would handle being this close to it?"

He took a moment to answer her, and in the silence between question and answer, they looked at each other. Again, her body responded. Her heart increased its beat so that it started pounding in her chest. And she felt nervous, very, very nervous. Unconsciously, without meaning to, she turned and faced him fully so that she could, now, only perceive the shimmer of Light out of the corner of her eye.

"You have been prepared," he said, "have you not?"

In lieu of replying, she asked him another question of her own. "How do you know that?"

"I know," he replied ambiguously, and then, "I know because I know you. Why have you not asked me if I've stepped through it?"

She broke eye contact with him, looking at the collar of his shirt. "Because I know you have," she said.

"How do you know?"

She raised her eyes to look into his again. "I know because I know you."

He smiled.

"The real question," she said, "is which side of it are you from?"

His smile deepened. "That is, indeed, the real question, is it not? And what is your answer?"

She turned to look at it again, and when she did, its Light lit her face, illuminating her features. "You are from the other side of it."

"As . . are . . you." He enunciated each word clearly, slowly, definitely.

She turned her head to look at him, but slowly. When she looked into his eyes again, she nodded, also slowly, and said softly, "Yes."

They looked at each other. They just looked, neither moving, neither speaking, for how long, neither she nor he could gauge. Finally, she broke the spell that had settled over them by asking a question.

"You wear a glamour?"

"Yes, I do. And do not ask me to release it. I always hold the glamour of the priest when I am in the priest's clothes. It's just something I have to do. You," he said, "wear a glamour, too, my Lady."

She closed her eyes briefly as pain, hot and potent, shot through her like an electric current. "I know," she said quietly. "But I cannot shed mine as easily as you do yours."

He reached out, laying gentle fingers on her cheek, and he caressed the soft skin of her cheek with his thumb. "Do not forget," he said as quietly, "the glamour has served you well, my Lady. It has protected you, shielded you while you Worked, and it has allowed you to be here."

"As one of them," she finished for him. "Yes, I know."

He nodded. "No more, though. There is not the need for you to be one of them anymore. So you may shed your glamour now, my Lady."

She laid a hand over his. "If only it were that easy."

They were standing so close, now, they could both see the variation of colour in each other's eyes. Pointedly, he looked at the shimmer of Light hanging in the air not ten paces from them. "It *is* that easy," he said.

She looked, too, following his line of vision. When she turned her head, he took his hand away from her cheek, but he held onto her hand and he didn't step back. She knew she wasn't quite ready to go there, through the shimmer, just yet.

"How do you handle playing the part of the priest and presiding over those horrible rituals?" she asked him, turning towards him again.

"I do it because it serves Purpose to do so. I do it because I must play the part of the priest to remain here. 'Tis a perfect disguise. 'Tis part of the glamour. I become like an actor, donning a costume, playing a part, reciting a well-rehearsed script. 'Tis not hard since the script is always the same, week in, week out. It has absolutely no meaning, therefore. It is just a bunch of words that I say over and over again. As for the rituals, my intent is neither to help the people here nor to harm them, and I imbue no meaning in the rituals because they mean nothing to me. Thus is the power and the effect on the people minimised. They," he said, referring to the congregation, "concern me not at all. I am not here for them. I did not come for them."

"Then why are you here?"

"Need you ask? I am here for you. Why else do you think you were so drawn to this church? And before you ask, there is no safer place to create a portal than in the bowels of a church. No one comes here, to this place. And I needed the power of this site to create the portal. That's why here. I knew you would come, no matter where you were physically. Such is your power, and such is the power of your vision. I knew you would be drawn here."

"So you have awaited me."

"I have."

"Did you know who I was when first you laid eyes on me?"

"I suspected you were you. I felt you as soon as you walked into the church. The conversation we had confirmed it."

She smiled a crooked smile at him. "You are not so young, then, as first I thought."

He smiled, too. "I am not young at all. I am, in fact, as old as you."

She raised an eyebrow. "That old, eh? I noticed there were no depictions of the crucified Jesus in the church. That's unusual in a church like this. Was that your doing?"

He nodded. "It was. I could not have been here if any such images had remained in the church. As symbols, they are harmful because they are pure deceit."

"How did you convince the priests to remove them?"

"I explained to them they were focussing too much on the death and not the life of 'Jesus', and I used my powers of persuasion to aid the penetration of my words. And, no, before you ask. I did not tell them who I was. They would not have handled the truth of me."

She nodded, understanding, knowing he spoke the truth. And then she turned to look, once again, at the beautiful shimmer of Light hanging in the air. "Will you come with me?"

A strange expression flickered in his eyes and across his features. Although she did not see it because she was looking away from him, she felt it. "How can you ask that of me? Of course I will come with you. Of course."

The intensity in his response brought a smile up and out of her. And then she laughed softly. "All right, then, let us waste not a moment more."

She moved away from him, breaking physical contact, but only temporarily. He would not allow any break in contact between them to be permanent from now on. They had both endured the torture of separation and Separation for long enough. And so, as she walked towards the shimmer, he came with her, and he entwined his fingers with hers. She responded, curling hers around his. She ignored her bag and coat, leaving both on the floor beside the pillar. When they reached the shimmer, he released her hand to reach up and take the collar from around his neck. When he dropped it on the stone floor of the crypt, he shed the glamour he was holding so that she could see him as he really was. Then, he stepped through the shimmer, becoming a part of it, and turned to help her through it.

As she stepped through it, there was only a blazing impression of Light – Light all around her – and warmth, but not warmth of temperature, warmth of embrace and welcome. The Light passed over her and through her, and it filled her to the brim. Where once she had been vacant, now she was filled to overflowing. Where once there had been a cold, dark, empty place within her, now there was Light and warmth and incredible substance. She was home. At long, long last, she had come home.

When both he and she had stepped into and through the shimmer of Light, it disappeared, as if they took it with them. The crypt was, then, filled with a darkness so dark, it was oppressively heavy. The crypt became, once again, what it had really always been – the bowels of a Catholic church – a cold, dark, empty place.

~

2

The Temple

Once again, she hesitated on the threshold of a large religious building, this time because she knew there would be a place where she could take her shoes off and leave her bag, and she looked around for just such a place. There was a monk, or a priest, dressed in his orange robe, sitting calmly on a chair against the left wall of the temple, facing the entrance, and just inside it. When she caught his eye, he indicated the long line of shoes placed neatly against the wall beside him. She smiled at him in acknowledgement and walked towards him, slipping her shoes off her feet and adding them to the long, neat line, and then slipping her bag off her shoulder and leaving it near the monk on his chair. She stood in front of him, then, and bowed slightly towards him, her hands held prayer-like against her chest. He acknowledged her thanks by repeating the same gesture back to her.

She turned to face the inner sanctum of the temple.

On the other side of the entrance, a man stood watching her, his arms folded as he leaned on one of the temple's wooden posts. He wore jeans, and his feet, like everyone else's in the temple, were bare. His blue t-shirt matched his blue eyes, and his hair was dark, almost black, and neither short nor long. She was completely unaware of him and so, as she moved further into the temple, she was not aware of the fact that he moved with her, matching her on the other side, his eyes never leaving her.

The first thing she noticed about this temple was that the temperature was exactly the same inside as it was outside. The weather in this country was usually hot, especially at this time of the year, but today, the temperature was mild. It was one of those days when one could wear whatever it was one wanted to wear, so she, like the man watching her, was dressed in jeans and a light, cream, long-sleeved, lace blouse, although she had pulled the sleeves up. Her long, dark-brown hair was pulled back and wound into an untidy bun at the back of her head so that curls escaped it and framed her face, and she wore only minimal make-up, enough, really, to enhance her green eyes.

This temple was not empty. On the contrary, there were many people in the temple, only a handful of them tourists. Usually she thought tourists possessed an unfortunate ability to suck the life and soul out of a place, but not here, not in this temple. The temple was not allowing it. Despite the numerous people, the temple was silent. It was, she thought, a little like a library, only with the added element of reverence. The people were moving around silently, respect and reverence in their stance, their demeanour, and in the hushed tones of any conversations they were engaging in. For the most part, the people did not speak, just as she and the monk at the temple's entrance had not spoken verbally.

It seemed to her as she moved further into the interior that the temple offered something for all her senses. The sweet scent of incense filled the temple, satisfying her sense of smell, and there were colourful flowers everywhere. Visually, the interior space was beautiful. The silence and tranquillity of the atmosphere were both welcomed and welcoming, and the peace and calm of the place wrapped itself around her, soothing and calming her inwardly so that she felt the tension in her muscles slowly ease, and her muscles relaxed as a consequence.

The temple itself, she observed, was all natural materials – wood, stone and thatch – and its interior was adorned with gold and colourful cloth and real flowers. Nothing artificial.

Noticing a wooden bench against the wall more than half way into the temple's interior, she moved towards it and then sat so she could observe her surroundings. A substantial group of people from many different cultures, both male and female, and a curious mix of different ages, sat cross-legged on a large mat woven from some kind of grass or reed. The mat obviously demarcated the space in the temple for meditation, as if it was its own room within the temple, and there were not many empty spaces on it, although the people left enough space between them in consideration of each other's privacy and personal space. They were all absolutely still, most with their hands resting on their knees or in their laps, many with their hands resting palm up, thumb and third finger touching, and all had their eyes closed. She watched them for a long time admiring the utter stillness they were able to achieve, and feeling herself become affected by it. Their stillness was infectious. She wondered how successful they were at truly stilling their thoughts. She found it impossible to still her thoughts, which was, at times, definitely not to her advantage. Most of the time, though, there was much to be gained in the movement of her thoughts and so she had no desire to attempt to still them. Meditation was not for her. And, in fact, she had been powerfully stopped from doing it when first she had tried, and was told exactly that. Everyone must find their own way, and meditation was not a part of hers. Contemplation was an entirely different matter, of course. She passionately believed in contemplation, and she wondered, now, as she watched the people on the mat if at least some of them were actually contemplating. From their stillness, she doubted it.

"May I join you?"

The voice was heavily accented, but its owner spoke flawless English, and, her reverie gently interrupted, she took her eyes from those meditating, turned her head and looked up. A monk stood over her wearing the orange robe that was typical for monks in the temple, one shoulder left bare, and his robe almost reaching his feet. Unlike many others in the temple, he wore leather sandals on his feet, and he wore a long necklace of carved wooden beads around his neck and another entwined around his left wrist and snaking between his fingers. He looked to be old but in such good health it was impossible to estimate his age. His head was shaven, his eyes were dark but gentle, and if she'd stood up next to him, she would have been at least a head taller than him.

She smiled her welcome. "Of course," she said, and then moved over to make room for him. When he sat beside her, she resumed her observation of those meditating, and so she and he became, for a long, long moment, silent companions. She felt comfortable in the silence, and she felt comfortable with him. He it was who broke the silence first.

"You are not Buddhist."

He said the words matter of factly, as if he was merely stating the obvious, which he was.

"No, I am not," she responded without taking her eyes from those meditating, even though he hadn't asked a question.

"May I ask you why you have come here?"

She took a long time to answer him because she wasn't sure, exactly, why she was there. "I was guided to come here," she finally answered. "Actually, I was brought here, but why, exactly, I am not yet sure."

"Ah," he said. "I see."

Another long and companionable silence fell between them. Again, she was not at all uncomfortable in the silence, and she could sense he was not either. Again, it was he who broke the silence that had descended upon them.

"You are one who walks the path of enlightenment," he observed. "A powerful path it is, too, the path you walk. And, like Gautama Buddha, you walk a solitary path, although you do not walk it alone."

Even though her eyes remained fixed on those meditating, her internal focus shifted, and she concentrated her attention on him, frowning ever so slightly as she did so. If he'd wanted her attention, he'd certainly got it. "How do you know all that?" she asked him.

"Well," he said matter of factly, "you changed the light in here when you walked in. I saw it and felt it, and so I searched out the source of the change. My eyes fell upon you, and I knew you were the one who had changed the light. So I watched you, and I saw that even though you sat alone on the bench, you were not alone. There are many beside you, around you, many who walk with you. I think maybe you all changed the light in here."

She smiled at that, and her smile sparkled in her eyes with depth and intensity and real, deep-seated amusement. She turned to look at him, altering her position on the wooden bench. "Well they would do that," she said, still amused. "They would definitely do that."

He nodded, returning her smile. "They *and* you," he said. "They are a part of you, so they could not change the light in here without you."

Again, she smiled. "Yes," she said softly, "that is exactly what they would say."

His eyes returned her smile, and then they became serious. "Lady of Light, can you acknowledge that many souls find peace and nourishment here?"

"Yes, I can acknowledge that. I know that is so."

"Can you also acknowledge that many souls find what they seek here?"

"Yes, I can acknowledge that. I know that is so. Can you acknowledge that, for many souls, this can become a trap?"

He nodded. "Yes, I can acknowledge that. I know that is so. It is like moving through different rooms in a house, is it not? Some souls find their home in this, our room," he spread his hands to indicate the temple and its occupants, "and they are meant to stay here. But some souls are meant to take the Knowledge and Wisdom from this room, build on it, and move on to the next room, and then the next, and then the next. Those souls are, in truth, too evolved to stay for long in this, our room, and so they must move on until they find their home. You are one such soul."

"Yes, I am, only, I have not spent any time in this, your room," she said. "I began my journey in another room entirely."

"Ah, yes," he said. "So you did. And even though you think that room did not serve you, it *did* serve you when you were a child. It gave you a foundation from which to move forward, to grow from, and from which you *could* move on. It also allowed you to see and to know the limitations of that room because there is, really, no substitute for personal experience, and it allowed you to know why and how those limitations affect all the souls who reside in it. And then, of course, it allowed you to know true freedom when you stepped beyond it. 'Tis the very nature of duality, is it not, beautiful Lady? In this human reality, humans come to know what hot is because they experience cold, and in experiencing cold, they know such an absence of heat that it makes them understand it, and appreciate it."

She nodded thoughtfully. "Yes," she agreed. "I do believe you are right. As a child consciousness, I did benefit from both the doctrine itself and the boundary offered by it. You are right. It gave me something to build on, and something to alter within myself as I outgrew it. So what about you?"

He smiled. "This is my home, Lady of Light. I would not be anywhere else."

She nodded her acknowledgement of that. "I envy you in a way. I have not yet found my home."

"Oh but you will. You will. Your room, though, is unlike any other. Indeed, we could say, you are creating a whole new room, although it is also a very ancient room you are creating, and a powerful one. 'Tis a room for highly evolved souls. Rooms like the one you are creating once existed here, but no more." He shook his head sadly. "No more." And then his demeanour changed as he smiled and reached out and jabbed her gently with a playful finger. "But they *will* again exist here when you create yours."

She laughed softly. "Just as Gautama Buddha did. He created a whole new room, did he not?"

Her new friend nodded earnestly. "Yes, he did." He looked around the temple. "And we have done good things with his room, and we have done bad things with it," he admitted.

"Yes," she agreed, "and is that not the very reason why some souls find peace and nourishment here, and some souls become trapped here."

"Yes. Indeed, yes." He looked at her intensely for a long moment, and she wondered at his thoughts. While he looked at her, she maintained eye contact with him, looking back. "You struggle sometimes to remember not all souls are like you. You do so because the dregs of identification still cling to you like mud. You think you are like them when you are not. Is that not the expression you use sometimes – the dregs of identification?"

He paused, seeking her response, and in the pause, she nodded, her expression intense as she wondered how he knew these things about her. She didn't bother asking him again, though, because she knew the answer would come when she was ready.

"You came to be identified with human souls in this place," he said. "And so you were. But no more, beautiful Lady. So you must find a way to let those last dregs of identification fall from your shoulders, like a robe no longer required. Or," he added, lifting his playful finger, "as one sheds a glamour one has held on to. You are not one of these souls, and you must allow yourself to *know* this, and to *be* what you are."

Again, she nodded, although she wasn't fully aware of doing so.

"Not all souls hold the Wisdom within them as you do," he continued. "Not all souls know what you know in here." He bunched the fingers of his left hand, with the beads weaved through them, and held it up to and against his chest, indicating his heart. "There are many temptations in this world, now, to lead souls off their path, and to tempt them into bad and harmful choices. This you know, Lady of Light."

She nodded and said very quietly, "Yes, this I know."

"Well," he said, "many souls do not wish to be bad, or to harm either themselves or others, and they do not wish to make bad choices. Many such souls recognise their bad choices will lead to hurt and suffering. For those souls, our room offers them the means by which they might stay true to the path of their destiny and make choices that honour and serve them."

She listened intently, watching him as he talked, her whole body turned towards him, her left shoulder leaning against the wall behind her for support, her legs crossed for comfort, and her hands relaxed in her lap.

Unbeknownst to them both, the man in the blue t-shirt stood, still and silent, almost directly opposite them, on the other side of those meditating, leaning against one of the internal columns of wood, watching them closely, his eyes never leaving them both. He watched them talk, back and forth, and he saw that she was listening to her companion intently. Her body language told him who watched that she was very engaged in the conversation, very connected to it, and very, very focussed on it, and on her companion.

"You are saying religions, like this one, protect people, from themselves more so than from anything else," she said.

"Yes," he replied, nodding once as he said the word. "This you know, Lady of Light, but I will remind you. All souls are at different levels of evolvement, or different stages of growth. In fact, we could say there are as many different levels of evolvement as there are souls. Some souls are very young, in a very real sense, especially here, in the human realm, and so they have need of the solidity and certainty, and the support, and the boundaries offered by well-defined doctrine. Just as humans themselves grow from childhood to adulthood to old age, so, too, does the soul evolve. And as children, humans need kindergartens to learn those skills they must learn at that age, and then they need pre-schools and then high schools and then universities or colleges. So, too, is it so for consciousness itself."

"Ah," she said, drawing out the word as enlightenment dawned. "And that is why you are here, in this room." She raised her hands and spread them wide, indicating the religion of which this temple was a vital part. "You are a guide and a teacher and a mentor to those souls whose room this is, even though you are an old and evolved soul. In truth, although you are at home and comfortable in this room, you are one who holds the Knowledge and Wisdom of many different rooms."

He grinned like a young child who's just been caught with a hand in the cookie jar, and his grin was infectious. "Yes. That is why I am here, in this room. And that is also why I am able to recognise the value of the room *you* are creating."

"And what would you say this, your room, is for in terms of the development of consciousness?"

"Well, it is not for little children – little children who want, want, want. That I can say for certain. Perhaps we could say it is for those souls who are truly developing and evolving. Or perhaps we could say it is for those souls who *recognise* the necessity for growth and evolvement, and in particular, growth and evolvement beyond the base desires of materiality. This, our room, offers the means by which those souls who wish to do so *may* do so. But I know it can take them only so far, as we have already acknowledged."

"Yes, I see it," she said. "This, your room, is not for those who are stuck and stagnant, nor is it for those who are so young all they can see is what they want."

"Yes," he said, nodding deeply when he said the word.

"What is your name?" she asked him.

He smiled and bowed towards her with his hands held prayer-like against him, just as she had bowed to the monk at the door. "Mani, at your service, beautiful Lady."

She repeated the gesture back to him. "And I am Jennifer, at *your* service, Mani."

"Ah," he said quickly. "I think that is not your name."

She chuckled again, thoroughly enjoying both the conversation and his company, his presence. "By which name would you call me, then?"

"I have already used your true name, beautiful Lady. I have just said it in English, its newest rather than its oldest form."

"Do you know its oldest form?" she asked curiously.

"Yes, Ushara, Lady of Light, I do."

She sat for a moment, and although a smile sparkled in her eyes, tears also filled them. "You are a unique and special soul, Mani. This world is fortunate to have you here."

He bowed, lowering his eyes. "I thank you."

"Mani," she said, drawing his eyes to hers once more, "I think the doctrine offered to the people of this world by your religion *does* have the best interests of the soul at its heart. The same cannot be said for the doctrines of other religions, though, particularly the so-called western religions. You of all people know well that old adage: by their fruit shall ye know them." Again, she spread her hands to indicate the temple and its religious doctrine. "This religion brings peace to those who practice it, even when those who practice it believe in different variations of its doctrine. Buddhists do not fight each other in the name of their variant doctrines. The same cannot be said of the other of the world's religions. Those other religions are divisive, and when they are, the people fight each other and kill each other in the name of their god, even though they are all supposed to believe in the same god. Not so your religion."

He watched her while she spoke. He watched her closely.

"And this saddens you?" he asked her.

"Yes, it does, but it also bewilders me. How anyone can kill and maim and harm another soul in the name of any god is something I simply cannot comprehend. I do not understand how they can justify it."

"Ah, yes, but remember what I said. Most souls are not like you. They do not see the way you see, and they do not know what you know. Many souls are very young, are they not? 'Tis a childish practice, killing another in the name of one's god. 'Tis very much like two children fighting over a toy, one hurting the other to have the toy and win the fight. 'Tis certainly *not* the behaviour of an evolved soul. And there are many reasons why people kill and fight in the name of their god, many of which are not at all authentic. In other words, killing in the name of their god is just an excuse. They want to kill, and they use their god as justification for doing exactly what they want to do, even though they know, deep down, their god does not approve of or endorse their actions. They *want* to kill because it makes them feel powerful to do so. Thus do they *want* to kill because the truth is they feel powerless deep, deep within."

She nodded, took a deep breath and let it out in a soft, gentle sigh. "True, Mani. Very true. And many of the souls here are stuck in their childish ways, are they not, unable to move on?"

He nodded. "Yes. Those souls labour under the burden of their karmic imbalances."

"Yes, they do. And they have not the wherewithal to move on because this reality does not provide them the means. So there is nothing offered here, like a kindergarten, to help them understand and resolve those imbalances. If anything, the religions they fight in the name of are a reflection of those imbalances, and, as such, perpetuate those imbalances."

"Yes." Again, he nodded as he said the word, as was his way.

And then he looked at her in silence for a long moment. She allowed him his gentle scrutiny, knowing he was seeing into her very soul, and feeling the need neither to hide nor to cover herself. She felt very safe with him. After an elongated moment of silence, he reached over and lifted one of her hands in his own.

"You care for all souls, Lady of Light. You care greatly so that it is, in part, a burden for you because you know you cannot help them individually. This has been one of the hardest parts of your journey – knowing that you are unable to help those around you. This is why you came here – to help all souls. But not individually. You are here for the collective, are you not?"

She nodded. "I am."

"So you struggle with the existence in this reality of the religions you can see, particularly the institutionalised religions of the western cultures, with their monotheistic god. Is this not so?"

"This is so."

"And so, because of what you see and what you have experienced, you do not wish to become the foundation stone of a new religion, I think, as have those of the Guardians who preceded you. In fact, you are quietly determined this will not happen."

"Yes."

He smiled. "'Tis human nature to turn Wisdom such as yours into rules and doctrines and recipes for living one's life. And if souls begin to live their lives in accordance with *your* Wisdom, then this world will be a greater place, even a *great* place."

She didn't respond. She just sat beside him and allowed her hand to rest in his. But she absorbed his words. In fact, his words penetrated deeply, so deeply, in fact, tears welled in her eyes once again. Finally, when the lump in her throat had eased somewhat, she responded.

"I take your point, Mani. 'Tis a good point you make. Actually, it is an excellent point you make. It would be hard to turn my Wisdom into a religion, though, I think."

"I think not. I think you would be surprised at the form such a religion would take."

She laughed softly at that. "Yes, no doubt you are right. What would be its god, then?"

He grinned again. "The same as for this, our room. Each soul would be its own god. Is that not your message, beautiful Lady?"

"Yes," she said, laughing softly. "That is my message." And then she sobered. "You are saying religion has its place in the human experience. That is your whole point, is it not, Mani?"

"Yes," he said, nodding again as he said the word, "so long as the religions of this world offer a real place for all souls at different levels of evolution the nourishment they require to keep growing. You are right, of course. Some of the religions of this world are counterfeit religions such that they harm the souls of this world. They pretend to be what they are not, and they pretend to give when they only take. Those religions do not have the welfare of the soul at heart, but, rather, serve only their own power base. *That* is exactly why they are harmful.

"But young souls need boundaries, as you well know, Lady of Light, and as we have already said. Is it not the human penchant to put boundaries, or definitions, on everything? It makes them feel secure because it gives them an infrastructure within which to operate. Is that not one of your own personal observations?"

"Yes, it is," she replied, narrowing her eyes at him. "Mani ... ? How do you know all these things about me? How do you know my deepest thoughts and observations?"

He grinned his childish grin, obviously relishing the fact that he knew something she did not. "How do you think I know?"

With the question, as simple as it was, enlightenment dawned.

"Are you a Guardian, Mani?"

Again, he grinned, but he was not given a chance to reply verbally.

The enormous statue of the Buddha at the very end of the temple caught her attention, and her eyes snapped to it. He, the very large Buddha, was sitting, cross-legged, facing the people meditating on their mat. She looked, again, at Mani.

"Are you *that* Guardian?" she asked quickly, loudly, as the realisation struck her.

"Yes," he replied. "Gautama Buddha was one of my incarnations. Does it not make sense that I would walk here and Work here in the room I created?"

"Yes," she breathed, still reeling from the shock of realisation, "it makes perfect sense that you would tend all those souls who chose to reside in your room. It makes perfect sense."

He nodded. "Indeed. Only," he paused to turn and look at the image of himself, or him in a previous incarnation, and then he looked back at her with a mischievous expression on his face, "I did not look like that. I have never looked like that."

She laughed softly, more at the expression on his face than at his words. "Iconification," she said. "Or deification. And veneration. 'Tis unfortunate." She observed the statue, the iconic image, for a long moment, and then she said, "At least they have you sitting comfortably, cross-legged. In Yeheshua's case they have him permanently pinned to a cross by his hands and feet, often with a crown of thorns around his head."

Mani threw his head back and laughed heartily, uninhibitedly, and, as a consequence, loudly. She caught his laugh – it was utterly impossibly not to – but she kept her eye on those meditating closest to them, for surely, she thought, his laughter had disturbed them. But, no. Not one moved or gave any indication whatsoever of having heard anything at all.

"Yes," Mani agreed when his laughter had subsided somewhat, "'tis most unfortunate for Yeheshua. I must agree." And then he pointedly looked over the heads of all those meditating, right at the man in the blue t-shirt who was still watching them as he leaned against the wooden pillar of the temple. The two exchanged smiles and subtle nods of their heads. "Most unfortunate, indeed," he repeated, and both his tone and his words caused her to follow his line of vision, looking across the temple, too.

The man in the blue t-shirt looked at her when she looked at him such that their eyes locked. She could not look away, even if she'd wanted to, which she did not.

"Well, well," she said softly, "so here we all are. If Socrates was here, we could be having a family reunion right now."

Again, Mani threw his head back and laughed heartily, and this time, a dozen or so people stirred on their mat, and a few of them opened their eyes and turned their heads to cast a disapproving glance his way. That only served to fuel his laughter. "Not so impervious to external distractions as they would like to think," he observed, not-so-quietly.

His laughter had made her look at him again, breaking eye contact with that other Guardian who stood across the temple from them, observing them, and she was wholly unable to stop herself grinning like that famous Cheshire Cat. "You enjoyed that, didn't you? You enjoyed disturbing them."

"Yes," he confessed, the mischief still surrounding him like an aura. "I did indeed."

She smiled as she watched the people resettle themselves. "You are a gentle soul, Mani," she said.

"And you are not?"

She looked at him. "I used to be."

He smiled a gentle smile at her. "Those events and circumstances that shaped you in those early years of your life caused you to develop a tough skin. In a very real sense, there was no safe place for you, so you had to create one for yourself. 'Tis one of the important roles and functions of parents to provide a safe place for a young consciousness to develop, but your parents did not, did they? Your father would never have abused you sexually, never. But he did abuse you spiritually and psychologically and even, in the name of discipline, physically, beautiful Lady, although not by himself, of course. He had much help. Such abuse is brutal, and it leaves bruises.

"But are you really so tough? If you were so tough then you would not sob uncontrollably when you watch all those documentaries on the big war and its aftermath. You would not hold your hands over your mouth in horror when you see an item on the news showing a bunch of teenage children hitting an autistic boy with spanners and wrenches. You would not be moved to tears when an eighty-one-year-old man – one whose blood contains a special anti-body that has saved millions of children whose blood is not compatible with that of their mother's – breaks the world record for blood donations. He did his bit to make a difference, did he not?"

"Yes," she agreed, "he did."

"You are not tough, beautiful Lady. You are just not given any opportunities to *be* gentle. That will not always be so. *That* is my promise to you."

This time, it was she who reached over and took one of his hands in her own. "I will do you the honour of believing you, Mani." She smiled into his gentle eyes. "I have bemoaned the necessity of enduring the shallow conversations I must endure in the human reality. I have missed the true connection and communion and fellowship of meaningful dialogue. So, I thank you for this. Our conversation will itself endure, in my heart, but not just there. You have enriched me and nourished me beyond my ability to express it to you. Thank you."

He smiled back. "Well, it was my very great pleasure, of course, Lady of Light. Yes," he repeated, nodding solemnly, "a very great pleasure indeed."

~

The End

www.ingramcontent.com/pod-product-compliance
Lightning Source LLC
Chambersburg PA
CBHW031052020726
47495CB00007B/1843